MAIGRET'S PIPE

Georges Simenon

MAIGRET'S PIPE

Seventeen Stories

Translated from the French by
Jean Stewart

A Harvest Book
A Helen and Kurt Wolff Book
Harcourt Brace & Company
San Diego   New York   London

Copyright © 1977 by Georges Simenon
English translation copyright © 1977 by Georges Simenon

All rights reserved. No part of this publication may be reproduced or transmitted in any form or by any means, electronic or mechanical, including photocopy, recording, or any information storage and retrieval system, without permission in writing from the publisher.

Requests for permission to make copies of any part of the work should be mailed to: Permissions Department, Harcourt Brace & Company, 6277 Sea Harbor Drive, Orlando, Florida 32887-6777.

Maigret is a registered trademark of the Estate of Georges Simenon.

"Maigret's Pipe" first published in France 1947 under the title *La Pipe de Maigret*, copyright 1947 by Georges Simenon; "Death Penalty," "Mr Monday," "The Open Window," "Madame Maigret's Admirer," "The Mysterious Affair in the Boulevard Beaumarchais," "Two Bodies on a Barge," "Death of a Woodlander," "In the Rue Pigalle," "Maigret's Mistake," "The Old Lady of Bayeux," "Stan the Killer," "The Drowned Men's Inn," "At the Etoile du Nord," "Mademoiselle Berthe and her Lover," "The Three Daughters of the Lawyer," and "Storm in the Channel" first published in France 1944 in *Les Nouvelles Enquêtes de Maigret* under the titles *Peine de mort, Monsieur Lundi, La fenêtre ouverte, L'amoureux de Madame Maigret, L'affaire du boulevard Beaumarchais, La péniche aux deux pendus, Les larmes de bougie, Rue Pigalle, Une erreur de Maigret, La vieille dame de Bayeux, Stan le tueur, L'Auberge aux Noyés, L'Etoile du Nord, Mademoiselle Berthe et son amant, Le notaire de Châteauneuf* and *Tempête sur la Manche*, copyright 1944 by Georges Simenon.

Library of Congress Cataloging-in-Publication Data
Simenon, Georges, 1903–1989
Maigret's pipe.
"A Helen and Kurt Wolff book."
Translation of La pipe de Maigret.
1. Detective and mystery stories, French — Translations into English. 2. Detective and mystery stories, English — Translations from French. I. Title.
[PZ3.S5892Mair]   843'.9'12   78-4169
ISBN 0-15-655146-2 (Harvest: pbk.)

Printed in the United States of America

First Harvest edition 1985

B C D E F

CONTENTS

MAIGRET'S PIPE

MAIGRET'S PIPE

I. *The House Where Things Change Places*

It was half past seven. In the Director's office, Maigret had heaved a sigh of mingled relief and exhaustion, the sigh of a heavy man at the close of a hot July day, and he had automatically pulled his watch from his waistcoat pocket. Then he had reached out to collect his files from the mahogany desk. The baize door had closed behind him and he had gone out through the waiting-room. Nobody was sitting on the red armchairs. The old office messenger was in his glazed cubby-hole. The corridor of Police Headquarters was a long, empty stretch of sunlit greyness.

His movements were familiar ones. He went back into his own room, where a persistent smell of tobacco lingered in spite of the wide open window overlooking the Quai des Orfèvres. He laid his files down on a corner of the desk, knocked out his pipe, which was still warm, against the window ledge, came back to sit down and automatically reached out for a different pipe to the right, where it ought to have been.

It was not there. There were three pipes, one of them a meerschaum, lying beside the ashtray, but his favourite, the one he was looking for, the one he came back to with the most pleasure and always carried about with him, a thick briar pipe with a slightly curved stem which his wife had given him for a birthday present ten years before, and which he called his good old pipe, was not there.

Surprised, he felt his pockets and thrust his hands into them. He looked on top of the black marble chimney piece. Actually, he was scarcely thinking. There was nothing extraordinary about not finding one of one's pipes right away. He walked round the room two or three times and opened the cupboard where there was an enamel wash-basin.

He was hunting as anyone might have done, but it was rather stupid of him, since he had not opened that cupboard all afternoon, whereas when Judge Coméliau had rung him up a few minutes after six he had been smoking that very pipe.

Then he rang for the office messenger.

'I say, Emile, has nobody come in here while I was with the Chief?'

1

'Nobody, sir.'

He hunted through his pockets once again, his jacket pockets and his trouser pockets. He was looking sulky and the fruitless search made him feel hot.

He went into the Inspectors' room, because he had occasionally left one of his pipes there. There was nobody in the room, and it was odd and pleasant to find the premises of Headquarters so empty, with a holiday feeling about the place. There was no pipe there. He knocked at the door of the Chief's room; the Chief had just gone out. He went in, but he knew beforehand that his pipe was not there, because he had been smoking a different one when he had gone in at about half past six to talk about certain pending cases and also about his forthcoming departure for the country.

Twenty minutes to eight. He had promised to be back home in the Boulevard Richard-Lenoir by eight o'clock, for his sister-in-law and her husband were expected for dinner. What else had he promised to do? To bring back some fruit. That was it. His wife had asked him to buy peaches.

But on the way home, in the sultry evening air, he went on thinking about his pipe. It worried him almost unconsciously, as any trivial but inexplicable incident worries one.

He bought the peaches, went home, and kissed his sister-in-law, who had put on weight again. He poured out drinks. That was when he should have been smoking his favourite pipe.

'Had a busy day?'

'No. Things are fairly quiet.'

There are periods like that. Two of his colleagues were on holiday; the third had rung up in the morning to say that relatives from the country had just descended on him and that he was taking two days' leave.

'You've got something on your mind, Maigret,' his wife commented during dinner.

And he dared not confess that it was his pipe that was preoccupying him. To be sure, he wasn't treating the matter over-seriously, but it dampened his spirits nonetheless.

At two o'clock – yes, he had sat down at his desk at a few minutes past two. Lucas had come to talk to him about a case of currency fraud, then about Inspector Janvier, whose wife was expecting another child.

Then, quite peacefully, having taken off his jacket and loosened his tie, he had drawn up a report on a suicide which had for a short time been mistaken for a crime. He had been smoking his big pipe then.

Next, Gégène, a petty pimp from Montmartre who had wounded his girl with a knife – 'just given her a little jab', as he said. But Gégène had not gone near the desk. In any case he had been handcuffed.

Liqueurs were being handed round. The two women were talking cookery. The brother-in-law was listening vaguely as he smoked a cigar, and the noises from the Boulevard Richard-Lenoir drifted up to the open window.

He had not even left his office that afternoon to go for a beer to the Brasserie Dauphine.

Then there had been that woman . . . what was her name? Roy or Leroy. She had made no appointment. Emile had come in to announce 'a lady and her son'.

'What's it about?'

'She won't say. She insists on speaking to the Chief.'

'Bring her in.'

By pure chance there was a gap in his timetable, for otherwise he would not have seen her. He had attached so little importance to this visit that now he could scarcely remember the details of it.

His sister-in-law and her husband left. His wife commented, as she tidied the room: 'You weren't very talkative this evening. Is something going wrong?'

No. Everything was fine, except for the loss of the pipe. Night had begun to fall and Maigret, in his shirt sleeves, sat with his elbows on the window sill, like thousands of other Parisians who were now enjoying the cool of the evening at their windows, smoking their pipes or cigarettes.

The woman – her name must have been Leroy – had sat down exactly opposite the Superintendent, stiffly, as people do who have determined to be on their dignity. A woman of about forty-five, one of those who, towards middle age, begin to shrivel up. Maigret himself preferred those who grow plump with age.

'I have come to see you, Monsieur le Directeur . . .'

'The Director isn't here. I am Superintendent Maigret.'

And here one detail recurred to him. There had been no reaction from the woman; presumably she did not read the papers and had never heard speak of him. She had seemed somewhat annoyed at not being taken to the Head of the Police Judiciaire in person, and had given a little wave of the hand as though to say:

'Well, it can't be helped, I'll have to put up with it.'

On the other hand the youth, whom Maigret had as yet scarcely noticed, had given a sudden start and turned a keen, eager gaze on the Superintendent.

'Aren't you coming to bed, Maigret?' asked Madame Maigret, who had just turned down the bed and begun to undress.

'Presently.'

Now, exactly what had that woman been telling him? She had

talked so much! Volubly, insistently, like those people who attach considerable importance to their slightest words and who are always afraid of not being taken seriously. It's an obsession with some women, particularly with those who are nearing fifty.

'We live, my son and I . . .'

Perhaps it was just as well she went on talking, for Maigret was only listening to her with half an ear.

She was a widow, for one thing. She had said she'd been a widow for some years, five or ten, he didn't remember. A longish period, since she complained of the hard time she'd had bringing up her son.

'I've done everything for him, Superintendent.'

How could one pay attention to the sort of remarks made by all women of the same age in the same position, with identical pride and a similar plaintive look? The mention of her widowhood, by the way, had provoked an incident. What was it? Oh yes . . .

She had said: 'My husband was a professional army officer . . .' And her son had corrected her:

'Sergeant-major, Maman. In the Commissariat, at Vincennes.'

'Excuse me . . . When I say officer, I know what I'm talking about. If he hadn't died, if he hadn't killed himself working for superiors who couldn't hold a candle to him and who left him all the work to do, he'd have been an officer today . . .'

Maigret had not forgotten about his pipe. On the contrary, he was on the right track; the proof being that the name Vincennes was somehow associated with the pipe. He had been smoking it, he was certain, when the word was uttered. After which there had been no further mention of Vincennes.

'Excuse me. Where do you live?'

He had forgotten the name of the quai, but it was close to the Quai de Bercy, at Charenton. He remembered visualizing a very broad quai, with warehouses and barges unloading.

'A small one-storeyed house between a café at the corner and a big block of flats.'

The young man was sitting at the corner of the desk, with his straw hat – for he had a straw hat – on his knees.

'My son didn't want me to come and see you, Monsieur le Directeur – excuse me, Superintendent. But I said to him: "If you've nothing on your conscience, there's no reason why . . ."'

What colour was her dress? Blackish, with touches of mauve; one of those dresses worn by middle-aged women who want to look distinguished. A rather elaborate hat, which had probably been altered more than once. Dark cotton gloves. She was listening to herself speaking. She began all her sentences with:

'Just imagine . . .' or else: 'As everyone will tell you . . .'

Maigret, who had put on his jacket again to receive her, felt hot and drowsy. It was a chore; he wished he had sent her straight to the Inspectors' room.

'More than once, on coming home I've noticed that somebody had been there during my absence.'

'Excuse me. Do you live alone with your son?'

'Yes. And at first I thought it might have been him. But it happened while he was at work.'

Maigret glanced at the youth, who was looking vexed. A familiar type: probably about seventeen, tall and thin, with a spotty face, reddish hair and freckles round his nose.

Was there something shifty about him? His mother was to say so presently, for there are some people who like speaking ill of their nearest and dearest. Shy, in any case, and withdrawn. He stared at the carpet, or at some object or other in the room, and when he thought himself unobserved he would cast a keen glance at Maigret.

He was not happy to be there, that was obvious. He did not feel that his mother was doing the right thing. Perhaps he was somewhat ashamed of her, of her pretentiousness, of her loquacity?

'What is your son's occupation?'

'He's a hairdresser.'

And the youth declared with some bitterness:

'Just because one of my uncles has a hairdressing salon at Niort, mother has got it into her head that . . .'

'There's nothing to be ashamed of in being a hairdresser. The point is, Superintendent, that he couldn't have left the place where he works, near the République. In any case, I made sure of that.'

'Forgive me. You suspected your son of coming home in your absence and so you kept a watch on him?'

'Yes, Superintendent. I don't suspect anyone in particular, but I know that men are capable of anything.'

'What could your son have come home to do without your knowledge?'

'I don't know.'

Then, after a pause:

'Brought in women, perhaps! Three months ago I found a letter from a girl in his pocket. If his father . . .'

'How can you be certain that someone came into your house?'

'For one thing, one can feel it immediately. As soon as I opened the door I could tell . . .'

Not very scientific, but natural enough and not unconvincing. Maigret had himself experienced such impressions.

'And what else?'

'Next, various small details. For instance, although I never lock the door of the wardrobe, I found that the key had been turned.'

'Is anything valuable kept in your wardrobe?'

'Our clothes and our linen, plus some family heirlooms, but nothing has gone, if that's what you mean. And in the cellar a packing-case had been moved.'

'What did it contain?'

'Some empty jars.'

'In short, nothing is missing from your house?'

'I don't think so.'

'How long is it since you first had the impression that somebody was visiting your home?'

'It's not an impression. It's a certainty. About three months.'

'In your opinion, how many visits have there been?'

'Perhaps ten altogether. After the first occasion there was a long gap of about three weeks when nobody came. Or else I didn't notice. Then two visits in quick succession. Then another gap of three weeks or longer. During the last few days there have been several visits, and the day before yesterday, when there was that terrible storm, I found footmarks and traces of damp.'

'You don't know whether they were a man's or a woman's footmarks?'

'Probably a man's, but I'm not sure.'

She had said a great deal more. She had poured forth information unsolicited! The previous Monday, for instance, she had deliberately taken her son to the cinema, because hairdressers don't work on Mondays. So she'd kept him under her eye. They had been together all afternoon. They had gone home together.

'And somebody had been there!'

'And yet your son didn't want you to speak to the police?'

'That's just it, Superintendent. That's what I can't understand. He saw the marks, just as I did.'

'You saw the marks, young man?'

He preferred not to speak, assuming a stubborn look. Did this mean that his mother was exaggerating, that she was talking nonsense?

'Do you know how the person or persons got into the house?'

'Through the door, I suppose. I never leave the windows open. The wall is too high for anyone to get in through the yard and they'd have to come through the yards of the neighbouring houses.'

'Did you see any marks on the lock?'

'Not a scratch. I even examined it with my late husband's magnifying glass.'

'And nobody has the key to your house?'

'Nobody. There's my daughter, of course' (here the young man gave a slight start) 'but she lives at Orléans with her husband and her two children.'

'Are you on good terms with her?'

'I've always told her she shouldn't have married such a useless fellow. Apart from that, since we never see one another . . .'

'Are you often out? You told me you were a widow. I imagine the pension you get from the Army is inadequate?'

She assumed an air of modest dignity.

'I work for my living. To begin with, I mean after my husband's death, I took in lodgers – two of them. But men are such dirty creatures. If you'd seen the state in which they left their rooms!'

At the time, Maigret had not been consciously listening, yet now he could recall not only her words but her intonations.

'For the past year I have been companion to Madame Lallemant, a very respectable lady, the mother of a doctor. She lives alone, near to Charenton lock, just across the way, and every afternoon I . . . She's more like a friend, if you see what I mean.'

Actually Maigret had not taken the matter very seriously. The woman might have been a crackpot; he was not interested. She was typical of those visitors on whom one is forced to waste half an hour. As it happened, the Director had come into the office, or rather had peeped in as he often did. He had cast one glance at the visitors, and he too had realized from the look of them that nothing of importance was involved.

'Can you spare a moment, Maigret?'

They had stood together for a short while in the next room, discussing a warrant for arrest which had just been telegraphed from Dijon.

'Torrence will see to it,' Maigret had said.

He had not been smoking his best pipe, but a different one. He must, presumably, have laid down his best pipe on the desk a little earlier, when Judge Coméliau had rung him up. But at that point he had not been thinking about it.

He had gone back into the room and stood by the window, his hands behind his back.

'In short, Madame, you've had nothing stolen?'

'I suppose not.'

'I mean you're not lodging a complaint of burglary?'

'I cannot do so, since . . .'

'You simply have the impression that in your absence somebody, during the last few months and particularly during the last few days, has taken to entering your house?'

'And even once during the night.'

'Did you see anyone?'

'I heard someone.'

'What did you hear?'

'A cup fell down in the kitchen and broke. I went downstairs immediately.'

'Were you armed?'

'No. I am never frightened.'

'And there was nobody there?'

'Nobody was there any longer. The broken pieces of the cup were lying on the floor.'

'And you have no cat?'

'No. No cat and no dog. Animals make too much mess.'

'Couldn't a cat have got into the house?'

The young man, on his chair, looked increasingly anguished.

'You're trying the Superintendent's patience, Maman.'

'In short, Madame, you don't know who breaks into your house and you have no idea what they could be looking for there?'

'None whatsoever. We've always been respectable people and . . .'

'If I may give you one piece of advice, it's to get your lock changed. Then we shall see if the mysterious visits persist.'

'And the police will do nothing?'

He was propelling them towards the door. It was nearly time for him to visit the Director in his office.

'In any case, I'll send round one of my men tomorrow. But short of keeping watch on the house all day and all night, I can't really see . . .'

'When will he come?'

'You told me you were at home in the mornings.'

'Except when I'm doing my shopping.'

'Will ten o'clock suit you? . . . Tomorrow at ten. Goodbye, Madame. Goodbye, my boy.'

He pressed the bell. Lucas came in.

'It's you? . . . Will you go to this address tomorrow morning at ten o'clock. You'll find out what it's all about.'

He spoke without conviction. Police Headquarters share with newspaper offices the privilege of attracting every sort of crank and crackpot.

Now, sitting at his window where the cool evening air was beginning to steal over him, Maigret was grumbling:

'That blasted kid!'

For it was the boy, without a shadow of a doubt, who had pinched his pipe from the desk.

'Aren't you coming to bed?'

He went to bed. He was cross and sulky. He felt hot and sticky in bed and he grumbled again before going to sleep. And next morning he woke up without zest, as one does after falling asleep with something unpleasant on one's mind. It was not a presentiment and yet he was very conscious – as was his wife, though she dared not mention it

– that the day was starting badly. Moreover, there were thunder-clouds about and the air was already sultry.

He walked along the embankment to the Quai des Orfèvres, and twice he automatically felt in his pocket for his favourite pipe. He climbed the dusty staircase, breathing heavily. Emile greeted him with:

'There's somebody to see you, sir.'

He cast a glance into the glass-walled waiting-room and there he saw Madame Leroy, sitting on a chair upholstered in green plush, perched on the edge as though ready to spring. She caught sight of him and duly rushed up to him, tense and angry and anxious, a prey to countless varied feelings; grasping the lapels of his jacket, she shouted:

'What did I tell you? They came back last night. My son has disap-peared. Will you believe me now? Oh! I quite realized that you thought I was crazy. I'm not such a fool. And see here, see here . . .'

She was fumbling wildly in her handbag, and pulled out a blue-edged handkerchief which she brandished triumphantly.

'This . . . Yes, isn't this a proof? We've got no handkerchiefs with blue on them at home. And yet I found this on the floor beside the kit-chen table. And that's not all.'

Maigret stared gloomily down the long corridor, where the morn-ing's activities were in full swing and where people turned back to stare at them.

'Come with me, Madame,' he sighed.

It was just his bad luck. He had felt it coming. He pushed open the door of his office and hung up his hat in its usual place.

'Sit down. I'm listening to you. You tell me that your son . . .'

'I tell you that my son disappeared during the night and that heaven knows what's become of him now!'

II. *Joseph's Slippers*

It was not easy to know exactly what she thought about her son's fate. A short while before, at Police Headquarters, during the fit of weeping that had broken out with the suddenness of a summer storm, she had lamented:

'You see, I'm convinced they've killed him. And there you were, doing nothing at all. Don't imagine I don't realize what you were thinking. You took me for a lunatic. Yes, you did! And now he's prob-ably dead. And I shall be left all alone and helpless.'

But now, as their taxi sped along under the spreading branches that overshadowed the Quai de Bercy like an avenue in some country town, her features had resumed their hardness, her glance its keenness, and she said:

'He's a weak creature, you see, Superintendent. He'll never be able to resist women. Just like his father, who gave me such a dreadful time!'

Maigret was sitting beside her in the taxi and Lucas in front beside the driver.

Outside the boundaries of Paris, in the Charenton district, the embankment still bore the name Quai de Bercy. But there were no more trees; factory chimneys on the other side of the Seine, and on this side warehouses and suburban villas, built while the area was still almost rural and now hemmed in by blocks of flats. At a street corner, a café-restaurant painted aggressively red, with yellow lettering, a few iron tables and two skimpy bay-trees in tubs.

Madame Roy – no, Leroy – tapped on the window excitedly.

'It's here. Please don't pay attention to the untidiness. I needn't tell you I never thought about doing the housework.'

She searched her bag for a key. The door was dark brown and the outer walls a smoky grey. Maigret had time to make sure that there were no traces of housebreaking.

'Please come in. I suppose you'll want to go round all the rooms. Look! the pieces of the cup are still lying where I found them.'

She had spoken the truth when she said the place was clean. There was no dust anywhere. Tidiness prevailed. But good heavens, how depressing it was! More than depressing, dismal. An excessively narrow passage, the lower half painted brown and the upper half dark yellow. Brown doors. Wallpaper that had been there for at least twenty years, so faded as to be colourless.

The woman went on talking. Perhaps she talked to herself when she was all alone, because she could not bear the silence.

'What surprises me most is that I didn't hear anything. I sleep so lightly that I wake up several times during the night. But last night I slept like a log. I'm wondering . . .'

He looked at her.

'You're wondering whether somebody didn't give you a drug to make you sleep?'

'That's impossible. He couldn't have done that. Why? Tell me, why should he have done that?'

Was she going to become aggressive again? Sometimes she seemed to be accusing her son and at other times to be making him out a victim. Meanwhile Maigret moved through the little house with such ponderous slowness as to give the impression of immobility. Like a sponge, he was steeping himself in the surrounding dankness.

And the woman dogged his footsteps, observing his every gesture, his every look, mistrustful, trying to guess at his thoughts.

Lucas, too, was watching his Chief's reactions, baffled by this odd and somewhat eccentric investigation.

'The dining-room is on the right, on the other side of the passage. But when we were alone – and we were always alone – we used to eat in the kitchen.'

She would have been highly surprised and possibly indignant if she had suspected that what Maigret was automatically hunting for as he looked around was his pipe. He went up the staircase, which was even narrower than the passage, with a rickety handrail and creaking steps. She came up behind him, explaining – for she felt a perpetual urge to explain:

'Joseph slept in the room on the left . . . Good heavens, I said slept, as if . . .'

'You've not touched anything?'

'Nothing at all, I give you my word. As you see, the bed's unmade. But I'd wager he hasn't slept in it. My son is a very restless sleeper. In the morning I always find the sheets all tangled up and the blankets on the floor. He sometimes talks in his sleep and even calls out . . .'

The Superintendent peered into a wardrobe that stood facing the bed.

'Are all his clothes here?'

'No, and that's just it. If they were, I'd have found his suit and his shirt on a chair, for he was hopelessly untidy.'

It might have been surmised that the young man, hearing a noise in the night, had gone down into the kitchen and been attacked by the mysterious visitor or visitors.

'Did you see him in bed last night?'

'I always came to kiss him goodnight in bed. Last night I came up as usual. He was undressed. His clothes were on the chair. As for the key . . .'

An idea occurred to her. She explained.

'I always stayed downstairs last and locked the door. I kept the key in my room, under my pillow, so that . . .'

'Did your late husband often spend a night out?'

She replied, with pained dignity:

'He did so once, after we'd been married three years.'

'And from then on you took to keeping the key under your pillow?'

She made no reply, and Maigret felt convinced that the father had been kept under as strict a watch as the son.

'So this morning you found the key in its usual place?'

'Yes, Superintendent. I didn't think of it right away, but now it comes back to me. So he can't have wanted to run away, can he?'

'One moment. Your son went to bed. Then he got up and dressed again.'

'Look! Here's his tie on the floor. He didn't put on his tie.'

'And his shoes?'

She quickly turned towards a corner of the room where two well-worn shoes lay at some distance one from the other.

'Nor his shoes. He's gone off in his slippers.'

Maigret was still looking for his pipe, unsuccessfully. He did not exactly know what else he was looking for. He was making a haphazard search of this shabby, dreary room in which the young man had lived. There was a blue suit in the wardrobe, his 'best suit' which presumably he wore only on Sundays, and a pair of patent leather shoes. A few shirts, almost all worn and mended at collar and cuffs. A packet of cigarettes that had been opened.

'By the way, did your son smoke a pipe?'

'At his age, I'd not have allowed him to. A fortnight ago he came home with a small pipe that he must have bought in some cheap store, for it was shoddy stuff. I took it out of his mouth and threw it in the fire. His father, even at the age of forty-five, had never smoked a pipe.'

Maigret sighed as he went on to Madame Leroy's bedroom. She kept saying:

'You must excuse the untidiness. The bed isn't made.'

The banal pettiness of the whole thing was nauseating.

'Upstairs there are attics where we slept during the early months of my widowhood, when I took lodgers. Tell me, since he hasn't put on his tie or his shoes, do you suppose . . .'

And Maigret, at the end of his tether:

'I've no idea, Madame!'

For the past two hours, Lucas had been conscientiously searching the house in every nook and cranny, while Madame Leroy followed him, saying from time to time:

'Look, on one occasion this drawer was opened. The pile of linen on the upper shelf had been disturbed.'

Outside, the heavy sunlight poured down like honey, but in the house a perpetual grey twilight reigned. Maigret went on soaking things in like a sponge; but he could not face following the others as they went back and forth.

Before leaving the Quai des Orfèvres, he had got a detective to telephone to Orléans to make sure the married daughter had not paid a visit to Paris recently. That trail led nowhere.

Could it be that Joseph had had a key made for himself without his mother's knowledge? But then, if he had planned to leave last night, why had he not worn his tie, and above all his shoes?

Maigret now knew what those slippers of Joseph's were like. Out of thrift, Madame Leroy had made them herself from scraps of stuff and cut the soles from a piece of felt.

Everything in the place looked poverty-stricken, and the poverty was all the more distressing because it was never admitted.

The former lodgers? Madame Leroy had told him about them. The first who had come, when she had put a notice in the window, was an old bachelor, a clerk at Soustelle's, the wholesale wine merchants whose house he had noticed while driving along the Quai de Bercy. 'A respectable, well-bred man, Superintendent. Or rather, can you call a man well-bred when he empties his pipe all over the place? And then he had a habit of getting up in the night and going downstairs to heat himself some tea. One night I got up and I met him in his nightshirt and underpants on the stairs. And yet he was an educated man.'

The second room had first been occupied by a stonemason, a foreman, she said, though her son would probably have corrected her. The stonemason had wanted to marry her.

'He kept on telling me about his savings, about a house he owned near Montluçon to which he wanted to take me when we were married. Note that he never said or did anything I didn't approve of. When he came in I would tell him: "Wash your hands, Monsieur Germain." And he would go and wash them under the tap. It was he who cemented the yard for me one Sunday, and I had to insist on paying for the cement.'

Then the mason had left, possibly discouraged, and he had been replaced by a Monsieur Bleustein.

'A foreigner. He spoke French very well, but with a slight accent. He was a commercial traveller and he only spent one or two nights a week in the house.'

'Had your lodgers their own keys?'

'No, Superintendent, because in those days I was always at home. When I had to go out, I slipped the key into a crack in the front wall of the house, behind the drainpipe, and they knew where to find it. One week Monsieur Bleustein did not come back. I found nothing in his room but a broken comb, an old cigarette-lighter and some tattered underwear.'

'Had he not given you notice?'

'No. And yet he was a well-bred man too.'

There were a few books on the sewing machine, which stood in one corner of the dining-room. Maigret glanced through them casually. They were cheap novels, chiefly adventure stories. Here and there, in the margin of a page, two interlaced initials had been traced, sometimes in pencil, sometimes in ink: J and M, the M almost always larger and more elaborately drawn than the J.

'Do you know anyone whose name begins with M, Madame

Leroy?' he called up the stairs.

'With M? . . . No, not that I can think of. Let's see . . . There was my husband's sister-in-law whose name was Marcelle, but she died in childbirth at Issoudun.'

It was noon when Lucas and Maigret met outside.

'Shall we have a drink, Chief?'

And they sat down together in the little red bistro at the street corner. They were both equally depressed; Lucas was in rather a bad temper.

'What a set-up!' He sighed. 'By the way, I discovered this scrap of paper. And guess where? In the kid's packet of cigarettes. He must have been scarred stiff of his mother, since he actually hid his love letters in his cigarette packets!'

It was, in fact, a love letter:

> *Joseph dear,*
>   *You hurt my feelings yesterday when you said I despised you and would never marry a man like you. You know that I'm not that sort of person and that I love you as much as you love me. I'm sure you're going to become somebody one day. But please, don't wait for me so near the shop. You've been noticed, and Madame Rose, who does the same thing herself but who's an old cat, has been making remarks about it. Wait for me by the métro from now on. Not tomorrow, because mother's coming to take me to the dentist. And above all, don't get any more such ideas into your head. Love and kisses,*
>
> > *Mathilde*

'So that's it!' said Maigret, thrusting the paper into his wallet.

'That's what?'

The J and the M. Life! It begins like that and it ends in a dismal little house redolent of resignation.

'When I think that young bastard pinched my pipe!'

'Do *you* really believe he was kidnapped?'

Lucas clearly did not. Nor did he believe in any of old Madame Leroy's stories. He was sick of the whole case already and could not understand the attitude of his chief, who seemed to be gravely pondering over some idea or other.

'If he hadn't pinched my pipe . . .' Maigret began.

'Well, what does that prove?'

'You can't possibly understand. I'd be easier in my mind. My bill, please, waiter.'

They waited for the bus side by side, looking at the almost deserted quai where, since it was the lunch break, cranes stood idle with their jibs in the air and barges seemed to be asleep.

In the bus, Lucas remarked: 'Aren't you going home?'

'I want to call in at the office.'

And suddenly, with an odd brief laugh through lips that held the stem of his pipe:

'Poor wretch . . . I mean that sergeant-major who may have been unfaithful to his wife once in his life and who for the rest of his days was locked into his own house every night!'

Then, after brooding for a moment: 'Have you noticed, Lucas, in cemeteries, that there are many more husbands' graves than widows'? "Here lies so and so, died 1901." And underneath, a more recent inscription: "Here lies so and so, widow of so and so, died 1930." She's gone to join him, true, but twenty-nine years later!'

Lucas did not attempt to understand, but took another bus to go home and have lunch with his wife.

While the Records Department was busy investigating all the Bleusteins who might have been in trouble with the Law, Maigret was busy with pending business and Lucas spent most of the afternoon in the République district.

The thunder still held off. The heat was increasingly oppressive, with a leaden sky tinged with purple like an infected boil. Ten times at least Maigret had involuntarily reached out for his favourite pipe, which was not there; and each time he had muttered:

'That blasted kid!'

Twice he called the switchboard to ask: 'Anything from Lucas?'

Surely it couldn't have been such a complicated business to question Joseph's workmates at the hairdresser's and through them to identify the girl Mathilde who wrote him affectionate notes.

For one thing, Joseph had stolen Maigret's pipe.

For another, that same Joseph, although fully dressed, had been wearing slippers – if you could call them slippers – the night before.

Maigret suddenly broke off reading a police report and asked to be put through to the Records Department. He enquired with uncharacteristic impatience:

'Well, what about those Bleusteins?'

'We're working on them, Superintendent. There are lots of them, some genuine and some bogus. We're checking dates and addresses. In any case I've found none recorded as living in the Quai de Bercy at any time. As soon as anything turns up I'll let you know.'

Finally Lucas appeared, sweating, having taken time to swallow a glass of beer at the Brasserie Dauphine before coming up.

'We've got it, Chief. It wasn't easy, I can tell you. I'd have thought it would be plain sailing. Not at all! Our Joseph is a queer fish, who keeps himself to himself. Imagine the hairdressing establishment – it calls itself *Palace-Coiffure* – a long narrow room, with fifteen or twenty

swing-back chairs in a row facing mirrors, and the same number of at-
tendants . . . It's a mad rush from morning till night there. There are
customers hurrying in and out, being trimmed and lathered and
lotioned . . .

'"Joseph?" the boss said to me – he's a fat grizzled little fellow –
"which Joseph, anyway? Oh yes, the spotty one. Well, what has
Joseph been up to?"

'I asked his permission to question his staff, and there I was, going
from one chair to the next, and they were all grinning and winking at
one another.

'"Joseph? No, I never went out with him. He always left by himself.
Did he have a girl? Maybe . . . although with a mug like that . . ."

'And they'd snigger.

'"Secrets? He was a regular clam. His lordship was ashamed of
being a hairdresser and he wouldn't have condescended to keep company with the likes of us."

'You see the sort of thing, Chief. And, besides, I had to wait till each
customer had been dealt with. The boss was beginning to find me in
the way.

'At last I got to the cash desk. The cashier was a dumpy little lady of
about thirty, with a gentle sentimental expression.

'"Has Joseph been doing something silly?" she asked first.

'"No, no, Mademoiselle. Quite the contrary. He had a girl friend in
the neighbourhood, hadn't he?"'

Maigret grunted: 'Cut it short, will you?'

'Particularly as it's high time to get going if you want to see the girl.
In short, it was through the cashier that Joseph used to get the messages from Mathilde when she couldn't keep her dates with him. The
one I found in the packet of cigarettes must have been sent the day
before yesterday. A kid used to dash into the hairdresser's and hand
over the note to the cashier, whispering: "For Monsieur Joseph".

'Luckily the cashier saw the boy, on several occasions, going into a
leather-goods shop in the Boulevard Bonne-Nouvelle.

'That was how, one thing leading to another, I eventually ran
Mathilde to earth.'

'You've said nothing to her, I hope?'

'She doesn't even know I'm interested in her. I simply asked her
employer if he had an assistant called Mathilde. He pointed her out to
me behind the counter. He offered to call her; I asked him to say
nothing. If you'd like . . . It's half past five. The shop closes in half an
hour.'

'Excuse me, Mademoiselle . . .'

'No, Monsieur.'

'Just one word . . .'

'Please leave me alone.'

A rather pretty little person, who assumed that Maigret . . . Well, he had no alternative. 'Police.'

'What? And you want to speak to me?'

'I'd like a word with you, yes, about your boyfriend.'

'Joseph? . . . What has he done?'

'I don't know, Mademoiselle. But I should like to know where he is at this moment.'

And just as he said the words, he thought: 'Damn, that was a silly thing to do.'

He had blundered, like any beginner. He realized it when he saw her glancing round anxiously. What had impelled him to speak to her instead of following her? Hadn't she arranged to meet Joseph beside the métro station? Hadn't she expected to see him there? Why did she slow down her pace instead of going on her way?

'I suppose he's at work as usual.'

'No, Mademoiselle. And probably you know that as well as I do, or even better.'

'What d'you mean?'

It was rush hour on the boulevards. Long processions of people were moving towards the entrance to the métro and diving down the stairs.

'Let's wait here a moment, please,' Maigret said, forcing her to remain in the neighbourhood of the station.

She was evidently on edge. She kept looking around wildly. She was an eighteen-year-old with a fresh, round little face and the self-assurance of a typical Parisian girl

'Who told you about me?'

'Never mind that. What do you know about Joseph?'

'What do you want to know about him that I can tell you?'

The Superintendent was also scanning the crowd, aware that if Joseph caught sight of him with Mathilde he would probably make himself scarce.

'Did your boyfriend ever talk to you about an imminent change in his position? Come on! You're going to lie to me, I feel sure.'

'Why should I lie?'

She had bitten her lip.

'You see! You're asking me questions so as to give yourself time to make up a lie.'

She tapped on the pavement with her heel.

'For one thing, what proof is there that you really are police?'

He showed her his card.

'You'll admit that Joseph had a complex about the mediocrity of his situation.'

'What of it?'

'He suffered from it painfully, to an excessive degree.'

'Maybe he didn't want to remain a hairdresser's assistant. Is that a crime?'

'You're well aware that that's not what I mean. He loathed the house he lived in and the sort of existence he led. He was even ashamed of his mother, wasn't he?'

'He never said so to me.'

'But you sensed it. So recently he must have spoken to you about a change in his way of life.'

'No.'

'How long have you known one another?'

'A little over six months. It was during the winter. He came into the shop to buy a wallet. I realized that he thought they were too expensive, but he dared not tell me so and he bought one. That evening I saw him on the pavement. He followed me for several days before he ventured to speak to me.'

'Where did you use to go together?'

'Most of the time, we could only meet for a few minutes outside the shop. Sometimes he would take the métro with me as far as Championnet station, which is near my home. Occasionally we went to the cinema together on a Sunday, but that was difficult on account of my parents.'

'Did you never go to his home in his mother's absence?'

'Never, I swear. Once he showed me his house from a distance, so that I should understand.'

'That he was very unhappy . . . Don't you see?'

'Has he done anything wrong?'

'No, no, young lady. He has simply disappeared. And I'm depending on you a little, not very much I must admit, to find him again. I needn't ask you whether he had a room somewhere in town.'

'You obviously don't know him. In any case he nadn't enough money. He handed over all his wages to his mother. She left him barely enough to buy himself a few cigarettes.'

She blushed.

'When we went to the cinema we each paid for ourselves, and once when . . .'

'Go on . . .'

'Goodness, why not . . . there's no harm in it . . . Once, a month ago, when we went into the country together, he hadn't enough money to pay for lunch.'

'Whereabouts did you go?'

'Towards the Marne. We got off the train at Chelles and went for a walk between the Marne and the canal.'

'Thank you, Mademoiselle.'

Was she relieved to have seen no sign of Joseph in the crowd? Or disappointed? Both, probably.

'Why are the police looking for him?'

'Because his mother asked us to. Don't worry, Mademoiselle. And believe me: if you have any news of him before we do, let us know immediately.'

When he turned back, he saw her moving hesitantly down the métro stairs.

A note was waiting for him on his desk at Police Headquarters.

A certain Stéphane Bleustein, aged thirty-seven, was killed on February 15th, 1919, in his apartment in the Hôtel Negresco at Nice, where he had been staying for a few days. Bleustein had a good many visitors, often late at night. The crime was committed with a revolver of 6mm/35, which has not been found.

The inquest held at the time failed to identify the criminal. The victim's belongings had been thoroughly searched by the murderer and the room was found next morning in indescribable disorder.

As for Bleustein himself, he remains a somewhat shadowy figure and inquiries have failed to discover where he came from. When he arrived in Nice he had been travelling on the express train from Paris.

Fuller information can no doubt be obtained from the Security Branch at Nice.

The date of the murder corresponded with that of Bleustein's disappearance from the Quai de Bercy, and Maigret, reaching out once more for his missing pipe and not finding it, grumbled irritably:

'The blasted little fool!'

III.   *Inquiries on Behalf of the Next of Kin*

There are certain phrases which, on a railway journey for instance, stick in one's mind and which fit the rhythm of the train so closely that one can't get rid of them. One such was haunting Maigret while driving in an old creaking taxi, and the rhythm was emphasized by the beating of heavy rain against the floppy roof.

In-qui-ries-on-be-half-of-the-next-of-kin. In-qui-ries-on-be-half . . .

For after all he had no reason to be here, plunging along in the darkness with a pale-faced, tense young girl beside him and little Lucas sitting meekly on the folding seat. When somebody like Madame Leroy comes to bother you, one ought to cut short her lamentations.

'Nothing has been stolen from you, Madame? You're not lodging a complaint? In that case I'm sorry, but . . .'

And even if her son has disappeared:

'You say he's left home? If we had to look for all the people who leave home, the entire police force would do nothing else and even so we'd not have enough men available.'

'Inquiries on behalf of the next of kin.' That's what they call them. Undertaken only at the expense of those who request them. As for the results . . .

They are always very worthy people, moreover, whether old or young, men or women, with kindly expressions, gentle puzzled eyes, humble insistent voices:

'You can take my word for it, Superintendent, that my wife – and I know her better than anyone – has not gone off of her own free will.'

Or someone's daughter, 'such an innocent, affectionate girl . . .'

And there are hundreds like that every day. 'Inquiries on behalf of the next of kin.' No point in telling them that it would be better for them if their wife or daughter were not to be found again, because that would mean disillusionment! *Inquiries on behalf* . . .

And Maigret had let himself become involved yet again! The car had left Paris and was speeding along the highway, outside the scope of the Police Judiciaire. He had no business to be there. He would not even get his expenses refunded.

It was all on account of a pipe. The thunderstorm had broken out just as he was alighting from a taxi in front of the house in the Quai de Bercy. When he rang, Madame Leroy was all alone in the kitchen eating bread and butter and a pickled herring. In spite of her anxiety she had tried to conceal that herring!

'Do you recognize this man, Madame?'

And she replied unhesitatingly, though with surprise:

'It's my former lodger, Monsieur Bleustein. It's funny . . . In the photograph he's dressed like a . . .'

Like a gentleman, yes, whereas at Charenton he had looked like a nobody. That photograph had had to be hunted for in the archives of a leading newspaper because, for some unknown reason, it was not to be found in those of the police.

'What does this mean, Superintendent? Where is this man? What has he done?'

'He's dead. Tell me now. I see,' and he glanced round the room, noticing that cupboards and drawers had been emptied, 'that you've had the same idea as myself.'

She reddened. She was already on the defensive. But this evening the Superintendent was short of patience.

'You've been making an inventory of everything in the house. Don't deny it. You wanted to know whether your son had taken anything away, didn't you?'

'There's nothing missing, I give you my word. What are you thinking? Where are you going?'

For he was rushing off in a great hurry, getting back into his taxi. More time wasted, stupidly, too. A short while ago, he had had the girl there in front of him, in the Boulevard Bonne-Nouvelle. But he had forgotten to ask her for her exact address. And now he needed her. Luckily the owner of the leather-goods shop lived on the premises.

Another taxi. Heavy raindrops were pattering on the tarmac People were hurrying; the taxi kept skidding.

'Rue Championnet, no.67 . . .'

He burst into a small room where four people – father, mother, daughter, and a twelve-year-old boy – were sitting round a small table, eating soup. Mathilde sprang up, terrified, her mouth open to cry out.

'Please excuse me; I need your daughter's help to identify a customer she has seen in the shop. Mademoiselle, will you be good enough to follow me?'

Inquiries on behalf of the next of kin! Oh, it's a very different matter when you're faced with an obliging corpse that gives you hints straight away, or when you're running after a murderer whose possible reflexes are easily guessed.

Whereas when you're dealing with amateurs, with their weeping and worrying! And there are Father's and Mother's feelings to consider!

'Where are we going?'

'To Chelles.'

'Do you think he's there?'

'I haven't the slightest idea, Mademoiselle. Driver, please stop first at the Quai des Orfèvres.'

And there he had picked up Lucas, who was expecting him.

Inquiries on behalf of the next of kin. He was sitting in the back of the cab with Mathilde, who tended to keep slipping against him. Heavy drops of water seeped through the battered roof and fell on to his left knee. In front of him was the glowing tip of Lucas's cigarette.

'Can you remember Chelles clearly, Mademoiselle?'

'Oh, yes!'

Of course she could! Wasn't it her happiest romantic memory? The only time they had escaped from Paris and had run along together through the long grass beside the river!

'Do you think you'll be able to show us the way, in spite of the darkness?'

'I think so. Provided we start from the station. Because we went there by train.'

'You told me you had lunch at an inn?'

'Yes, a tumble-down sort of inn, so dirty and sinister-looking that we were frightened. We took a road alongside the Marne. At one point it became just a path. Wait a minute . . . On the left there's an abandoned lime-kiln. Then about five hundred metres further on, a small one-storey house. We were quite surprised to find it there.

'We went in. There was a zinc counter on the right . . . whitewashed walls with a few colour-prints, and a couple of iron tables and a few chairs . . . The man . . .'

'You're speaking of the landlord?'

'Yes. A little dark fellow who looked as if he might be something else. I don't quite know how to tell you. One imagines things. We asked if we could get something to eat and he gave us some pâté and sausage and then he warmed up some rabbit for us. It was very good. The landlord chatted with us, he told us about the anglers who use his inn. Besides, there was a whole heap of fishing rods in a corner. When you don't know, you imagine things.'

'Are we there?' Maigret asked through the pane of glass, for the driver had stopped.

A little station with a few lights amid the blackness.

'To the right,' the girl said. 'Then second on the right again. That was where we asked our way. But why do you think Joseph might have come here?'

For no reason! Or rather because of that pipe, although he dared not admit that.

Inquiries on behalf of the next of kin! It would make him a laughing-stock. And yet . . .

'Straight on, now, driver,' Mathilde broke in. 'Until you come to the river. There's a bridge, but instead of crossing it you turn left. Take care, the road's narrow.'

'Admit it, my dear; your Joseph must have talked about a possible and even a probable change in his situation.'

Later on, she might perhaps become as hard as old Madame Leroy, who had once been a girl herself, probably a pretty affectionate girl.

'He was ambitious.'

'I'm not speaking about the future. I mean right away.'

'He wanted to be something other than a hairdresser.'

'And he expected to have some money, didn't he?'

She was in agonies. She was so afraid of giving her Joseph away!

The taxi was crawling along a rough road beside the Marne, and on their left they could make out some shabby bungalows and a few more pretentious villas. Here and there a light showed, or a dog barked. Then suddenly, at about a kilometre's distance from the bridge, the ruts grew deeper and the taxi stopped. The driver declared:

'I can't go any farther.'

The rain was falling harder than ever. When they got out of the car it drenched them, and everything around them was wet, the slimy mud under their feet, the bushes through which they pushed their way. A little farther on they had to walk in single file, while the taxi-driver sat grumbling in his cab and probably settled down for a nap.

'It's funny. I didn't think it was so far. Can't you see any house yet?'

The Marne was flowing close by them. They were splashing through puddles. Maigret walked in front, parting the branches. Mathilde followed close behind him and Lucas brought up the rear, as calm as a Newfoundland dog.

The girl was beginning to be frightened.

'I certainly recognized the bridge and the lime-kiln. We can't possibly have taken the wrong road.'

'There's every reason,' Maigret muttered, 'why the way seems longer to you today than when you came with Joseph. Look, there's a light on the left.'

'That's the place, I'm sure.'

'Hush! Try not to make a noise.'

'Do you believe that . . .?'

Maigret said, with sudden sharpness: 'I don't believe anything. I never believe anything, Mademoiselle.'

He let them come level with him, and spoke in a low voice to Lucas.

'You wait here with the girl. Don't move unless I call you. Lean forward, Mathilde. From here one can make out the front of the house. Do you recognize it?'

'Yes, I'd swear to it.'

Maigret's broad back was already blocking out the small light from her.

And she was left to herself, her clothes soaking, in total darkness, in pouring rain, by the riverside, with a little man she did not know and who was calmly smoking one cigarette after another.

IV.   *The Anglers' Rest*

Mathilde had not exaggerated when she described the place as shady-looking and almost sinister. A sort of dilapidated arbour stood beside the little house, whose shutters were closed over grimy windows. The door had been left open, since the storm had only just begun to cool the air.

Yellow light shone on a dirty floor. Maigret suddenly emerged from the darkness. He stood in the doorway, looking larger than life-size, and raising a finger to the brim of his hat he muttered, with his pipe between his lips:

'Good evening, gentlemen.'

Two men were sitting talking at an iron table on which stood a bottle of marc and a couple of thick glasses. One of the men, a small dark fellow in shirt-sleeves, looked up calmly, showing some slight surprise, then rose to his feet, hitching up his trousers, and muttered: 'Good evening . . .'

The other man had his back turned, but he was obviously not Joseph Leroy. He was a heavily built man in a light grey suit. Oddly enough, in spite of the unusual character of Maigret's belated appearance, he never moved: it even looked as though he was restraining himself from giving a start. A china clock on the wall, advertising something or other, said ten past twelve, but it must have been later than that. Was it natural that the man should not have had sufficient curiosity to turn round and see who was coming in?

Maigret stood there, near the counter, the water streaming down from his clothes and making dark patches on the grey floor.

'Can you let me have a room, *patron*?'

The landlord, to gain time, had gone over to stand behind the bar counter, where there were only three or four dubious-looking bottles on a shelf, and asked:

'Can I give you something?'

'If you want to. I asked if you had a room vacant.'

'I'm sorry, no. Have you come on foot?'

It was Maigret's turn to avoid replying, and he said:

'I'll have a marc.'

'I fancied I heard a car engine.'

'That's quite possible. Have you or haven't you a room vacant?'

The other man's back was still turned, a few metres away from him, a back as motionless as though it were carved out of stone. There was no electricity. The room was lit only by a wretched oil lamp.

Why had the man not turned round . . . why had he kept so stiffly, painfully still . . .

Maigret felt anxious. He had just made the rapid calculation that, in view of the dimensions of the café and of the kitchen that could be glimpsed behind it, there must be at least three rooms on the upper floor. He could have sworn, judging from the appearance of the *patron*, the shabbiness of the premises, and a certain look of general neglect and disorder, that there was no woman about the house.

Now he had just heard someone walking stealthily overhead. This must be significant, for the landlord automatically glanced up and looked annoyed.

'Have you many people staying just now?'

'Nobody. Apart from . . .'

He indicated the man, or rather the man's motionless back, and

Maigret suddenly felt aware of imminent danger; he understood that he must act very quickly, without a blunder. He had time to see the man's hand reach towards the lamp on the table, and he sprang forward.

He was too late. The lamp had crashed to the ground with a clatter of broken glass, while a smell of paraffin filled the room.

'I thought I knew you, you bastard!'

He had managed to grab the man by the jacket. He tried to get a firmer hold, but the other struck out to free himself. They were in total darkness. The open door was a vaguely glimmering rectangular shape. What was the landlord doing? Would he attempt to rescue his customer?

Maigret hit out in his turn. Then he felt his hand being bitten; he flung himself with all his weight upon his opponent, and they rolled on to the floor together, amongst fragments of glass.

'Lucas!' Maigret shouted with all his might. 'Lucas . . .'

The man was armed; a hard shape in his jacket pocket was unmistakably a gun, and Maigret struggled to prevent him from slipping his hand into the pocket.

The landlord did not stir. He made no sound. He must have been standing motionless, perhaps unconcerned, behind his bar counter.

'Lucas!'

'Coming, Chief.'

Outside, Lucas was running over ruts and through puddles, calling out:

'You stay where you are, I tell you. D'you hear? I forbid you to follow me.'

He was presumably speaking to Mathilde, who must have been pale with fright.

'If you dare to bite me again, you brute, I'll knock your face in. Understood?'

Maigret, with his elbow, was preventing the man from getting at his gun. His opponent was as vigorous as himself, and alone in the darkness Maigret might not have got the better of him. They had collided with the table, which had overturned on top of them.

'Over here, Lucas. Your torch.'

'Coming, Chief.'

And suddenly a shaft of pale light shone on the two men whose limbs were intertwined.

'Good Lord, it's Nicolas! Fancy meeting you here!'

'Of course I'd recognized you myself, just from your voice.'

'Give us a hand, Lucas. He's a dangerous customer. Give him a good knock to keep him quiet. Don't be afraid; he's tough!'

And Lucas hit the man on the head as hard as he could with his little rubber truncheon.

'Now hand me the bracelets. I didn't expect to find this brute here. There, that's it now. You can get up, Nicolas. You needn't pretend to have passed out. You've got a harder head than that. Patron!'

He had to shout a second time, and it was odd to hear the landlord's voice speaking quietly out of the darkness, from beside the bar-counter:

'Messieurs . . .'

'Isn't there another lamp or a candle in the house?'

'I'll get you a candle. If you'll shine your torch into the kitchen . . .'

Maigret had bound his wrist with his handkerchief to staunch the blood; the man had given it a sharp bite. Sobs were heard beside the door; Mathilde, presumably, who did not know what was going on and who thought perhaps that it was Joseph with whom the Superintendent . . .

'Come in, my dear. Don't be afraid. I think it's nearly over. You, Nicolas, sit here, and if you dare to move . . .'

He laid his gun and his opponent's on a table, within his reach. The landlord came back with his candle, as calmly as though nothing had happened.

'Now,' Maigret said, 'go and fetch me the young fellow.'

There was a moment's hesitation. Was he going to deny all knowledge?

'I tell you to go and fetch me the young fellow, d'you understand?'

And, as the landlord moved towards the door:

'Has he got a pipe, by the way?'

Between sobs, the girl was asking:

'You're sure he's here and nothing's happened to him?'

Maigret made no reply; he was listening intently. Upstairs the landlord was knocking at a door. He was speaking urgently, in a low voice; now and then a sentence could be overheard:

'It's some gentlemen from Paris and a young lady. You can open the door. I promise you . . .'

And Mathilde, in tears: 'He might have been killed . . .'

Maigret shrugged and went towards the staircase himself.

'Mind that parcel, Lucas. You recognized our old friend Nicolas, didn't you? I thought he was safely locked up in Fresnes!'

He went slowly up the stairs and pushed the landlord away from the door.

'Why don't you go downstairs now? Give the girl something to set her up, a toddy or something of the sort. Well, Joseph?'

At last a key turned in the lock. Maigret pushed open the door.

'Isn't there any light?'

'Wait a minute. I'll light a candle. There's a bit of one left.'

Joseph's hands were shaking, and his face, when the candlelight shone on it, was convulsed with terror.

'Is he still down there?' he gasped.

His mind was in a whirl and his words poured forth in confusion.

'How did you find me? What did they tell you? Who's the girl?'

It was a rustic bedroom with a high bed, unmade, and a chest of drawers which must recently have been pushed against the door as though to withstand a siege.

'Where have you put them?' asked Maigret, as though it was the most natural thing in the world.

Joseph looked at him in stupefaction and realised that the Superintendent knew everything. He could not have shown more amazement if God the Father had come bursting into his room.

He fumbled wildly in the back pocket of his trousers and pulled out a tiny parcel wrapped in newspaper.

His hair was untidy and his clothes creased. Maigret instinctively glanced at his feet, which were shod in shapeless slippers.

'My pipe . . .'

This time the boy was on the verge of tears and his lips trembled in a childish pout. Maigret wondered whether he was not about to fall on his knees and beg for pardon.

'Keep calm, young man', he warned him. 'There are people downstairs.' And with a smile he accepted the pipe that the boy held out to him, trembling more desperately than ever.

'Hush! Mathilde is coming up the stairs. She hadn't the patience to wait for us to come down. Tidy your hair.'

He picked up a jug to pour some water into the basin, but the jug was empty.

'No water?' Maigret asked in some surprise.

'I drank it.'

Of course! Why had he not thought of it? That pale face, those drawn features, those lifeless eyes.

'You're hungry?'

And, conscious of Mathilde's presence on the dark landing, he remarked without turning round:

'Come in, my dear . . . You'll keep it cool, if you'll take my advice. He loves you very much, of course, but what he needs first of all is something to eat.'

V. *How Joseph Ran Away*

It was a pleasure, now, to listen to the rain pattering on the leaves all round them and especially to breathe the cool, damp night air through the wide open door.

Joseph was still so tense that despite his hunger he had scarcely been able to swallow the pâté sandwich brought him by the landlord, and his Adam's apple kept rising and falling.

As for Maigret, who was at his second or third glass of marc, he was now smoking his favourite pipe, restored to him at last.

'You see, young man, without wishing to encourage you to petty larceny, I must point out that if you hadn't pinched my pipe I really believe your body would have been fished up some day out of the rushes in the Marne. Maigret's pipe, eh?'

And in fact Maigret spoke these words with a certain satisfaction, like a man whose pride is pleasantly tickled. Somebody had pinched his pipe, as others might pinch the pencil of a great writer, the paint-brush of a famous painter, a handkerchief or other trivial object belonging to a favourite star.

This the Superintendent had understood from the start. 'Inquiry on behalf of the next of kin' . . . A case with which he ought not really to have been concerned

The point was that a boy who suffered from a sense of inferiority had stolen his pipe. And the following night that boy had disappeared. And he had constantly tried to dissuade his mother from consulting the police.

Because he wanted to conduct the inquiry himself, of course. Because he felt capable of doing so. Because, with Maigret's pipe between his teeth, he fancied himself . . .

'When did you realize that it was diamonds that the mysterious visitor was looking for in your home?'

Joseph nearly lied, out of vanity, then changed his mind after a glance at Mathilde.

'I didn't know it was diamonds. I thought it must be something small, because the smallest crannies had been searched and even tiny pillboxes opened.'

'Say, Nicolas! Hey, Nicolas!'

Nicolas sat glaring fixedly, slumped on a chair in a corner, his handcuffed fists on his knees.

'When you killed Bleustein at Nice . . .'

Not a flicker of reaction passed over the man's bony face.

'D'you realize I'm talking to you? When you did Bleustein in at the Negresco, didn't you understand that he was swindling you? Aren't you going to come clean? Well, that'll come. What did Bleustein tell you? That the diamonds were in the house in the Quai de Bercy? Sure. But you ought to have realized that little things like that are easy to hide. Perhaps he'd told you the wrong hiding-place? Or had you thought yourself cleverer than you are? No, no. Don't talk so much.

I'm not asking you where the diamonds came from. We'll know that tomorrow, after the experts have looked at them.

'It was bad luck that you got picked up on an old charge just at that moment. What was it? A burglary in the Boulevard Saint-Martin, if I'm not mistaken? By the way, that was jewellery too, wasn't it? After all, you're a specialist . . . You got three years for that. And just three months ago, when you were let out, you came prowling round that house. You'd got the key that Bleustein had had made for himself . . . What's that you say? . . . Okay, just as you please.'

The youth and the girl were looking at him in amazement. They could not understand Maigret's sudden cheerfulness, because they did not know what a strain he had been undergoing during the last few hours.

'You see, Joseph – hello, so I've begun to *tutoyer* you – it was all quite simple. A stranger gets into a house three years after that house has stopped taking lodgers . . . I immediately thought of someone who'd been released from jail. An illness wouldn't have gone on for three years. I should have examined the lists of discharged prisoners straight away and I'd have happened on our friend Nicolas . . . Have you a light, Lucas? My matches are soaked.

'And now, Joseph, tell us what took place that crucial night.'

'I was determined to find out. I thought it must be something very valuable, something worth a fortune . . .'

'And since your mother had brought me into the case you wanted at all costs to find out that very night.'

Joseph hung his head.

'And in order not to be disturbed, you poured Lord knows what into your mother's tisane.'

He did not deny it. His Adam's apple rose and fell faster.

'I did so want a different sort of life!' he stammered almost inaudibly.

'You went downstairs in your slippers. Why were you so sure you'd find whatever it was that night?'

'Because I'd already searched the whole house except the dining-room. I'd divided the house into sections. I was sure it could only be in the dining-room.'

A trace of pride was perceptible under his dejection and humility, as he declared:

'I found them!'

'Where?'

'You may have noticed that in the dining-room there's an old ceiling lamp with sconces holding imitation candles made of china. I don't know why it occurred to me to unscrew the candles. Inside there were little twists of paper and in these there were some hard objects.'

'One minute! When you came down from your room, what were you planning to do if you should be successful?'

'I don't know.'

'You weren't planning to run away?'

'No, I swear.'

'But perhaps to hide the treasure somewhere else?'

'Yes.'

'In the house?'

'No. Because I was expecting you to come and search it yourself and I was sure you'd find the diamonds. I'd have hidden them at the hairdresser's. Then, later on . . .'

Nicolas laughed derisively. The landlord was standing quite still with his elbows on his bar-counter, and his shirt made a white patch in the semi-darkness.

'When you discovered about the sconces . . .'

'I was just putting the last of them back in place when I felt someone beside me. At first I thought it was Mother. I switched off my torch, which I'd been using to see with. There was a man there and he kept coming nearer, and then I rushed to the door and out into the street. I was very frightened. I ran. The door slammed. I was in my slippers, I had no hat and no tie on. I went on running and I could hear steps behind me.'

'You couldn't keep up with this young greyhound, Nicolas!' mocked Maigret.

'Near the Bastille there were some policemen on the beat. I walked while I was near them, because I was sure the man wouldn't dare attack me just then. So I reached the Gare de l'Est, and that's what gave me the idea . . .'

'The idea of Chelles, to be sure. A romantic memory! And then?'

'I stayed in the waiting-room until five in the morning. There were people there. And so long as I was in a crowd . . .'

'I understand.'

'Only, I didn't know who was after me. I kept looking at everybody in turn. When the booking office opened I slipped between a couple of women. I asked for my ticket in a whisper. Several trains were leaving at about the same time. I got into one after another, crossing the railway lines.'

'Say, Nicolas, it seems as though this kid gave you even more trouble than he gave me!'

'So long as he didn't know where my ticket was for, you see? At Chelles I waited till the train was moving before I got out.'

'Not bad! Not bad!'

'I rushed out of the station. There was nobody in the streets. I started running again. I didn't hear anyone behind me. I got here and

I asked for a room straight away, because I was all in, and I was anxious to get rid of . . .'

He was still trembling at the thought of it.

'Mother never allowed me much pocket money. In the room I discovered that I only had fifteen francs and a few telephone tokens. I wanted to go off again and get home before Mother . . .'

'And then Nicolas came.'

'I saw him through the window, getting out of a taxi five hundred metres away. I realized straight away that he must have gone as far as Lagny and taken a cab and that at Chelles he had picked up my trail. Then I locked myself in. When I heard steps in the stairway I pulled the chest of drawers against the door. I was sure he would kill me.'

'Without a qualm,' muttered Maigret. 'Only he didn't want to give himself away in front of the landlord. Isn't that so, Nicolas? So he settled down here, assuming that you would come out of your room at some point, if only to get something to eat.'

'I ate nothing. I was afraid, too, that he might take a ladder and come in at night by the window. So I kept the shutters closed. I dared not go to sleep.'

Steps could be heard outside. Now that the storm was over, the taxi-driver had begun to worry about his fares.

Then Maigret knocked out his pipe against his heel, filled it again and stroked it with satisfaction.

'If you'd been unlucky enough to break it . . .' he grunted. Then, without a break:

'Come on, all of you, let's go! By the way, Joseph, what are you going to tell your mother?'

'I don't know. It'll be terrible.'

'Not at all, not at all! You went down into the dining-room to do some detecting. You saw a man going out. You followed him, proud of playing policeman.'

For the first time, Nicolas opened his lips. He commented contemptuously:

'If you think I'm going to help you play that game!'

Maigret replied, imperturbably:

'We'll see about that presently, won't we, Nicolas? You and I together, in my office . . . Say, driver, it's going to be a tight fit in your car! Shall we be off?'

A little later he whispered to Joseph, who was huddled in a corner of the seat beside Mathilde:

'I'll give you another pipe, you know! An even bigger one if you like.'

'Only,' the boy retorted, 'it won't be *your* pipe!'

June 1945

DEATH PENALTY

The greatest danger, in this kind of case, is that one may get fed up with it. They had been playing a waiting game for twelve days already; Inspector Janvier and Sergeant Lucas took it in relays, indefatigably patient, but Maigret had contributed at least a hundred hours himself, since only he really knew what he was aiming at.

That morning Lucas had called him from the Boulevard des Batignolles:

'The birds look like flying . . . The maid has just told me they're fastening their cases . . .'

By eight o'clock Maigret was on the look-out in a taxi not far from the Hôtel Beauséjour, with a suitcase at his feet.

It was Sunday; rain was falling. At a quarter past eight the couple emerged from the hotel with three suitcases and hailed a taxi. At half past eight this taxi stopped in front of a brasserie near the Gare du Nord, facing the big clock. Maigret, too, got out of his cab and, making no attempt to conceal himself, sat down outside the café at a table immediately next to his 'birds'.

Not only was it drizzling, it was cold. The couple had settled down beside a brazier. When he noticed the Superintendent, the man involuntarily raised his hand to his bowler hat, while the woman clutched her fur coat closer round her.

'A hot toddy, waiter!'

The others were drinking toddies too; and passers-by brushed past them, the waiter hurried to and fro, life went on as it does on any Sunday morning in the neighbourhood of a big railway station, just as though a man's life were not at stake.

The minute hand moved jerkily forward on the clock face, and at nine o'clock the couple rose and made their way over to the ticket booth.

'Two second-class singles to Brussels . . .'

'One second-class single to Brussels,' echoed Maigret.

Then followed the bustle of the crowded platforms, the search for seats on the express train, until finally the couple climbed into a compartment at the far end, close to the engine, where Maigret followed them and lifted his suitcase on to the rack. People were kissing one another goodbye. The young man in the bowler got out to buy papers, and returned with a pile of weeklies and magazines.

It was the Berlin express, crowded with people talking every language under the sun. Once the train had left, the young man, without removing his gloves, began to read a paper, while his companion, who seemed to be feeling cold, instinctively laid her hand on his.

'Is there a restaurant car?' somebody asked.

'After the frontier, I believe!' another person replied.

'Do we stop for the customs?'

'No. The examination takes place in the train, after Saint-Quentin . . .'

The train passed through suburbs, then through endless forest, then stopped briefly at Compiègne. From time to time the young man looked up from his paper and cast a rapid glance at Maigret's placid face.

He was tired, no doubt of that. Maigret, who was casting similar stealthy glances, thought that he was looking paler than usual, even tenser and more nervous, and that he could clearly have no idea what he had been reading for the past hour.

'Aren't you hungry?' the young woman asked.

'No . . .'

People were smoking pipes and cigarettes. It was a dark day. They passed villages with wet empty streets, and churches where High Mass was probably being sung.

And Maigret no longer even tried to put the facts together one by one, precisely through fear of getting fed up with the whole thing, since for the past two and a half weeks he had thought of nothing but this case.

The young man sitting opposite him was soberly dressed, more like an Englishman than a Parisian: an iron grey suit, a grey overcoat with concealed buttons, a bowler hat and, to complete his outfit, an umbrella which he had laid on the lower rack.

If his name had been spoken in the compartment everybody would have been startled, since at least half of the newspapers spread out on passengers' knees were still talking about him.

He had a fine name: Jehan d'Oulmont. An excellent Belgian family, which had figured repeatedly in his country's history.

Jehan d'Oulmont was fair, with finely cut features but an over-sensitive skin, flushing readily, and his face was subject to nervous twitches.

Twice already Maigret had held him closeted in his office at Police Headquarters, and twice, for hours on end, he had tried in vain to make the young man give way.

'You admit that for the past two years you've been the despair of your family?'

'That's my family's business!'

'You began studying law at the University of Louvain, but you were expelled for notorious misconduct.'

'I was living with a woman . . .'

'Excuse me! With a woman who was being kept by an Antwerp merchant!'

'That's an unimportant detail!'

'When your family cast you off you came to Paris . . . You were seen chiefly at race-courses and nightclubs . . . You called yourself the Comte d'Oulmont, although you have no right to the title.'

'Some people like it . . .'

Despite his sickly pallor he maintained his unshakable coolness.

'You made the acquaintance of Sonia Lipchitz, and you knew all about her past . . .'

'A woman's past is no concern of mine.'

'At twenty-three Sonia Lipchitz had been the mistress of a number of men. . . . The latest of these left her a considerable fortune, which she squandered in less than two years.'

'That proves that I'm not mercenary, for in that case I'd have been too late on the scene.'

'You know that your uncle, Count Adalbert d'Oulmont – they like fancy names in your family – used to spend a few days in Paris every month, staying at the Hôtel du Louvre.'

'To make up for the austere life he felt compelled to live in Brussels.'

'That's as it may be! . . . Your uncle, an old habitué of the hotel, invariably reserved the same suite, no. 318 . . . Every morning he went riding in the Bois, then lunched in a fashionable restaurant, after which he retired to his hotel rooms until five o'clock.'

'He must have needed a rest!' the young man retorted cynically. 'At his age!'

'At five o'clock he would send for the barber and the manicurist and . . .'

'And then until two in the morning he visited the places where you can meet pretty women.'

'That's true, too.'

For if the Comte d'Oulmont, at one period of his life, had been a distinguished diplomat, it had to be admitted that with age he had gradually become the typical elderly dandy, wig and all.

'Your uncle was a rich man.'

'I've always been told so.'

'He repeatedly helped you out with subsidies.'

'And with sermons . . . which made us quits.'

'Two days before his death, you introduced him to your mistress Sonia Lipchitz in a Champs-Elysées bar.'

'As you yourself might have introduced him to your wife.'

'Please! You all three had an apéritif together, then under pretext of a business engagement, you left the two of them alone . . . At that moment you and Sonia were at the end of your tether. After living for a long time at the Hôtel de Berry near the Champs-Elysées, in a smart penthouse, you'd sunk to a seedy hotel in the Boulevard des Batignolles.'

'Are you blaming me for that?'

'Apparently your uncle did not take to Sonia, since he left her immediately after dinner and went off to some small theatre.'

'Is that my fault too?'

'Two days later, on Friday, at about half past three, the Comte d'Oulmont was murdered in his hotel suite, where he was taking his usual siesta. According to the forensic experts, he was killed by a violent blow from a lead pipe or an iron bar.'

'And they searched me,' the young man sneered.

'I know! And you even had an alibi. You showed me your betting book next morning – you're a racing addict. On the afternoon of the murder you were at Longchamp, and you laid bets on two horses in every race. This was confirmed by the tote tickets found in your coat pocket and by some of your friends, who noticed you once or twice during the afternoon.'

'You see!'

'Nonetheless you would have had time, during the race meeting, to jump into a taxi and dash off to your uncle's hotel.'

'Did anybody see me there?'

'You're sufficiently familiar with the Hôtel du Louvre to know that they don't pay attention to the comings and goings of guests. All the same, a page-boy thinks he remembers . . .'

'Surely that's rather vague?'

'A sum of thirty-two thousand francs in French notes had been stolen from your uncle.'

'If I'd had them, I'd have had time to get across the frontier!'

'I know that, too. No money was found at your hotel. Indeed, two days later, your mistress pledged her last two remaining rings at the municipal pawn-office, and now you are living on the five thousand francs she got for them . . .'

'You see . . .'

That was the whole case! An almost perfect crime! An alibi of the sort that cannot be successfully challenged. Jehan had been seen at the races that afternoon. But at what time?

He had laid bets. But for certain races his mistress might have laid them for him, and it's no great distance from Longchamp to the Rue de Rivoli.

A piece of lead piping, an iron bar? Anyone can obtain these and get rid of them without difficulty. And anyone, with a little skill, can slip into a grand hotel without being noticed.

What about Oulmont's betting book? And the pawning of the two rings next day?

'You've admitted yourself,' Oulmont remarked, 'that my late lamented uncle had women in to visit him. Why don't you look in that direction?'

Logically, his argument was irrefutable, so much so that when he had turned up at the Quai des Orfèvres, after being twice questioned, and had asked to be allowed to return to Belgium, they had had to grant him permission for lack of sufficient evidence.

This was why for the past twelve days Maigret had been making use of his well-tried tactics: having his man followed step by step, minute by minute, for twenty-four hours a day, and followed ostentatiously, so that he would be the first to give up through sheer exhaustion and disgust.

And this was why Maigret had chosen, that morning, to take his seat in the railway carriage facing the young man who, on seeing him, had given a sketchy greeting and had then been forced, for hours on end, to affect an offhand manner.

It had been a shocking, inexcusable crime, the more odious in that it had been committed by a relative of the victim, an educated man without any obvious moral taint!

The jury would require him to pay for it with his head. And that head, somewhat pale indeed, barely flushed on the cheekbones, was now lifted to confront the customs officers.

There was nearly a scene of protest in the compartment. Maigret had given his orders by telephone, and the examination of the young couple's luggage was so thorough as to be indiscreet.

The result was negative. Jehan d'Oulmont gave his wan smile. He was smiling at Maigret. He knew Maigret was his enemy. He, too, felt that this was a war of attrition, but a war in which his head was at stake.

One of them knew everything: the murderer. When, how, at what exact moment, in what circumstances the crime had been committed.

But the other, Maigret, smoking his pipe in spite of the frowns of the woman next to him, who disliked tobacco smoke – what did he know, what had he discovered?

It was indeed a war of attrition! Past the frontier, Maigret would no longer even have the right to intervene, and already the first miners' dwellings of the Borinage were discernible.

So why was he here? Why did he persist? Why did he follow the couple to the restaurant car, where they had gone for an aperitif, and sit down at the same table, silent and threatening?

And when they reached Brussels, why did he stop at the Palace Hotel, where Jehan d'Oulmont and his mistress had taken a room?

Had he discovered a flaw in the alibi? Had Jehan d'Oulmont forgotten some detail which had given him away?

This was not so; in that case he would have been arrested in France, and handed over to French lawcourts where he would undoubtedly have been sentenced to death. . . .

In the Palace Hotel, Maigret took a room next to the couple's. Leaving his door open, he went down behind them into the restaurant, walked behind them past the shop-fronts of the Rue Neuve, and entered the same brasserie, apparently as calm and resolute as ever.

Sonia was almost as feverishly tense as her companion. Next day she did not get up until two o'clock, and the couple took lunch in their room. And they heard the telephone bell ring as Maigret ordered his!

A day passed . . . Two days . . . The five thousand francs must be melting away. Maigret was still there, pipe in mouth and hands in pockets, sombre and patient.

But what did he know? Who could have said what he knew?

In fact Maigret knew nothing! He merely *felt.* Maigret was sure of the answer, he'd have staked his reputation on being right. But it was in vain that he had gone over the problem a hundred times in his head, questioned Parisian taxi-drivers and race-course specialists.

'You know, we see so many people . . . Possibly? . . .'

Particularly as there was nothing unusual about Jehan d'Oulmont's appearance, and those who were shown his photograph promptly recognized somebody else.

Flair is not enough; nor is conviction. The law demands proof, and Maigret went on hunting without knowing who was going to tire first. He walked behind the couple in the Botanical Gardens. He spent evenings in the cinema. He lunched and dined in excellent brasseries of the sort he liked, and drank his fill of beer.

The rain had been followed by a sort of melting snow. By Tuesday the Superintendent calculated that his victims could only have three hundred Belgian francs left, and wondered whether they might perhaps have recourse to the secret hoard.

It was an exhausting life, and at night he had to wake up at the slightest sound in the next room. But he was like those boar-hounds which, once launched in pursuit of their quarry, will let themselves be disembowelled sooner than retreat.

Around them, nobody suspected anything. Waiters served Jehan d'Oulmont as they might any other customer, unaware that his head was none too secure on his shoulders. At a dance hall a very respectable-looking young man danced with Sonia, then disappeared, returning an hour later to ask her for another dance; he began fiddling with her handbag as though to tease her; then he greeted d'Oulmont with a friendly wave.

This was a trivial incident, on their third day in Brussels. And yet from that moment Maigret at last felt some hope of success.

What he did next was so unlike him that Madame Maigret would have been astonished. He went up to the bar of the nightclub, drank several glasses in company of the girls who crowded round him, became excessively lively and eventually, practically reeling, went over to Sonia and asked her to dance.

'If you want to!' she said curtly.

She left her handbag on the table and glanced at her lover, who, however, was now obliged to dance with one of the girls of the establishment.

At this moment, while the two couples mingled with so many others under an orange light, who could have foreseen what was going to happen?

The dance over, Maigret was no longer alone. A little man in black walked beside him to the young couple's table and said:

'Monsieur Jehan d'Oulmont? . . . Quiet, please . . . No scenes . . . On behalf of the Belgian Criminal Investigation Department it is my duty to arrest you.'

The handbag still lay there on the table. Maigret looked as if he was thinking of something else.

'To arrest me on what charge?'

'I have a warrant for your extradition which . . .'

Then d'Oulmont's hand reached out for the handbag. Suddenly the young man stood up, levelled a gun at Maigret and . . .

'You won't have the last laugh,' he snarled.

A shot rang out. Maigret still stood there, hands in pockets. Jehan, clutching his gun, was panic-stricken. The dancing couples scattered in the inevitable disorder . . .

'You understand?' Maigret said to the Chief of the Brussels Police. 'I had no proofs. Only clues! And I knew he was just as intelligent as myself . . .

'I couldn't prove that he had killed his uncle. And he would probably have got away with it if . . .'

'If what?'

'If he had not formerly studied law, and if the death penalty had still existed in Belgium. I'll explain . . . In France he killed his uncle because he needed money. He knew that his life was at stake there. He took refuge in Brussels, realising that he would be extradited if his crime could be proved . . . And I was always there at his heels! In other words, I might have clues, I might even have proofs . . . In that case nothing could save him . . .

'Or rather there was one thing that might save him from the guillotine, as happened with the murderer Danse. *If he should commit another murder before being extradited, he would be subject to the jurisdiction of the Belgian courts, in which the death penalty no longer exists but which would send him to prison for life.*

'This was the dilemma I was seeking to confront him with by following him so closely. He had no weapon. The action of his mistress this evening suggested to me that they had managed to secure one, thanks to the complicity of an old acquaintance, and that this was in the handbag.

'During the dance a policeman replaced the loaded revolver by one charged with blanks.

'Then came the arrest.

'Jehan d'Oulmont, now panic-stricken, knowing what fate awaited him, opted for a life sentence in Belgium.

'Is it clear?'

Yes, it was clear enough! A second crime had saved the life of old Count d'Oulmont's murderer. Moreover, the young man's sarcastic smile proclaimed:

'You see, you won't have my head!'

His head, indeed, was safe; nonetheless he was henceforward incapable of doing further harm. And Maigret was at last entitled to think about something else!

MR MONDAY

Maigret stood still for a moment in front of the black iron gate that separated him from the garden, and on which an enamel plate bore the number 47b. It was five o'clock in the evening, and darkness had fallen. Behind him a branch of the Seine flowed sullenly round the deserted Île de Puteaux, with its thickets and tall poplars and patches of waste ground.

In front of him, however, on the other side of the gate was a small modern private house, a typical Neuilly house with all the elegance and comfort of the Bois de Boulogne district, its garden now carpeted. with autumn leaves.

No. 47b was at the corner of the Boulevard de la Seine and the Rue Maxime-Baès. On the first floor some rooms were lit up, and Maigret, hunching his shoulders under the rain, decided to ring the bell. It is always embarrassing to disturb a peaceful house, particularly on a winter's evening when it seems to be guarding its privacy and its cosy warmth, and above all when the intruder has come from Police Head-quarters with his pockets full of horrible documents.

A light went on downstairs, a door opened and a servant, before crossing the garden in the rain, tried to catch a glimpse of the visitor.

'What is it?' he asked through the gate.

'Dr Barion, please . . . ?'

In the elegant hallway Maigret automatically thrust his pipe into his pocket.

'Who shall I say?'

'You must be Martin Vignolet, the chauffeur,' said the Superintendent, to the man's considerable surprise.

At the same time he slipped his visiting card into an envelope, which he then closed. Vignolet was a man of about forty-five to fifty, with prominent bones and thick hair, obviously of peasant origin. He went up to the first floor, and returned a few minutes later; Maigret followed him up, passing a child's pram on the way.

'Please come in,' said Dr Armand Barion, opening the door of his consulting room.

He had the deeply shadowed eyes and the pallor of a man who has not slept for several days. Maigret had not even begun to speak when he noticed the sound of children's voices at play on the ground floor.

*   *   *

Before entering the house, he already knew what the household consisted of. Dr Barion, a specialist in lung diseases and a former intern at Laennec Hospital, had only lived in Neuilly for the past three years, and besides his practice he kept up his laboratory research. He was married and had three children, a boy of seven, a girl of five and a baby a few months old, whose pram Maigret had observed.

The domestic staff consisted of Martin Vignolet, who was both chauffeur and valet, of his wife Eugénie who did the cooking, and finally, until three weeks previously, of an eighteen-year-old Breton girl, Olga Boulanger.

'I assume, doctor, that you're aware of the reason for my visit. Following the post mortem, the Boulanger family have taken legal advice and have lodged an action, as plaintiffs; and I have been instructed . . .'

His whole attitude seemed apologetic and indeed it was not without a sense of embarrassment that he had begun to tackle this case.

Three weeks earlier Olga Boulanger had died in somewhat mysterious circumstances, nonetheless the registrar had issued a death certificate and the burial had taken place. The parents had come from Brittany for the funeral, typical peasants, tough and mistrustful, and they had learnt, heaven knows how, that their daughter was four months pregnant. Someone had put them in touch with Barthet, a particularly acrimonious lawyer, and on his advice they had, a week later, demanded exhumation and an autopsy.

'I have the report with me,' Maigret sighed, indicating his pocket.

'Don't bother! I know all about it, particularly as I got permission to assist the pathologist.'

He was calm, although exhausted and probably feverish. He was wearing his lab coat; with the lamplight full on his face, he looked Maigret in the eyes without ever flinching.

'I needn't add that I was expecting you, Superintendent.'

On his desk, in a metal frame, stood a photo of his wife, a pretty woman of barely thirty with an air of delicate refinement.

'Since you have Dr Paul's report in your pocket, you must be aware that we found the unfortunate girl's intestine riddled with tiny perforations, which quickly brought on septicaemia. You must know, too, that after meticulous researches we succeeded in establishing the cause of these perforations, which my distinguished colleague and I found most disturbing: It worried us so much that we called in a colonial doctor to our aid, and he solved the problem.'

Maigret nodded. Barion, who seemed to guess what he was longing for, broke off to say:

'Please smoke if you like. I don't myself, since my patients are

mainly children. A cigar? . . . No? . . . I'll go on . . . The method used
to kill my servant – for I'm positive she was killed – is apparently well
known in Malaya and the New Hebrides. The victim is induced to
swallow a certain number of those slender beards, as sharp as needles,
that grow on ears of various cereals, including rye . . . These beards
remain in the bowel, the lining of which they gradually pierce, and the
inevitable result . . .'

'Excuse me!' Maigret sighed. 'The post-mortem also confirmed
that Olga Boulanger was four and a half months pregnant. Could she
have got into bad company?'

'No! She seldom or never went out. She was rather a gawky little
thing with a freckled face . . .'

And he hastily returned to his subject.

'I must confess, Superintendent, that since that post-mortem ten
days ago I've thought about nothing but this case. I bear no grudge
against the Boulanger parents, who are simple folk and who clearly
lay the blame on me. Nonetheless I should be in a tragic position if I
failed to discover the truth. Fortunately I have partially succeeded in
doing so . . .'

Maigret could scarcely conceal his surprise. He had come to conduct an investigation, and now he found himself confronted, so to
speak, with one that had already been carried out, and of which a
calm, clear-headed man was making a report.

'What day is it today – Thursday? . . . Well, since last Monday,
Superintendent, I've had positive proof that poor Olga was not the
intended victim . . . How did I discover this? . . . In the simplest possible way. It was necessary to discover what food the girl had eaten
that could have contained the fragments of the rye . . . As she would
never have thought of killing herself, particularly in such an out-of-
the-way and extremely painful fashion, some outsider was obviously
responsible . . .'

'Don't you suspect your chauffeur Martin of having had relations
with her?'

'Indeed I'm certain he did,' agreed Dr Barion. 'I questioned him
on the subject and he ended by confessing.'

'Had he never lived in the colonies?'

'Only in Algeria . . . But I can assure you right away that you're on
the wrong track. With my wife's help and the cook's, I patiently drew
up a list of all the articles of food that have been eaten in the house
lately and I even analysed some of them. On Monday, when I was
here in the consulting room, in despair of ever reaching any result,
my attention was caught by the sound of footsteps on the gravel and I
saw an old man going towards the kitchen, where he was a regular
visitor.

'It was the man we call Mr Monday, whom I'd completely forgotten.'

'Mr Monday?' Maigret repeated with an amused smile.

'That's the name the children have given him, because he comes every Monday. A beggar of the old sort, I was going to say a pre-war beggar, clean and respectable, who goes on a different round each day. Here, it's a Monday . . . Traditions have grown up gradually, including that of keeping a complete meal for him – it's always the same, for that matter, because we have chicken with rice on a Monday and he eats it peacefully in the kitchen. He amuses the children, who go and chat with him . . . Quite a long time ago I noticed that he used to bring each of them one of those cream cakes that are called *religieuses*, and I objected . . .'

Maigret, who had been sitting too long, got up, and his interlocutor continued:

'You know how tradespeople would sooner give away goods to the poor than money . . . I suspected that these *religieuses* must come from some local pastry-cook's and that they were probably stale. Not to upset the old fellow, I said nothing about it, but I forbade my son and daughter to touch these cakes.'

'Which the maid then used to eat?'

'Probably.'

'And it was in these cakes . . . ?'

'This week Mr Monday came as usual with his two *religieuses* wrapped up in cream-coloured paper. When he had left I examined the pastries, which I'll show you presently, and I found there beards of rye in sufficient quantity to have caused the troubles that resulted in Olga's death . . . Do you understand now? The intended victims were my children, rather than that poor girl . . .'

Their voices could still be heard from the floor below. The room was warm and quiet, save for the occasional swish of a car on the asphalt of the embankment.

'I haven't told anyone yet . . . I was waiting for your visit . . .'

'Do you suspect this beggar of . . .'

'Mr Monday? Certainly not! Besides, I've not told you everything yet, and the rest of the story will completely exonerate the poor old fellow. Yesterday I went to the hospital, then I called on some colleagues. I wanted to know if any of them had recently recorded any case analogous to that of Olga Boulanger . . .'

Hoarse-voiced, he drew a hand across his forehead.

'And it appears practically certain that at least two people died in the same fashion, one nearly two months ago, the other only three weeks ago . . .'

'Had they eaten cakes?'

'I couldn't find out, for the doctors had mistaken the cause of death and had not thought an inquest necessary . . . There you are, Superintendent! . . . I know nothing more, but I've learnt enough, as you see, to be terrified. Somewhere in Neuilly there's a madman or a madwoman who, I don't know how, manages to introduce death into cream cakes . . .'

'You told me just now that your children were the intended victims . . .'

'Yes . . . I'm firmly convinced of that . . . I understand your question. How does the murderer manage to ensure that it's those particular cakes, Mr Monday's cakes, that . . .'

'Especially since there have been other cases!'

'I know . . . I can't explain it . . .'

He seemed sincere, and yet Maigret could not resist watching him stealthily.

'May I ask you a personal question?'

'By all means . . .'

'Forgive me if it's a painful one. The Boulangers accuse you of having had sexual relations with their daughter . . .'

The doctor hung his head and groaned:

'I knew we should come to that! I don't want to lie to you, Superintendent . . . It's true, it's stupidly true, for it happened stupidly, one Sunday when I was alone here with the girl . . . I'd give anything in the world for my wife not to find out, for it would hurt her too much. On the other hand I can give you my word as a doctor that by then Olga had already become the mistress of my chauffeur . . .'

'So that the child? . . .'

'Was not mine, I assure you . . . The dates don't even correspond! . . . In any case, Olga was a good creature who'd never have thought of blackmailing me. You see that . . .'

Maigret would not allow him time to pull himself together.

'And you don't know anyone who . . . Wait . . . You spoke of a madman or a madwoman . . .'

'I did! Only it's impossible, physically impossible! Mr Monday never goes to *her* place before coming here! And when he does, afterwards, she leaves him in the street and throws him some coins out of the window.'

'Who are you talking about?'

'About Miss Wilfur . . . It makes one believe in immanent justice! . . . I adore my wife and yet there are two things I keep secret from her. The first you know already . . . The second is even more absurd. If it were daylight you'd be able to see, through this window, a house where an Englishwoman, Laurence Wilfur, who's thirty-eight years old, lives with her invalid mother. They are the wife and daughter of the late Colonel Wilfur, a Colonial army officer. Over a year ago, when the two women came back from a long stay in the south of France, I was called in to attend the daughter, who was complaining of unspecified pains . . .

'I was rather surprised, for one thing because I'm not in general practice, and for another because I could find nothing wrong with my patient. I was even more surprised to learn, in the course of conversation, that she was acquainted with all my movements and even my most trivial habits, and I only understood when I came back to this room and noticed her window . . .

'I'll cut the story short, Superintendent. Ridiculous as it may seem, Miss Wilfur is in love with me, as may happen to a woman of her age who lives alone with an aged parent in a big gloomy house, hysterically in love . . .

'On two further occasions I let myself be caught . . . I visited her, and while I was sounding her she suddenly seized hold of my head and pressed her lips to mine . . .

'Next day I got a letter beginning: *My darling* . . . And the worst of it is that Miss Wilfur seems convinced that we are lovers!

'I can swear to the contrary. Since then I've avoided her. I even had to throw her out of this consulting room, where she came to pester me, and if I haven't mentioned it to my wife it's partly from professional discretion and partly to avoid arousing groundless jealousy . . .

'I know nothing more. I've told you everything, as I had made up my mind to do . . . I'm accusing nobody . . . I don't understand! . . . But I'd give ten years of my life to avoid having my wife . . .'

Now Maigret understood that his initial composure had been deliberate, contrived by a great effort of will, and the young doctor seemed by now ready to burst into tears in front of him.

'Make your own inquiry . . . I wouldn't want to influence you . . .'

As Maigret went through the hall a door opened and two children, a small boy and an even smaller girl, ran laughing past. Martin closed the gate behind the Superintendent.

Maigret came to know the district, that week, till he was sick of it. With stolid stubbornness, he spent hours pacing the embankment, in spite of the persistently rainy weather and the astonishment of various servants who had noticed him and who conjectured that this suspicious-looking prowler was up to no good.

Seen from outside, Dr Barion's house seemed an oasis of peace, industry and neatness. Several times Maigret caught sight of Madame Barion pushing her baby's pram along the riverside. One morning when the weather was fine he watched the two older children at play in the garden, where there was a swing.

As for the Wilfur woman, he saw her only once. She was tall and solidly built, totally lacking in grace, with large feet and a masculine gait. Maigret followed her, on the off-chance, but she merely went into an English bookshop in the neighbourhood, to change the library books which she took out on subscription.

Then Maigret gradually widened the scope of his rambles to take in the Avenue de Neuilly, where he noted two cake-shops. The first was dark and narrow, painted outside an ugly yellow, and seemed well enough suited to this sinister business of death-dealing cakes. But the Superintendent examined the display in vain, and inquired inside: *religieuses* were never made there.

The other was the elegant pastry-cook shop of the neighbourhood, with two or three small marble tables for tea; the Pâtisserie Bigoreau. Here it was all light and fragrance and sweetness. A rosy-cheeked girl moved cheerfully about the room, while the cash desk was kept by a very genteel lady in a black silk dress.

Could it be possible? . . . Maigret could not make up his mind to take action. With the passage of time, as his conversation with the doctor became more remote, the latter's accusations, closely scrutinised, seemed insubstantial; so much so that at times the Superintendent felt the whole thing was an absurd nightmare, a story invented, from beginning to end, by a megalomaniac or a criminal at bay . . .

And yet the pathologist's report confirmed Barion's statement: poor freckled Olga really had died from swallowing beards of rye.

And the cakes brought on the following Monday by the mysterious old beggar had also contained a large number of such beards, inserted between the two layers of pastry. But might not this have been done at a later time?

To crown it all, although Olga's father, who kept an inn somewhere in Finisterre, had gone back to his village, his wife, in deep mourning, was still in Paris and spent hours in the waiting-room of Police Headquarters, looking out for Maigret in the hope of getting news from him. Like so many others, she assumed that the police were omnipotent! Tight-lipped, stern-faced, on the verge of anger, she would ask:

'And when are you going to arrest him?'

The doctor, obviously! And it even seemed as if she were going to accuse Maigret of some devious complicity.

He decided, nevertheless, to wait until Monday, and felt almost remorseful about this, particularly as every morning he saw a huge trayful of *religieuses*, with coffee icing, in the window of the Patisserie Bigoreau.

Could he take his oath that they did not also contain death? That the girl who was carefully carrying three of them away, or the boy who was devouring one on his way home from school, would not suffer the same fate as Olga?

By one o'clock on Monday he was on guard not far from the pastry-cook's, and not until two o'clock did he see an old man whom he recognized without ever having seen him before. It was undoubtedly 'Mr Monday' stepping quietly forward, calm and philosophical, smiling at life, savouring the minutes, as it were, crumb by crumb.

He pushed open the door of the cake shop with a familiar gesture and Maigret, from outside, observed Madame Bigoreau and her daughter goodhumouredly joking with the old man.

They were obviously pleased to see him! His poverty was not of the depressing sort. He was telling them something that made them laugh, until the plump girl finally remembered Monday's ritual, leaned over the window display and chose two *religieuses* which, with a professional gesture, she wrapped in a twist of cream-coloured paper.

Mr Monday, quite unhurried, then went into the cobbler's shop next door, where he got nothing but a small coin, and finally to the tobacconist's at the street corner, where he was given a pinch of snuff.

There was patently nothing unforeseen about his daily life. And the Monday people here, the Tuesday people in another district, the Wednesday people somewhere else, could set their watches by his visits.

He soon reached the Boulevard de la Seine, and his gait became more sprightly the nearer he got to the doctor's house.

That was clearly the best house of all, where he was going to get a real meal, the same meal that the family had been eating a little while before, a meal eaten sitting at a table in a clean warm kitchen. He went in by the back door, like a regular visitor to the house, and Maigret rang at the other door.

'I'd like to see the doctor immediately,' he said to Martin.

He was shown upstairs.

'Will you ask for the two cakes to be brought up right away? The old man is downstairs . . .'

Old Mr Monday was eating his meal, unaware that the present he had just brought for the children was being examined by two men in the doctor's consulting room.

'Nothing there!' Barion concluded after a brief scrutiny.

So there must be some weeks when the cakes were deadly and others when they were harmless.

'Thank you . . .'

'Where are you going?'

Too late! Maigret was on his way out already.

'Come in this way, Monsieur . . .'

Poor Madame Bigoreau was horrified at the thought that one of her customers might know she was being visited by a policeman. She showed him into a comfortable little parlour with stained glass in the windows, adjoining the shop. There were jam tarts cooling on every available piece of furniture, even on the arms of the chairs.

'I'd like to ask you why you always give two *religieuses*, rather than any other cakes, to the old man who comes on a Monday . . .'

'It's quite simple, Monsieur. To begin with we used to give him any cakes that were slightly damaged, or left over from the day before. Two or three times it happened to be *religieuses*, which are pretty fragile. Then we gave him something different and I remember that on that occasion he insisted on buying two *religieuses* all the same . . .

' "They bring me luck," he declared.

'So as he's a decent old fellow we got into the habit . . .'

'Another question . . . Have you a customer called Miss Wilfur?'

'Yes. Why do you ask that?'

'No special reason . . . She's a charming person, isn't she?'

'Do you think so?'

The tone in which this was said encouraged Maigret to insist:

'I mean that she's somewhat eccentric . . .'

'You're right there! She's eccentric, as you put it, and she never knows what she wants! If there were many customers of her sort we'd have to double our staff! . . .'

'Does she often come in?'

'Never! . . . I don't believe I've ever seen her. But she rings up and talks half in French and half in English, so that there are very often mistakes . . . Do sit down, Monsieur . . . I apologize for leaving you standing . . .'

'I've finished. It's I who apologize, Madame, for having taken up your time.'

Three brief sentences, which had been enough to explain everything, were buzzing away in Maigret's head. The cake-shop lady had said of Miss Wilfur:

'*An eccentric, who never knows what she wants* . . .'

And then: '*If there were many customers of her sort we'd have to double our staff* . . .'

And a minute later she had admitted that she had never seen the woman, who gave her orders by telephone, '*half in French and half in English.*'

Maigret had not pressed her further. There would be time enough for that when it came to official questioning, in an atmosphere less sickly-sweet than that of the cake shop. Moreover, Madame Bigoreau might easily recover her professional pride and keep silence rather than admit to accepting 'returned goods'.

For that must be what happened! The remarks she had made could have no other meaning! The Englishwoman gave her orders by telephone, half in French and half in her own language. Then she would send back the cakes that were delivered, on the pretext that there had been some mistake . . .

She would send back the *religieuses!* . . . The cream cakes into which she'd had time, while the messenger was waiting in the kitchen, to slip some beards of rye!

Maigret, with his hands in his pockets, walked towards Dr Barion's house, and as he reached the gate he almost collided with Mr Monday emerging from it.

'So you have brought your two *religieuses*?' he called out gaily.

And as the old man stood there dumbfounded:

'I'm a friend of Barion's . . . I gather that every Monday you bring the children some cakes . . . I just wondered why it's always *religieuses.*'

'Don't you know? . . . It's quite simple! . . . Once I was carrying some that I'd been given and the children saw them. They told me those were their favourite cakes. And so, since they're real nice people such as you don't often meet, who give me the same sort of food as themselves, with dessert and coffee, the lot, you see? . . .'

Next day, when Maigret called at Miss Wilfur's with a warrant for her arrest, she adopted a haughty attitude, threatened to appeal to her ambassador, and then defended herself at all points with remarkable self-possession.

'Such self-possession is a further proof of her insanity!' said the psychiatrist who examined her.

So, in fact, were all her lies. For she claimed to have been the doctor's mistress over a long period and even to be pregnant by him.

The medical examination, however, showed her to be *virgo intacta*. A thorough examination of the house, furthermore, disclosed a large quantity of ears of rye hidden in a desk.

It was learnt, finally, through the woman's mother, that Colonel Wilfur had died in the New Hebrides of multiple perforation of the intestine, resulting from a native plot.

Maigret saw Martin again for final questioning.

'What would you have done with the kid?' he asked.

'I'd have gone off with Olga and we'd have set up a pub in the country somewhere . . .'

'And your wife?'

Martin merely shrugged his shoulders.

Miss Laurence Wilfur, who had been infatuated with Dr Barion to the point of wanting to kill his children out of spite, of spying on all his most trivial actions, of poisoning a pastry-cook's cakes in her desperate determination to attain her end, and who had had the inspired notion of using the innocent 'Mr Monday' without his knowledge, was confined for life to a mental home.

And there, for the past two years, she has been informing her companions that she is about to give birth to a son!

THE OPEN WINDOW

At five minutes to twelve the three men were standing opposite no. 116b Rue Montmartre, almost at the corner of the Rue des Jeûneurs.

'Shall we go up?'

'Let's have a drink first and then go up . . .'

They had a quick one at the nearby bar counter and then, their coat collars turned up and their hands in their pockets, for it was a cold day, they entered the courtyard of the building, looking for staircase C; they found it at last and climbed up two flights. On every door of this complicated house there were brass or enamel plates denoting here a maker of artificial flowers, there a film society. On the second floor, at the end of a dark corridor, the plate bore the words *Le Commerce Français*, and Sergeant Lucas, stepping in front, opened the door and touched his hat.

'Is Oscar Laget here?'

In the waiting-room a man of about fifty was sitting at a green baize-covered table sticking stamps on envelopes. He first shook his head, then something about the visitors' appearance must have struck him, for he looked at them more attentively and, seeming to understand, got up.

'He's never in the office in the morning,' he explained. 'What d'you want him for?'

'I have a warrant for his arrest,' replied Lucas, showing a paper that was protruding from his pocket. 'Where can we find him at this time of day?'

'You're not likely to find him . . . He must be at the Bourse, or in some restaurant in the neighbourhood. He'll be back here by four o'clock.'

Lucas exchanged a glance with his companions.

'Let's see his office . . .'

The man walked meekly in front of him, led him across a narrow passage and showed him an office which was, in fact, empty.

'Okay. We'll come back at four o'clock.'

If on this occasion Maigret was really in at the beginning of the case, it was due to pure chance. At three o'clock he was in his office in the Quai des Orfèvres when a telephone call informed him that some Algerians had been knifing one another in the neighbourhood of the

Porte d'Italie. Now Algerians were the special concern of Sergeant Lucas.

'I can't go, Chief. I have to be in' tne Rue Montmartre at four o'clock to make an arrest.'

'Who are you arresting?'

'Laget . . . You know? . . . The man from the *Commerce Français* . . . The warrant is signed by the financial section of the D.P.P.'

'You run off to the Porte d'Italie . . . I'll deal with the Rue Montmartre.'

He worked until ten minutes to four, then jumped into a taxi with the two inspectors, went through the archway and into the courtyard, and queried automatically at the sight of the network of dilapidated staircases:

'Isn't there another way in?'

'I don't think so . . .'

It didn't matter, after all! It was a straightforward business, the arresting of a shady little financier!

'Second floor, Chief. Turn to the right . . .'

It was all just a chore. The fifty-year-old clerk, Ernest Descharneau, was still sitting at his table in the waiting-room; this time he was not sticking on stamps but copying addresses on to envelopes. In front of him four or five people were waiting wearily.

'Has Oscar Laget come in?' asked Maigret without removing his pipe.

'Not yet . . . He won't be long . . . These gentlemen are waiting for him too . . .'

Maigret glanced at the said 'gentlemen', obviously creditors, seedy-looking people who had been there for an hour or two in the hope of extracting a few francs from Laget. Maigret had time to fill his pipe, after emptying it on the floor, which was already filthy.

'It's draughty in here!' he grumbled, turning up the velvet collar of his overcoat.

Ernest Descharneau, leaning over sideways a little, listened attentively and muttered:

'I think I hear him coming.'

'Why? Doesn't he come in by this door?'

'He always comes in by the back . . . I'll go and tell him . . .'

He got up as he spoke the last word, and suddenly a report rang out, from the direction of Laget's room. Descharneau started forward, but Maigret waved him aside and went in ahead of him.

There was a bend in the passage, and at the end of it an open window – the source of the draught! – overlooking a small courtyard. Maigret, with a shiver, closed it as he passed. He expected to find Laget's door locked, but this was not so. The businessman was in his office, sitting in his chair; his squat figure had slumped back and there was a gaping wound in his right temple; on the carpet, just beneath the dangling hand, lay a revolver.

Maigret swung round. 'Don't let anybody in,' he growled.

Something had immediately surprised him, but he didn't yet know what it was. He sniffed the air and looked about him, still keeping his hands in his pockets and his hat pushed back in characteristic fashion. Finally his glance fell on a pair of woman's shoes showing under the window curtain, and he muttered:

'What are *you* doing there?'

And then a youngish woman in a fur coat came out of her hiding-place and stammered, with an anguished look at the three men:

'Who are you? What have you come here for?'

'And yourself?'

'I am Madame Laget!'

The detective who had been bending over the body now stood up and declared, very calmly:

'He's dead! . . .'

Inspector Janvier was commissioned to inform the District Police Superintendent, the people from the D.P.P. and the Records Department, while Maigret, scowling, paced about the room in the bleak afternoon light.

'How long have you been in this room?' he suddenly asked, with a sideways glance at Madame Laget.

'I came here almost at the same time as you did . . . When I heard footsteps I hid behind the curtain to make sure . . .'

'Why?'

'I don't know . . . I wanted to find out first . . .'

'To find out what?'

'What had happened . . . Are you sure he's dead?'

She was not weeping, but she looked distraught; Maigret did not insist, but instead went over to the second detective and whispered:

'Stay in the room and make sure she doesn't touch anything.' Then he went back to the waiting-room, where the creditors were still sitting.

'Don't go away, any of you . . . I may need you . . .'

'Is he dead?'

'Very much so . . . As for you,' he turned to Descharneau, 'I'd like to speak to you in private . . .'

'We can go into Madame's office. Unless she's in there . . .'

Her room was opposite Laget's. In order not to be disturbed, Maigret locked the door; he fiddled automatically with the key of the stove, which was drawing badly, and then motioned his companion to a chair.

'Sit down . . . Your name . . . Your age . . . Tell me everything you know.'

'My name is Ernest Descharneau, fifty-four years of age; I am a former tradesman, a lieutenant in the reserve . . .'

'And now an office clerk?' growled Maigret.

'Not quite that,' Descharneau corrected him with a touch of bitterness. 'But you're right: it's something of the sort.'

Although his clothes were worn, he was well-groomed, and there was a certain distinction about his bearing, that drab, muted distinction peculiar to people who have come down in the world.

'Before the war I had a shop in the Boulevard de Courcelles, and business wasn't too bad.'

'What sort of a shop?'

'I sold arms and ammunition, and sporting equipment. Then I went to the front as a private, and by the third year of the war I was a lieutenant in the artillery . . .'

Maigret now noticed a slender red ribbon on the lapel of the man's jacket. He also observed that although speaking with somewhat feverish haste, the man kept an ear cocked for the sounds that came from the other room.

'It was in Champagne that I got to know Oscar Laget, who was serving under me . . .'

'As a private?'

'Yes. Later on he rose to the rank of sergeant. When we were demobbed I found my shop closed down and my wife ill. I had a little money left and I was unlucky enough to invest it in a concern that collapsed soon after . . . Then my wife died . . .'

Footsteps sounded, and Maigret realised that it was the local police, but he paid no attention. Perched on the edge of the desk, he questioned the man:

'And after that?'

'Laget had just started a chemical products business and I went to see him. He had an office in the Boulevard Haussmann and he took me on as canvasser. Since you came here in order to arrest him, you must know what sort of man he was . . .'

'Carry on!'

Sometimes Maigret seemed not to be listening.

'The chemical products firm lasted three years, and I saved a little money. One fine day Laget shut up shop, and I was back on the streets. At that point there was some talk of prosecution, which did not prevent Laget, a year later, from launching a new concern, *Le Commerce Français*, with a great deal of publicity . . .'

Descharneau seemed reluctant to go on, wondering whether or not

Maigret was taking any interest in his story, and the sound of footsteps and voices could still be heard in the other room.

'At one point he had as many as sixty people on his staff, and the
offices took up three floors in a new block in the Rue Beaubourg.
Laget published trade journals, *Le Journal de la Boucherie, Le Bulletin des
Mandataires, Le Moniteur des Cuirs et Peaux,* and various others.'

'You were involved?'

'When I went back to see him, he took me on with no specific func-
tion, but I was his right-hand man after a fashion . . . He appointed
me to the board of most of the firms he set up, sometimes even as director . . .'

'So that now you're liable to prosecution too?'

'It's very probable,' snarled Descharneau. 'You can't imagine
what it was like . . . Even when there was a staff of sixty, we were
sometimes hard put to it to lay our hands on two thousand francs . . .
Laget had his own car and Madame Laget had hers. They had built
themselves a country house for eight hundred thousand francs, but
the servants were left without wages for three months at a time. We
had to rob Peter to pay Paul. Laget would disappear for two or three
days, then come back in a state of great excitement by a side door and
make me sign some papers:

'"Hurry! . . . This time we're going to make our fortunes! . . ."

'I didn't even know what I was signing. Whenever I hesitated, he'd
accuse me of ingratitude, reminding me that he'd rescued me out of
the gutter . . .

'He had his moments of generosity. When he was in funds he
wouldn't think twice about giving me twenty or thirty thousand
francs, although he was quite liable to ask for them back next day . . .'

Maigret, taking his pipe from his mouth, suddenly asked a question
which, for all its simplicity, startled Descharneau:

'Where did you lunch?'

'When? . . . Today? . . . Wait a minute . . . I went out briefly to buy
some bread and some sausage . . . you'll find the skins and crumbs in
my waste-paper basket . . .'

'Has nobody been here?'

'What do you mean? At two o'clock, some creditors turned up as
usual. That's why Laget dared not come up by the main staircase.
There's another way in, in the Rue des Jeûneurs. You have to go
through some buildings, along passages, and a long way round
through both blocks, but he preferred that . . .'

'And his wife?'

'She did the same!'

'Does she usually come to the office at four o'clock?'

'No! She's generally here by two. But this is the first Wednesday in the month and she's been to the Ministry to collect her pension. She was a war widow before she married Laget . . .'

'Do you think her capable of killing her husband?'

'I don't know.'

'And do you think Laget capable of committing suicide?'

'I don't know . . . I've told you all I know . . . I wonder what's going to become of me now . . .'

Maigret went to open the door.

'I'll see you again presently.'

When he entered Laget's office he found ten or fifteen people busy there. The electric light had been switched on. The photographer from Records had just finished his job, and was packing up his apparatus. The examining magistrate and a young deputy were talking in low voices, while Madame Laget, her features taut, sat in a corner, seemingly dazed by the noise and bustle.

'Have you found anything?' the police superintendent asked Maigret.

'Not yet. And you?'

'We've found the cartridge case, which was certainly fired from this gun. Madame Laget has identified it as her husband's revolver, which was always kept in the drawer of his desk . . .'

'Will you come for a moment, Madame Laget?'

And Maigret took her into the room where he had been questioning Descharneau.

'Please forgive me for bothering you just now . . . I've only two or three questions to ask you. First, what do you think of Descharneau?'

'My husband did everything for him . . . He saved him from destitution . . . He trusted him completely . . . Why? Has Descharneau been saying things against him? . . . He's quite capable of it . . . He's an embittered man . . .'

'Second question,' Maigret cut in. 'What time did you last come into the office?'

'At two o'clock, to fetch my identity papers before going to the Ministry. Until these last few months I hadn't wanted to draw my war widow's pension . . . But in view of the situation . . .'

'What time did your husband usually come back in the afternoon?'

'Actually, at three o'clock . . . I'll try and explain . . . He had to have business lunches with his clients, at which there was rather too much to eat and drink. Since he slept badly at night he had formed the habit of taking an hour's nap in his office.'

'And today?'

'I don't know . . . At two o'clock, Descharneau merely told me that my husband wanted to see me at four o'clock precisely on an important matter . . .'

'And he didn't mention the police?'

'No!'

'Thank you.'

As he escorted her back to the door, Maigret kept trying to pin down the sensation he had experienced on first entering Laget's office. At some moments he thought he was near his goal, but next minute the recollection would become blurred again.

Now he was feeling warm and, still with his pipe between his teeth and his hat pushed back, he wandered into the waiting-room. Four people who had been waiting for Laget to ask him for money were still there, and Maigret looked them over in turn. He picked on a tall young man who looked shabby and undernourished.

'How long have you been here?'

'Since ten past or a quarter past two, Monsieur . . .'

Descharneau, who had gone back to sit at his desk, was listening.

'Has nobody come in since then?'

'Only these gentlemen . . .' And he pointed to his companions, who nodded.

'Nobody's gone out? . . . No? . . . Wait a minute . . . Did the office. clerk stay put the whole time?'

'The whole time.' But the young man immediately had second thoughts.

'Wait a sec . . . Just once, he went into the passage, because the telephone had rung . . .'

'At what time?'

'I really couldn't say! . . . It might have been a quarter to four? . . . Yes, it was shortly before you got here.'

'Tell me, Descharneau, who was the call from?'

'I don't know . . . It was a wrong number . . .'

'You're sure?'

'Yes. They asked me . . . they asked me if this was the dentist's . . .' Now, just before he said the last words, he had glanced down, as though seeking inspiration, at the envelopes lying on the table, circulars that Laget used to send out to thousands of people. Automatically, Maigret looked down too, and he read on the top envelope of the pile: *M. Eugène Devries, dental surgeon, Rue* . . .

He found it hard to restrain a smile!

'Well, what's your verdict?' the Superintendent asked, when he had gone back to join the examining magistrate and his deputy.

'Suicide!' the latter declared. 'According to the pathologist the shot was fired less than fifteen centimetres from the face. So unless Laget was really determined to put up no resistance . . .'

The two men looked up sharply when Maigret cut in:

'Or was asleep!'

'So you really think it's a . . . ?'

And the magistrate's glance turned to Madame Laget, who was just then submitting, with an air of injured dignity, to having her finger-prints taken.

'I don't know yet,' Maigret admitted. 'If it's a crime, it's certainly a very subtle one . . . For you'll observe that we were present, so to speak . . . You might almost think the murderer waited on purpose till the police were there . . .'

Maigret stopped the pathologist as he went by.

'And you, doctor, did you notice nothing abnormal?'

'Why, no . . . Death was certainly instantaneous . . .'

'And what else?'

'What d'you mean?'

'Nothing . . . Laget must have felt the cold even more than I do . . . Notice that the back of his chair is up against the radiator . . .'

The magistrate and the deputy exchanged glances. Maigret once more knocked out his pipe against his heel. For decency's sake, the face of the dead man had been covered with a honeycomb towel taken from the washroom. The investigators had practically finished their job and were only waiting for a signal to leave.

'Tell me, Superintendent,' Maigret said suddenly to the local police officer, 'I notice that there are two telephones on the desk: one connected with the exchange and the other an extension. It must be connected with the waiting-room. Would you go in there and call me?'

The officer went out. Everyone waited, watching Maigret, whose mind seemed to be elsewhere. A minute passed, then another. Then the police superintendent returned, looking surprised:

'Didn't you hear? . . . I kept on ringing . . .'

Then Maigret said:

'Would you come with me a minute, Monsieur le Juge?'

And he took him into the office where he had previously interviewed Descharneau and Madame Laget.

He stood with his back to the fire in his favourite position, speaking in an unemphatic voice as though to excuse himself for having gone about things so fast, and to avoid humiliating the magistrate.

'I just happened to be there at the right moment, and was able to watch the clerk . . .'

'Was it he who . . . But that's impossible, since . . .'

'Wait! Physically as well as morally, you must have recognized in him one of those failures who are perhaps the most pitiful legacy of the last war, or at any rate its most lamentable victims. A man who had been Lieutenant Descharneau and whose character must then have been above reproach. At the armistice he found nothing left of his former life. His business was ruined, his wife died. And it was Laget, whose vulgarity and unscrupulousness had worked wonders in that uneasy period, who took him on . . .'

There was a pause. Maigret filled his fourth pipe.

'I was going to say that's all!' he sighed. 'Laget made use of Descharneau as a man of his sort makes use of a decent man. And the man's decency jibs frequently, then gradually weakens, rebelling by fits and starts, so that by the end Descharneau's strongest feeling towards the man who claims to be his benefactor is hatred . . . A hatred that becomes all the keener when Laget himself starts to go downhill, so that finally Descharneau turns out to have sold his decency for a mess of pottage . . .'

'I don't see what you're . . .'

'Getting at? Nor do I. At least I couldn't a short while ago. I just imagined the two men, the boss and the clerk, the former N.C.O. and the ex-lieutenant with their roles reversed. I imagined this office overrun by seedy creditors and process-servers, and then the expedients, the accommodation bills, the drafts left unpaid, the cheques that bounced, all the wretched accompaniment to a downfall of this sort . . .'

'That was in fact why a warrant was issued for his arrest.'

'Excuse me one moment.'

Maigret opened the door and called in Descharneau, who was clearly in some terror.

'Tell me, Descharneau . . . How many times had Laget been prosecuted already?'

'I don't know . . . Five or six?'

'And each time he managed to get out of it, didn't he?'

'Yes. He could pull strings . . .'

'Thank you! You can go now.'

When the clerk had left, Maigret turned to the magistrate again.

'There you are! Descharneau didn't want Laget to get out of it this time. He's a sick man, you'll have noticed . . . I bet he's got a stomach ulcer, if not cancer . . . He stands no chance of setting himself up again. Once Laget was arrested he'd have ended up as a down-and-out of the sort you see at charity soup-kitchens. Now, rightly or wrongly, Descharneau considers Laget responsible for turning him into a down-and-out . . .'

'But how could he have done it, practically?'

'I'll give you my opinion, and it won't take more than a couple of minutes to confirm it . . . Today, at twelve o'clock, a sergeant and two inspectors came to arrest Laget, who was not there, and Descharneau told them to come back at four . . .

'Don't forget that for days and months at a time our man sat in the waiting-room with nothing to do but stick stamps and address envelopes, and that he had time to turn over and over in his head endless plans for revenge, one more complicated than the other . . .

'He admitted to me that, contrary to his usual custom, he had not gone out for lunch today, and I suspect him of having spent the time over a meticulous task the traces of which we shall look for presently . . .

'For it was a splendid, an almost unique opportunity! Most days Madame Laget is in the office by two o'clock, as a member of the staff. Only on the first Wednesday in the month she goes to the Ministry of Finance to draw her pension.

'When she looked in to collect her identity papers, Descharneau told her that her husband would be expecting her in his office at four o'clock precisely, and she had no reason to disbelieve him . . .

'After that, everything was almost too easy . . . The waiting-room was, as usual, full of creditors who would be able to confirm that Descharneau had never left them . . .

'Only for one minute . . . At a quarter to four, note the time! . . . a bell was heard ringing, presumably the telephone bell; but Descharneau informed me casually, though somewhat unconvincingly, that it had been a wrong number.

'We shall see presently if, under the table in the waiting-room, there may not be a button that would set a bell ringing. That's all the more likely since the clerk must have had some method of warning his employer of unwelcome visitors.'

'It can easily be checked,' said the magistrate.

'So can everything else. At a quarter to four, then, Descharneau goes into his employer's room, having heard him return there half an hour previously. Laget was having his usual nap. Descharneau, a former gunsmith, had had no difficulty in getting hold of a silencer, which he fitted to the revolver in the drawer, and he fired point blank . . .'

'But . . .'

'Wait a minute! He puts the silencer back into his pocket, or more likely throws it down the lavatory. He returns to the waiting-room and sits there till we come . . .

'Then he tells us that Laget will be back shortly. We wait, like everybody else. Descharneau, listening attentively, hears Madame Laget coming back at four o'clock, and while she is still coming up the back stairs he presses the button of the telephone extension . . .'

'I don't follow . . .'

'Don't you see that there had to be a report to make it seem that *it was only at that moment that Laget was killed or committed suicide?* . . . A moment ago the District Superintendent tried to call me on the extension, and failed to do so . . . I bet you that the wire was connected with some sort of fire-cracker resting on the window-ledge in the corridor, which I forgot to tell you was open when we arrived. So it was in our presence, under our noses . . . We rushed in and unwittingly scared Madame Laget, who hid behind a curtain.'

Maigret smiled.

'I was struck by something unusual when I entered that room . . . Now I understand what it was . . . As an old pipe-smoker I can distinguish between warm smoke and smoke that has gone cold. Now in Laget's office there was certainly a smell of gunpowder, *but it was cold powder* . . . As for the pathologist, with whom we'll discuss it later, he was misled about rigor mortis of the body by the fact that it was propped against the radiator, so that . . .'

On the window-ledge were found the remains of the fire-cracker and a bit of wire connected with the telephone extension.

'It's not true!' cried Descharneau, the first day. But they found him next morning dead in his cell, having hanged himself with strips of linen torn from his shirt.

MADAME MAIGRET'S ADMIRER

1

In the Maigrets' household, as in many others, certain traditions had grown up which had eventually become as important to them as are religious rites for some people.

Thus, during the many years they had lived in the Place des Vosges, the Superintendent had formed the habit, in summer, of undoing his dark tie as soon as he came in from the courtyard and started up the staircase, completing the process by the time he reached the first floor.

The staircase of the building which, like all those in the square, had once been a splendid private mansion, ceased at that point to rise majestically between wrought-iron banisters and walls of imitation marble; it became steep and narrow, and Maigret, panting a little, reached the second floor with his shirt collar open.

He still had to go along a poorly lit corridor as far as his own door, the third on the left, and as he put his key into the lock, carrying his jacket over his arm, he invariably called out:

'It's me!'

And he would sniff, so as to guess from the smell what was cooking for lunch, then make his way into the dining-room, whose tall window was open on to the dazzling sight of the square where four fountains were plashing musically.

It was June. The weather was particularly hot and at Police Head-quarters the talk was all of holidays. There were people in their shirt-sleeves on the boulevards and beer was flowing freely on the *terrasse* of every café.

'Have you seen your admirer?' the Superintendent asked, mopping his brow as he settled down by the window.

Nobody would have guessed at that moment that he had just spent hours in that sort of anti-crime laboratory known as Police Headquarters, studying the darkest and most sordid recesses of the human heart.

Away from work, he was ready to be amused by trifles, particularly when it was a matter of teasing his naive wife. For the past fortnight the standing joke had been to ask her for news of her admirer.

'Does he still go for his two little turns round the Square? Is he still just as mysterious and distinguished-looking? When I think that you've a weakness for distinguished-looking men and yet you married me!'

Madame Maigret was going back and forth, laying the table, since she would not have a maid, merely a cleaning woman in the mornings for the rough work. She took up the game.

'I never said he was distinguished-looking!'

'But you described him to me: a light grey hat with a bound brim, a small turned-up moustache, probably dyed, a walking-stick with a carved ivory knob . . .'

'You may laugh! . . . One of these days you'll realise that I was right . . . I'm convinced that he's no ordinary man and that his behaviour means there's something strange going on . . .'

From the window one could automatically watch the comings and goings through the Place des Vosges, which was fairly empty in the mornings but where, in the afternoons, the mothers and nannies of the neighbourhood sat on benches watching children at play.

All around the public garden, which, fenced in by its railings, is one of the most formal in Paris, stand identical houses with arcades and steeply sloping roofs.

To begin with, Madame Maigret had paid only casual attention to the stranger, who could scarcely have passed unnoticed, since everything about his dress and attitude was twenty or thirty years out of date, and he reminded one of the typical old dandy only to be seen nowadays in the illustrations of humorous magazines.

It was early in the morning, the time when all the houses had their windows wide open and one could see maids busy with housework in the various homes.

'He seems to be looking out for something,' Madame Maigret had commented.

That afternoon she had gone to visit her sister, and next day, at exactly the same time, she had seen the stranger again, walking round the square at a steady pace once and then twice, and finally disappearing in the direction of the République district.

'Probably an old fellow who fancies little housemaids and comes to watch them shaking the carpets!' Maigret had said when his wife, in the course of conversation, had mentioned her old dandy.

And at three o'clock that afternoon, to her considerable surprise, she had seen him sitting on a bench immediately opposite her window, motionless, with his hands folded on the knob of his walking-stick.

At four o'clock he was still there. At five o'clock he was still there. Not until six o'clock did he get up and take himself off along the Rue des Tournelles, without having spoken a word to anyone or even unfolded a newspaper.

'Don't you think it's odd, Maigret?' For she had always addressed her husband by his surname.

'I've already told you: there must certainly have been some pretty servant-girls around him . . .'

And next day Madame Maigret returned to the attack:

'I watched him carefully, for he spent three hours again sitting on the same bench, in the same place . . .'

'Perhaps he wanted to have a good look at you? From that bench one must be able to see into our apartment, and the gentleman's in love with you . . .'

'Don't talk such nonsense!'

'For one thing, he carries a walking-stick, and you've always liked men who use walking-sticks . . . I bet he wears pince-nez . . .'

'Why?'

'Because you've a weakness for men with pince-nez!'

They were bickering gently, after twenty years of marriage, enjoying the pleasant peace of their home.

'Listen . . . I looked carefully all round him . . . There was indeed a nursemaid sitting just opposite him, on a chair. A girl I'd already noticed in the fruiterer's shop, for one thing because she's very pretty, and furthermore because she's distinguished-looking . . .'

'There you are!' said Maigret triumphantly. 'Your distinguished-looking maid was sitting in front of the old gentleman. You've already noticed that women sometimes sit down without realising what they're showing, and your admirer spent the afternoon ogling her.'

'That's all you think about!'

'So long as I haven't seen your mystery man . . .'

'Can I help it if he only comes when you aren't here?'

And Maigret, who was in constant contact with so many sensational happenings, revived his spirits by such simple pleasantries, and never failed to ask for news of the man whom they had come to describe as Madame Maigret's admirer.

'You can laugh as much as you like! All the same there's something about him, I don't know what, that fascinates and rather frightens me . . . I don't know how to explain . . . When you look at him you can't take your eyes off him. For hours on end he can sit in the same place without stirring, and even his eyes don't move behind his pince-nez . . .'

'Could you see his eyes from here?'

Madame Maigret almost blushed, as though caught in the act.

'I went up to have a closer look . . . I particularly wanted to know if you'd been right . . . Well, the blonde nursemaid, who always has two children with her, behaves very properly and there's nothing to be noticed . . .'

'Does she stop there all afternoon too?'

'She arrives about three o'clock, usually after the man. She always has some crochet work with her. They leave at roughly the same time. For hours on end she works at her crochet without raising her head except sometimes to call back the children if they wander off . . .'

'Don't you think, darling, that there are hundreds of nursemaids sitting in the public gardens of Paris doing crochet or knitting for hours on end while they look after their employers' children?'

'Quite possibly!'

'And lots of old retired gentlemen who have nothing to do but warm themselves in the sun, casting lustful glances at pretty girls?'

'This one isn't old . . .'

'You told me yourself that his moustache was certainly dyed and that he must be wearing a wig.'

'Yes, but he doesn't seem old.'

'The same age as me?'

'Sometimes he seems older and sometimes younger . . .'

And Maigret, pretending to be jealous, grumbled:

'One of these days I shall have to get a close-up view of this admirer of yours!'

He did not give the matter serious thought, and neither did Madame Maigret. In the same way they had once amused themselves for quite a while observing a courting couple who met each evening under the arches, noting their quarrels and reconciliations, until the day when the girl, who worked in the local dairy, had appeared at exactly the same spot with a different young man.

'You know, Maigret . . .'

'What?'

'I've been thinking it over . . . I wonder whether the man couldn't be there to spy on somebody . . .'

Days passed, and the sun grew ever hotter; in the evenings the crowd in the square became denser, as all the working people from neighbouring streets came to take the air beside the four fountains.

'What I find so strange is that he never sits down in the mornings. And why does he walk twice round the square, as if he were expecting a signal?'

'What does your pretty blonde do meanwhile?'

'I never see her. She works in a house on the right hand side and from here one can't see what's happening there. I see her in the market, where she doesn't talk to anyone, except to tell the tradesmen what she wants. She never argues about prices, so that she's cheated of at least twenty per cent . . . She always seems to have her mind on something else . . .'

'Well, next time I have a tricky job of watching to be done I'll put you on to it instead of my men.'

'You can laugh at me! But sooner or later we shall see whether . . .'

It was eight o'clock. Maigret had dined already, which was unusual, since he was generally kept rather late at the Quai des Orfèvres.

He was sitting at the window in his shirt-sleeves, his pipe between his lips, gazing absent-mindedly at the pink sky which was shortly to be overrun by dusk, and at the Place des Vosges, now crowded with people whom the precocious summer heat had made listless.

Behind him he heard sounds which implied that Madame Maigret was finishing the washing up and would soon come to sit beside him with some piece of needlework.

Evenings such as this, with no unpleasant case to solve, no murderer to discover, no thief to watch, evenings when his thoughts could roam in peace as he watched the pink sky, were rare, and Maigret had never been enjoying his pipe more, when suddenly, without turning round, he called out:

'Henriette?'

'D'you want something?'

'Come and look . . .'

With the stem of his pipe he pointed to a bench just opposite them. At one end of this bench an old fellow who looked like a tramp was taking a nap. At the other end . . .

'It's him!' declared Madame Maigret. 'Fancy that!'

It struck her as almost indecent that 'her' afternoon stroller should have disrupted his timetable so as to be sitting on the bench at such a time.

'He looks as if he'd fallen asleep,' muttered Maigret, relighting his pipe. 'If there weren't two floors to climb up afterwards, I'd go and have a closer look at your admirer, so as to find out what he's really like . . .'

Madame Maigret went back into her kitchen. Maigret watched a squabble between three small boys who ended up by rolling in the dust, while others rushed round them on roller skates.

He stayed there till he had finished his second pipe, and the stranger was still in the same place, whereas the tramp had set off slowly towards the embankment. Madame Maigret settled down with some needlework in her lap, being incapable of spending an hour doing nothing.

'Is he still there?'

'Yes.'

'Aren't they going to shut the gates?'

'In a few minutes . . . The attendant has begun driving people towards the exits.'

As it happened, the attendant did not notice the stranger, who was sitting there motionless, and three of the gates had already been closed; the attendant was about to turn the key in the lock of the fourth, when Maigret, without a word, picked up his jacket and went downstairs.

From up above, Madame Maigret saw him arguing with the man in green, who took his duties as guardian of the square very seriously. Eventually, however, he let the Superintendent in, and Maigret walked straight up to the man in the pince-nez.

Madame Maigret had sprung to her feet. She realised that something was up, and she signalled to her husband as though to ask:

'Has it happened?'

What, she could not have said exactly; but for many days she had been apprehending some incident. Maigret replied with a nod, got the attendant to stand watch by the gate and came back upstairs.

'My collar and tie . . .'

'Is he dead?'

'As dead as can be! He's been dead for at least two hours, if I'm any judge.'

'Do you think he's had a stroke?'

Maigret did not speak; he always had some difficulty tying his tie.

'What are you going to do?'

'Start the inquiry, of course! Inform the D.P.P., the pathologist and all the rest . . .'

A velvety darkness had fallen over the Place des Vosges, where the tinkle of the fountains rang out more loudly, one of the four, always the same one, having a shriller note than the others.

A few minutes later Maigret was in the tobacconist's shop at the corner of the Rue du Pas-de-la-Mule, where he made a series of phone calls; then he posted a policeman in the attendant's place at the gate of the garden.

Madame Maigret did not want to go down. She knew that her husband hated having her involved in his cases. She also understood that for once he was working undisturbed, since nobody had seen him coming and going or noticed the dead man with the pince-nez.

Furthermore, the square was almost deserted. Only the couple who kept the florist's shop down below were sitting by their door, and the man who sold motor-car accessories, wearing a long grey overall, had come for a chat with them.

They were surprised to see the first car stop at the gate and drive into the garden; they eventually went up to look when they saw a second car and an imposing gentleman who must belong to the Department of Public Prosecution. Finally, by the time the ambulance arrived, the group of onlookers had grown to fifty people, but none of them suspected the cause of this strange gathering, for the crucial scene was concealed by bushes.

Madame Maigret had not switched on the light; she often sat in the dark when she was alone. She kept looking out over the square; she saw windows being opened, but there was no sign of the pretty blonde nursemaid.

The ambulance went off first, towards the Forensic Institute. Then a car with a few passengers . . .

Then she saw Maigret on the pavement; he chatted with some gentlemen for a few minutes before crossing the street on his way home.

'Aren't you going to turn on the light?' he grumbled, peering through the darkness.

She switched on the light.

'Shut the window. It's getting chilly . . .'

He was a different Maigret now, no longer relaxed as he had been so short a while before, but the Maigret whose bursts of ill-temper terrified young detectives at Police Headquarters.

'Stop that sewing! You get on my nerves! Can't you sit for a minute with your hands idle?'

She stopped sewing. He was walking back and forth in the small room, hands behind his back, from time to time casting a peculiar glance at his wife.

'Why did you tell me he sometimes looked old and sometimes young?'

'I don't know . . . I got that impression . . . Why? . . . How old is he?'

'Under thirty, at any rate.'

'What are you saying?'

'I'm telling you that your friend is far from being what he seems . . . I'm telling you that he had fair hair hidden under his wig, that his moustache was a false one and that he wore a sort of corset that gave him the stiff look of an old dandy . . .'

'But . . .'

'There's no but about it . . . I'm still wondering by what miracle you happened to smell out this affair.'

He seemed almost to hold her responsible for what had occurred, for his spoilt evening, for the work in store for him.

'Do you realise what's been going on? Well, your admirer was murdered on that bench . . .'

'You can't mean it! . . . In front of everybody?'

'Yes, in front of everybody, and probably just when there were most people about . . .'

'Do you think that maid . . . ?'

'I've just sent the bullet to an expert who's going to call me in a few minutes . . .'

'How could anyone have fired a revolver and . . .'

Maigret shrugged his shoulders and waited for the phone call, which, as he expected, came without delay.

'Hello! . . . Yes, that was what I thought . . . But I needed your confirmation.'

Madame Maigret was impatient; but he deliberately kept her waiting, and muttered as though the matter did not concern her:

'A compressed air rifle of a special type, extremely uncommon . . .'

'I don't understand . . .'

'It means that the fellow was killed from a distance, possibly by someone in ambush at one of the windows round the square, who had plenty of time to take aim . . . He must have been a first-class marksman, moreover, for the man was shot through the heart and death was instantaneous . . .'

Thus in broad daylight, while the crowd . . .

Madame Maigret was so upset that she burst into tears, then apologised awkwardly:

'I'm sorry . . . I couldn't help it . . . I feel involved, somehow . . . It's silly, but . . .'

'When you've calmed down, I'll hear your evidence.'

'*My* evidence?'

'Of course! You're the only person, so far, who can provide any useful information, since your curiosity led you to   .'

And Maigret deigned to give her a few details, although still apparently talking to himself.

'The man had no personal papers on him . . . His pockets were practically empty, apart from a few hundred-franc notes, a little small change, a tiny key and a nail file . . . We shall try and identify him nonetheless.'

'Only thirty!' Madame Maigret repeated.

It was bewildering! And she understood now why she had been so strangely fascinated by the sight of this young man so rigidly maintaining the pose of an old one, like a waxwork dummy.

'Are you ready to answer?'

'I'm ready!'

'Please observe that I am questioning you in the course of my duties and that tomorrow I shall be obliged to draw up a report of this interrogation . . .'

Madame Maigret smiled wanly, for she was somewhat awestruck.

'Did you notice the man today?'

'I didn't see him in the morning, because I went to the Halles. In the afternoon he was in his usual place . . .'

'And the blonde girl?'

'She was there too, as usual.'

'Did you ever notice them speaking to one another?'

'They'd have had to speak very loud, for they were more than eight metres apart . . .'

'And they sat motionless like that all afternoon?'

'Except that the girl was doing her crochet . . .'

'Always crochet? For the past fortnight?'

'Yes . . .'

'You didn't notice what stitch she was using?'

'No . . . If it had been knitting I'd have known all about it, but . . .'

'What time did the woman go away?'

'I don't know . . . I was busy preparing a custard . . . Probably about five o'clock, as usual . . .'

'And according to the pathologist, death occurred about five p.m. Only now it's a matter of minutes . . . Did the woman leave before or after five o'clock, before or after the man's death? . . . I wonder what possessed you, today of all days, to make a custard. If one's going to spy on people one may as well do it thoroughly and conscientiously . . .'

'Do you believe that woman . . . ?'

'I don't believe anything at all! I only know that I have nothing to go on for my inquiry but your information, for what it's worth. Do you know, for instance, where the blonde girl works?'

'She always goes into no. 17b.'

'And who lives at no. 17b?'

'I don't know that either . . . Some people who have a big American car and a foreign-looking chauffeur . . .'

'And that's all you noticed? Well, you'd make a fine detective, you can take my word for it . . . A big American car and a foreign-looking chauffeur . . .'

He was putting on an act, as he often did in moments of puzzlement, and his anger ended with a warm smile.

'Do you know, old dear, if you hadn't taken an interest in your boyfriend's behaviour I should be in a tight corner now? I don't say the situation is very promising, nor that the inquiry will be plain sailing, but all the same we've got something to work on, however slight.'

'The pretty blonde?'

'The pretty blonde, as you say! That gives me an idea . . .' He rushed to the telephone and summoned a detective, whom he stationed in front of no. 17b, with orders, should a handsome blonde girl come out, on no account to lose sight of her.

'And now to bed . . . It'll be time enough tomorrow morning . . .

He was just falling asleep when his wife ventured timidly:

'Don't you think it might be as well to . . .'

'No, no, no!' he shouted, half sitting up in bed. 'Just because you almost showed some flair, that doesn't entitle you to start giving me advice! Anyhow, it's time to go to sleep!'

It was the time when the moon was touching the slate roofs of the Place des Vosges with silver, while the four fountains kept up a sort of chamber music in which one of them was always in a hurry and, as it were, out of tune.

II

When Maigret, his face lathered with shaving cream and his braces dangling, cast a first glance through his window at the Place des Vosges, there was already a considerable crowd of people around the seat where, the night before, a man had been found dead.

The florist's wife, better informed than the rest since she had witnessed from afar the visit of the Department of Public Prosecution, gave wordy explanations and, even seen from a distance, her emphatic gestures showed that she was speaking with conviction.

The whole neighbourhood was there, and women who, a short while before, had been hurrying to get to their workshop or office punctually, had suddenly found time to linger, since a crime was involved.

'Do you know that woman?' asked the Superintendent, pointing with his razor at a youngish lady who stood out among the rest because she wore an extremely elegant light-coloured suit of English cut, suitable for morning outings in the Bois de Boulogne.

'I've never seen her . . . At least I don't think so . . .'

That meant nothing. The first floor apartments in the Place des Vosges are inhabited by the wealthy middle class and by fashionable people. Nonetheless, the sort of woman whom Maigret was now scrutinizing with some irritation seldom goes for a walk at eight in the morning, unless it be to take her dog for an airing.

'Look here! This morning you must do a lot of shopping . . . You're to go into all the shops. You're to listen to what people are saying and above all you must try to get some information about the blonde maid and her employers . . .'

'This time you won't call me a gossip?' Madame Maigret teased him. 'When do you expect to be back?'

'How can I tell?'

For while he had been asleep, the inquiry had been going on, and he hoped to find some substantial grounds for his investigation when he reached the Quai des Orfèvres.

Thus, at eleven o'clock last night, Dr Hébrard, the famous pathologist, had received a message while attending a first night at the
Comédie Française, in white tie and tails. He had stayed till the last
act, had gone to congratulate an actress friend in her dressing-room,
and a quarter of an hour later, at the Forensic Institute (which is the
same as the new morgue), one of his assistants helped him to slip on
his lab coat while another extracted from one of the many drawers
lining the walls the body of the unknown man from the Place des
Vosges.

At the same moment, on the top floor of the Palais de Justice, where
files hold the records of all the criminals in France and most of the
criminals in the rest of the world, two men in grey overalls were
patiently checking finger-prints.

Not far from these, on the other side of a spiral staircase, the experts
on duty in the lab were beginning their meticulous study of various
articles: a dark suit of old-fashioned cut, buttoned shoes, a malacca
cane with a carved ivory knob, a wig, pince-nez and a tuft of fair
hair cut from the dead man's head.

When Maigret, after shaking hands with his colleagues and having
a brief interview with his Chief, went into his office, which, despite the
open window, smelled of stale tobacco, three reports were awaiting
him, tidily set out on his desk in folders of different colours.

Dr Hébrard's report first: the victim had died almost immediately
on being hit, and the shot had been fired from a distance of over
twenty metres, possibly as much as a hundred, with a small-calibre
gun which nonetheless gave its missiles great penetrative force.

Probable age: twenty-eight.

In view of the absence of professional marks, it was probable that
the man had never engaged continuously in manual work. On the
other hand he had practised sport, particularly rowing and boxing.

He was in perfect health, and particularly robust. A scar on the left
shoulder showed that about three years previously the young man
had been wounded by a revolver bullet which had struck his shoulder
blade.

Finally, a certain compression of the finger-tips suggested that he
must have done a considerable amount of typing.

Maigret read all this slowly, puffing at his pipe and looking up from
time to time to watch the Seine flow past in the dazzling morning sunlight. At other moments he would scribble a word or two, compre-
hensible only to himself, in the notebook which was notorious not only
for its ordinariness but because, during long years of use, it had ac-
cumulated comments bewilderingly superimposed on one another in
all directions.

The laboratory report was scarcely more sensational.

The garments had been worn by others before belonging to their recent owner, and everything implied that he had bought them in some junk shop or in the Carreau du Temple.

The walking-stick and the buttoned shoes seemed to have come from the same source.

The wig, which was of fairly good quality, was of a very ordinary type such as can be found at any wig-maker's.

Finally, the examination of the dust found in the garments disclosed a largish quantity of very fine flour, not purified but still mingled with fragments of bran.

The pince-nez were of plain glass, useless as an aid to sight.

There was nothing in the records! No card bearing finger-prints corresponding to those of the victim.

Maigret sat for a few minutes with his elbows on his desk, lost in thought, and possibly overcome by some degree of lethargy. The case promised neither well nor badly, rather badly on the whole, however, since there had been no help at all from chance, which was usually fairly generous.

Finally he rose, put on his hat and spoke to the janitor on duty in the corridor.

'If anyone wants me, I shall be back in about an hour.'

He was too close to the Place des Vosges to take a taxi, and he went there on foot along the Seine; at the fruiterer's shop in the Rue des Tournelles he caught sight of Madame Maigret in animated conversation with three or four gossiping housewives.

He averted his head to conceal a smile and went on his way.

During Maigret's early days in the police force, one of his bosses who had a passion for the scientific methods which had recently been introduced used to tell him:

'Careful, young man! Not so much imagination! Police work is not done with ideas but with facts!'

Which, however, had not prevented Maigret from going on in his own way and carving out a pretty successful career for himself.

Thus, as he reached the Place des Vosges, he was worrying less about the technical details contained in that morning's reports than about what he would have called the atmosphere of the crime.

He tried to imagine the victim, not dead as he had seen him but alive: a young fellow of twenty-eight, fair-haired, strong and muscular, probably elegant, dressing up every morning in that old dandy's outfit bought at some second-hand market stall, and under which he still wore fine linen . . .

And walking twice around the square before disappearing along the Rue de Turenne.

Where did he go? What did he do until three o'clock in the afternoon? Did he still look like a character from some nineteenth-century comedy, or did he change clothes somewhere in the neighbourhood?

How could he then stay motionless for three hours on end, never opening his mouth, never making a gesture, just staring into space?

How long had this performance been going on?

Finally, at night, where did the stranger disappear to? What was his private life? Whom did he see? Whom did he speak to? To whom did he confide the secret of his personality? How was one to account for the flour and the fragments of bran in his clothing, which suggested a mill rather than a bakery? What could he have been doing in a mill?

All this made Maigret forget to stop at no. 17b and he had to retrace his steps. He went in under the archway and spoke to the concierge. She showed no surprise when he showed her his police badge.

'What is it you want?'

'I'd like to know which of your tenants employs a rather pretty, smart, fair-haired maid . . .'

She interrupted him to say, without the least hesitation:

'Mademoiselle Rita?'

'Maybe. Every afternoon she looks after two children in the square . . .'

'They're her employers' children: Monsieur and Madame Krofta, who have had the first floor flat for well over fifteen years . . . They were here even before me. Monsieur Krofta runs an import and export business. He has an office somewhere in the Rue du Quatre-Septembre.'

'Is he at home?'

'He's just gone out, but Madame must be upstairs.'

'And Rita?'

'I don't know . . . I haven't seen her yet this morning . . . Actually, I've been doing the stairs . . .'

A few minutes later Maigret rang at the door of the first floor flat, and although he could hear noises going on in the depths of the apartment, he was kept waiting for quite a while at the door. He rang again. Finally the door was half opened, and Maigret saw a youngish woman, trying to disguise her state of undress beneath a pale blue housecoat.

'What do you want?'

'To speak to Monsieur or Madame Krofta. I'm a Superintendent of the Police Judiciaire . . .'

She let him in, resignedly, folding her housecoat about her, and Maigret found himself in a splendid apartment with large high rooms, furnished with great taste and displaying valuable bibelots.

'I apologize for receiving you like this, but I'm alone with the children. How can you have got here so soon? My husband only left a quarter of an hour ago . . .'

She was a foreigner, as was clear from her slight accent and from her typically Central European charm. Maigret had already recognized her as the woman he had noticed that morning, wearing a light-coloured suit and listening to the housewives gossiping in the middle of the Place des Vosges.

'Were you expecting me?' he said quietly, trying to conceal his surprise.

'You or somebody else . . . But I must confess I didn't know the police acted so swiftly . . . I suppose my husband will be back soon?'

'I don't know . . .'

'Haven't you seen him?'

'No . . .'

'But then . . .'

There was obviously some misunderstanding, and Maigret, who hoped to gain some information thereby, did nothing to clear it up.

The young woman, meanwhile, possibly in order to give herself time to think, stammered out:

'Will you excuse me a moment? The children are in the bathroom and I wonder if . . . if they're not up to some mischief.'

She moved smoothly away; she had real beauty both of face and figure, with a certain majesty in addition to her supple grace.

She could be heard exchanging a few words with her children in the bathroom; then she came back with a slight smile of welcome.

'Forgive me, I never even asked you to sit down . . . I'd rather my husband had been here, for he knows more than I do about the value of the jewels, since it was he who bought them.'

To what jewels was she referring? And what was it all about, and why did the young woman appear so tense as she impatiently awaited her husband's return?

It looked as though she were afraid of talking, and was trying to drag out the conversation without giving anything away.

Maigret, who was conscious of all this, was careful not to give her any help; he looked at her with the utmost detachment, assuming what he called his 'plain man's' expression.

'One's constantly reading about thefts in the papers, but oddly enough one never imagines such things happening to oneself. And yesterday evening I had no suspicion . . . It was this morning . . .'

'When you came in again?' Maigret suggested.

She gave a start.

'How do you know I'd been out?'

'Because I saw you . . .'

'You were in the neighbourhood already?'

'I'm here all the year round, for I'm one of your neighbours.'

She was disturbed at this. She was clearly wondering what this mysteriously simple remark might imply.

'I went out, true, as I often do, to take the air before getting the children dressed. That's why you find me in déshabille . . . When I come back I put on my housecoat and . . .'

She could not restrain a sigh of relief. Footsteps had halted on the landing. A key turned in the door.

'It's my husband,' she murmured.

And she called out:

'Boris! Come in here . . . There's somebody waiting for you.'

The man was goodlooking, too; older than his wife, about forty-five years of age, well-dressed and well-groomed, a Hungarian or a Czech, Maigret thought, but speaking perfect, polished French.

'The Superintendent has got here before you, and I was telling him you'd soon be back . . .'

Boris Krofta was scrutinizing Maigret with a polite attention which did not wholly disguise mistrustfulness.

'I beg your pardon,' he murmured. 'But . . . I don't quite understand . . .'

'Superintendent Maigret of the Police Judiciaire.'

'It's odd . . . You wished to speak to me?'

'To the employer of a girl called Rita, who looked after two children in the Place des Vosges every afternoon.'

'Yes . . . But . . . you're not going to tell me that you've already traced her, or that you've recovered the jewellery? . . . I know I must strike you as peculiar . . . The coincidence is so strange that I'm trying to understand it. You must realize that I've just got back from the local police station, where I went to lodge a complaint against Rita . . . On my return I find you here, and you tell me . . .'

'What was the subject of your complaint?'

'The theft of the jewellery. The girl disappeared yesterday without warning. I thought she must have run off with a young man, and I decided to put an advertisement in the newspaper. Last night we never left the house. This morning, while my wife was out, it suddenly occurred to me to look in her jewel case . . . That was when I understood why Rita had run away, for the jewel case was empty . . .'

'What time was it when you made this discovery?'

'Barely nine o'clock in the morning. I was in my dressing-gown. I dressed quickly and hurried off to the police station . . .'

'And at this point your wife came back?'

'That's right . . . While I was dressing . . . What I still fail to understand is your coming here this morning . . .'

'Just a coincidence!' Maigret murmured, in a tone of the utmost innocence.

'And yet I'd like to be in the picture . . . Did you know, this morning, that the jewels had been stolen?'

Maigret made an evasive gesture which meant nothing and which served to intensify Boris's anxiety.

'At any rate, please do me the favour of telling me the reason for your visit. I don't think it's customary for the French police to enter people's homes, to sit down and . . .'

'And to listen to what they're told!' Maigret finished. 'Admit that it's nothing to do with me. Ever since I came here you've been talking about a theft of jewellery which doesn't interest me, whereas I came on account of a crime . . .'

'A crime?' the young woman exclaimed.

'Didn't you know that a crime had been committed yesterday in the Place des Vosges?'

He saw her obviously take thought, remembering that Maigret had said he was her neighbour, and instead of saying no as she might have done she murmured with a smile:

'I heard vague rumours of something this morning as I went through the square . . . some housewives were gossiping . . .'

'I don't see how . . .' the husband put in.

'How this business concerns you? I don't know either, so far, but I'm convinced that we shall know sooner or later. At what time did Rita disappear yesterday afternoon?'

'Shortly after five o'clock,' replied Boris Krofta without a trace of hesitation. 'Isn't that so, Olga?'

'That's right. She came in at five o'clock with the children. She went up into her bedroom and I didn't hear her come down again. About six o'clock I went upstairs, because I was beginning to wonder why she wasn't getting the dinner ready . . . And her room was empty . . .'

'Will you take me up to it?'

'My husband will go up with you. I can hardly do so, dressed as I am . . .'

Maigret was already acquainted with the house, since it was exactly like his own. After the second floor the staircase grew still narrower and darker, and eventually they reached the attic floor. Krofta opened the third door.

'It's here . . . I left the key in the lock . . .'

'Your wife just told me it was she who had gone up!'

'That's true. But I went up myself afterwards.'

The open door disclosed a maid's bedroom which would have been quite unremarkable, with its iron bed, its wardrobe and wash-stand, but for the view over the Place des Vosges to be seen through the window.

Beside the wardrobe there was a fibre suitcase of a familiar type; inside the wardrobe, some clothes and underwear.

'So your maid must have gone off without any luggage?'

'I suppose she chose to take the jewellery instead; it was worth about two hundred thousand francs . . .'

Maigret's big fingers were fiddling with a small green hat, then he picked up another, trimmed with a yellow ribbon.

'Can you tell me how many hats your maid had?'

'I've no idea . . . My wife may perhaps be able to tell you, but I doubt it . . .'

'How long had she been in your service?'

'Six months . . .'

'Did you find her through an advertisement?'

'Through an employment agency, which had warmly recommended her. For that matter, she was an excellent servant.'

'You have no other staff?'

'My wife likes to look after the children herself, so that one maid is quite enough for us. Particularly as we spend a good part of the year on the Riviera, where we have a gardener and his wife to help in the house.'

Maigret suddenly felt impelled to blow his nose, in spite of the weather; he dropped his handkerchief and bent down to pick it up.

'That's odd . . .' he muttered as he stood up again.

Then, looking his companion up and down, he opened his mouth and closed it again.

'Did you want to say something?'

'I wanted to ask you one more question. But it's so indiscreet that you may think it uncalled for . . .'

'Please go on!'

'If you insist . . . Well, I wanted to ask you, on the off-chance, whether, your maid being such a pretty girl, you had ever had any relations with her other than those between an employer and his servant? I'm asking you this off the record, and you're quite entitled not to reply.'

Oddly enough, Krofta seemed to ponder, suddenly much more preoccupied than he had been. He took his time before replying; he cast a slow glance all around him, and then said with a sigh:

'Must my reply become official?'

'In all probability there will be no question of that.'

'In that case I'd rather admit to you that, in fact, I have occasionally . . .'

'In the rooms on the first floor?'

'No . . . That would be difficult because of the children . . .'

'Did you meet outside the house?'

'Never! . . . I came up here from time to time, and . . .'

'I understand the rest!' Maigret said with a smile. 'And I'm very glad to have your answer. Actually, I had noticed that a button was missing from the sleeve of your jacket, and I've just picked up that button on the floor, at the foot of the bed. Obviously some violent exertion must have been needed to wrench it off and . . .'

He handed the button to his companion, who seized it with surprising eagerness.

'When was the last time this happened?' Maigret asked casually, as he went towards the door.

'Three or four days ago . . . Wait a minute! . . . Four days, yes . . .'

'And Rita was willing?'

'I think so.'

'Was she in love with you?'

'At any rate she let me think she was.'

'Have you any rival that you know of?'

'Oh, Superintendent! . . . There was no question of that, and if Rita had had a lover I'd certainly not have considered him as a rival . . . I adore my wife and my children, and I don't know myself why I . . .'

And Maigret, as he went down the stairs, said to himself with a sigh:

'Well, my fine fellow, I have the impression that you've not been telling the truth for a single moment!'

He stopped in the concierge's lodge, and sat down opposite the woman, who was shelling peas.

'So you've been to see them? They're no end upset about that jewellery business!'

'Were you in your lodge yesterday at five o'clock?'

'To be sure I was . . . And my son was sitting just where you are now, doing his homework . . .'

'Did you see Rita and the children come in?'

'As clear as I see you now!'

'And did you see her come down again a few minutes later?'

'That's what Monsieur Krofta came to ask me just now. I told him I hadn't seen anything. He insists that's not possible, that I must have gone out of the lodge or that I wasn't paying attention. After all, so many people go past! Yet I think I'd have noticed her, seeing as it wasn't her usual time of day . . .'

'Have you ever met Monsieur Krofta going up to the third floor?'

'What would he have gone up there for? Oh, I understand . . . You think perhaps he'd have gone up to be with the maid . . . You obviously don't know Mademoiselle Rita . . . They're saying now that she

was a thief . . . That's as may be! . . . But she wasn't one for gadding
about or letting her master have his way with her . . .'

Maigret, resignedly, lit his pipe and moved off.

III

'Well then, Madame Superintendent Maigret?' he teased her affec-
tionately as he sat down by the window, his shirt-sleeves gleaming in
the sunlight.

'Well, for lunch today you'll have to make do with some grilled
steak and an artichoke. And I bought that ready-cooked to save time.
According to gossip . . .'

'What do they say? Come on! Give us the results of your
inquiry . . .'

'For one thing, Mademoiselle Rita wasn't really a servant . . .'

'How do you know?'

'All the tradespeople noticed that she didn't know how to count in
sous, which implies that she's never had to do the shopping. The first
time the butcher tried to give her change for a franc she stared at him,
and if she accepted it I'm sure it was in order not to call attention to
herself . . .'

'Good! So she was a young lady playing maid at the Kroftas' . . .'

'I think rather she was a student. In the local shops they talk all
sorts of languages, Italian, Hungarian, Polish. Apparently she always
seemed to understand and when jokes were made in her presence she
used to smile . . .'

'And hadn't they anything to say about your admirer?'

'Some people had noticed him, but not to the same extent that I
had . . . Oh yes, there's something else. The Gastambides' maid, who
often goes to sit in the square of an afternoon, declares that Rita didn't
know how to crochet and that it would have been impossible to use the
things she made except for floor-cloths . . .'

Maigret's narrowed eyes were twinkling with amusement at the
care which his wife had taken to put together her recollections and
express them in an orderly and methodical way.

'That's not all! Before Rita, the Kroftas had a maid of their own
nationality, but they dismissed her because she became pregnant.'

'By Krofta?'

'Oh no! He's too much in love with his wife. Apparently he's so jealous that they don't entertain anybody . . .'

Thus all this petty gossip, these assertions which might be true or
untrue, sincere or otherwise, helped to alter and sometimes to complete Maigret's picture of the people concerned.

'Since you've done such good work,' Maigret murmured as he lit a fresh pipe, 'I'm going to give you a hint myself. The shot that killed our unknown friend in the wig and pince-nez was fired from Rita's attic window, as can easily be proved in a reconstruction of the crime. I checked the angle of fire, which corresponds absolutely with the position of the body and the trajectory of the bullet . . .'

'Do you believe it was she who . . .'

'I've no idea . . . Think it over yourself!'

And with a sigh he resumed his collar and tie; she helped him into his jacket. Half an hour later, he sank into his chair at Police Headquarters and mopped his face, for it was even hotter than on the previous day, and there was thunder in the air.

An hour later, Maigret's three pipes were warm, the ash tray was overflowing, and the blotter was covered with a tangle of words and scraps of sentences scrawled in all directions. As for the Superintendent, he was yawning, patently drowsy, and staring round-eyed at what he had written in the course of his reverie.

Supposing Krofta had got rid of Rita, the theft of jewellery was a clever invention to divert suspicion from himself.

It was a nice idea, but there was no proof of it and the maid might well have run off with her employer's jewels.

Krofta had hesitated before admitting that he had made love with his servant.

That might mean that it was true and that he was embarrassed by it; it could equally well mean that it was not true, but that he had seen Maigret picking up the button, or that he suspected the Superintendent's question of concealing a trap of this sort.

Could the button have been left for four days on the floor, which seemed to have been recently swept?

And why had Madame Krofta been for an early morning walk today? Why had she seemed reluctant to admit that she had heard people talking about the crime, when Maigret had seen her spend a considerable time listening to the gossiping housewives?

Why had Krofta asked the concierge if she had seen Rita go out? Was he conducting a personal investigation? Wasn't it more likely that he knew the police would ask the same question, and that by speaking of it beforehand he had the chance of influencing the good woman by suggestion?

Suddenly Maigret sprang up. The final result of this accumulation of trivial facts and observations was not merely to irritate him but to arouse a secret anxiety in him, for it led inevitably to the question: where was Rita?

She was on the run, if she was guilty of theft and murder. But if she was guilty of neither, then . . .

A minute later, he was in the Chief's office where, putting on his surliest air, he demanded:

'Can you let me have a blank search warrant?'

'Things not going right?' the head of the Police Judiciaire chaffed him; he was more familiar than most people with Maigret's moods. 'We'll try and get it for you. But you'll have to be prudent, eh?'

As it happened, while the Chief was seeing about the search warrant, Maigret was summoned to the telephone. It was his wife, and there was acute anxiety in her voice.

'I've just thought of something . . . I don't know if I ought to say it over the telephone . . .'

'Say it, anyway!'

'Supposing it wasn't the person you're thinking of who fired the shot . . .'

'I understand. Carry on . . .'

'Supposing, for instance, it was her employer . . . You follow me? . . . I wonder if, by any chance, she could still be in the house? . . . Dead, perhaps? . . . Or else a prisoner? . . .'

It was touching to see Madame Maigret eagerly following a trail for the first time in her life.

But what the Superintendent would not admit was that she had practically reached the same point as himself.

However, he queried ironically: 'Is that all?'

'You're making fun of me? . . . You don't believe that . . .'

'In short, you imagine that by searching no. 17b from cellar to attic . . .'

'Just think, suppose she were still alive . . .'

'We'll see! Meanwhile, let's hope dinner will be a bit more substantial than lunch . . .'

He hung up, and went back to the Chief's room for the warrant he needed.

'Doesn't this case suggest espionage to you, Maigret?'

The Superintendent, who hated committing himself in such cases, merely shrugged his shoulders.

But as soon as he had left the room he retraced his steps and called out briefly:

'I'll answer that question tonight.'

Madame Lecuyer, the concierge of no. 17b, was no doubt a worthy woman, who did her best to bring up her children decently, but she had one terrible fault: she panicked readily.

'You understand,' she admitted, 'with all these people asking me questions from first thing this morning, I don't know if I'm coming or going . . .'

'Keep calm, Madame Lecuyer,' said Maigret, as he sat by the window, not far from the small boy who was doing his homework as on the previous day.

'I've never done any harm to anyone and . . .'

'You're not being accused of doing any harm to anyone . . . You're only being asked to try and remember . . . How many tenants have you?'

'Twenty-two, because I must tell you that the flats on the second and third floors are very small, just one or two rooms, so that we have a lot of people . . .'

'Did any of these tenants have anything to do with the Kroftas?'

'How could they? The Kroftas are rich people, with their own car and a chauffeur . . .'

'By the way, do you know where they garage their car?'

'Somewhere along the Boulevard Henri IV . . . The chauffeur hardly ever comes here, for he has his meals out . . .'

'Did he come yesterday afternoon?'

'I can't remember . . . I believe he did . . .'

'With the car?'

'No! The car wasn't parked here yesterday, nor this morning . . . It's true that the Kroftas hardly went out . . .'

'Let's see! Was the chauffeur in the house yesterday at about five o'clock?'

'No! He left again at half past four . . . I remember, because my boy had just come back from school . . .'

'That's true!' confirmed the boy, looking up.

'Now another question: have any large cases been taken out of the house since five o'clock yesterday? For instance, has a removal van been parked in the neighbourhood?'

'No, I'm sure of that!'

'Nobody has taken out any cupboards or chests or unwieldy packages?'

'What d'you expect me to say?' she moaned. 'How can I tell what you mean by an unwieldy package?'

'One that might, for instance, contain a human body . . .'

'Good heavens! Is that what you're thinking of? Are you supposing now that somebody's been murdered in my house?'

'Go back over your recollections hour by hour . . .'

'No! I saw nothing of the sort . . .'

'No lorry, no cart, not even a handcart, came into the courtyard?'

'I've told you so!'

'There's no empty room in the house? All the flats are occupied?'

'All, without exception! There was just one room on the third floor, and that's been let for the past two months.'

At that point the boy raised his head, and with his pen between his lips mumbled:

'What about the piano, Mum?'

'What can that have to do with it? That wasn't a case being taken out, it was a case being brought in . . . and they had a hard job getting it up the stairs!'

'A piano was delivered here?'

'Yesterday at half past six.'

'What firm?'

'I don't know . . . There was no name on the van. This one didn't come into the courtyard . . . There was a great big case and three men were at it for a good hour . . .'

'Did they take the case away with them?'

'No . . . Monsieur Lucien went down with the workmen to stand them a drink at the bistro round the corner.'

'Who is this Monsieur Lucien?'

'The tenant of the little room I was telling you about . . . He's been there two months . . . He's very quiet and respectable . . . They say he writes music . . .'

'Does he know the Kroftas?'

'I shouldn't think he's even seen them . . .'

'Was he at home at five o'clock yesterday?'

'He came in about half past four . . . about the time the chauffeur left.'

'Did he tell you then that he was expecting a piano?'

'No . . . He simply asked if there were any letters for him.'

'Did he usually get many?'

'Very few.'

'Many thanks, Madame Lecuyer . . . Try to keep calm; there's no need for you to worry yourself . . .'

Maigret went out and gave instructions to two inspectors who were pacing up and down in the Place des Vosges; then he returned to no. 17b, going quickly past the lodge lest the concierge should start questioning him again and confiding all her anxiety.

Maigret did not stop on the first floor nor on the second. On the third, bending down, he noticed the scratches made by the piano as the men dragged it along. It seemed to him that the scratches stopped at the fourth door, and he knocked at it; he heard shuffling footsteps, like those of an old woman in slippers, then a cautious voice mumbled:

'Who's there?'

'Monsieur Lucien, please?'

'It's next door . . .'

But at the same moment another voice muttered a few words and the door was partially opened; a stout old woman tried to make out Maigret's features in the half-darkness.

'Monsieur Lucien isn't in just now. Can I take a message for him?'

Maigret instinctively leaned forward to try and see the second person who was in the room.

In the dim light, it was difficult to make out anything. The room was cluttered with old furniture, old fabrics, hideous trinkets, and pervaded by the peculiar smell of places where old people live.

Beside the sewing-machine a woman was sitting, upright as though on a formal call, and the Superintendent was more surprised than he had ever been in his life when he recognized his own wife.

IV

'I heard that Mademoiselle Augustine undertook little sewing jobs,' Madame Maigret hurriedly explained. 'I came to see her about this. We chatted. Her room happens to be next door to the maid's room, the girl who stole . . .'

Maigret gave a shrug, wondering what his wife was getting at.

'The oddest thing is that yesterday they brought up a piano for the neighbour on the other side, in a huge case which must still be there . . .'

This time Maigret frowned, enraged that his wife should, heaven knows how, have reached the same conclusions as himself.

'Since Monsieur Lucien isn't here I shall have to go downstairs,' he announced.

And he did not waste a minute. The two inspectors whom he had left in the Place des Vosges, in front of the house, were now posted in the stairway, not far from the Kroftas' door. A locksmith was sent for, and also the local police superintendent.

The result was that shortly afterwards the door of Monsieur Lucien's room had been forced open. In the room there was merely a very ordinary piano, a bed, a chair, a wardrobe, and, standing against the wall, the case which had contained the piano.

'Get this case opened,' ordered Maigret, who was playing high and was intensely nervous.

He did not want to touch the case himself, for fear of finding it empty. He filled his pipe with assumed calm, and pretended to be quite unmoved when he heard a shout.

'Superintendent! . . . There's a woman here! . . .'

'I know!'

'She's alive!'

'I know!' he repeated.

Of course! If there was a woman in the packing-case, it must be the notorious Rita, and he was practically certain she must be alive, tightly bound and gagged.

'Try to bring her round . . . Send for a doctor . . .'

He walked past his wife, who was in the corridor with Mademoiselle Augustine, and who gave him a smile unparalleled in their domestic history, a smile which suggested that Madame Maigret might be going to exchange her role of docile spouse for that of detective.

As the Superintendent reached the first floor, the door of the Krofta apartment opened. Krofta was there in person, in a state of considerable excitement, yet wholly master of himself.

'Is Monsieur Maigret there?' he asked the two detectives on sentry duty.

'Here I am, Monsieur Krofta.'

'You're wanted on the telephone . . . It's the Ministry of the Interior . . .'

Actually, it was the Director of the Police Judiciaire calling his subordinate.

'Is that you, Maigret? . . . I thought I might catch you here . . . While you were up to heaven knows what elsewhere in the house, the person in whose apartment you're now taking this call got in touch with his embassy . . . They contacted the Ministry of Foreign Affairs, who . . .'

'I understand!' growled Maigret.

'Just as I told you! A case of espionage! Our orders are to keep mum, to avoid any leakage to the press . . . Krofta has been for a long time now his country's unofficial agent in France; he centralizes the reports of secret agents . . .'

Krofta, the man in question, was standing in a corner of the room, pale but smiling.

'May I offer you something, Superintendent?'

'No, thanks!'

'I understand you have found my servant?'

And the Superintendent replied, stressing each syllable:

'I found her just in time, yes, Monsieur Krofta! Good day to you!'

'I was sure,' Madame Maigret said as she finished making her chocolate custard, 'when I heard that the girl didn't know how to crochet . . .'

'Of course!' her husband agreed.

'They must really have managed to tell each other some interesting things by this system, spending several hours a day at it. If I understand it aright, this girl Rita who had taken a post as domestic servant with the Kroftas actually spent her time spying on her employers.'

Maigret was never fond of explaining his cases, but under the circumstances it would have been too cruel to leave Madame Maigret in the dark.

'She spied on spies!' he growled. And he added sullenly, shrugging his shoulders:

'That's why, just as I was about to pounce on the gang at last, I got the order: "Give it up! Silence and discretion!"'

'Indeed, that can't be very pleasant,' she sighed as though she thus excused all Maigret's past ill-humour.

'It was a pretty case, though, with strokes of genius. Try to understand the situation. On the one hand the Kroftas, with all the information that passes through their hands and which they transmit to their own government.

'On the other hand the maid Rita and a man, the old gentleman on the bench, your mysterious admirer. For whom were they working? That doesn't concern me now. It's up to Intelligence. They were probably the agents of another power, or perhaps of a dissident faction, since the internal and external policies of certain countries are peculiarly mixed up.

'The fact remains that they needed the information centralized every day by Krofta, and Rita got hold of this without too much difficulty. But how could it be passed on outside? Spies are very vigilant, and any suspicious behaviour on her part would have ruined her.

'And so they hit on the idea of the old dandy on the bench! And the idea of the crochet hook which, used by hands more expert than they seemed, might communicate by its jerky movements long messages in Morse code.

'Sitting opposite Rita, her accomplice recorded everything in his memory. It's just one more example of the incredible patience of certain secret agents, for he had to retain everything he had learnt, word for word, for hours on end, until the time when, back in his home at Corbeil, near Moulins, he would spend the night typing it out.

'I wonder how the Kroftas discovered this extremely cunning device? They probably learnt of it through the chauffeur, when he came in at about four o'clock.'

Madame Maigret was so afraid of his stopping that she listened without daring to display the least sign of emotion.

'Now you know as much as I do. The Kroftas had to do away with the man first, and next to question Rita, to get her to say for whom she was working and how much she had already given away.

'For some time past Krofta has been housing a killer, Monsieur Lucien, who's a first-class shot. He rings him up. Lucien wastes no time, and from the girl's bedroom he shoots down his allotted victim.

'Nobody has seen or heard anything, except Rita who has to take the children home and who is forced to keep up a pretence of ignor ance on pain of being shot down in her turn.

'She knows what to expect. They try to get her secret from her. She holds out. They threaten her with death, and they have that piano brought up to Monsieur Lucien's room so that the case can be used to remove her body. Besides, who would think of looking for her in the musician's room?

'Krofta has already planned his defensive strategy. He lodges a complaint, reports his maid's disappearance, invents the theft of the jewels and . . .'

A pause. Night was falling. The blue of the sky was darkening, and the silvery sound of the fountains harmonized with the liquid silver of the moonlight.

'And you coped with it!' Madame Maigret suddenly said with ad-miration.

He looked at her half seriously, half smiling. She went on:

'How maddening that at the crucial moment they prevented you from finishing the job . . .'

Then he said, with mock indignation:

'D'you know what's even more maddening? To have found you at that Mademoiselle Augustine's! For, after all, you got there before me . . . But then, of course, the victim was your admirer!'

THE MYSTERIOUS AFFAIR IN THE BOULEVARD BEAUMARCHAIS

At ten minutes to eight, when Martin of the Gaming Squad left his office, he was surprised to see the corridor still full of journalists and photographers. It was very cold, and some of them, with their coat collars turned up, were munching sandwiches.

'Hasn't Maigret finished yet?' he asked as he went by.

At the far end of the long corridor Martin, instead of taking the stairs, pushed open a glazed door. The room he entered was as sparsely lighted as the rest of the building at Police Headquarters. It was the waiting-room of the Head Office; in the middle of it stood a huge round sofa covered in red velvet. A man was sitting there, wearing an overcoat and a hat. A few steps away two inspectors stood smoking cigarettes, while the old porter, in his glass cage, was eating his dinner.

Martin filled his pipe. In a quarter of an hour he would be at home, dining with his family. He had come out of curiosity, to see what was happening here, because people had been talking of nothing else for the past two days.

'How's it going?' he whispered to one of the detectives.

The latter, with a sigh, pointed to the second door, that of Maigret's office.

'Who's with him?'

'Still the sister-in-law . . .'

The man on the sofa looked up slowly on hearing the whispering voices, and cast a sad, reproachful glance at the two policemen. He was a thin, sickly-looking person of about forty, or maybe a little less, with deep rings under his eyes and a small dark moustache.

'He's been here ever since this morning . . .' the detective whispered to Martin.

Just at that moment Maigret's door opened, and the Superintendent emerged. As he left the door ajar, the men caught a glimpse of his smoke-filled office and of the figure of a very young blonde woman sitting in a green armchair.

'Lucas!' Maigret called out, peering at the detectives as though in a daze, 'run and fetch me some sandwiches . . . Call in at the brasserie and have some beer sent up . . .'

Martin took this opportunity to shake hands with his colleague.

'How's it going?'

Maigret, flushed and with a hectic glitter in his eyes, was clearly longing for a breath of fresh air.

'Listen,' he said, lowering his voice. 'I'll tell you something. If I don't finish this inquiry this evening I shall give it up. Don't you understand my feeling? . . . I can't go on living in this set-up any longer . . .'

The man on the sofa, who could not hear his words, sat quivering with anxiety, but the Superintendent went back into his office, the door closed, and Martin left the room at last, while the minute-hand of the clock moved forward and snatches of talk from the waiting journalists could be heard.

And yet the case had seemed entirely commonplace to begin with. The previous Sunday, on the fourth floor of an apartment house in the Boulevard Beaumarchais where the ground floor was occupied by a pipe manufacturer, Louise Voivin, aged twenty-six, had died suddenly, having to all appearances been poisoned.

In this comfortable, potentially cheerful middle-class dwelling there lived, apart from the dead woman, her husband Ferdinand Voivin, a dealer in precious stones, and her sister Nicole, aged eighteen.

This was the young woman who had been closeted with Maigret for several hours and who showed no signs of breaking down; although she kept nervously biting at her handkerchief she remained clearheaded, despite the stifling atmosphere of the room.

On the desk stood a lamp, darkened by a huge green shade. Maigret's face, above it, was in shadow, but light fell full on that of the girl, as she sat on a low chair. The window curtains had not been drawn, so that drops of rain could be seen trickling down the dark panes, amidst the gleams of light from the riverside lamps.

'They're going to bring us something to drink,' Maigret sighed with relief.

He felt so hot that he wanted to take off his jacket and collar, whereas the girl was still wearing her grey fur coat; a round hat of the same fur set on her very fair hair gave her a peculiarly Nordic look.

What question could he ask her that he had not already asked? And yet he could not bring himself to let her go. He had a vague feeling that he must keep her under his eye, while her brother-in-law waited in the room next door.

To keep himself in countenance Maigret flicked over the pages of his file, as though the repeated re-reading of the same details might give rise to some inspiration.

For all its simplicity, there had been something disturbing about the first report, made by the local police, concerning the events of that Sunday.

'. . . *On the fourth floor, in a room at the far end of the apartment, we found the body of Louise Voivin lying on the floor. Dr Blind, who had been called in by the relatives half an hour previously, declared that she had died a few minutes earlier with horrible convulsions, and he unhesitatingly ascribes the death to poisoning, presumably from a heavy dose of digitalis, administered either intentionally or accidentally . . .*'

Then, a little further on:

'. . . *we questioned the husband, Ferdinand Voivin, 37 years of age, who declared he knows nothing. He asserts however that his wife had been showing signs of neurasthenia for several months past . . .*

'. . . *We questioned the sister of Louise Voivin, Nicole Lamure, 18 years of age, born at Orléans, whose statements correspond to those of her brother-in-law . . .*

'. . . *We questioned the concierge, who declares that for a long time now Louise Voivin had suffered from ill-health and was afraid of being poisoned . . .*'

That Sunday had been All Saints' Day, actually. A cold rain had been falling, and the smell of chrysanthemums and incense from churches filled the air, while towards evening the officials from the Department of Public Prosecution, soaking wet and muddy-footed, made their way towards the Bouulevard Beaumarchais, where the pipe-maker's shop was closed.

But all this was usual enough; it was the dramatic atmosphere common to almost all such cases. The real tragedy was as yet unsuspected by the waiting journalists, for it was only now, in his overheated office, that Maigret had discovered it.

And he waited impatiently for the refreshing tang of his draught of beer, while keeping his eyes averted from the tense-faced girl who sat staring fixedly at a corner of his desk.

'Come in!' he called.

The waiter from the Brasserie Dauphine who brought in beer and sandwiches cast a glance at Maigret's companion.

'Will that be all?'

'Yes . . . Take some to the gentleman who's sitting in the waiting-room.'

But Voivin, when he was offered something to eat and drink, shook his head as though he had not the heart for it.

Maigret stood there taking great bites at his sandwich, while his companion nibbled at hers.

'How long had they been married?'

'Eight years . . .'

A commonplace story about insignificant people. Ferdinand

Voivin, a small-scale broker in precious stones, during a visit to Orléans where he was in charge of an appraisal, had made the acquaintance of Louise Lamure, whose parents ran a shoe shop.

'You yourself were only a child at the time?'

'I was ten . . .'

'I suppose,' he tried to speak jokingly, 'you weren't as yet in love with your brother-in-law?'

'I don't know . . .'

He glanced obliquely at her and did not feel like laughing.

'So, a year ago, when your father died, your sister and her husband took you in . . .'

'I came to live with them, that's true . . .'

'And since when, precisely, have you been Voivin's mistress?'

'Since the seventeenth of May . . .'

She said this clearly, almost proudly.

'Do you love him?'

'Yes . . .'

To look at this fragile passionate creature, one might have imagined Voivin as a handsome romantic figure to have inspired such love. And one of the disturbing features of this affair was that the broker was such a nondescript person that one could not remember his face without an effort. Even his profession lacked any sort of glamour. For hours at a time he would hang about the cafés of the Rue La Fayette where dealers in gems forgather, and it was not until a month ago that he had been able to afford a modest secondhand car. He suffered from ill-health into the bargain.

'And your sister?'

'She was jealous.'

'Did she love him?'

'I don't know . . .'

'What did she say when she surprised you together?'

'She didn't say anything. She wrote to me. Since then we've never spoken a word to one another.'

'And that was when?'

'The second of June . . It was the third time we had . . .'

'In the Boulevard Beaumarchais?'

'Yes . . . In my bedroom . . . Ferdinand thought Louise had gone out, but she was in the kitchen with the cleaning woman.'

'Did you never think of going to live elsewhere?'

'I wanted to . . . Louise insisted on my staying.'

'Why?'

'So that she could keep an eye on us better . . . She said that if I left the apartment it would be too easy for her husband to visit me secretly.'

'And at home?'

'She never left us alone together. She always wore felt slippers so that one couldn't hear her coming.'

'How could you live together all those months without speaking a word to one another?'

'We used to exchange notes . . . For instance my sister would write: "Get your washing ready for tomorrow", or "Don't use the bath, there's a leak."'

'And Voivin?'

'He was very unhappy. From the beginning, he refused to sleep in the same room as his wife and he fixed up a divan in the living-room. He assured me they'd given up having any relations.'

Maigret counted on his fingers.

'June . . . July . . . August . . . September . . . October . . . Five months! . . . So you went on living like that for five months?'

She nodded, as though it had been quite natural.

'Did Ferdinand Voivin never speak to you about getting rid of his wife?'

'Never! I swear he didn't . . .'

'And he never suggested your going away with him?'

'You don't know him,' she sighed, shaking her head. 'He's a decent man, can't you understand? He's the same in business matters. When he's signed a contract he carries it out, come what may. Ask anyone who's worked with him . . .'

'All the same, for the past few months your sister seems to have had forebodings. She wrote three letters to a former schoolfriend, and in all three she speaks of being poisoned . . .'

'I know! My sister had gone out of her mind from constantly spying on us. Almost every night she'd open my bedroom door quietly, and in the darkness I could feel her hand touching my face to make sure I was in bed and alone there.'

'One question. Since the second of June, have you never been alone with Voivin?'

'Three or four times, outside the house. But my sister found out. Each time she was waiting for us at the door of the hotel. She followed me everywhere. Once she went out into the street in her slippers because she hadn't had time to put on her shoes.'

Maigret had visited the apartment, which was as nondescript as Voivin himself. He imagined the life of those three people. And he kept coming back to the same questions, like horses on a roundabout endlessly going round in a circle.

'Did you know that there was a packet of bicarbonate of soda in the bathroom medicine-cabinet?'

That was the crucial question. After the death of Louise Voivin the

police had searched the apartment, and they had soon found a glass
that had contained medicine, which analysis showed to be digitalis
diluted in a little water. Only, beside the glass there had been a packet
labelled 'Bicarbonate of soda', which contained enough digitalis to
kill a hundred people.

'How did you spend last Sunday afternoon?'

'Like any other Sunday. It was the worst day of the week for us. Ferdinand stayed in his room, looking over bills. I was in my own room,
reading. My sister must have been in hers . . .'

'What had you eaten for lunch?'

'I remember quite well . . . A hare, which one of Ferdinand's customers had sent him.'

And she kept uttering Ferdinand's name as fervently as though he
had been the most splendid and remarkable of men.

'Were you much distressed by your sister's death?'

'No!'

She made no secret of it. She even looked up to show her face.

'My sister made him too unhappy . . .'

'And how did he react himself?'

'Was it his fault? . . . I know he never loved her. He lived eight years
with her but he was never happy. My sister was always depressed and
ill. She'd had an operation in the first year of her marriage and she
was no longer quite a normal woman' . . .

Maigret left the room for a moment again and, from the doorway,
looked at the man slumped on the sofa. He had already questioned
him once, the day before, but briefly, and he was reluctant to embark
again on one of those endless examinations that are equally distressing for both parties.

'Won't he have anything to eat?' Maigret asked one of the two inspectors, in a whisper.

'No. He says he's not hungry.'

Maigret shrugged, and, bracing himself, went back into his office,
where Nicole still sat motionless.

'By the way . . . Talking of illnesses . . . Which of you in the family
had stomach trouble?'

'Ferdinand did,' she said unhesitatingly. 'Not often, but occasionally, particularly when he'd been having palpitations.'

'He had palpitations, then?'

'That's to say he'd been treated for a heart condition about two
years ago, I think, but it was practically cured.'

'Do you know whether your brother-in-law had stomach trouble
during the last few weeks?'

'Yes, he did,' she said, as categorical as ever.

'Which day?'

'The day we were all taken ill . . .'

'You don't know what you had eaten?'

'I can't remember . . .'

'Was the doctor called in?'

'No! Ferdinand didn't want that. During the night we all suffered from headaches and nausea, and Ferdinand thought there might have been an escape of gas.'

'Was that the only time?'

'Yes . . . At least the only time it was so bad . . .'

'You mean that there had been other occasions?'

'I see what you're getting at, Superintendent . . . But you're not going to shake me . . . I shall hold out to the end, in spite of everything, because I know Ferdinand is innocent . . . If anyone could have poisoned my sister it wouldn't have been him but myself, and as you see I'm not afraid to say so . . .'

'But you didn't do it?' he said in a strange tone of voice.

'No . . . I never even thought of it . . . I might have killed her some other way, I don't know how. It's true that we'd all been unwell lately . . . Only just put yourself in my place. Can you imagine the sort of life we led? At meals there was always one or other of us who couldn't eat anything. Do you know how many cleaning women we had in five months? . . . Eight! . . . As they said, they didn't want to stay in such a crazy household.'

She broke into hysterical tears. It was not the first time she had wept during the interrogation, but she quickly resumed her self-control and looked Maigret straight in the eyes as though to anticipate his question.

'I don't even know if we still opened the windows. And it had come to the point when I dared not go as far as the end of the street because I knew my sister would be on my heels . . .'

'So, in your opinion, your sister committed suicide?'

She did not answer immediately; the question clearly made her uneasy.

'In other words, you assume that your sister managed to get hold of a large quantity of digitalis and that instead of trying to poison you she deliberately took her own life?'

'I don't know . . .' she admitted.

And it was obvious that she did not believe that either, that it did not fit in with her sister's character.

'So then?'

'It's a mystery . . . In any case, Ferdinand did not kill her!'

'And you yourself?'

But if he hoped to trip her up he was disappointed. She raised her head once more and met his eyes with a certain irony in hers.

'I think we'd better call in your brother-in-law,' Maigret muttered. 'Or rather . . . Just a minute . . . will you go into the waiting-room while I see him in here . . .'

'What have you got to say to him?'

She was standing up now, growing impatient, and tearing at her handkerchief with her teeth.

'Send him in!' called Maigret, opening the door. 'The young lady will wait . . .'

He ushered her out, and showed Voivin to the chair she had just vacated.

'A glass of beer?'

Voivin merely shook his head.

'Not hungry? . . . I apologize for having kept you waiting. Your sister-in-law had so much to tell me. By the way, what are you intending to do now?'

The broker reluctantly raised his head and looked at the Superintendent with amazement, then with suspicion, as though it was obvious that he was not going to be released.

'One question, Voivin . . . Since Nicole could not speak freely to you on account of your wife, I suppose she used to write to you?'

He tried to see the connection, and shook his head.

'No.'

'Why not? Being in love as you both were . . .'

'It was impossible . . . My wife would have found the letters. She spent her whole time hunting through the apartment, my clothes and even my shoes . . .'

Maigret sighed. He would have given a good deal to see Nicole's love lavished on somebody else, on anybody rather than on this second-rate man, second-rate even in his despair.

'Couldn't you have found a hiding-place?'

'I tell you Louise would have discovered it . . .'

The Superintendent appeared to give up the idea.

'Well, it can't be helped . . . By the way . . . I wanted to ask you one thing. When you had that heart trouble . . .'

Ferdinand gave a sad smile.

'I was waiting for that question . . .'

'Then answer it!'

'Well then, yes, I was prescribed digitalis. But it's two years since I stopped taking it.'

'All the same you knew its effects and you must have been warned that a massive dose of it . . .'

'Believe me, Superintendent, I didn't kill my wife . . .'

'And I'm convinced that Nicole did not poison her either.'

'Did you suspect her?'

'No, no! Keep calm! You tell me that you did not kill your wife. And Nicole did not kill her. And now I shall ask you a question to which you are entitled not to reply. Listen carefully, Voivin . . . You know your wife was a jealous woman, who was prepared to put up with her sister's presence rather than give her the chance to meet you secretly; knowing her as you did, can you maintain that she may have simply envisaged the possibility of killing herself and thereby leaving the pair of you a clear field? . . . Think carefully . . .'

'I don't know . . .'

'Come on! Answer or don't answer, but no lies, Voivin, no evasions . . .'

The man's lips were trembling, and suddenly a fetid smell pervaded the room, betraying the physical effects of his panic.

Maigret without a word went to open the window, then returned to his desk, slowly filled his pipe and tossed off the few remaining drops of beer.

'I'll help you, shall I?' he said gently.

'I suppose you'd rather I did not bring in your sister-in-law?'

Voivin was weeping, perhaps from mortification as much as from distress, and Maigret walked to and fro as he spoke, averting his eyes from the man.

'If I make a mistake, you must stop me . . . But I think I'm not mistaken . . . You go to Antwerp from time to time?'

'Yes . . .'

'I thought so . . . To Antwerp and Amsterdam, where the main diamond markets are. There you were able to get hold of a certain quantity of digitalis more easily and with less risk than in France, which explains why our searches in Paris and the suburbs met with no success.'

'I'm thirsty!' moaned Voivin, choking . . .

His extreme humility embarrassed Maigret. Taking a bottle of brandy from his cupboard he poured a large glass of it for the broker.

'You're not a naturally cheerful fellow. You marry a young woman and in the very first year of your marriage an operation suddenly makes her years older. You go on working without joy, but as meticulously as you do everything, and at one point your heart gives you trouble . . . Isn't that so?'

'It wasn't serious . . .'

'That's not the point . . . And then your sister-in-law descends on you, and all of a sudden you discover youth and zest for life. You're in love! You're madly in love! . . . But you've too much respect for your given word to desert your wife and start life afresh. You're a weak man, I might even say you're a coward. The day your wife took you by surprise you showed no fight.'

'I'd like to know what you'd have done in my place!'

'It doesn't matter. Your life at home had become daily and hourly torture. Though you were unable to leave your wife, you were even less capable of giving up your sister-in-law. Stop me if . . .'

'It's quite true!'

'You're one of those weak men who provoke catastrophes! I know what I'm saying . . . Yes, you're one of those who, from fear of loneliness, are capable of dragging many others to death with them . . . Since life had become intolerable you envisaged death for the three of you, which is why you bought such a large quantity of poison . . . Is that true?'

'How could you guess?'

'So far, it was quite easy. It was the death of your wife, and of nobody else, that I couldn't explain. But you've given me the explanation yourself . . . I'm coming to it. To begin with, admit that on at least two occasions you made some preliminary experiments, that's to say you put small doses of digitalis into the food which made you all ill . . .'

'I wanted to know . . .'

'That's just it. You were afraid . . . You hadn't made up your mind to die . . . And you tried to find out with small doses . . . As to the rest, your answer to one of my last questions made things clear to me. Your wife kept watch on all your actions, searched every corner of the apartment, down to your shoes. Under the circumstances, where could you put digitalis? And what was the medicine that nobody took but yourself?'

Voivin raised desperate eyes in silence.

'Everything follows from that. The digitalis was hidden under the innocuous label 'bicarbonate of soda'. And probably you'd have gone on hesitating for weeks, maybe months . . .'

'I don't believe I'd ever have done it!' moaned Voivin.

'All right . . . You'd have hesitated for a long time, in any case, if the accident had not occurred. One of your customers made you a present of a hare. Your wife, being in poor health, suffered from indigestion, went to the medicine cupboard, saw the packet of bicarbonate of soda and put a spoonful of it into a glass.'

Voivin hid his face in his hands.

'That's all!' Maigret broke off, opening the window even wider. 'Look here . . . there's a washroom next door. Do you want to go there before I call in your sister-in-law?'

The broker glided like a shadow into the neighbouring room. Maigret opened the door.

'Will you come in, Mademoiselle Nicole? Your brother-in-law is just coming back . . .'

And then, abruptly: 'You don't want to die?'

'No!'

'All the better, then! Take care . . .'

'Of what?'

'Nothing . . . Not to let yourself be carried away . . .'

'What has he told you?'

'He's told me nothing!'

'Do you still think he's guilty?'

'You can settle matters with him . . .'

'Where is he?'

Maigret had to turn aside to conceal a smile.

'He's . . . he's collecting his wits,' he said.

And he relit his pipe, which had gone out, while Voivin, like a man dazzled by the light, groped his way back into the office.

'Ferdinand!' exclaimed Nicole.

'No, not here, please! . . . I beg you . . .' growled Maigret.

TWO BODIES ON A BARGE

The lock keeper of Le Coudray was a lean, depressed-looking fellow in a corduroy suit, with drooping moustaches and a suspicious eye, like a typical estate bailiff. He made no distinction between Maigret and the fifty other people – gendarmes, journalists, policemen from Corbeil and representatives of the Department of Public Prosecution – to whom he had told his story over the past two days. And as he spoke he kept a watchful eye, upstream and downstream, over the grey-green surface of the Seine.

It was November. The weather was cold and a bleak pale sky was reflected in the water.

'I had to get up at six this morning to look after my wife,' (and Maigret reflected that these decent, sad-eyed men are always the ones who have sick wives to look after) . . . 'While I was lighting the fire I thought I heard something. But it was only later, while I was up on the first floor preparing her poultice, that I realized somebody was calling . . . I came downstairs . . . I went out on to the lock, and there I could vaguely make out a dark mass against the weir . . .

' "What's up?" I shouted.

' "Help!" somebody called out hoarsely.

' "What are you doing there?" I asked.

'And he went on shouting: "Help!" '

'I took my wherry to go after him. I could see it was the *Astrolabe*. As it was beginning to get light at last, I made out old Claessens on deck. I could take my oath that he was still tight and that he had no idea what his barge was doing up against the lock. The dog was loose, and indeed I asked him to hold on to it. And that's it . . .'

The important thing, from his point of view, was that a barge had run into his lock and might have damaged it if the current had been stronger. He seemed totally unconcerned by the fact that, apart from the drunken old carter and a big Alsatian dog, there had been nobody on board but two corpses, a man and a woman, both hanged.

The *Astrolabe* had been released and was now moored a hundred and fifty metres away, guarded by a constable who kept himself warm pacing up and down the tow-path. It was an old barge without a motor, a 'stable-boat' as they call those barges that travel along canals with their horses on board. Passing cyclists turned to stare at this

100

greyish hull, about which all the papers had been talking for the past two days.

As usual, when Superintendent Maigret had been brought in, it was because there were no fresh clues to be noted. Everybody had gone into the case, and the witnesses had already been questioned fifty times, first by the local gendarmerie, then by the Corbeil police, by magistrates and by reporters.

'You'll see it was Emile Gradut who committed the crime,' he had been told.

And Maigret, after spending two hours questioning Gradut, was back on the scene of the incident, his hands in the pockets of his heavy overcoat, looking cross and staring at the gloomy landscape as though he was considering buying a plot of land there.

The interest lay not in the lock at Coudray into which the barge had crashed, but at the other end of the reach, eight kilometres higher upstream at the lock of La Citanguette.

The setting here was much the same as lower down. The villages of Morsang and Seine-Port were on the opposite bank, a longish way off; so that there was nothing to be seen but the quiet water with copses beside it and the occasional scar of an old gravel pit.

But at La Citanguette there was a bistro, and boats did their utmost to spend the night there. It was a real boatmen's bistro where they sold bread, canned goods, sausage, tackle, and oats for the horses.

And that was really where Maigret conducted his inquiry, without appearing to do so, taking a drink from time to time, sitting down by the stove or taking a turn outside while the *patronne*, who was so fair as to be almost an albino, watched him with a slightly ironical respect.

About that Wednesday evening the following facts were known. When it was beginning to get dark, the *Aiglon VII*, a small tug from the Upper Seine, had brought her six lighters, like a brood of ducklings, up to the Citanguette lock. It was drizzling at the time. When the boats were moored the men forgathered as usual in the bistro for a drink, while the lock keeper took in his cranks.

The *Astrolabe* came round the river bend only half an hour later, by which time darkness had fallen. Old Arthur Aerts, the skipper, was at the wheel, while Claessens walked along the tow-path in front of his horses with his whip over his shoulder.

Then the *Astrolabe* had moored behind the string of boats, and Claessens had taken his horses on board. At that point nobody had paid attention to them.

It was seven o'clock at least and everyone had finished eating when Aerts and Claessens came into the bistro and sat down by the stove. The skipper of *Aiglon VII* was doing most of the talking and the two old men did not speak. The white-haired *patronne*, with a baby in her arms, served them with four or five glasses of marc, but she had taken little notice of them.

That was how it had been, Maigret now realized. All these people were more or less acquainted with one another. They would come in with a brief gesture of greeting and sit down without a word. Sometimes a woman would come in, just to buy provisions for next day and then to warn her husband, as he sat there drinking: 'Don't be too late back . . .'

That had been the case with Aerts's wife Emma, who had bought bread, eggs and a rabbit.

From that point onwards every detail acquired crucial importance, every piece of evidence became extremely valuable. And so Maigret persisted.

'You're sure that when he left about ten o'clock Arthur Aerts was drunk?'

'Quite tight as usual . . .' the proprietress replied. 'He was a Belgian, a good fellow on the whole, who always sat in his corner saying nothing and went on drinking till he'd just got strength enough left to go back to his boat.'

'And Claessens the carter?'

'He could take a bit more. He stayed about a quarter of an hour longer, then he went off, after coming back for his whip which he'd forgotten.'

So far, so good. It was easy to picture the banks of the Seine at night, below the lock, the tug with its six lighters behind it, then Aerts's barge, with a lamp hanging over each boat and the steady drizzle pouring down over it all.

About half past nine Emma had gone back on board the barge with her provisions. At ten, Aerts had gone back himself, quite tight, as the *patronne* had said. And at a quarter past the carter had at last made his way back to the *Astrolabe*.

'I was only waiting for him to leave to close down, because boatmen go to bed early and there was nobody else left.'

So much was reliable evidence and could be confirmed; but it was all. After that, not the smallest piece of exact information. At six in the morning the skipper of the tug had been surprised not to see the *Astrolabe* behind his lighters, and a little later he had noticed that the moorings had been cut.

At the same moment the lock keeper at Le Coudray, who was looking after his sick wife, had heard the shouts of the old carter, and soon afterwards had discovered that the barge had run into his weir.

The dog was running loose on the deck. The carter, woken up by the collision, knew nothing and declared that he had been asleep all night in his stable as usual.

Only, in the cabin at the back of the boat, Aerts's body was discovered; he had been hanged, not with a rope but with the dog's
chain. Then, behind a curtain that concealed the wash-basin, his wife
Emma was found hanging too; she had been hanged with a sheet
taken from the bed.

And that was not all, since just before setting forth, the skipper of the
Aiglon VII, after vainly calling for his stoker Emile Gradut, discovered
that the man had disappeared.

'Gradut was the murderer . . .'

Everybody was convinced of it, and that very evening the newspapers were full of such headlines as: 'Gradut seen prowling round
Seine-Port', 'Man-hunt in forest of Rougeau', 'Aerts's hoard still not
found . . .'

For all evidence went to prove that old Aerts had had a hoard, and
indeed everyone agreed on the sum: 100,000 francs. It was a long yet
quite simple story. Aerts, who was sixty and had two grown-up, married sons, had married as his second wife Emma, a tough Strasbour-
geoise twenty years his junior.

Things were not going at all well between the couple. At every lock
they stopped at, Emma would grumble about the miserliness of the
old man, who scarcely gave her enough to eat.

'I don't even know where he keeps his money,' she would say. 'He
wants his sons to have it when he dies . . . And meanwhile I have to
kill myself looking after him and steering the boat; not to mention . . .'

She would add crude details, sometimes in front of Aerts himself,
while he just shook his head stubbornly; then, after she had left, he
would mutter:

'She only married me for my hundred thousand francs, but she's
going to be disappointed . . .'

Emma would comment, furthermore:

'As though his sons needed it to live on!'

In fact the elder son, Joseph, was the skipper of a tugboat at Antwerp, while Théodore, with his father's help, had bought a fine self-
propelled barge, the *Marie-France*; he had been notified of his father's
death while passing through Maestricht, in Holland.

'But I'm going to find those hundred thousand francs of his . . .'

She would tell you all this out of the blue, when she'd only known
you five minutes, giving the most intimate details about her old husband, and adding cynically:

'He surely can't suppose that it was out of love that a young woman
like myself . . .'

And she was unfaithful to him. The evidence was indisputable.
Even the skipper of the *Aiglon VII* knew about it.

'I can only tell you what I know . . . But it's a fact that during the fortnight we were lying idle at Alfortville and the *Astrolabe* was being loaded, Emile Gradut often went to meet her, even in broad daylight . . .'

So what next?

Emile Gradut, twenty-three years of age, was a bad character, that was obvious. He had, in fact, been caught after twenty-four hours, half starved, in the forest of Rougeau, less than five kilometres from La Citanguette.

'I've done nothing!' he yelled at the policemen, as he tried to ward off their blows.

A nasty little ruffian with whom Maigret had been closeted for two hours in his office and who kept stubbornly repeating:

'I've done nothing . . .'

'Then why did you run away?'

'That's my business!'

As for the examining magistrate, convinced that Gradut had hidden the hoard in the forest, he had fresh searches made there in vain.

There was something infinitely dreary about it all, as dreary as the river which reflected the same sky from morning till night, or those strings of boats that announced their arrival with a blast from a hooter (one blast for each barge being towed) as they threaded their way into the lock in an endless stream. Then, while the women stayed on deck to look after the children and keep an eye on the movements of the boat, the men went up to the bistro for a drink and then walked slowly back.

'It's plain sailing,' one of his colleagues had said to Maigret.

And yet Maigret, as sullen as the Seine itself, as sullen as a canal in the rain, had returned to his lock and could not bring himself to leave it.

It's always the same story: when a case seems too clear-cut, nobody bothers to probe it in detail. Everybody agreed that Gradut was the criminal, and he had such a villainous look about him that it seemed self-evident.

Nonetheless, the results of the post mortem had now come in and they led to some curious conclusions. Thus in the case of Arthur Aerts, Dr Paul said:

'. . . *Slight bruising at the base of the chin . . . From the state of rigor mortis and the contents of the stomach it can be specified that death by strangulation occurred between 10 and 10.30 p.m.*'

Now Aerts had gone back on board at ten o'clock. According to the white-haired *patronne*, Claessens had followed him a quarter of an hour later, and Claessens declared that he had gone straight into his cabin.

'Was there a light in the Aerts's cabin?'

'I don't know . . .'

'Was the dog tied up?'

The poor old fellow had thought for a long time, but had finally made a helpless gesture. No, he didn't know. He hadn't noticed . . . How could he have foretold that it would matter so much what he did that particular evening? He had been drowsy with drink as usual; he slept in his clothes, on the straw, lying cosily beside his horse and his mare.

'You heard no noise?'

He didn't know! He couldn't have known! He had gone to sleep and when he woke up he had found himself in midstream, up against the weir.

At this point, however, there was a piece of evidence. But could it be taken seriously? It came from Madame Couturier, the wife of the skipper of the *Aiglon VII*. The head of the Corbeil police had questioned her like everyone else before letting the train of boats carry on its journey towards the Loing canal. Maigret had the report in his pocket.

Q. Did you hear anything during the night?

A. I wouldn't swear to it.

Q. Tell us what you heard.

A. It's so uncertain . . . I woke up at one point and looked at the time on my alarm clock . . . It was a quarter to eleven . . . I thought I heard people speaking near the boat . . .

Q. Did you recognize the voices?

A. No. But I thought it must be Gradut meeting Emma . . . I must have fallen asleep immediately after . . .

Could one rely on this? And even if it was true, what did it prove?

Below the lock, the tug-boat and its six lighters and the *Astrolabe* had been lying quiet that night and . . .

As regards Aerts, the report was definite: he had died of strangulation between 10 and 10.30 p.m.

But things became more complicated when it came to the second report, the one about Emma.

'. . . *The left cheek shows contusions produced either by a blunt instrument or by a violent blow with someone's fist . . . Death, due to asphyxia by hanging, must have taken place at about 1 a.m.*'

And Maigret became ever more deeply absorbed in the slow, ponderous life of La Citanguette, as though only there was he capable of thought. A self-propelled barge flying a Belgian flag reminded him of Théodore, Aerts's son, who must by now have reached Paris.

At the same time, the Belgian flag suggested the thought of gin. For on the table in the cabin there had been found a bottle of gin, more than half empty. Somebody had made a thorough search of the cabin itself and even tore open the mattress covers, scattering the flock stuffing.

Obviously, in an attempt to find the hidden hoard of 100,000 francs!

The first investigators had declared: 'It's quite simple! Emile Gradut killed Aerts and Emma. Then he got drunk and hunted for the treasure, which he hid in the forest.' Only . . . Yes! Only Dr Paul, in his post mortem on Emma's body, had found in her stomach all the gin that was missing from the bottle!

Clearly, since Emma had drunk the gin, it couldn't have been Gradut!

'Sure!' the investigators had replied. 'Gradut, after killing Aerts, had made the woman tipsy in order to overcome her more easily, for she was a strong creature, don't forget . . .'

So that if they were right, Gradut and his mistress must have stayed on board from 10 or 10.30 p.m., the time of Aerts's death, until midnight or 1 a.m., the time of Emma's.

It was possible, of course . . . Everything was possible . . . Only, Maigret wanted, somehow or other, to get to understand the bargees' way of thinking.

He had been as harsh as the rest with Emile Gradut. For two hours he had grilled him thoroughly. To begin with he had tried the wheedling method, *la chansonnette* as they said at the Quai des Orfèvres.

'Listen, old fellow . . . You're involved, that's clear . . . But to be frank with you, I don't believe you killed the pair of them . . .'

'I've done nothing!'

'You didn't kill them, that's for sure . . . But admit that you knocked the old fellow about a bit . . . It was his own fault, of course . . . He caught you together, and so in self-defence . . .'

'I've done nothing!'

'As for Emma, of course you didn't touch her, since she was your woman . . .'

'You're wasting your time! I've done nothing . . .'

Afterwards Maigret had become harsher, even threatening.

'Oh, so that's how it is . . . Well, we shall see if, once you're on that boat with the two bodies . . .'

But Gradut had not even flinched at the prospect of a reconstruction of the crime.

'Whenever you like . . . I've done nothing . . .'

'All the same when we find the money you've put away somewhere . . .'

Then Emile Gradut gave a smile . . . a smile of pity . . . an infinitely superior smile . . .

That evening the only vessels moored at La Citanguette were one motorized barge and a 'stable-boat'. By the lower lock, a policeman was still on duty on the deck of the *Astrolabe*, and he was greatly surprised when Maigret, climbing up on board, announced:

'I haven't time to go back to Paris . . . I shall sleep here . . .'

The soft lapping of water could be heard against the hull, and the footsteps of the policeman as he paced the deck for fear of going to sleep. The poor man began to wonder whether Maigret was not going out of his mind, for he was making as much noise, all alone inside the boat, as if the two horses had been let loose in the hold.

'Excuse me, officer . . .' Maigret emerged from the hatchway, 'could you possibly get hold of a pickaxe for me?'

Get hold of a pickaxe at ten o'clock at night, in such a spot? However, the policeman woke up the sad-looking lock keeper, who, being a gardener, owned a pickaxe.

'What does your Super want to do with it?'

'Blessed if I know . . .'

And they exchanged significant glances. As for Maigret, he went back into the cabin with his pickaxe, and for an hour after that the policeman heard muffled blows.

'Look here, officer . . .'

It was Maigret again, sweating and out of breath, thrusting his head through the hatchway.

'Go and put through a phone call for me . . . I'd like the examining magistrate to come as early as possible tomorrow morning and have Emile Gradut brought along . . .'

The lock keeper had never looked so lugubrious as when he guided the examining magistrate to the barge, while Gradut followed, flanked by a couple of policemen.

'No . . . I swear I don't know anything!'

Maigret was asleep on the Aerts's bed. He did not even apologize, and seemed unaware of the magistrate's stupefaction at the sight of the cabin.

The floorboards had been lifted. Underneath there was a layer of cement, but this had been smashed with the pickaxe, and the mess was indescribable.

'Come in, *Monsieur le juge* . . . I was very late getting to bed and I haven't had time to tidy myself up yet . . .'

He lit a pipe. He had found some bottles of beer somewhere and he poured himself a drink.

'Come in, Gradut . . . And now . . .'

'Yes, now?' asked the magistrate.

'It's quite simple,' Maigret declared, puffing at his pipe. 'I'll explain to you what happened the other night. You see, there was one thing that struck me from the first: old Aerts had been hanged *with a chain* and his wife *with a sheet*.

'You'll soon understand. Study police records and I'll swear you'll never find a single case of a man hanging himself with a wire or a chain. It may be odd, but it's so . . . Suicides are sensitive people and the thought of those links bruising their throats and pinching the skin of their necks . . .'

'So Arthur Aerts was murdered?'

'That's my conclusion, yes, particularly since the bruise that was noticed on his chin seems to prove that the chain, having been slipped round his neck from behind while he was drunk, struck his face first . . .'

'I don't see . . .'

'Wait a minute! Now note that his wife, on the other hand, had been hanged with a twisted sheet . . . Not even a rope, whereas there are plenty of them on board a boat . . . No, a sheet off a bed, which is the gentlest way of hanging oneself, so to speak . . .'

'And that means?'

'That she hanged herself . . . She even had to swallow half a litre of gin to get up courage, whereas normally she never drank . . . Remember the forensic report . . .'

'I remember it . . .'

'So we have one murder and one suicide, the murder committed at about a quarter past ten, the suicide at midnight or 1 a.m. And that makes everything as clear as daylight . . .'

The magistrate was watching him somewhat suspiciously, and Emile Gradut with ironical curiosity.

'For a long time now,' Maigret went on, 'Emma, who had not got what she hoped for from her marriage to old Aerts and who was in love with Emile Gradut, had been obsessed by one idea: to get hold of the hoard and run away with her lover. Suddenly an opportunity arose. Aerts came home dead drunk. Gradut was close by, on board the tug. She'd already noticed, when she went to buy her provisions in the bistro, that her husband was pretty tipsy. So she unfastened the dog and waited, with the chain all ready to be slipped round the man's neck . . .'

'But . . .' the magistrate objected.

'Presently! Let me finish . . . Now, Aerts is dead. Emma, elated with her triumph, runs to fetch Gradut; don't forget, at this point, that the wife of the tugboat skipper had heard voices close to her boat at a quarter to eleven . . . Isn't that true, Gradut?'

'It's true!'

'The couple come on board to look for the treasure, search everywhere, even inside the mattress, but fail to find those hundred thousand francs. Is that true, Gradut?'

'It's true!'

'Time passes and Gradut grows impatient. He even wonders, I'd be willing to bet, if he's not been had, if those hundred thousand francs really exist. Emma swears they do . . . But what use are they if they can't be found? . . . So they keep on searching. Then Gradut gets fed up . . . He knows he'll be accused of the crime. He wants to clear off. Emma wants to go with him . . .'

'Excuse me . . .' the magistrate tried to put in.

'Presently! . . . I tell you she wants to go off with him and, since he has no desire to be burdened with a woman who hasn't even any money, he solves the problem by knocking her out with his fist. Having floored her, he cuts the moorings of the barge . . . Is that true, Gradut?'

This time Gradut seemed reluctant to reply.

'That's about all!' Maigret concluded. 'If they had discovered the treasure they'd have gone off together, or else they'd have tried to make the old man's death look like suicide . . . Since they've failed to find it, Gradut takes fright, and roams through the countryside trying to take cover . . . Emma, when she comes round, finds the boat drifting downstream and the hanged man swinging by her side. No hope left for her, not even the hope of escape. It would mean waking Claessens to guide the barge with the boathook . . . In short, the whole thing has been a fiasco. And she decides to kill herself . . . Only as her courage fails her, she drinks first and then takes a soft sheet from the bed . . .'

'Is this true, Gradut?' asked the magistrate, watching the young thug.

'Since the Super says so . . .'

'But . . . wait a minute . . .' the magistrate objected. 'What is to prove that he didn't find the treasure and, in order to keep it . . .'

Then Maigret merely kicked aside some pieces of cement and disclosed a hiding-place in which lay Belgian and French gold coins.

'Do you understand now?'

'More or less . . .' the magistrate muttered, without much conviction.

And Maigret, filling a fresh pipe, growled:

'One had to know, in the first place, that they use a cement foundation for repairing old barges. Nobody had told me that . . .'

Then, with a sudden change of tone:

'The oddest thing about it is that I've counted, and there really are a hundred thousand francs . . . A peculiar household, don't you think?'

DEATH OF A WOODLANDER

This was one of the rare cases which might have been solved from diagrams and documents, by deduction and by scientific police methods. Indeed, when Maigret left the Quai des Orfèvres he was already acquainted with its every detail, even down to the casks of wine.

He expected to make a brief journey through space, and it proved to be an exhausting journey through time. Barely a hundred kilometres from Paris, at Vitry-aux-Loges, he alighted from a preposterous little train such as one only sees in old-fashioned picture books, and his request for a taxi was taken for a joke and met with disapproval. He nearly had to complete his journey in the baker's cart, but at the last minute he persuaded the butcher to drive him in his van.

'Do you often go there?' asked Maigret, referring to the little village to which his investigation was taking him.

'Twice a week. Thanks to you they'll be getting an extra delivery of meat . . .'

Maigret had been born forty kilometres away, on the banks of the Loire; and he had not expected to find tragedy lurking in the forest of Orléans.

For now they were in the depths of the forest. They drove for about ten kilometres with high trees on either side before reaching a village that stood in the midst of a clearing.

'Is it here?'

'Next village . . .'

It was not raining, but the forest was damp and the sky oppressive in its bleak whiteness. The trees had lost almost all their leaves, which lay rotting, while here and there branches creaked and an occasional distant shot rang out.

'Is there much shooting?'

'That must be Monsieur le Duc.'

And now in a clearing even smaller than the previous ones some thirty low, poky little houses huddled round a church with a pointed steeple. Every one of these houses must have been at least a hundred years old, and their black slate roofs added to their grimness.

'Will you take me to the Potru sisters' place?'

'I thought as much. It's opposite the church . . .'

Maigret got down, while the butcher, a little further on opened the back of his van and attracted a few housewives, who seemed rather reluctant to buy meat on an unscheduled day.

Maigret had so closely studied the diagram prepared by the original investigators that he could have found his way about the house with his eyes shut.

And that was practically what he had to do, because the rooms were so dark. It really was a journey backwards through time that faced the Superintendent as he entered the shop, which seemed to have ignored the present century.

The sparse distribution of light, the sombre colour of walls and furniture were reminiscent of some old painting, with hazy patches of greyness amid the chiaroscuro and here and there a sudden gleam of light on glass or copper.

For the past sixty-five years, since the day they were born, the Potru ladies (the elder of them at any rate, for the second was only sixty-two) had lived in this house, like their parents before them.

Nothing, presumably, had changed, neither the shop-counter with its scales and boxes of candy, nor the haberdashery department, nor the grocery corner which exuded a sickly smell of cinnamon and chicory, nor the zinc shelf on which drinks were served.

In one corner a cask of paraffin stood next to a smaller cask containing cooking oil. There were a couple of tables at the far end of the shop, and another on the left hand side, long tables, polished by time, flanked by backless benches.

A door opened on the left. A woman of thirty-two or thirty-three, with a baby in her arms, looked at Maigret.

'What do you want?'

'Don't bother about me . . . I've come for the inquiry . . . You're a neighbour, I suppose?'

The woman, heavily pregnant under her apron, replied:

'I'm Marie Lacore, the blacksmith's wife . . .'

Noticing an oil lamp hanging from the roof, Maigret realized that the hamlet had no electricity.

The second room, into which he made his way uninvited, was so dark that Maigret was glad of the glow provided by a couple of logs, which enabled him to make out a huge bed, piled high with mattresses and topped by a ballooning red quilt. In this bed an old woman was lying motionless, her eyes the only sign of life in a rigid pale face.

'Is she still not speaking?' he asked Marie Lacore.

She shook her head. With a shrug of his shoulders, the Superintendent sat down on a straw-bottomed chair and pulled some documents from his pockets.

There had been nothing sensational about the incident itself, which had taken place five days earlier. The Potru sisters, who lived alone in this shabby dwelling, were reputed to have some money put by. They even owned three other houses in the village, and they had a well-deserved reputation for meanness.

During the Friday night some neighbours had thought they had heard a noise, but had not worried about it. At daybreak on the Saturday a peasant, passing by, had noticed the bedroom window wide open, had gone up and then had called for help.

Beside the window Amélie Potru, in her nightgown, was lying in a pool of blood. On the bed, her face turned to the wall, her sister Marguerite lay dead, with three stab wounds in her chest; her right cheek and her eye had been savagely slashed.

Amélie was still alive. She had tried to give the alarm by opening the window, and she had then collapsed, weakened by loss of blood. None of her eleven wounds was serious; almost all of them were on her shoulder and her right side.

The second drawer of the chest was open, the linen lay in disorder and on it was found a leather briefcase, green with age, in which the two sisters must have kept their papers. On the floor lay a savings book, title deeds, rent books and tradesmen's bills.

The Orléans police had held an inquiry. Maigret had been provided with a detailed plan of the premises and also of photographs and the report of the interrogation.

The dead woman, Marguerite, had been buried two days later. As for Amélie, when it had been proposed to take her to hospital she had resisted wildly, clinging with her nails to the bedclothes, and conveying by her fierce glare her desire to be left at home.

The pathologist asserted that since none of her organs was affected her sudden mutism could only be accounted for by shock. In any case, for the past five days no sound had issued from her lips and she lay there, immobilized and bandaged and yet watching all that went on around her. Even now she never took her eyes off Maigret.

However, three hours after the visit from the Public Prosecutor's Department from Orléans, a man had been arrested, all the evidence pointing to his guilt. He was Marcel, a natural son of the sister who had been killed, born when she was twenty-three. He was now thirty-nine, and after having been a stud-groom to 'Monsieur le Duc', according to the local people, now worked as a woodcutter in the forest and lived in a ruined farm ten kilometres away, close to the Loup-Pendu pond.

Maigret had been to see the man in his cell. He was a brute in every sense of the word. He had repeatedly stayed away from home for weeks on end without giving any sign of life to his wife and five children, who got from him more kicks than sous. A drunkard into the bargain, a real bad one.

Maigret read through Marcel's account of the crucial evening in the atmosphere in which it had developed.

'I got there on my bike about seven o'clock, when the women were about to have their supper. I had a drink at the counter, then I went into the yard to kill a rabbit. I skinned it and my mother cooked it for me. As usual my aunt raised hell, she's never been able to stand me . . .'

The local people confirmed the fact that Marcel used frequently to descend on his mother in this way for a good feed, since she dared not refuse him anything and his aunt was afraid of him.

'There was another row because I took a cheese out of the shop and ate some of it . . .'

'Where did the wine come from?' asked Maigret.

'Out of the shop . . .'

'How was the room lit?'

'By the oil lamp . . . After supper my mother, who was feeling poorly, went to bed and asked me to fetch her papers out of the second drawer of the chest of drawers. I went to sit beside her with the papers and we went through the bills together, because it was the end of the month . . .'

'What else was there in the briefcase?'

'Certificates and bearer bonds, a big bundle of them, thirty thousand francs' worth or more . . .'

'You never went into the coach-house? You didn't light the candle?'

'Never. At half past nine I put the papers back into the drawer and left. I had another drink of brandy as I went through the shop. If anyone says I killed the two old women they're lying. You'd do better questioning the Yugo . . .'

To the great surprise of Marcel's lawyer, Maigret did not pursue the matter.

As for Yarko, more generally known as the Yugo because he came from Yugoslavia, he was another peculiar character, who had landed in these parts after the war and had stayed there, living by himself in a wing of the next-door house and working as a carter in the forest.

He, too, was a drunkard, and recently the Potru sisters had refused to serve him because he already owed them too much money. On one occasion Marcel, who happened to be present, had had to turn the Yugo out of the house and had punched him on the nose.

The Potru sisters hated him, particularly since they had leased him an old stable at the end of their yard, where he kept his horses, and for which he owed them a quarter's rent. At the present moment he was presumably carting wood in the forest.

And Maigret, papers in hand, followed out his idea; he went up to the fireplace where, on the morning when the crime was discovered, a stout kitchen knife with its handle completely burnt had been found among the ashes. It was obviously the weapon which had been used, and on which all trace of finger-prints had been obliterated by fire.

On the other hand, the drawer of the chest and the leather briefcase showed a great many of Marcel's prints, and nobody else's!

On the candlestick which had been found on the table, the only prints were those of Amélie Potru, who lay there watching Maigret's movements with her icy glare.

'I suppose you still won't make up your mind to talk,' he growled on the off chance, lighting his pipe.

And he bent down to mark in chalk on the floor the bloodstains which were reproduced on his plan of the place.

'Are you stopping for a little?' asked Marie Lacore. 'That would give me the chance to go and put my dinner in the oven . . .'

So the Superintendent was left alone in the house with the old woman. It was his first visit to the place, but he had already spent a day and a night studying the file and the plan. Orléans had done such an efficient job that there had been nothing to surprise him, except the painful experience of finding reality even more sordid than he had imagined.

And yet he came from a peasant family! He *knew* that certain hamlets still live today as they did in the thirteenth or fourteenth century. But to find himself suddenly plunged into this woodland village, in this house, this room, beside this injured woman of whose alert mind he was aware, was as distressing to him as a visit to those homes or hospitals where some of the worst deformities of the human race are concealed.

At the start of his job, in Paris, he had made a few notes in the margin of the report:

'*(1) Why should Marcel have burned the knife without bothering about the finger-prints he had left on the chest of drawers and on the briefcase?*

(2) Why, if he had used the candle, did he bring it back into the bedroom and extinguish it?

(3) Why did the trail of bloodstains not form a straight line from the bed to the window?

(4) Why, when he left the house at half past nine, did Marcel leave by the front door, thus risking discovery, instead of by the yard door, which leads into the countryside?'

On the other hand, there was one factor which disheartened Marcel's lawyer: one of his coat buttons had been discovered actually in the old ladies' bed, distinctive buttons from an old corduroy hunting-jacket.

'It must have got caught and come off while I was skinning the rabbit,' he had maintained.

Maigret, having re-read his notes, stood up and looked at Amélie with a peculiar smile, for she was going to be very disappointed at losing sight of him. He now opened the door of the coach house, which was a narrow place lit only by a skylight and containing piles of wood and, on the left, against the wall, the notorious casks of wine.

The two first were full, one of red wine, the other of white. The next two were empty, and on one of them the police experts from the Records Department had noticed drips of candle wax which had come from the candle found in the bedroom.

In his report the special Superintendent from Orléans said:

'. . . It is probable that these traces were left by Marcel when he came to get a drink. His wife admits that when he got home he was completely drunk, and the zigzag track of his cycle on the road confirms this . . .'

Maigret looked around for something which he failed to find, went back into the bedroom, opened the window, but saw nobody on the village square but a couple of small boys watching the house.

'Say, sonny, could you go and fetch me a saw?'

'A saw for sawing wood?'

Behind him there was still that cadaverous face, whose watchful eyes followed the movements of his thickset figure. The boy returned with two saws of different sizes. At the same time, Marie Lacore came back.

'I've not kept you waiting? . . . I've left the kid at home. . . . Now I'm going to have to attend to her . . .'

'Wait a few minutes longer . . .'

'I'll just put the water on to boil.'

Maigret, indeed, preferred not to witness the next scene; he'd had quite enough! He went back into the coach house and, making for the barrel with the smears of candle-wax, he introduced the saw into its bung-hole and set to work.

He knew what he was going to discover. He was self-confident. If he had still had some doubts that morning, the atmosphere of the house had confirmed his hunch. And Amélie Portu was just as he had expected to find her!

The walls of the place exuded not merely avarice but hatred. And when he first went in he had caught sight of a pile of newspapers on the counter. This was very important, and the reports had not mentioned it: the Potru ladies acted as newsagents. Amélie owned a pair of spectacles, and did not wear them during the day; she must therefore need them for reading; she must therefore have read . . .

And the biggest objection to the Superintendent's theory now vanished.

The basis of his theory was hatred, a hatred exacerbated by long years spent tête à tête, by life together in this constricted house, nights spent in the same bed, identical interests . . .

Marguerite had had a child, she had known love, whereas her elder sister had not even had that joy! For fifteen or twenty years the boy had hung around the house with the two women, then, once on his own, he had kept coming back to eat and drink and demand money.

Money which belonged as much to Amélie as to Marguerite! Even more, indeed, *since she was the elder and had worked longer to earn it!*

A hatred fomented by the countless incidents of daily life, such as Marcel's killing of the rabbit, his eating of the cheese which was there to be sold and which he had quite shamelessly spoiled without protest from his mother . . .

Yes, Amélie read the newspapers; she must eagerly have studied the law reports and realized the importance of finger-prints!

Amélie was afraid of her nephew. She bore a grudge against her sister for showing him the hiding-place where their money was kept and, as on that very evening, letting Marcel handle the certificates which he must have coveted.

'Some day he'll come and murder us . . .'

Maigret could have sworn that such words must often have been uttered in that house. He kept on sawing. He was warm now, and he took off his hat and coat and laid them on the nearest cask.

The rabbit . . . The cheese . . . Then suddenly the realization that Marcel had just left his finger-prints on the drawer and on the shabby old briefcase . . . And into the bargain that button which had come off his jacket and which his mother, lying in bed, could not sew on for him.

For, if Marcel had been the murderer, why should he have emptied the contents of the briefcase on the scene of his crime rather than take the whole thing away? This argument applied even more to Yarko, who, as Maigret had ascertained, could not even read!

Amélie's wounds, which were all on her right side, were too numerous and too superficial; this had been Maigret's starting-point. He had pictured her, clumsy and fearful of pain . . . She did not want to die nor to suffer too long, and she had counted on summoning her neighbours by opening the window and calling for help . . .

Would a murderer have given her time to run to the window?

By the irony of fate, she had fainted before anyone had heard her cries, and had been left unattended all night!

This must have been what had happened! She had killed her sister, who was lying half asleep, and then, no doubt wrapping a rag round her hand, she had opened the chest of drawers and emptied the brief-case, since in order for Marcel to be suspected the money had to disappear!

Which explained the candle . . .

After which, sitting on the edge of the bed, she had wounded her-self, clumsily, half-heartedly, then had walked to the fireplace, as the trail of bloodstains showed, so as to obliterate her fingerprints by burning the knife!

Then she had got as far as the window and . . .

Maigret, who was nearing the end of his task, turned round sharply. He heard voices, and what sounded like a struggle. He saw the door open and, framed in the doorway, a grotesque and sinister figure appeared: that of Amélie Potru, dressed in a strange sort of petticoat and bodice, with bandaged arms and trunk, staring at him, while Marie Lacore, behind her, was protesting against such rashness.

Well, Maigret had not the heart to speak. He chose rather to com-plete his task, and when at last the cask fell apart he did not even heave a sigh of relief on discovering rolls of paper: the missing share certifi-cates and railway debentures which had been pushed through the bung-hole.

He would have liked to leave immediately, or else, like that coarse fellow Marcel, to treat himself to a hefty draught of rum straight from the bottle.

Amélie still spoke no word. Her mouth was half open. If she were to faint she would fall into the arms of Marie Lacore, a much smaller woman whose pregnancy rendered her fragile.

There was nothing for it! The scene seemed to belong to a different era, to a different world. Maigret collected the certificates and stepped forward, while Amélie drew back; finally he laid the papers down on the bedroom table.

'Go and fetch the mayor,' he said to Marie Lacore, speaking curtly because his throat felt constricted. 'He shall be my witness.'

And to Amélie: 'As for you, you'd better go back to bed.'

In spite of his professional curiosity, and although he was hardened, he did not want to look at her. He merely heard the springs of the bed creak. He stayed there with his back turned until the arrival of the farmer who was mayor of the hamlet, and who hardly dared enter the house.

There was no telephone in the village. A man was sent on a bicycle to Vitry-aux-Loges. The police arrived almost at the same time as the butcher's van.

The sky was still as bleakly white and the west wind was shaking the trees.

'Have you found something?'

He replied evasively, dejectedly, and yet he already knew that this case would provide the subject for long studies in the criminal archives not only of Paris but also of London, Berlin, Vienna, even New York.

To see him, you'd have thought he was drunk!

IN THE RUE PIGALLE

A chance visitor to Marina's might well have been misled. Lucien, the proprietor, wearing a thick beige sweater that made him look even shorter and broader, was fiddling with his bottles behind the bar, decanting, re-corking, carefully changing the washer on his tap, and his sullenness might well have been put down to the time of day and the weather.

For it was a grey morning, colder than usual, the sort of morning when snow seems imminent and you want to stay in bed. It was barely nine o'clock, and there was little activity in the Rue Pigalle.

The casual visitor would probably have wondered about the identity of the thickset man in a heavy overcoat, who stood with his back to the stove, smoking a pipe and nursing a glass of spirits in his hand; he would certainly not have expected to find here Superintendent Maigret of the Police Judiciaire.

He would also have seen a slatternly Breton servant girl, Julie, with a permanently scared look on her freckled face, kneeling on the floor and wiping the legs of the table.

In the restaurants of the Pigalle district, things seldom start very early. The place had not been cleaned; dirty glasses were still lying around, and in the kitchen, through the open door, the *patronne*, Marina herself, could be seen, looking even grubbier and more ungainly than her maid.

The general effect was quiet and homely. At the farthest table there were two men who although they were unshaven and their rumpled suits had clearly been slept in, didn't look in too bad shape.

In fact, the casual visitor would just have thought the place a modest restaurant like any other, with its regular customers, a place not of the cleanest, to be sure, but not unattractive on this chilly morning.

He would doubtless have changed his mind on seeing Maigret suddenly glance at the camelhair overcoat belonging to one of the customers and hanging on the coat-rack, go up to it, thrust his hand into the pockets and pull out a knuckle-duster; and then on hearing the Superintendent remark goodhumouredly:

'Hey, Christiani . . . Is this the one that knocked me out?'

119

Half an hour earlier, on his arrival at the Quai des Orfèvres, Maigret had been called to the phone by somebody who insisted on speaking to him personally, and who was obviously making an effort to disguise his voice.

'That you, Superintendent? . . . Look here, there was a row going on last night at Marina's . . . If you were to look in there you might meet your old friend Christiani . . . And it might occur to you to ask him for news of Martino . . . You know, the kid from Antibes, whose brother has just been shipped off to Guiana? . . .'

Before five minutes were up, Maigret had learnt from the exchange that the telephone call came from a tobacconist's in the Rue Notre-Dame-de-Lorette. A quarter of an hour later, he alighted from a taxi at the corner of the Rue Pigalle, just as the gutters were carrying their fullest load of refuse alongside the pavement.

Although he was still in the dark, Maigret was convinced that the affair must be taken seriously, indeed very seriously, since such denunciations are seldom unfounded.

He had the proof of this right away, as he walked slowly up the street. Almost opposite Marina's he noticed a small bar, kept by an Auvergnat, unexpectedly wedged between two nightclubs. In this bar, keeping watch close to the window, the Superintendent recognized two men, the Niçois and Pepito, who are not usually seen about so early, particularly in such a place.

The minute after, he pushed open the door of the restaurant across the street, at the far end of which he saw Christiani with a young recruit, René Lecoeur, known as the Accountant because he had formerly been a bank clerk in Marseilles.

In this sort of situation it is better not to be surprised at anything. Raising his hand to his bowler hat, Maigret greeted the assembled company, like any harmless regular dropping in for a drink.

'How goes it, Lucien?'

Which did not prevent him from noticing the way the napkin shook in Lucien's hands, while the maid, looking up with a start, bumped her head against a table.

'Did you have a lot of company last night? . . . Give me a coffee and a small calvados . . .'

Then, entering the kitchen:

'How are things, Marina? . . . I saw you'd had a mirror broken above the bar . . .'

For he had noticed at a glance that a mirror had been smashed by a bullet from a revolver.

'That was done some time ago,' Lucien hurriedly explained. 'Somebody I don't know, who had just bought a gun and didn't know it was loaded . . .'

After that things moved very slowly. Maigret had been there for over a quarter of an hour and they had not exchanged more than a score of remarks. The maid went on with her work, Lucien remained behind the bar, and Marina busied herself in the kitchen. Meanwhile the Superintendent smoked his pipe and drank his calvados, going from time to time to glance out at the bistro over the way and then returning to stand by the stove.

He knew the household like the back of his hand. Lucien, who had been in trouble in Marseilles, had subsequently gone straight and opened this little restaurant in Montmartre with his wife. His customers were chiefly old acquaintances, people from the underworld of course but who had settled down, for the most part, and become almost respectable.

This was the case with Christiani who, ten years previously, when arrested, had promptly struck Maigret with his knuckle-duster and who was now owner of a couple of 'houses' in Paris and another at Barcelonnette.

It was more or less the case, too, with the men in the bistro over the way, particularly the Niçois, who also owned 'houses' like Christiani's and unfortunately in competition with his.

'Say, how long has your pal been staying at the Auvergnat's across the street?'

'I'm not interested in such people!' retorted Christiani with contempt.

'That may be. But he certainly seems to be interested in you, and if I didn't know you're a stout fellow I'd think that it's his presence in the little bistro that keeps you from going out . . .'

A pause, and another sip of calvados.

'Yes . . . That's how I'd picture things . . . Last night, for one reason or another, there could have been some unpleasantness. And since then, Pepito and the Niçois could have been waiting for you outside, so that the two of you had to sleep on the restaurant benches.'

As he spoke he went up to the Accountant and fingered the creases on the young man's jacket.

'Only I wonder what could have happened, seeing that everyone knows Lucien doesn't like trouble and that you're no longer the sort to take risks. By the way, Martino's brother, who set off yesterday from the Île de Ré, sends you his greetings . . .'

All very friendly, almost goodhumoured. Nevertheless Christiani had given a start, and since the Accountant was standing there Maigret took the opportunity to feel his pockets and extract a stout knife with a safety-catch.

'That's dangerous, son! You shouldn't go about carrying that kind of toy. What about you, Christiani? Haven't you anything for me in your pockets?'

Christiani, with a shrug, pulled out a Smith and Wesson revolver which he handed over to the Superintendent.

'Why, hello, there's one bullet missing . . . Maybe the one that smashed the mirror . . . What surprises me, by the way, is that you didn't reload it and that you didn't bother to clean the barrel . . .'

He slipped the knife, the knuckle-duster and the revolver into his overcoat pocket, and with apparent unconcern searched in every corner of the place, even opening the ice-box and the telephone booth. Meanwhile his mind was hard at work; he was trying to understand. He built up hypotheses which he rejected one after the other.

'Did you know that the Niçois told Martino that someone had informed on his brother? At any rate, that's the story I've just heard. If I let you go, it's so that you may avoid him, for he might hold it against you and he generally carries a gun.'

'What are you getting at?' growled Christiani, who to all appearances was just as calm as Maigret.

'Nothing . . . I'd like to see Martino . . . I don't know why, but I'd be interested to see him.'

Meanwhile he had made sure that nobody, alive or dead, was hidden in the restaurant, or in the kitchen, or in the adjoining bedroom where Lucien and Marina slept.

At half past nine a messenger brought in a case of aperitifs, and then, almost immediately afterwards, a huge yellow van belonging to the Voyages Duchemin agency stopped in front of the building, leaving again shortly after.

'I'd like a slice of sausage, Marina, one of your own make . . .'

Then Maigret gave a sudden frown on seeing a new figure emerge from the bedroom, looking as surprised as himself.

'Where have *you* come from?'

'I was . . . I was lying on the bed . . .'

It was Fred, who had been Christiani's accomplice on various occasions; he was lying, since Maigret had just ascertained that the bedroom was empty.

'It seems to me,' muttered the Superintendent, 'that you're all so fond of the house that you won't leave it . . . You give me your gun, too.'

Fred hesitated, then held out his revolver, another Smith and Wesson, from which no cartridge was missing.

'Will you give it me back?'

'Maybe . . . It depends on what Martino has to tell me . . . I'm expecting him at any moment. Yes, I told him to meet me here . . .'

He was watching their faces and he saw René Lecoeur turn pale and gulp down a mouthful of spirits.

Maigret made one more effort. He had to find the answer, at all
costs, and he found it just as he was looking out into the street, where a
lorry was passing.

'Lift the receiver . . .' he ordered Christiani.

He did not want to go into the phone booth himself, for that would
have meant taking his eye off his suspects.

'Ask for Police Headquarters . . . Get Lucas on the line . . . You've
got him? Pass me the receiver . . .'

Fortunately the cord was long enough.

'That you, Lucas? . . . Ring up the Voyages Duchemin Agency
right away . . . We must get hold of a van of theirs which has just delivered or collected something in the Rue Pigalle . . . Understood? . . .
Find out what it was . . . Quick as you can! . . . Yes, I'm stopping
here . . .'

Then, turning towards the kitchen:

'What about that sausage, Marina?'

'Coming, Superintendent . . . Here you are . . .'

'I don't expect these gentlemen want any . . . Unless I'm very much
mistaken, they can't be feeling very hungry . . .'

At ten minutes past eleven, they were all still in their places, including the Niçois and his companion at the Auvergnat's over the way. At
eleven minutes past eleven, Lucas jumped out of a taxi in a state of
great excitement, pushed open the door and signalled to Maigret that
he had something important to tell him.

'You can speak in front of these gentlemen, they're all friends.'

'I got hold of the van, in the Boulevard Rochechouart . . . They collected a trunk. They'd had a phone call from this house . . . A third-
third-floor tenant, Monsieur Béchevel . . . It was a huge trunk, or
rather a chest, to be sent by goods train to Quimper . . .'

'You let it go, I hope!' teased Maigret.

'I had it opened . . . There was a body in it, Martino's, the man
whose brother . . .'

'I know . . . And then . . .'

'Dr Paul was at home and he came round right away. I've got the
bullet, which was still embedded in the wound . . .'

Maigret fingered it nonchalantly, and muttered as though to himself:

'A Browning, 6 mm 35 . . . You see how it is: these gentlemen,
who spent the night here, only have Smith and Wessons . . .'

Nobody could foresee what he was going to do. Even now, a
casual visitor would not have realized the tenseness of the situation.
Lucien was exercising all his ingenuity finding things to do behind
the bar.

'Shall I tell you what I think happened? . . . Strictly between ourselves, of course . . . Last night Martino, who'd had too much to
drink, got it into his head that Christiani was responsible for his
brother's arrest. He came to settle accounts with him. And then, as he
was a bit over-excited, he had an accident . . . You get my meaning?'

Lucas, too, was wondering what his chief was getting at. Christiani
had lit a cigarette and was blowing out the smoke with assumed indif-
ference.

'Only, the Niçois and Pepito were waiting in the street . . . They
dared not come in, but they thought they'd wait for the others outside.

'Are you with me now? . . . That's why these friends of ours slept on
the restaurant benches while the Niçois kept watch outside, and then,
at daybreak, settled down at the Auvergnat's . . . The trickiest part
was what to do with that wretched corpse; they couldn't really leave it
on Lucien's hands. What would *you* have done, Christiani? . . . You're
an intelligent fellow . . .'

Christiani gave a disdainful shrug.

'You tell me, Lucien . . . Who's this Béchevel on the third floor?'

'An old gentleman, an invalid . . .'

'Just what I thought . . . Someone went up there in the small hours
and made it clear to him that he'd got to keep quiet . . . Before anyone
was awake in the house they took the body up there by the back stairs
and put it into a chest belonging to the old man. Then they rang up
the Voyages Duchemin. Go up to the third floor and see if I'm
right . . . I'm sure you'll be given the description of our friend Fred,
who was in charge of the job . . .'

So far there was nothing sensational about the scene. In fact a bank
messenger who had called was able to settle his business with Lucas
without noticing anything untoward.

'You've still got nothing to tell me, Christiani?'

'Nothing . . .'

'And you, Lecoeur? After all, it's the first time I've seen you
involved in serious trouble . . .'

'I don't know what you're talking about,' the boy said in a tense
voice.

'Then we shall just have to wait for Lucas . . .'

They waited. And the other lot, across the street, waited too. And
the street grew busier, while the clouds lifted a little and the light became brighter.

'Too bad it had to happen here, Lucien! . . . Never let anyone break
a mirror . . . It brings bad luck . . .'

Lucas was soon back, announcing:

'You were quite right! . . . I found the poor fellow bound and
gagged. He described Fred, but there was somebody else there last

night whom he didn't see. They jumped on him while he was still asleep.'

'That'll do! Ring for a taxi ... Wait! ... Call Headquarters too, and get them to send somebody to watch the fellows over the way, and see that they don't make trouble.'

Maigret, scratching his head, looked at his three toughs and said with a sigh:

'In the meantime, perhaps we shall find out which of you fired the shot ...'

As if he had all the time in the world and didn't know how to spend it, Maigret selected one of the tables and spread out on it a regular panoply of weapons, setting Christiani's knuckle-duster by the side of his revolver and Fred's, then putting Lecoeur's knife a little further off.

'Don't panic about what I'm going to tell you, kid,' he said to the young man, who seemed about to faint. 'This is the first time you've been in trouble, but it probably won't be the last ... This gun, you see, undoubtedly belongs to Christiani, who's been too long in the business to play about with a little Browning like the one that killed Martino. Fred, too, is an old hand who likes serious weapons. When the row broke out, Christiani fired and someone must have knocked his arm, for he only hit the mirror. Then you, with your little Browning ...'

'I haven't got a Browning,' the Accountant managed to stammer out.

'Exactly! *It's the fact that you haven't got one that proves you fired the shot.* Fred kept his gun because he knew it would prove his innocence. Christiani didn't even clean his, to show that he had only fired one shot which hit nobody ... They both know all about experts' reports and they played the game accordingly. Whereas you had to get rid of your revolver because it would have proved you were the murderer. Where did you put it?'

'I didn't kill him!'

'I'm asking you where you put it ... Ask Christiani ... It's too late to play the clever boy ...'

'You won't find any Browning ...'

Maigret looked at him with pity and muttered under his breath:

'You poor sucker!'

The more of a sucker, the more to be pitied since Martino had borne him no grudge and he had only fired to prove to the others that he had guts.

When Lucas returned, Maigret whispered to him:

'Look everywhere ... specially on the roof ... They won't have been such fools as to hide the gun in Lucien's place or in the old man's. See if, at the top of the stairs, there's a window opening on to the roof . . .'

He took his lot with him, while two or three harmless-looking strollers kept watch on the bistro across the street.

Christiani, in his camelhair overcoat, looked like some respectable citizen who has been arrested by mistake and who will promptly be released with apologies. Fred had assumed a jaunty air. The Accountant was tense in every nerve.

The case was an absolutely classic one. Maigret had always claimed that, but for chance, fifty per cent of criminals would escape punishment and that, but for informers, another fifty per cent would remain at liberty.

It sounded like a wisecrack, particularly when uttered in his cheerful gruff voice.

All the same an informer had played a part here, and so had chance, which had enabled him to notice the yellow van of the Voyages Duchemin.

But was there not also a considerable factor due to professional skill, knowledge of human nature and even what is known as flair?

At three o'clock that afternoon the Browning was discovered on the roof, where it had been thrown through the skylight.

At half past three the Accountant had confessed with tears, while Christiani, giving the address of a celebrated lawyer, asserted:

'You'll see, it'll get me about six months!

At which Maigret sighed, without looking at him:

'And your knuckle-duster only cost me a couple of teeth . . .'

MAIGRET'S MISTAKE

There are some people whose faces one cannot even bear to punch, for fear of fouling one's fist! For the past three or four hours, ever since he had been landed with this case in the Rue Saint-Denis, Maigret had been in one of his worst moods, tense and edgy, in that state of sullen, irritated disgust that made him, on such occasions, unapproachable at Police Headquarters.

'Call me a taxi!' he snapped at the office messenger.

And while he followed his 'customer' along passages, then down the stairs, into the courtyard and along the pavement, he really seemed to be holding him at arm's length with a pair of tongs.

'27b Rue Saint-Denis . . .'

He wrapped his overcoat closely round his body, as though to avoid any contact with the man.

And yet this was not an old offender. His police record was clean. He was a tradesman, a fellow of about forty-five, respectably but simply dressed in a suit that was not very new but quite well cut and a frieze overcoat. Physically, he looked the sort of person one often meets in business districts, vacuum-cleaner salesmen or dubious brokers.

His name was Eugène Labri. He was a Frenchman, born in Cairo or Port Said. He was fat. He had dark, brilliant eyes. He was obsequious.

'After you, please, Superintendent.'

And Maigret growled between his teeth:

'You rotter!'

He would rather have been dealing with one of those youngsters who, corrupted by the false glamour of delinquency, knock down a concierge one evening or rob a small shopkeeper. He would have enjoyed an argument with a real burglar, one of those who know their job and set about it with a sort of professional scrupulousness.

But the man before him was an informer, a mean little bounder with pretensions to respectability, who was bowing and scraping to him.

The man before him was the owner of the *Special Bookshop* in the Rue Saint-Denis, and the mere name spoke volumes.

*　　*　　*

127

It stood between a pork butcher's and a hairdresser's; Labri had to use his key to open one of the shutters, for the bookshop was closed. It was a long narrow room, almost a corridor. The window was only one metre wide, but that metre had been put to good use, for it contained a whole collection of books with enticing titles, with suggestive covers, wrapped in cellophane so as to intensify their secret character.

It was five in the afternoon, just the time when, on the previous day, the tragedy had taken place. A crowd was passing along the pavement, people carrying little parcels of food, and taxis were gliding by all unsuspecting.

Maigret closed the door, put back the chain – for there was a chain; people of that sort are cautious! – and pushed his man ahead of him.

'Show me your office . . .'

He would almost rather not have used the familiar *tu*! The man, meanwhile, displayed as much eagerness as if he had been receiving one of his customers.

'Careful of the staircase . . . It's rather steep.'

At the end of the room, behind the counter, there was a narrow staircase of the sort you find in certain bistros where a rudimentary toilet has been fitted up in the cellar.

'Allow me to lead the way,' simpered Labri.

Down below there hung a red velvet curtain, and behind it was a peculiar closet, a library to judge by the bookshelves, a boudoir to judge by the red divan and the big mirror behind it.

Beside the curtain, in the shadows, stood a door of which customers must have been unaware and which Labri pushed open like one well used to doing so, before switching on the light:

'You see it's a very modest place . . .' he excused himself with one of those smiles that Maigret wanted to wipe out with a blow of his fist. The set-up was indeed modest enough: a desk of light-coloured wood, of a mass-produced model, a green-painted metal file, a small gas-ring on the right, with a teapot and some cups. A coat-rack and a wash-basin.

Maigret was too tall and too broad for this basement, which had been cunningly devised as a snare for the depraved, and where his hat brushed the ceiling. He felt as though he were choking.

'How did you see what was going on next door?'

Like any good tradesman showing his current accounts, Labri lifted a calendar hanging against the wall and disclosed an opening that gave on to the boudoir next door.

'Through here . . . I used to put out the light . . . There's a piece of plate-glass over the opening . . .'

And Maigret longed to repeat, like a leitmotiv:

'You rotter!'

He was a rotter, undoubtedly, but a prudent one, who knew his Code Civil and had come to some agreement with the police. The *Special Bookshop* attracted connoisseurs of erotic literature by means of judicious publicity.

'Connoisseurs will enjoy the personal guidance of Mademoiselle Emilienne,' promised the prospectus.

And indeed Mademoiselle Emilienne, the assistant, sometimes came down into this boudoir with some important customer to show him a limited edition worth four or five hundred francs.

While Labri, at his spy-hole . . .

The tragedy seemed straightforward. Two days previously, Labri had sold his business, which he was to go on running for another week before handing it over to the new proprietor.

'*The assistant will remain at the disposal of the purchaser* . . .' declared the contract

And at eleven o'clock the night before, policemen had been surprised to notice lights on in the shop. A sergeant had gone in, and finding nobody on the ground floor had gone down into the basement as Maigret had just done, to find a young woman lying dead in the boudoir.

This was Mademoiselle Emilienne, the assistant who was being handed over to the new owner together with the rest of the stock.

Labri, who lived in a small apartment in the Rue de Metz, had been questioned that morning by the local Superintendent, and had begun by telling lies.

'About five o'clock,' he had declared, 'I made some tea on the gasring as usual. Mademoiselle Emilienne came in to fetch a cup, which I suppose she drank next door. I took my tea alone, then, as I had appointments in town, I went off and left my assistant in charge of closing the shutters . . . I had every confidence in Mademoiselle Emilienne, who had been with me for the past four years.'

Now it was quite clear that Mademoiselle Emilienne had been poisoned by the cup of tea she had drunk.

The local Superintendent, who had had Labri in his clutches before Maigret, had not dealt gently with him, as was proved by a bruise on the man's right temple. An hour later he obtained the following confession:

'The truth is that at about six o'clock I found my assistant lying motionless in the boudoir . . . I thought she was asleep . . . I went away, intending to return a little later . . .'

This was almost plausible, since the pathologist attributed the girl's death to an overdose of sleeping tablets.

'So Mademoiselle Emilienne was not dead when you left?'

'No, I'd have seen . . . She was not cold . . .'

'It never occurred to you to send for a doctor?'

'In our profession, it's wiser to avoid scandal . . . You know that as well as I do . . .'

He stressed these words, thus reminding the Superintendent that he sometimes made himself useful to the police by procuring certain information for them.

In short, he had left Mademoiselle Emilienne while she was still alive. He had, so he asserted, been prevented from returning to the Rue Saint-Denis and, thinking no more about the incident, had gone home to bed.

Maigret, his lips pursed bitterly, was brooding over these facts while all along the Rue Saint-Denis the ordinary life of a working-class district went on and while, in this revoltingly scented basement, Labri posed as an honest tradesman on good terms with his country's laws and his own conscience.

'I swear I've nothing to blame myself for . . . You can examine all the books I've got here . . . The covers may be alluring but there's nothing reprehensible inside . . . That's just why I needed a clever young woman to sell them . . . You follow me? . . . When customers came down here with her, they tried to take liberties . . . She put them in their places, and obliged them to buy expensive books . . .'

He actually smiled, as though it had been a good joke!

'If I hadn't treated her well she would not have stayed with me for four years . . . I used to make the tea myself. The afternoons are long.'

Particularly in that airless office, that basement that seemed so cut off from real life!

'I can guess what you're thinking . . . I'm suspected of trying to kill Emilienne . . . But for one thing I'd have had nothing to gain since the sale contract specifies that she was included in the assets of the shop. I might have got into trouble over bills, for my purchaser had signed a certain number of drafts . . . You see!'

He was speaking goodhumouredly, winking as though to take Maigret into his confidence.

'In any case, how could I have poisoned her? . . . I was told this morning that, according to the doctor, she had swallowed eight sleeping tablets . . . Have you ever taken them? . . . No? . . . Well, I have had one occasionally, and they're so bitter that you couldn't make anyone swallow one unawares . . .'

'Oh yeah?' retorted Maigret, because he had an answer to this. Mademoiselle Emilienne, whose body he had seen at the Forensic Institute, had been a young woman in poor health whose very pallor must have interested her customers. Now Labri could quite well have simulated paternal concern and made her swallow the bitter tea on the pretext of administering some medicine or other.

'I assure you you're on the wrong track, Superintendent! If I had given her the sleeping tablets I'd have arranged for them to take effect somewhere else, so that I shouldn't have been involved . . .'

He'd thought of that, the bastard! He was forestalling accusations. He seemed to be running a counter-investigation of his own.

'What interest could I have had?'

Yes, what interest? That was the question Maigret was asking himself too, for he knew the fellow well enough to realise that he would not have done the job for nothing.

Maigret, smoking his pipe, hunted through the drawers of the desk and, in a file, discovered some letters clipped together as though they were business letters, which nevertheless were love letters.

Granville, August 6

My darling,
It's three days now since we were together, and I don't think I can bear living any longer without you, my lover, without . . .

There were two pages of it. It was signed:

Your mistress for life,
Emilienne.

Maigret, still smoking his pipe, glared at his plump companion.

'A tragic love-story?' he asked with savage irony.

And the other, smirking, replied: 'Why not?'

It seemed a very long way from the real world, where people healthy in mind and body were walking in the sharp winter air on the other side of the basement window!

Maigret looked at the spy-hole through which one could keep watch on the adjoining boudoir, then he looked at his vile companion and could hardly control his heavy fists.

'You're surely not going to tell me she committed suicide?'

'It was certainly not in my interest to kill her and get myself into trouble, particularly when I was on the point of retiring to the neighbourhood of Nice, where I've bought a villa.'

Labri defended himself at every point, or rather, slimy fellow, he slipped out of one's grasp, and Maigret's fury increased. He could understand the psychology of some foolish youngster who has acted on impulse. He knew all the secrets of the traders in flesh of Montmartre, the traders in dream of Montparnasse. He knew his Paris street by street, so to speak; but never before, and he now regretted it, had he gone down into a basement of this sort, nor peered through the spy-hole of a fellow like Labri.

'The more you think about it, the more convinced you'll be that I am innocent and that the whole story does me a grave injustice . . .'

That was the way he talked! He referred to his business as though it were a respectable trade! He seemed almost prepared to produce his account books!

'The more I think about it,' Maigret could not resist retorting emphatically, 'the more I want to smash your face in!'

He had taken a violent dislike to that face, which had its beauty as well as its ugliness, for Labri's languorous eyes counter-acted the meanness of his mouth and chin.

He was that nastiest type of blackguard who can get away with anything by exerting a certain charm.

Maigret, facing him, felt a mounting rage which was almost that of a father prepared to avenge his own daughter.

Suddenly he went up to him and shook his fist in the man's face.

'Confess!' he growled.

The other's blatant terror, betraying his cowardice, only acted as a further stimulus.

'Confess, you swine! . . . Of course I know you've covered your tracks . . .'

And Labri shrank back against the wall in a state of total collapse.

'Emilienne was your mistress. She knew all the filthy business that went on here. That was why you felt impelled to put her out of the way before going to live on your private means in your villa at Nice.'

'Monsieur le Commissaire . . .'

'Confess, I tell you! . . . Confess that, under pretext of making her take some medicine or other, you poisoned her . . . Then, since she took some time to die, you went off like the mean little skunk you are . . .'

'Monsieur le Commissaire . . .'

Maigret was by now oblivious of the cold east wind which, outside, made people turn up their coat collars and which swept away the miasmas of the city. He could envisage the girl with the long face and thin lips and the dead eyes, who had never enjoyed good health and whom this fellow had kept locked up in a basement selling fake vice to old men.

'Confess, you swine . . .'

'I swear, Superintendent . . .'

'Don't swear! Confess!'

'You're going to be sorry for what you're doing now . . .'

This was the wrong argument to use, since it finally drove Maigret beside himself with rage.

'What's that you said?'

'I said you'd be sorry for it . . . You're making a mistake . . . You're going too far . . .'

'What are you saying?'

'You're going too far . . .'

'You dare say that after those letters from the girl? . . . You dare assert that you were not her . . .'

He was just about to hit out. He had raised his fist, when the telephone bell rang.

'Hello . . . That you, Superintendent? . . . We've just received the pathologist's report after the post-mortem . . . Are you there? . . .'

Labri was standing motionless, with his back to the wall. Maigret, exacerbated, shouted down the telephone:

'Well?'

And he restrained himself from hitting out . . .

'Well? . . . What is it? . . .'

Sergeant Lucas's voice came over the line:

'Yes . . . As I was just telling you . . . She's . . . Well, apparently the girl was a virgin . . .'

Maigret hung up, mechanically. He had suddenly understood. He had apparently made a mistake, but he had not been slow to realise it.

'I'm glad to see you're feeling calmer,' Labri was rash enough to remark.

'What's that?'

'Nothing . . . I . . .'

And Maigret clenched his fists with all his might, because now he knew that it was something even worse than he had supposed. He glared almost coldly at this vile creature against whom he was now powerless. He sighed:

'It's correct . . . You didn't kill her . . .'

Not with his hands, no! Not with poison! He had killed her with his basement, lurking like some foul disease under a street that was teeming with life.

So an inexperienced little girl had one day answered his advertisement, asking for a pretty saleswoman. She had come from the depths of the country, and all she had seen of Paris was this trap for old gentlemen whom she was supposed to keep on tenterhooks . . .

The only man she had known was Labri . . .

Labri with his podgy face and those velvet eyes, who, cautious businessman that he was, had led her to believe that people can be lovers without . . .

For he had told the truth! He had not touched her! He was too clever for that. He was not going to kill the goose that laid the golden eggs for the sake of a brief satisfaction. And she, writing from Granville, where she was on holiday, addressed him as 'my lover', without knowing that in order to be lovers . . .

Why yes! everything had become clear! Maigret had made a mistake! Emilienne knew nothing! Emilienne, when she sold her books in the room on the other side of the peep-hole, had need of all her innocence to play the part of an innocent! To help the business! To be convincingly frank, convincingly naive! To be the sort of person of whom the old customers whispered to one another:

'She really *is* ignorant!'

They used a different term which more clearly defined Emilienne's physical condition . . .

Until the day when she learnt that she was part of the stock, that she was to be handed on to the purchasers of the shop, that Labri was going off without her, Labri whom she thought of as her lover . . .

And Emilienne, driven out of her mind, had chosen to kill herself! Labri, panic-stricken, had abandoned her lying in his basement, leaving someone else to discover her body!

'What did I tell you?' Labri murmured with a queer sort of smile on seeing Maigret's discomfiture.

Then the Superintendent glanced round to reassure himself that he really was down in a cellar, far from ordinary life and its laws.

'I made a mistake,' he growled. 'That may happen to anyone.'

After which, since the thing really needed doing, he sent his fist flying into the man's face, heaved a sigh of relief, and said as he watched Labri feeling a loosened tooth:

'You can always say you fell down the staircase! It's so steep!'

THE OLD LADY OF BAYEUX

I

'Sit down, Mademoiselle,' sighed Maigret, regretfully removing his pipe from his mouth.

And he glanced again at the note from the magistrate which read: 'A family affair. Interview Cécile Ledru, but act only with the utmost circumspection.'

It was at Caen, where Maigret had been sent to reorganize the Flying Squad. He was not yet used to the harsh and secretive atmosphere of provincial life and felt far less at ease than in his office in the Quai des Orfèvres.

Moreover he was puzzled by that note: 'A family affair . . . the utmost circumspection . . .'

Did this mean that once again he was going to be involved with the family problems of some high-up official or local bigwig? It was incredible how many people of standing in this part of the world had cousins, brothers- or sisters-in-law who had taken a wrong turning!

'I'm listening, Mademoiselle Ledru.'

Mademoiselle Cécile was not bad-looking. In fact she was very good-looking, especially in the black dress that gave a poetic quality to her naturally pale smooth skin.

'Your age?'

'Twenty-eight.'

'Profession?'

'I suppose I'd better explain it all to you, so that you can understand my position. I was an orphan, and my first job was as a maid of all work. I was only fifteen, with my hair still down my back, and I couldn't read or write . . .'

This was all the more surprising in that the person now confronting the Superintendent had an unmistakable air of distinction.

'Go on, please . . .'

'I happened to find employment with Madame Croizier at Bayeux. Have you heard speak of her?'

'I'm afraid not.'

All provincials are the same, they assume that their local personages are known throughout the world!

'I'll tell you about her presently. I'll just explain that she took a great liking to me and had me educated. Later she kept me on as her

135

companion and she insisted that I call her Aunt Joséphine . . .'

'So you lived at Bayeux with Madame Joséphine Croizier?'

Tears rose to the girl's eyes and she drew out her handkerchief to wipe them away.

'All that's in the past,' she said, sniffing back her tears. 'Aunt Joséphine died yesterday, here at Caen, and it's to tell you that she was murdered that I . . .'

'Excuse me! Are you quite sure that Madame Croizier was murdered?'

'I'd stake my life on it.'

'Were you present?'

'No!'

'Did somebody tell you?'

'My aunt herself!'

'What! Your aunt told you she'd been murdered?'

'Please, Superintendent . . . Don't take me for a lunatic . . . I know what I'm saying . . . My aunt told me repeatedly that if anything happened to her at the house in the Rue des Récollets, my first duty would be to demand an inquiry . . .'

'One minute! What's this house in the Rue des Récollets?'

'It's the home of her nephew, Philippe Deligeard . . . Aunt Joséphine had gone to Caen for a few weeks to have her teeth seen to, for she had only just begun to have trouble with them, at sixty-eight! . . . She had gone to stay with her nephew and I had stopped in Bayeux because Philippe isn't fond of me . . .'

On a scrap of paper, Maigret noted: 'Philippe Deligeard.'

'How old is this nephew?'

'Forty-four or forty-five.'

'Profession?'

'He has none. He used to be well off, or at least his wife was; but I think that for some years now this wealth has been non-existent . . . However the couple still live in a private house in the Rue des Récollets, and they have a cook, a valet and a chauffeur. Philippe has been to Bayeux several times to beg his aunt to lend him money.'

'And did she?'

'Never! She used to tell her nephew he must just be patient and wait for her death . . .'

While the girl was talking, Maigret summed up the situation in his own mind.

In the first place, at Bayeux, in one of those quiet streets near the cathedral where the sound of footsteps set the curtains twitching at every window, lived Madame Joséphine Croizier, widow of Justin Croizier.

The story of her wealth was both macabre and funny. Croizier, who had been a mere solicitor's clerk when he married, had an obsession with insuring himself. He spent his time signing policies with every conceivable company, and everyone laughed at him for it.

Once and only once he had gone by boat to Southampton. The sea was rough. A sudden lurch had sent Croizier spinning against the bulwarks so disastrously that he had broken his skull, and shortly afterwards his widow, to her astonishment, received a million francs from various insurance firms.

Since then, the sole interest of Joséphine Croizier, in her gloomy house at Bayeux, had been the management of this fortune, which had increased, and meanwhile to spend whole afternoons chatting with her protégée Cécile Ledru.

It was said that the original million had proliferated and that, thanks to fortunate investments, Joséphine Croizier now owned four or five million francs.

Philippe Deligeard, her sister's son, had on the contrary made a showy start when he married the daughter of a rich horse-dealer. He had bought a splendid mansion which was said to be one of the most handsomely furnished in all Caen.

Unlike his aunt, he had made some unfortunate investments, and according to public rumour, for the past three or four years he had been living on credit, borrowing from money-lenders against a future inheritance from his aunt.

'In short, Mademoiselle Cécile, there is no serious basis for your accusation, except that Philippe needed money and that his aunt's death would provide him with it?'

'I've already told you that Madame Croizier herself always declared that if she were to die in the Rue des Récollets . . .'

'Forgive me, but you must be aware how little trust one can place in old ladies' apprehensions . . . Will you now give me the actual facts of the situation?'

'My aunt died yesterday, about five o'clock in the evening. They're trying to make out that she had a fatal heart attack.'

'Had she a weak heart?'

'No more than most people! Nothing that was likely to kill her . . .'

'Were you in Bayeux at the time?'

It seemed to Maigret – it might only have been an impression – that the girl hesitated slightly.

'No . . . I was at Caen . . .'

'I thought you had not gone there with Joséphine Croizier . . .'

'That is correct . . . But it's hardly half an hour's bus ride to Caen from Bayeux. I came in to do some shopping.'

'And you didn't try to see your aunt, as you call her?'

'I called at the Rue des Récollets . . .'

'At what time?'

'About four o'clock. They told me Madame Croizier had gone out . . .'

'Who told you so?'

'The manservant.'

'After consulting his employers?'

'No! Of his own accord.'

'Therefore one must assume that it was the truth, or else that he had been given orders in advance?'

'That was what I thought.'

'Where did you go next?'

'Into town. I had a good many small errands. Then I went back to Bayeux, and this morning I read in the Caen newspaper that my aunt had died . . .'

'It's odd . . .'

'What did you say?'

'I said it was odd. At four in the afternoon, when you called at the Rue des Récollets, you were told your aunt had gone out. You went back to Bayeux and next morning you learned from the newspaper that she had died a few minutes, an hour at most, after your visit. Is it true that you have made an indictment, Mademoiselle Cécile?'

'Yes, Superintendent. I'm not well off, but I'd give the little money I have to help find out the truth and get the criminals punished.'

'One second! Since you mention your financial position, may I ask you if you expect to inherit from Joséphine Croizier?'

'I'm sure I shall inherit nothing, for I drew up the will myself and I formally refused to gain by it. Otherwise nobody would have believed in my disinterestedness during the years I devoted to my bene-factress . . .'

She was almost too perfect. Maigret, observing her carefully, could find no weak spot in her armour.

'So you're left without a penny?'

'I didn't say that, Superintendent. Madame Croizier paid me as her companion. Since I had no expenses, I was able to put aside a fair sum of money which will enable me to face the future. I'm prepared to spend the whole of that sum if necessary to avenge my aunt.'

'May I ask one further question? Philippe is the heir, isn't he? Sup-posing it is proved that he killed his aunt, he will be unable to inherit. What will happen to her millions?'

'They will go to charitable societies for the protection of girls.'

'Was Madame Croizier interested in these charities?'

'She was sorry for young women and realized the dangers they incur . . .'

'Was she very prudish?'

Cécile hesitated for a moment, reflecting:

'Yes, very prudish!'

'Somewhat obsessive on the subject?'

'Almost . . .'

'Thank you, Mademoiselle.'

'You'll hold an inquiry, won't you?'

'I'm going to find out certain things and, if need be . . . By the way, where can I find you?'

'During the two days before the funeral, which is to take place at Caen, I shall spend most of my time in the mortuary chapel in the Rue des Récollets . . .'

'In spite of Philippe?'

'We don't speak to one another and I don't set foot in the rest of the house. I mourn and I pray . . . At night I stay in the Hôtel Saint-Georges.'

Maigret was finishing his pipe, looking with oddly narrowed eyes at the huge grey house, the carriage gate with its brass knocker, the great courtyard with its bronze lamp-posts.

It was what he called a no-smoking case, in other words an investigation to be carried on in places where he could not decently keep his pipe in his mouth.

This was why he was having a brief smoke now before going in, and meanwhile watching people coming and going, ladies in black, gentlemen in formal dress, all the top people of Caen coming to pay their respects.

'This is going to be great fun!' he sighed, as he knocked out his pipe against his heel.

And he went in like all the rest, walked past the silver tray that was full of visiting-cards with their corners turned down, and at the far end of a passage paved with blue and white tiles came to a big door hung with black; this was the mortuary chapel, and here he saw the coffin surrounded with flowers and tapers, and black figures standing or kneeling.

The odour of burning wax and chrysanthemums was enough to convey the atmosphere immediately, and there was much whispering, much dabbing of the nostrils with handkerchiefs, together with that air of high dignity that people assume only in the face of the Law and of death . . .

Cécile Ledru was there in a corner, on a prayer-stool, her face covered by a thin crape veil through which her regular features and her moving lips could be discerned, while her fingers ran over a rosary of jade beads.

A man, also in black, red-eyed, with irregular features, was looking at Maigret as though to inquire his business there, and the Superintendent went up to him.

'Monsieur Philippe Deligeard, I presume? I'm Superintendent Maigret. Could you spare me a few minutes' conversation?'

Maigret had the impression that his interlocutor cast a resentful glance at the girl before they left the black-draped room.

'Kindly follow me, Monsieur. My study is on the first floor . . .'

A marble staircase with a very handsome wrought-iron banister. On the landing wall, an authentic Aubusson tapestry; then a large study furnished in Empire style, whose three windows overlooked grounds which were more extensive than might have been expected in the centre of a town.

'Please sit down. I suppose that young woman has been carrying on her intrigues and that she is responsible for your visit?'

'You refer to Cécile Ledru?'

'Yes, I mean that low-class adventuress who, over a certain period, succeeded in exercising a disastrous influence over my aunt . . . Cigar?'

'No, thank you . . . You say over a certain period . . . Am I to understand that this influence did not last?'

Maigret needed no close scrutiny of Philippe Deligeard to recognize the type. Dressed with studied elegance in deep mourning, he was every inch the rich bourgeois whom one meets in all provincial towns, fashionably correct, living in style, a stickler above all for decorum, for certain details of dress, certain forms of speech and bearing which distinguish him from the common herd.

'You realise, Superintendent, that it is extremely painful, extremely disagreeable for me to receive a visit from the police at such a distressing moment. However, I will reply to your questions, because I am determined that this business shall be cleared up and that Cécile shall be punished as she deserves.'

'That is to say?'

'As I gather from your previous question that you have realised, my poor aunt was not permanently taken in by that young woman's hypocritical airs and her supposedly disinterested devotion. In fact, when my aunt came to spend a month with us, we offered to put up her companion too – we've plenty of room – so as not to disturb her habits. And my aunt refused, admitting to us that she had had enough of the girl and wanted some excuse for getting rid of her. She was only afraid that if she made too sudden a break, Cécile might try to get her revenge . . .'

Maigret, in spite of himself, was affected by the atmosphere, and murmured with an irony which was unnoticed by his interlocutor:

'How false and cruel people are!'

'As I was saying, sooner or later my aunt would have parted with this creature, who had tried in vain to stir up ill-feeling between us.'

'Is that what she did?'

'By asserting, among other things, that I had mistresses . . . Speaking as man to man, Superintendent . . . At my age and in my situation, you'll admit that it's only natural that I . . . Discreetly, of course! Like a man of the world . . . Obviously my poor aunt, with her obsession about virtue, would not have understood . . . Old people need not be told about such details . . .'

'Is that what Cécile did?'

'Otherwise how would my aunt have found out? It was bad strategy on the part of that treacherous young woman, for it turned against her in the end. When Aunt Joséphine learned that her virtuous companion used to receive a young man secretly, under her own roof, a young man whose family was, to say the least of it, scarcely respectable . . .'

'Cécile had a lover?'

Either Maigret's indignation was genuine, or it was a consummate piece of acting. True, he took advantage of it to extract his pipe from his pocket with an air of perfect innocence, as though oblivious of his grand surroundings and the Havana cigars lying on the desk.

'For the past two years they have been lovers and have met almost every night. His name is Jacques Mercier. He runs a transport business with a friend, but it should be noted that his parents went bankrupt a few years ago.'

'Incredible! And you told your aunt?'

'Of course . . . Why not? . . . It was my duty to do so!'

'Obviously . . .'

'And so my aunt had decided to get rid of Cécile at last. Once again, she was restrained only by fear of the girl's vindictiveness . . . That was why I suggested to my aunt that she should stay with us from then on . . . I would have put the whole of the second floor at her disposal.'

'When were these questions discussed?'

'Why . . . as recently as the day before yesterday . . .'

'And the decision had been taken?'

'Not formally . . . She had begun to accept the principle of the plan . . .'

'I suppose, nevertheless, that you are not accusing Cécile of having killed your aunt?'

Philippe looked at Maigret in sudden agitation.

'But . . . my aunt was not killed! . . . The girl must be mad as well as wicked to spread such stories . . . My aunt died of a heart attack, as the doctor's death certificate specifically states . . . I don't see how . . .'

'In short, you're not accusing Cécile of having killed your aunt?'

'I should accuse her if I were not sure, as I am, that my aunt died from natural causes. On the other hand if the girl continues her scandal-mongering about us I shall find myself obliged to bring an action against her for libel.'

'One question, Monsieur Deligeard . . . Your aunt died at about five o'clock in the afternoon, didn't she?'

'Yes, at a few minutes past five . . . My wife told me, for I was not present myself . . .'

'Good . . . Now, about four o'clock, Joséphine Croizier was not in the house?'

'Every day at four o'clock she had an appointment with her dentist, for she was having a plate made and it was a lengthy business.'

'Do you know what time your aunt came back?'

'About five o'clock, so I was told . . . It was almost immediately on her return that she had the attack, and she died without having had time to make arrangements.'

'Was she taken ill in her bedroom?'

'Yes. The Louis XIV room on the second floor.'

'Was your wife up there?'

'My wife went up soon afterwards, when my aunt opened her door to call for help.'

'May I ask where you were?'

'I presume, Superintendent, that this is not an official interrogation, for I could not submit to that.'

'Not at all! We just want to be able to provide an answer to the audacious young woman who . . .'

'I must have been at my club. I generally leave the house at half past four or a quarter to five, on foot, to get some exercise . . . I walk through part of the town. About five o'clock I play a rubber of bridge and at half past seven the car calls to take me home for dinner.'

'You were told the news by a telephone call to your club?'

'That's right . . .'

'And when you got back?'

'My aunt was dead and the doctor was already there . . .'

'The family doctor?'

'No! He lives too far away and my wife had sent for a young doctor who lives near by, but whose professional help was in fact not needed . . .'

'You have one son?'

'Yes, Gérard, who is twenty years old and a student at the Hautes Etudes Commerciales. At the time of my aunt's death he was probably at his college or in some café in the town, like others of his generation. Young men nowadays do not realize that a gentleman's place is in his club and not in some establishment frequented by all and sundry . . .'

'And the servants?'

'Arsène, my chauffeur, had the day off. The manservant is always on duty on the ground floor in the afternoons. As for the cook, I presume she was in the kitchen. Is there anything else you would like to know, Superintendent? I have to attend to the people who have come to present their condolences, and I am expecting, at any moment now, a visit from the Chairman of the Board of Magistrates, who is also Chairman of my club. I think the best thing you can do is to warn that young woman. If she goes on spreading her foul rumours I shall have her put in jail . . .'

Philippe Deligeard must have wondered what, at such a moment, could have brought a peculiar smile to Maigret's lips. The fact was that the Superintendent had for some time past been staring at a mirror which stood over the mantelpiece. In this he saw reflected a door, hidden by a curtain. Several times already this curtain had stirred. Once, the Superintendent had caught sight of a woman's pale face and he was sure this was Madame Deligeard.

Had she heard her husband's admissions about the necessity, for a man of the world, of discreetly conducted love affairs?

'Goodbye, Superintendent . . . I am sure that after the explanations I have taken the trouble to give you I shall no longer be disturbed in my bereavement by this foolish and indecent story. The manservant will show you out . . .'

Philippe rang, and after a curt bow to the policeman, made his way with dignity towards the interesting curtain, behind which sounds were presently heard.

A quarter of an hour later, Maigret was closeted with the Public Prosecutor, in placid but ironical mood, fingering his pipe in his pocket since the Public Prosecutor of Caen was not the sort of person in whose office one was allowed to smoke.

'Well, have you heard what that young woman had to say?'

'I have also visited the scene of the old lady's death.'

'What's your opinion? It's just spiteful gossip, isn't it?'

'On the contrary, it's my impression that somebody helped good old Joséphine Croizier to her death. But who? . . . That is the question . . . And there's another: are you anxious to have the truth known?'

II

The Hôtel Saint-Georges was one of those small private hotels that are to be found in every town, although one would not suspect their existence unless somebody sent one there, hotels frequented chiefly by old people, priests, timid young girls, and in general by all those connected, however remotely, with piety, from vergers to candle-manufacturers.

Maigret had already been waiting for a good half-hour in the lounge, which was furnished with cane chairs and where an old lady, busy with her embroidery, cast a severe glance at him from time to time. The smoke of his pipe rose gently to form a bluish cloud around the hanging lamp.

'My dear fellow, I bet you and I are waiting for the same person,' he had thought on seeing a young man nervously pacing up and down and continually pulling out his watch.

Now, after that half-hour's wait, and in spite of not having exchanged a word, the two men knew one another. Examining Maigret from head to foot, the young man was undoubtedly reflecting: 'So that's the famous Superintendent Cécile told me about. He looks like a simple soul to me! But I suppose something fresh must have turned up, since he's come to see Cécile at her hotel . . .'

Maigret, meanwhile, was thinking: 'Not bad-looking, young Jacques Mercier! Good-looking, indeed, almost too good-looking! Not at all the typical young provincial; he's got quite an emancipated air! A handsome face, curly hair, bright eyes and plenty of spirit . . . Aha, Mademoiselle Cécile . . . It strikes me that you're fond of contrasts and that you're not as prim by night as by day . . .'

When the girl arrived, she saw Jacques Mercier first and a smile lit up her face. But the young man drew her attention to Maigret's presence, and she frowned as she stepped towards him.

'Did you want to speak to me?' she asked, obviously embarrassed at being found in her lover's company.

'I wanted to ask you a few details, yes. But it's not going to be easy in this hotel, which is so quiet that you can hear a moth flying. Shall we go into a café for a few minutes?'

Cécile glanced at Mercier, who nodded, and the three of them were presently installed in a brasserie where a game of billiards was going on.

'In the first place, let me point out, Mademoiselle Cécile, that it was not very kind of you not to have told me about Monsieur Mercier.'

'I thought this business was nothing to do with him, but I might have guessed Philippe would tell you about him. What else did he say about me?'

'Nothing very pleasant, as you may well imagine. His social manners may be perfect but he's got a nasty tongue. A beer, waiter! What will you take, Mademoiselle? A glass of port? And you, Monsieur? Two ports . . .'

Sprawling at ease on the imitation-leather-covered seat, his gaze automatically following the billiard balls, Maigret puffed with quiet enjoyment at his pipe, apparently relishing the dim but pervasive tranquillity of provincial life.

'So it's been going on for two years, has it?'

'We've known each other for two years, yes.'

'And how long is it since Monsieur Mercier started spending the night in the old lady's house?'

'More than a year . . .'

'You've never thought of getting married?'

'The old lady, as you call her, would never have allowed it. To be exact, she'd have considered such a plan as a betrayal. She was jealous of my affection. Having nobody in her life except nephews whom she detested, she had come to consider me as her property, in a way. It was for her sake that I agreed to keep my relations with Jacques secret, solely so as not to disappoint her and to spare her distress.'

Thus she meekly replied to Maigret's questions, while her companion, with an occasional anxious frown, seemed to be warning her to take care.

'Your turn now, Monsieur Mercier.'

'I don't see how I'm involved with . . .'

'That's not the point. What I want is your help in a task which Mademoiselle Cécile has asked the police to undertake. According to Philippe Deligeard, your financial affairs are going badly. Is that true?'

'That's to say . . .'

'Tell him, Jacques!'

'It's true! I joined up with a friend to buy three lorries to collect and transport fish in the small seaports of the Cotentin region. Unfortunately the lorries, which were not new, have cost us a lot to repair.'

'How long will it be?'

'What d'you mean?'

'Before you go broke.'

'The lorries have been out of action for three days, because the rent of the garage hasn't been paid.'

'Thank you. Would you remind me, Mademoiselle, what time you called at the Rue des Récollets?'

'The day before yesterday? . . . About four, wasn't it, Jacques?'

'Excuse me! So you were with her?'

'I drove her there . . . I waited at the corner of the street . . . It must have been five past four . . .'

'You brought her from Bayeux by car?'

And Maigret glanced severely at Cécile, who had told him she had taken the bus.

'Very good! Now tell me, Mademoiselle . . . When you learned of Joséphine Croizier's death through the newspaper, I suppose you asked Mercier to drive you to Caen. What time did you reach the Rue des Récollets?'

'About half past nine in the morning.'

'So a whole night had gone by since the old lady's death. Will you tell me exactly what you saw?'

'What do you mean? I first saw the manservant, then some men in the main passage, then Philippe Deligeard, who came up to me saying with a sneer: "I expected you to come rushing up!"'

'And then I saw my aunt . . .'

'Careful! This is where your story becomes interesting. You saw your aunt's body. Where?'

'In the coffin.'

'So it was already in the coffin, which was not yet closed?'

'They closed it a little later, in my presence. The men I'd met in the corridor were from the undertaker's.'

'So you recognized your aunt's face? You're certain of that?'

'Absolutely! What's in your mind?'

'You noticed nothing abnormal?'

'No, I didn't . . . I was crying . . . I was very upset . . . I'd have liked to stay beside her for a few minutes to collect myself, but it was impossible . . .'

'One last question. I know the main entrance to the house in the Rue des Récollets. But I suppose there's another way in?'

'There's a little door at the back giving on to the Rue de l'Echaudé. It's a lane rather than a street, for there aren't any houses there, only garden walls.'

'If you go in by this back way, can you get to the upper floors without meeting the manservant or the cook?'

'Yes. You take a little staircase that leads to the second floor.'

'My bill, waiter . . . Thank you, Mademoiselle, and you too, Monsieur Mercier.'

And having paid for the drinks, he stood up, looking more cheerful than the circumstances seemed to warrant. A few minutes later, with his pipe still between his lips, he made his way into Deligeard's club. He called on the secretary, to whom he put a number of questions. Then he meticulously noted the replies in his notebook with ever-increasing satisfaction.

'So you say you're certain of having seen Philippe Deligeard come in at a quarter past five, the day before yesterday? That's right, isn't it? His three usual bridge partners were waiting for him for the game, which regularly began at five o'clock. He sat down at the table. The cards had just been dealt when he was summoned to the telephone. When he emerged from the phone box he looked very pale and he announced that his aunt had just died at his home . . . You've nothing more to add? . . . Thank you . . . Good evening, Monsieur.'

And Maigret shrugged his shoulders as he walked through the solemn rooms where gloomy old men, sunk deep in their armchairs, were dozing behind their newspapers.

Dr Liévin, who had been called in when Joséphine Croizier had her heart attack, proved to be a very young man with bright red hair; Maigret found him cooking himself a chop on a gas ring. The young man was wearing his white lab coat, and the scene took place in the consulting room.

'Am I disturbing you, doctor? Forgive me, but I need a few precise details about the death of Madame Croizier.'

Liévin was barely twenty-seven years old and had only just come to Caen, where his practice, to judge by the look of the place, could not have been very large.

'I assume, to begin with, that you are the doctor nearest to the Rue des Récollets?'

'More or less . . . I believe there's one who has a consulting room in the Rue des Minimes, but I don't know him.'

'Had you ever been called in to Monsieur Deligeard's before?'

'Never! As you'll have gathered when you came in, I'm only just starting here and my patients are mostly humble people. I was rather surprised when I was summoned to one of the grandest houses in the town.'

'What time was it? Can you establish that point definitely?'

'Quite definitely, for I've a little nurse who comes every afternoon for consultations and leaves at five o'clock. Now she had just put on her hat and I was kissing her goodbye when the phone bell rang.'

'So it was exactly five o'clock. How long did it take you to reach the Rue des Récollets?'

'Altogether, seven or eight minutes.'

'Did the manservant show you in and take you up to the second floor?'

'No, not precisely. The manservant opened the door, but almost immediately a woman leaned over the banisters and called out: "Come up quickly, doctor . . ." It was Madame Deligeard, and she herself took me into the room on the right.'

'Excuse me, did you say the room on the right? It was a room with pale blue wallpaper, wasn't it?'

'You're mistaken, Superintendent. The room on the right has buttercup yellow wallpaper.'

'Furnished in Louis XIV style?'

'Excuse me! I know something about styles and I can give you my word that the room on the right is furnished in Regency style.'

To the astonishment of the doctor, who could not understand the importance of this question, Maigret wrote down in his notebook everything that had been said.

'All right. So you were up there and it was about ten minutes past five. Where was the body?'

'On the bed, of course.'

'Undressed?'

'Why, naturally . . .'

'Excuse me! It was ten minutes past five, and Joséphine Croizier was undressed. What was she wearing?'

'A nightgown and a dressing-gown.'

'Were her clothes lying about the room?'

'I don't think so. . . No. . . Everything was quite tidy . . .'

'And nobody was there but Madame Deligeard?'

'That's right. She seemed very upset. She described her aunt's attack to me. I immediately understood that death must have been practically instantaneous . . . Nonetheless I examined the dead woman, and I realized that she had been in very poor health. It must have been her tenth attack at least.'

'Were you able to determine the time of death approximately?'

'One does so automatically . . . Death must have occurred at a quarter past four, give or take a few minutes . . .'

The doctor was astonished and alarmed when Maigret jumped up and grabbed him by the shoulders.

'What did you say? A quarter past four?'

'Why, yes! Madame Deligeard admitted, moreover, that before calling me she had tried to get hold of two other doctors, and this had taken a certain time . . .'

'A quarter past four!' Maigret repeated, rubbing his forehead. 'I don't want to offend you, doctor . . . But you're a beginner . . . Are you quite certain of what you're saying? . . . Could you maintain your assertion if the life of a man or a woman were at stake?'

'I could only repeat what I've told you . . .'

'All right! I believe you . . . But I'd better warn you that it will almost certainly be necessary to repeat your statement in court, and that counsel will do their utmost to discredit your evidence.'

'They won't succeed.'

'Have you anything else to tell me? What happened next?'

'Nothing. I signed the death certificate ... Madame Deligeard insisted on paying me right away, and gave me two hundred francs.'

'Is that your fee?'

'No, she suggested it herself. She took me half way down the stairs and the manservant showed me out.'

'And you met nobody else?'

'Nobody.'

'Well, there's nothing for it,' growled Maigret, ringing at the door of a small house through whose windows could be seen a family at table.

He wanted to put a few questions to the doctor in charge of registering deaths, a little deaf old man who received him with a table-napkin in his hand, apologized and showed him into a study that smelled of cabbage soup, while the clink of spoons sounded in the dining-room next door.

'You knew Monsieur and Madame Deligeard before being called to certify the death of their aunt?'

'I had seen Monsieur Deligeard about the town. He's a prominent man, you know ... But we don't move in the same circles.'

'When did you go to certify the death?'

'I was informed by the municipal authorities about half past six. I called at the Rue des Récollets before seven o'clock.'

'Had you known Madame Croizier?'

'No. The manservant kept me waiting while he went to tell Monsieur Deligeard, who took me up to the second floor and showed me into a yellow bedroom.'

'You're sure it was a yellow bedroom?'

'Absolutely sure. It struck me particularly because my daughter wants a yellow room and my wife insists that it's not very respectable. I ascertained that the old lady had died of a heart attack and I filled in the usual forms.'

'She was undressed?'

'Yes, she was in her night clothes.'

'There was no disorder in the room?'

'I noticed none.'

'Did you meet anybody?'

'Nobody ... Why?'

'Finally, have you any idea of the time of death?'

'I didn't concern myself with that ... Between four and five o'clock, I would say.'

'Thank you ...'

Maigret, his appetite whetted by the smell of soup, went to sit down in a restaurant famous for its *soles normandes* and its tripe *à la mode de Caen*. The restaurant, like all the places Maigret had visited that day, had something dusty and solemn about it, an atmosphere of deliberate austerity.

'All the same there are some out-and-out scoundrels in this dump,' Maigret reflected as he ate his dinner. 'I don't believe I've ever seen the like in the whole of my career . . .'

After all, it was the sort of case he enjoyed: a respectable façade, solemn prudish people, all the outward signs of virtue carried to the point where it exudes boredom.

And he, Maigret, was to probe all this, to search in every corner, to sniff on every side, until at last, behind the freestone and the panelling, the sombre clothes and the haughty or sullen faces, he discovered the human beast, the nastiest and most unforgivable sort of beast, the kind that kills out of sordid self-interest, for motives of gain!

Exceptionally, he was in no hurry, and he took a sly delight in working with almost pleasurable slowness, as though he were playing cat and mouse with the murderer.

The Prosecutor had told him insistently:

'Do what's necessary, but be prudent! . . . You would pay dearly for one false step, and so should I . . . Philippe Deligeard is a prominent man who may owe money but who is received everywhere. As for the girl, Cécile as you call her, if you lay a finger on her you'll have all the left-wing press defending her as a victim of the rich . . . Watch out Superintendent!'

And Maigret muttered to himself, disrespectfully:

'Of course, old boy! But we're going to get them . . .'

The tripe was delicious, and when Maigret rose from table he was in a state of euphoria, particularly as he had been unable to refuse the proprietor's offer of a glass of calvados.

'Presently I'll straighten it all out!' he promised himself. 'Meanwhile I must have a talk with that manservant I've heard so much about . . .'

And he went off to ring at the Rue des Récollets. The servant was about to usher him into the waiting-room, but Maigret stopped him.

'No, old fellow, it's you I want to talk to. You know who I am, don't you? What were you doing when I rang?'

'We were having coffee in the kitchen . . .'

'Then I'll come and have coffee with you!'

He was inviting himself; he was thrusting himself upon the man, who dared not protest, but informed the cook and the chauffeur, Arsène:

'The Superintendent would like a cup of coffee . . .'

Arsène was wearing a very smart grey uniform, which he had

unbuttoned so as to relax, and the cook was a stout woman with blotchy red cheeks, who seemed uneasy at Maigret's intrusion into her kitchen.

'Don't let me disturb you, folks! I could have summoned you to the station, but I thought it wasn't worth it for such a slight matter . . Take it easy, Arsène! . . . By the way, why were you absent the day before yesterday? . . . Was it your regular day off?'

'Not exactly. In the morning the boss told me that since he couldn't spare me next week on account of a trip South, I could take the day off. I took advantage of it to visit my sister, who's married to a baker in Le Havre.'

'So Monsieur Philippe drove the car himself?'

'Yes . . . I thought he wouldn't be needing the car, but I noticed he'd been using it.'

'How did you find out?'

'There were muddy marks inside it.'

'He must have gone into the country then, since there's been no rain?'

'You know, hereabouts the country begins not far from the house. After a few hundred metres you don't see any more paved streets . . .'

As for the manservant, whose name was Victor, he answered every question with mathematical precision and Maigret was not surprised to learn that he had been an N.C.O. in the artillery.

'Where do you spend the afternoon?'

'In the pantry, which is not far from the entrance hall. The day before yesterday I was doing the silver . . .'

'Can you tell me at what time Madame Croizier went out?'

'A few minutes before four, as usual. She had an appointment for four o'clock with her dentist, who lives close by.'

'Was she looking well?'

'She always was! She was very well-preserved, a very cheerful person, not at all proud, and she never went past without a word for us.'

'Did she say anything special to you?'

'No! She just called out: "I'll be back soon, Victor . . ."'

'Did she go on foot to the dentist's?'

'Madame Croizier did not like going in the car. Even when she went back to Bayeux she preferred to go by train.'

'Could you tell me where the car was at that moment?'

'I couldn't say, sir!'

'It wasn't in the garage?'

'No, sir . . . Monsieur and Madame had gone out in it shortly after lunch. They came back about an hour later, but they must have left the car outside in the street. I must tell you that we never leave it in our street, which is too narrow, but in the next street, where it can't be seen from the doorway.'

'So, Monsieur and Madame, as you've told me, came back about three o'clock. An hour later, shortly before four o'clock, Madame Joséphine Croizier went out. And then?'

'Mademoiselle Cécile came . . .'

'At what time?'

'Ten past four. I told her that her aunt had just gone out, and she left.'

'Did she see anyone besides yourself in the house?'

'Nobody but me.'

'And then?'

'Monsieur went out. It was twenty-five past four . . . I looked at the clock, because it was a bit earlier than the usual time he goes to the club.'

'He wasn't carrying any parcel?'

'Certainly not!'

'Did he look just as usual?'

'I'd say so . . .'

'Go on . . .'

'I began doing the knives. Yes . . . Nothing else was happening just then. And it was nearly five o'clock when Madame Croizier got back.'

'Still looking quite well?'

'She was in good spirits. She said to me as she went by that it's quite wrong to think that dentists always hurt one . . . I told her that mine had pulled out one tooth in mistake for another . . .'

'Did she go up to her room?'

'Yes, she went upstairs.'

'Hers is the Louis XIV room, isn't it?'

'That's right.'

'The one on the right, with buttercup yellow wallpaper?'

'No, no! That's the Regency room which is hardly ever used.'

'What happened next?'

'I don't know. Some minutes went past. Then Madame came down, very upset . . .'

'Excuse me, how many minutes went past?'

'Twenty . . . In any case it was past five o'clock when Madame asked me to ring Monsieur at his club to let him know his aunt had had an attack.'

'And when you rang the club you said she had had an attack?'

'Yes . . .'

'You didn't say she was dead?'

'No . . . I didn't know then that she was dead . . .'

'Did you go upstairs?'

'No . . . None of us went up. A young doctor came and Madame went to meet him. It was only at seven o'clock that we were officially told of Madame Croizier's death and it was eight o'clock when we all went up to see her.'

'In the yellow bedroom?'

'No! In the blue bedroom . . .'

A bell rang. Victor grumbled:

'It's the master wanting his tisane . . .'

And Maigret made his way slowly towards the front door.

III

'The Public Prosecutor asks if you will kindly wait . . .'

Maigret was sitting at the end of a hard bench in the dusty corridor of the Palais de Justice of Caen, where lawyers occasionally walked past, the sleeves of their gowns flapping like ducklings' wings.

It was ten in the morning. Maigret, who had left his wife in Paris and was boarding with a family of decent people, had that morning been brought by a policeman a somewhat curt summons from the Public Prosecutor, asking him to be at his office at ten precisely.

At ten minutes past ten he rose from his bench and went up to the doorman.

'Is there somebody with the Prosecutor?'

'Yes.'

'Do you know if he's likely to be there long?'

'I expect so! He's been there since half past nine already. It's Monsieur Deligeard.'

A queer smile passed over Maigret's lips, and he made no bones now about filling his pipe. Each time he passed in front of a certain padded door he heard the murmur of voices, and each time his lips curled in the same smile.

Finally, just after half past ten a bell summoned the attendant, who came back to announce:

'The Public Prosecutor will see you now!'

Philippe Deligeard had not left the room. Maigret stuffed his lighted pipe into his pocket and went in with deliberately slow and ponderous steps. On certain occasions, particularly when he was feeling in a good humour, he enjoyed appearing unnaturally stupid, and then he looked stouter and more loutish, like a regular caricature of a policeman, lacking only a big moustache.

'My respects, Monsieur le procureur. Good morning to you, Monsieur Deligeard . . .'

'Close the door, Superintendent. Come here. You are putting me in an extremely delicate and disagreeable position. What did I ask you yesterday?'

'To be circumspect, Monsieur le procureur . . .'

'Didn't I also tell you that I gave no credence to the ill-natured gossip of that young woman, that Cécile who seems to me more than ever like a scheming adventuress?'

'You told me at any rate that Monsieur Deligeard is an important person in this town and that under the circumstances I must be very circumspect in my dealings with him . . .'

And Maigret, smiling affably, glanced at Philippe who, in his deep mourning, looked even more solemn than the magistrate. He had put on an air of total unconcern, averting his eyes from the Superintendent and waiting as though to say:

'You'll see, by and by!'

As for the Prosecutor, he was glaring at Maigret, whose irony he sensed, and he clearly found it hard to repress his rage.

'Sit down! Stop walking about! I hate people who walk about when one's speaking to them . . .'

'Gladly, Monsieur le procureur.'

'Where were you yesterday evening at about nine o'clock?'

'At about nine o'clock? . . . Wait a minute . . . I must have been at Monsieur Deligeard's . . .'

'What exactly do you mean by that?'

'At his house, obviously!'

'Of course! But you were there without his knowledge! You were acting illegally, seeing that you had not been given a search warrant.'

'I had a few questions to put to the servants.'

'That's precisely the subject of my criticism and of the complaint which Monsieur Deligeard here present has lodged against you. I am forced to record this complaint, for you have overstepped your rights. You might perhaps have been entitled to question the servants, but in that case the obvious course was to inform their employer first. I presume you understand me, Superintendent?'

'Of course, Monsieur le procureur.'

And Maigret took a sly delight in dropping his eyes humbly, like some minor official caught committing an offence.

'That is not all, and the rest is far more serious, so serious that I do not yet know what action the authorities will take as a result of your behaviour. After listening with indulgence to servants' gossip, and indeed inviting it, you left the house, but you shortly re-entered it by another door. I suppose you don't deny that?'

'Unfortunately I can't, Monsieur le procureur!'

'With what key did you open the garden door? Did you by any chance get it from Cécile Ledru? Consider carefully the consequences of your answer . . .'

'I had no key to the little door. To tell you the truth, I did not intend going into the garden. I just wanted to find out how they brought in the corpse . . .'

'What's that?'

The Prosecutor had risen to his feet and so had Philippe; they had both turned pale, presumably for different reasons.

'I'll tell you about that presently, if you like. As regards the door, I found that the lock is a very simple one, easily to be opened with any good master-key. I wanted to put it to the test, and I tried it. The night was dark, and the garden was deserted. I realized that the garage was not far off and, not wishing to disturb Monsieur Deligeard for so slight a matter, particularly under such distressing circumstances, I went to look for the traces of mud that Arsène had mentioned . . .'

The Prosecutor was now frowning anxiously. Philippe, clutching his gloves, tried to break in, but the Superintendent left him no time.

'That's all . . . I am aware that I committed an offence . . . I apologize for it and I will explain it as best I can . . .'

'That's to say that it's a blatant case of housebreaking! You, an officer of the Flying Squad, you took the liberty of . . .'

'I'm very sorry, Monsieur le procureur . . . Once again, if I hadn't been anxious not to disturb Monsieur Deligeard, who had just had his tisane taken up to him, I'd have asked to be shown up to ask him a few questions . . .'

'That's enough! I must add that I don't like the mocking tone you apparently feel entitled to adopt. This very day I shall transmit Monsieur Deligeard's complaint to the Ministry, and needless to say I forbid you to have anything more to do with this affair, in which you have exceeded your orders. Monsieur Deligeard, I think that until further notice we may consider this incident as closed, and I hope I have given you all the satisfaction you may desire . . .'

'Thank you, Monsieur le procureur. This man's behaviour was so presumptuous that I could not decently, if only for the good name of the police, allow . . .'

And he went up to shake hands with the magistrate, who meanwhile prepared to escort him to the door.

'Thank you! We shall meet again soon . . .'

'I shall be at the funeral tomorrow and . . .'

Suddenly Maigret's quiet voice was heard saying:

'Monsieur, I ask your permission, as Public Prosecutor of the Republic, to put one single question to this man.'

The Prosecutor frowned. Deligeard, already standing in the doorway, waited automatically, and Maigret said softly:

'Can you tell me, Monsieur, if you intend to go to Caroline's funeral?'

The Prosecutor was stupefied at the immediate effect of these words. Philippe's discomfiture was patent; his features were distorted, he dropped his gloves and he seemed ready to rush savagely at the Superintendent.

Maigret, still placid, over-placid, closed the door again.

'You see that we hadn't quite finished! I am sorry to delay you, but I'm afraid it may take quite a long time . . .'

'Superintendent . . .' began the Prosecutor.

'Don't be afraid, and don't suppose that my mention of this Caroline will entail what the press calls an unwarrantable intrusion into private life. Caroline was not a demi-mondaine, nor a working-girl seduced by Monsieur Deligeard, but just his old nurse . . .'

'Please explain yourself more clearly . . .'

'As clearly as I can without taking too much of your time, or making you visit the scene of the crime. I shall begin, if you allow me, with the mystery of the blue and yellow bedrooms, which was the basis for my discoveries, or rather which confirmed my suspicions. Don't glance towards the door, Monsieur Deligeard. You know it's useless.'

'I'm waiting!' the Prosecutor sighed nervously, fiddling with a paper-knife.

'I must tell you, then, that on the second floor of the house in the Rue des Récollets, Madame Joséphine Croizier occupied the room on the left, known as the Louis XIV room, which has a pale blue wallpaper. Now, at a few minutes to five, Joséphine Croizier, alive and well, came back to the house, made some joking remark to the manservant and went upstairs. She then went into her own room, the blue bedroom.

'But when Dr Liévin, having been summoned by telephone, arrived at ten minutes past five, he was shown into the room on the right, the Regency room, which has bright yellow wallpaper. And in that room the poor old lady was lying, not only dead but already undressed, in her night clothes, without any signs around her of the disorder entailed by hasty undressing . . . What's you view of the problem, Monsieur le procureur?'

'Go on!' replied the Prosecutor curtly.

'This isn't the only mystery about the case. Here is another: young Dr Liévin, who has only just begun to practise in the district and whose patients are mostly poor people from whom he gets a ten-franc fee, is summoned to the Deligeards' sumptuous mansion, in preference to any other practitioner. Now he states that death took place at about twenty minutes past four. Who is lying? Is the doctor lying, or the manservant who saw Madame Croizier come in shortly before five o'clock? And in this case the dentist is lying too, for he declares that at

4.20 the old lady from Bayeux was in his consulting room . . .'

'I don't understand . . .'

'Be patient! I didn't understand at first . . . Nor did I understand why, on that particular day, Monsieur Deligeard left his home earlier than usual and yet did not reach his club until a quarter past five, when his usual partners were becoming impatient and were on the point of looking for another player . . .'

'One's pace of walking may vary . . .'

The reply came from the Prosecutor, since Deligeard, his face ashen, stood rigidly motionless.

'Then answer this question, Monsieur le procureur. Monsieur Philippe had barely arrived when his manservant rang up to inform him that his aunt had just had a heart attack. The man said no more than that, since that was all he knew. Nonetheless Monsieur Deligeard went back to the card-room in a state of distress, announcing that his aunt had just died . . .'

The Prosecutor cast a hostile look at Philippe who, though still not moving, had finally cast down his eyes.

'Now, at random, some secondary questions. Why, precisely on that day, did Monsieur Deligeard give his chauffeur the day off, on the pretext that he would be needed every day of the following week? Co-incidence? Maybe. Why did he take out the car at two in the afternoon and then leave it outside? Where did he go, with his wife, between two and three?'

'To visit a sick-bed!' Philippe suddenly retorted.

'To visit Caroline's sick-bed, that's true, Caroline who lives outside the town, which explains the traces of mud. Now I can prove that these marks come from the road outside her house, where there is a lime-kiln.'

Automatically, but perhaps with malicious intent, Maigret began to fill his pipe and walk up and down the room.

'Monsieur le procureur, we are confronted with one of the vilest crimes I have ever met, which is at the same time an almost perfect crime. In order that you may understand, I must take you rapidly over the ground I covered myself . . . Philippe Deligeard, who has never done anything in his life except to marry a rich woman, to live on a grand scale and to speculate with so little commonsense that he lost all his fortune, has been in desperate straits for the past three years, and his only hope has been his aunt, who refused to come to his rescue . . .

'It's as clear as can be!

'Monsieur Deligeard will not contradict me when I add that on cer-tain days, in spite of the lavish style in which they still lived, there were not a hundred francs of cash in the house.

'Things had reached the point when on several occasions the gas and electricity were about to be cut off . . .

'One can't begin to learn a profession at his age. One can't change one's way of life overnight.

'His aunt was old . . . In spite of that disquieting person, the girl Cécile Ledru, she was not going to disinherit her nephew, particularly as Cécile herself was against such an idea . . .

'Philippe, moreover, had taken the precaution of revealing to the old lady that the girl was not a pure young thing, but was visited every evening by her lover in her patroness's house . . .

'Do you see, Monsieur le procureur? . . . You might say that the crime had been decided on, it had to take place . . . Joséphine Croizier had to die so that the Deligeards might go on living in the way they liked . . .

'On the other hand, whereas it is easy enough to cause someone's death it is difficult to conceal the cause of death from doctors.

'Poison is a risky weapon, particularly when an inheritance is involved and above all in the provinces, for it's the first thing that scandal-mongers think of. And everyone knew that the Deligeards were in desperate straits . . .

Firearms were out of the question. A knife would leave marks. Moreover Madame Croizier was quite tough enough to resist any attempt to jostle her on the stairs . . .

'The crime, as I said, had been practically decided on.

'All that was lacking was opportunity, the opportunity to do away with the old lady without running any risk.

'And suddenly the opportunity arose. Philippe had an old nurse, about the same age as Madame Croizier, who lived alone in a house on the outskirts of the town and had no relatives.

'This old nurse had already had a number of heart attacks, and on learning that she had just had another the Deligeards went to see her at two o'clock, returning home an hour later with the knowledge that old Caroline had only a couple of hours more to live . . .

'The lay-out of the house was convenient, but they could not afford to neglect any detail.

'Madame Deligeard left immediately by the back door and returned to the bedside of the old nurse, who breathed her last at about twenty minutes past four.

'Philippe, meanwhile, did not leave home until roughly his usual time, or slightly earlier because of his impatience; he picked up his car at the end of the street, drove to Caroline's, put her body into the car and brought his wife home at the same time.

'Together they carried the body into the house, still using the back door, and laid it in the yellow bedroom on the second floor.

'None of the servants knew that Madame Deligeard had been out Her husband meanwhile was supposed to be on his way to the club.

'They waited in the house together for the imminent return of Philippe's aunt . . .

'She came back and went into her own room, the blue bedroom, where they promptly murdered her . . .

'Philippe now merely had to go to his club – through the back gate, in his car – to establish an alibi for himself.

'The doctor, who had been chosen from among those unfamiliar with the house or with Joséphine Croizier, was shown the body of Caroline, who had died from natural causes, and of course he signed a death certificate to that effect.

'The same process was repeated with the doctor who came to register the death that evening.

'And then they merely had to take the nurse's body back to her house . . .'

'What made you think of Caroline?' the Prosecutor asked after a pause.

'Logic! The two doctors had not been able to examine the body of Joséphine Croizier. I therefore bought the paper next day and studied the list of deaths. I was sure I should find an old woman's name in it, and when I did I made some inquiries about her. The neighbours had noticed a car repeatedly coming and going, but thought no more about it, knowing that the old woman's former employers often came to see her. That is moreover the only thing to be said in favour of Philippe Deligeard . . .'

The silence grew oppressive. Suddenly the paper-knife was slammed down as the magistrate asked with a hesitant voice:

'Do you confess, Philippe Deligeard?'

'I refuse to answer except in the presence of my lawyer.' The traditional formula! He was white to the lips. When he stood up he tottered and he had to be given a glass of water.

The post-mortem on poor Joséphine Croizier showed, first, that her heart was in excellent condition, and next, that she had been clumsily killed, first by an attempt to strangle her with a shoe lace, and then, probably because she was still struggling, with two knife wounds in the chest.

'I can only congratulate you,' the Prosecutor told Maigret, accompanying his words with an icy smile. 'You are indeed the first-class fellow we had been promised. But I feel I ought to tell you that your methods, in a small town like ours, are risky, to say the least . . .'

'Which means, I take it, that I am not to stay much longer in Caen.'

'The fact is that . . .'

'Thank you, Monsieur le procureur.'

'But . . .'

'I felt somewhat ill at ease myself in this part of the world. My wife is expecting me back in Paris. I can only hope that the jurors of this town will not let themselves be overawed by the grand mansion of that utter scoundrel Philippe, and that he'll get the death penalty . . .'

And he muttered, between his teeth:

'Somebody else will have to make a fourth at bridge!'

STAN THE KILLER

I

Maigret, his hands behind his back, his pipe between his teeth, was walking slowly, thrusting his bulky form with some difficulty through the busy morning crowd in the Rue Saint-Antoine, while the sunshine poured down from a bright sky on to the little barrows loaded with fruit and vegetables and the stalls which took up almost the whole width of the pavement.

It was the time when housewives were shopping most busily, weighing artichokes in their hands and tasting cherries, while steaks and escalopes succeeded one another on the butcher's scales.

'Best asparagus, five francs the big bundle!'

'Fresh whiting! Just come in!'

Shop assistants in white aprons, butchers in checked linen aprons, smells of cheese in front of a dairyman's and, further on, the odour of roasting coffee; the bustling trade of food stores and the queues of canny housewives, the clang of cash registers, the heavy rumble of passing buses . . .

And Superintendent Maigret walked past, all unsuspected, and nobody guessed that one of the most distressing cases imaginable was involved.

Almost opposite the Rue de Birague there was a small café, the Tonnelet Bourguignon, with only three tables on its narrow terrace. This was where Maigret sat down, to all appearances the exhausted stroller. He did not even raise his eyes when a tall thin waiter came up to take his order.

'A small glass of white Mâcon,' growled the Superintendent.

And who would have guessed that the somewhat clumsy waiter of the Tonnelet Bourguignon was none other than Inspector Janvier?

He came back with the glass of wine uneasily balanced on a tray. With a napkin of doubtful cleanliness he wiped the table, and a scrap of paper fell to the ground. Maigret picked it up soon afterwards.

'*The woman has gone out shopping. Not seen One-Eye. The Beard went out early. The other three must have stopped in the hotel.*'

By ten o'clock the bustle was on the increase. Beside the Tonnelet a grocer's shop was offering bargains, and its touts stopped passers-by to

161

make them taste biscuits being sold at two francs a tin.

Just at the corner of the Rue de Birague stood a seedy hotel, the
type where you can take rooms 'by the month, the week or the day',
but where payment in advance is required; its sign, perhaps ironically, bore the name Hôtel Beauséjour.

Maigret was savouring his glass of dry white wine, and he seemed
to be looking for nothing in particular amid the motley crowd of
people milling round him in the spring sunshine. And yet his gaze presently fastened on a window on the second floor of a house in the Rue
de Birague. almost opposite that hotel. At that window a little old
man was sitting beside a canary's cage, and seemed to be concerned
only with warming himself in the sun so long as God deigned to grant
him life.

This was Lucas, Sergeant Lucas, who had skilfully added some
twenty years to his appearance and who, although he had picked out
Maigret on the terrace of the café, carefully avoided showing any signs
of recognition.

All this was part of a police ambush which had been going on for six
days already, and twice a day at least the Superintendent got the
latest news from his men, who by night were relieved by a policeman
on the beat who was really an inspector from the Criminal Investigation Department, and by a tart who, while walking the street in the
neighbourhood, took good care not to be accosted.

Maigret would get Lucas's information by and by, when he was
summoned to the telephone at the Tonnelet Bourguignon. And it
would probably be no more interesting than Janvier's.

The crowd passed so close to the tiny terrace that the Superintendent was continually obliged to tuck his feet under his chair.

Now, suddenly, he was taken by surprise as a man sat down beside
him, at the same table, a thin red-headed man with sad eyes, whose
mournful face recalled that of a clown.

'You again?' growled the Superintendent.

'I'm sorry, Monsieur Maigret, but I'm sure you'll end by under-
standing me and accepting my suggestion . . .'

And to Janvier, who now came forward, every inch a waiter:

'I'll take the same as my friend here . . .' He had a pronounced
Polish accent. He must have had a sore throat, for he was continually
chewing a creosote 'cigar' which added to the oddity of his appearance.

'You're beginning to get on my nerves!' Maigret told him curtly.
'Will you tell me how you knew I'd be here this morning?'

'I didn't know.'

'Then why did you come? Are you going to try and make me believe
that you just happened to catch sight of me?'

'No!'

The man's movements were as deliberate as those of certain music-hall acrobats who perform their acts in slow motion. He stared straight ahead with his yellow eyes, or rather he seemed to be staring into vacancy. And he spoke in a sad, monotonous voice, as though uttering endless condolences.

'You're not being kind to me, Monsieur Maigret . . .'

'That doesn't answer my question. How do you come to be here this morning?'

'I followed you!'

'From Police Headquarters?'

'Long before that . . . From your home.'

'So you admit you've been spying on me?'

'I'm not spying on you, Monsieur Maigret! I respect and admire you. I've already told you I shall be your collaborator some day . . .'

And he heaved a nostalgic sigh as he gazed at his creosote-flavoured 'cigar', tipped by artificial ash of painted wood.

Only one of the newspapers had mentioned the case, and moreover this paper, which had got the information heaven knows how, made the Superintendent's task very much more complicated.

The police have reason to believe that the Polish gangsters, including Stan the Killer, are at present in Paris.

This was true, but it would have been better kept quiet. During the past four years a gang of Poles, about whom practically nothing was known, had attacked five farms, always in Northern France and always using the same methods.

For one thing, the farms had always been isolated ones, and the farmers in each case had been elderly people. Moreover, the attack invariably took place on market day, when people who had sold a good many animals had a considerable amount of cash in their possession.

There was nothing scientific about the gang's method. It was a brutal assault, comparable to that of highway robbers in old days, with utter disregard for the value of human life.

The Poles were killers. They killed everyone they found on the farm, including children, knowing that this was the only way to avoid being recognized some day.

There might have been two of them, or five, or eight.

In each case, a van had been noticed. A twelve-year-old boy asserted that he had seen a one-eyed man. Some people declared that the bandits wore black masks when they were about their work.

At all events, on each occasion the farmers had had their throats slashed with knives.

*   *   *

The affair did not concern Paris. The various flying squads of France had been in charge of it. For two whole years the mystery had remained intact, which caused considerable unease in rural districts.

Then a piece of information had come from the neighbourhood of Lille, where certain villages are, as it were, Polish enclaves on French soil. The information was vague enough, and its source could not even be traced.

'The Poles say it's Stan the Killer's gang.'

But when the people of the mining villages, few of whom spoke French, were questioned one by one, either they knew nothing or else they stammered vaguely: 'I was told . . .'

'By whom?'

'I don't know . . . I've forgotten.'

On the occasion of a crime in the region of Reims, however, a servant at one of the farms who, unknown to the bandits, had been asleep in an attic, had been spared. She had heard the murderers speaking a language which she thought was Polish. She had seen faces in black masks, but she had noticed that one of the men had only one eye, and that another, a giant over six foot tall, had an extraordinarily hairy face.

So the police had taken to referring to the bandits as Stan the Killer, the Beard, and One-Eye . . .

For long months nothing more had been known until the day when a young detective from the Lodgings Squad had made a discovery. He was responsible for the Saint-Antoine district, which is swarming with Poles. He had noticed, at a hotel in the Rue de Birague, a suspicious-looking group which included a one-eyed man and a giant whose face was covered with shaggy hair.

They seemed to be poor people. The bearded giant had a room by the week, with his wife, but almost every night he took in a number of his compatriots, sometimes a couple, sometimes five of them; often, moreover, other Poles rented the room next door.

'Will you look into this, Maigret?' the head of the Police Judiciaire had suggested.

And next day, although the matter had been kept secret, a newspaper published the information!

The following day, Maigret's mail included a badly written letter, full of spelling mistakes and in an almost childish handwriting, on the sort of cheap paper that is sold in grocers' shops:

'Stan won't let himself be caught. Watch out. Before you've got the better of him he'll have had time to kill a lot of people round him.'

Of course the identity of Stan the Killer was as yet unknown, but there was good reason to believe that the tip about the Rue de Birague was reliable, since the murderer had taken the trouble to send a threatening letter.

And this letter was not meant as a joke, Maigret was sure of it. It 'smelled' authentic, as he said. Somehow it smacked of the underworld.

'Take care, old boy!' the Chief had warned him. 'No hasty arrests. The man who has cut the throats of sixteen people in the past four years will have no qualms about shooting all and sundry when he sees he's going to be caught ...'

That was why Janvier had become a waiter in the café opposite the Hôtel Beauséjour, and Lucas had been transformed into an elderly cripple spending his days basking in the sun at his window.

The noisy life of the district went on without anybody suspecting that at any moment a man at bay might start firing at random ...

'Monsieur Maigret, I've come to tell you ...' And there was Michel Ozep again.

His first meeting with Maigret had been four days ago. He had turned up at Police Headquarters and insisted on being seen by the Superintendent himself. Maigret had kept him waiting for over two hours, but this had not disconcerted the fellow.

Once in Maigret's office, he had clicked his heels and bowed, holding out his hand:

'Michel Ozep, formerly an officer in the Polish army, now teacher of gymnastics in Paris.'

'Sit down, I'm listening.'

The Pole spoke with a strong accent and in so voluble a fashion that it was not easy to follow him. He explained that he belonged to a very good family, that he had left Poland as a result of personal troubles – he implied that he had been in love with his Colonel's wife! – and that he was becoming increasingly desperate because he could not get used to an inferior way of life.

'You see, Monsieur Maigret ...' (he pronounced the name *Maigrette*) 'I'm a gentleman ... Here I give lessons to people who have no culture and no education ... I am poor ... I decided to kill myself ...'

Maigret had at first thought: 'A madman!' For visits of this sort are common at the Quai des Orfèvres; a great many crazy people feel impelled to go there and tell their stories.

'I tried three weeks ago ... I jumped into the Seine off the Pont d'Austerlitz, but the police from the River Squad saw me and pulled me out ...'

Under some pretext Maigret went next door and rang up the River Squad; the statement was quite true.

'Six days later I tried to gas myself, but the postman came with a letter and opened the door . . .'

A call to the local police station confirmed this too.

'I really want to kill myself, do you understand? There's no point to my life now. A gentleman cannot consent to go on living in this manner, in squalor or mediocrity. So I thought you might perhaps need a man like me . . .'

'What for?'

'To help you arrest Stan the Killer.'

Maigret was frowning.

'You know him?'

'No. I've only heard speak of him. It shocks me, as a Pole, that one of my countrymen should thus violate the laws of hospitality. I want to get Stan and his gang arrested . . . I know he's determined to defend himself desperately . . . So some people are sure to be killed when they arrest him. Isn't it better that I should be one of them, since I want to die in any case? . . . Tell me where to find Stan . . . I'll go and I'll disarm him. . . If need be I'll wound him, so that he'll no longer be dangerous . . .'

Maigret had no alternative but to use the traditional formula:

'Leave me your address . . . I'll get in touch with you.'

Michel Ozep lived in lodgings in the Rue des Tournelles, not far, as it happened, from the Rue de Biragrue. A detective had made inquiries about him, and the report had been relatively favourable. He really had been a sub-lieutenant in the Polish army when it was formed. Then all trace of him disappeared, until he turned up again in Paris, where he tried to give lessons in gymnastics to the sons and daughters of small tradesmen.

His suicide attempts had not been invented.

Nonetheless Maigret, in agreement with the head of the Police Judiciaire, had written him an official letter which ended:

. . . cannot to my great regret take advantage of your generous offer, for which many thanks . . .'

Twice since then Ozep had appeared at the Quai des Orfèvres and had demanded to see the Superintendent. The second time he had even refused to leave, asserting that he would wait there as long as was necessary and taking possession, almost forcibly, for hours on end, of one of the green plush chairs in the waiting-room.

Now Ozep was sitting at Maigret's table on the terrace of the Tonnelet Bourguignon.

'I want to prove to you, Monsieur Maigrette, that I can be of some use, and that you can accept my help. I've been following you for the past three days and I'm able to tell you all that you've been doing meanwhile. I also know that the waiter who had just been serving me is one of your inspectors and that there's another at a window opposite, sitting beside a bird-cage with a canary in it.'

Maigret gritted his teeth furiously on the stem of his pipe, averting his eyes from his interlocutor, who went on in a monotonous voice:

'I can understand that when a stranger comes up and tells you: "I'm an ex-officer of the Polish army and I want to commit suicide", you may think it's not true; but you have checked up on all that I've told you. You've seen that I wouldn't stoop to telling a lie . . .'

His words poured forth in a rapid, jerky stream, the more wearisome to listen to since his accent distorted the words, so that sustained attention was required to follow them.

'You are not Polish, Monsieur Maigrette. You don't understand our mentality. You don't speak our language. But I am seriously anxious to help you, because my country's good name must no longer be tarnished by . . .'

Maigret was choking with annoyance. And the other man, although he must have been aware of it, nevertheless went on speaking:

'If you try to arrest Stan, what will he do? He may have two or even three guns in his pockets . . . He'll fire on everybody . . . Who knows if women or children may not get wounded or killed . . . Then people will say that the police . . .'

'Will you be quiet?'

'But I want to die . . . Nobody will mourn poor Ozep . . . You'll say to me: "There's Stan!" and I'll follow him as I followed you . . . I'll wait till there's nobody about . . . I'll say to him: "You're Stan the Killer!"'

'Then he'll fire at me and I'll shoot at his legs . . . The fact of his firing at me will prove that he is really Stan and that you've made no mistake. And when he's wounded . . .'

Nothing stopped the man! He would have gone rambling on in despite of the whole world.

'Suppose I had you jailed?' Maigret interrupted him roughly.

'Why?'

'To have a little peace!'

'What could you say? What has poor Ozep done against the laws of France, which he has always sought to defend and for which he is ready to give his life?'

'Shut up!'

'What did you say? You'll agree?'

'Nothing of the sort!'

At that moment a woman came by, a blonde woman with a very pale complexion, whom everyone in the neighbourhood could recognize as a foreigner. She was carrying a shopping bag and making her way to a butcher's shop.

Maigret, who was watching her, noticed that his companion was
suddenly impelled to blow his nose violently, covering his face with his
handkerchief.

'That's Stan's mistress, isn't it?' he said when the woman was out of
sight.

'Are you going to leave me in peace or not?'

'You're convinced that she's Stan's mistress, but you don't know
which of them is Stan. You think it's the bearded one. But the bearded
one is called Boris. And the one-eyed man's name is Sasha. He's not a
Pole but a Russian. If you carry out the investigation yourself you'll
learn nothing, because they're all Poles in that hotel and they'll either
refuse to answer or they'll tell you lies. Whereas if I . . .'

None of the housewives in the busy Rue Saint-Antoine could have
guessed what was being discussed on the tiny terrace of the Tonnelet
Bourguignon. The fair-haired woman with the pale complexion was
bargaining over lamb chops at a nearby butcher's stall, and her eyes
betrayed something of the same weariness as did Michel Ozep's.

'Perhaps you're bothered because you think there'll be questions
raised if I'm killed? . . . For one thing, I have no relatives. For another,
I have written a letter in which I say that I alone, and of my own free
will, have sought death . . .'

Poor Janvier was hovering in the doorway, not knowing how to
explain to Maigret that there was a telephone message for him.
Maigret had noticed this, but he went on watching the Polish fellow
and puffing gently at his pipe.

'Listen, Ozep . . .'

'Yes, Monsieur Maigrette?'

'If you're found again hanging round the Rue Saint-Antoine, I'll
have you locked up!'

'But I live . . .'

'Go and live somewhere else!'

'You refuse the offer I . . .'

'Be off!'

'But . . .'

'Be off, or I'll have you arrested!'

The man rose, clicked his heels and bowed low, then moved away
with dignity. Maigret, who had caught sight of one of his detectives,
signalled to him to follow this peculiar gym instructor.

At last the coast was clear for Janvier to come up.

'Lucas has just called. He's seen arms in the room, and five Poles
spent the night in the next room, some of them on the floor, leaving the
door open between. What did that fellow want?'

'Nothing . . . Bill, please.'

And Janvier, resuming his role, pointed to Ozep's glass:

'Are you paying for this gentleman's? One-twenty and one-twenty makes two francs forty . . .'

Maigret took a taxi to Police Headquarters.

At the door of his room he found the detective whom he had sent to follow Ozep.

'You've lost his trail!' he shouted. 'Aren't you ashamed? I put you in charge of a simple shadowing job and . . .'

'I haven't lost him,' humbly muttered the detective, who was a novice.

'Where is he?'

'Here.'

'You brought him here?'

'He brought himself.'

And in fact Ozep had made straight for Police Headquarters and settled down calmly in the waiting-room, with a sandwich, after announcing that he had an appointment with Superintendent 'Maigrette'.

II

Maigret was busy with an unglamorous but nevertheless useful task: pressing the pen firmly on the paper, in his big round hand he was summarising the various pieces of information about the gang of Poles obtained by means of police traps during the past fortnight.

Thus set out side by side, their meagre nature was revealed, since it was not even possible to decide exactly how many members the gang comprised.

According to earlier information, that is to say according to the people who, at the time of the attacks, had seen or thought they had seen the bandits, these numbered four or five, but it was likely that other accomplices picked out the farms beforehand and frequented the cattle markets.

There were probably about six or seven of them in all, and this corresponded to the number of individuals who prowled around the nucleus in the Rue de Birague.

Only three or four of them were regular tenants, who had filled in their forms and produced passports in order:

1. Boris Saft, known to the investigators as 'the Beard', who seemed to be cohabiting with the pale fair-haired woman;

2. Olga Tserewska, 28 years old, from Vilna;

3. Sasha Vorontsow, nicknamed One-Eye.

The inquiry centred round this trio, which appeared also to form the basis of the gang.

Olga and bearded Boris shared a room; one-eyed Sasha occupied the neighbouring room, and the door between the two was always left open.

Every morning the young woman went out shopping and prepared a meal on a spirit lamp.

The bearded man seldom went out; he spent most of his days lying on the iron bedstead, reading Polish papers which were fetched for him from a news-stand in the Place de la Bastille.

The one-eyed man had gone out now and then, and on each occasion he had been followed by a detective. Was the man aware of this? At all events, he had merely taken them for a walk around Paris, sitting down at various cafés for a drink, without speaking a word to anyone.

The other Poles were what Lucas described as 'transients'. The same four or five people went in and out, Olga provided their meals, and they sometimes slept in one of the two rooms, on the floor, and left again the next morning.

There was nothing out of the way about this, for it was the general practice in this hotel, which was frequented by poor people, exiles who would share the cost of a room between several or put up compatriots they had met in the street.

About the 'transients' Maigret had a few notes:

1. The Chemist, so called because he had twice visited the Labour Exchange seeking a job with some chemical products firm. His clothes were very worn but of fairly good cut. For hours on end he would walk the streets of Paris, apparently seeking to earn a little money, and for one whole day he had been employed as a sandwich-man;

2. Spinach, so named because he wore an extraordinary spinach-green hat, the more noticeable since his shirt was of a faded pink. Spinach went out chiefly at night and was sometimes to be seen opening the doors at some Montmartre nightclub;

3. The Fat Boy, a rotund, short-winded little fellow, better dressed than the others although his shoes were not matching.

There were a couple more that used to visit the Rue de Birague, less regularly, and it was difficult to say whether they were really members of the gang.

Maigret made a note at the end of this list:

'*These people give the impression of being penniless foreigners in search of any sort of job. Yet there is always vodka in the rooms and on certain nights they have a regular binge.*

'*It is impossible to know whether or not the gang, aware that they are being watched, assume this attitude to mislead the police.*

'*Moreover, if one of them is really Stan the Killer, it seems likely to be either One-Eye or the Beard. But this is only a guess.*'

Without the least enthusiasm, he took his report to the Chief.

'Nothing new?'

'Nothing definite. I could swear the artful dodgers have recognized all our men and are deliberately keeping us on the move with perfectly innocent comings and goings. They've decided that we cannot permanently mobilize a section of the Police Judiciaire to watch them. They've got time . . .'

'Have you a plan?'

'You know, Chief, that I gave up having ideas a long time ago. I just go about sniffing. Some people think I'm waiting for inspiration, but they're wrong. What I'm waiting for is the significant fact which never fails to emerge. The important thing is to be there when it happens and to take advantage of it.'

'So you're waiting for some little fact?' the Chief murmured with a smile, for he knew his man.

'I'm convinced of one thing: we really are dealing with the Polish gang. Thanks to that idiotic journalist who's always prowling about our corridors and must have overheard some conversation, the rascals have been warned.

'Now, why did Stan write? that's what I'm wondering. Perhaps because he knows the police are always reluctant to make a large-scale arrest? Perhaps, and this is the most likely, out of sheer bravado. Killers have their pride, I almost said their professional pride . . .

'Which of them is Stan? And why this diminutive, which sounds more American than Polish?

'You know I take my time about forming an opinion . . . Well, it's beginning to come. Over the past two or three days I've become familiar with the psychology of these rascals, and it's very different from that of French murderers . . .

'They need money, not in order to retire into the countryside or to go on the spree in nightclubs, or to take refuge abroad, but simply to live the way they like, that's to say doing nothing, eating, drinking and sleeping, spending whole days lying about on filthy beds, smoking cigarettes and putting away quantities of vodka . . .

'And they feel the need to be together, to daydream together, to chat and, some nights, to sing together . . .

'As I see it, after committing their first crime they went on living this way until the money was exhausted, then they planned the next job. As soon as funds are low they begin again, coldly, remorselessly, without the least pity for the old people whom they murder and whose savings they run through in a few weeks or months . . .

'Now that I've understood that, I'm waiting . . .'

'I know! For the little fact . . .' teased the head of the Police Judiciaire.

'Make fun of me as much as you like. Nonetheless the little fact may be there already . . .'

'Where?'

'In the waiting-room. The fellow who calls me Maigrette and who's determined to help me with the arrest, even if it should cost him his life. He declares it's as good a way as any of committing suicide.'

'A madman?'

'Maybe! Or one of Stan's accomplices who has discovered this means of finding out our intentions. Any hypothesis is permissible, and that's just what makes my man so fascinating. For instance, why shouldn't he himself be Stan the Killer?'

And Maigret emptied his pipe gently on the window-sill, so that ash fell down on to the quayside, possibly on to the hat of a passer-by.

'Are you going to make use of this man?'

'I think so.'

With these words the Superintendent made for the door, avoiding any further explanation.

'You'll see, Chief! It would surprise me if we need set any more traps after the end of this week.'

And it was now Thursday afternoon!

'Sit down there! Aren't you fed up with sucking that disgusting creosote "cigar" all day?'

'No, Monsieur Maigrette.'

'I'm getting rather tired of your "Maigrette" . . . However, let's talk seriously . . . You're still determined to die?'

'Yes, Monsieur Maigrette.'

'And you still want to be entrusted with a dangerous mission?'

'I want to help you to arrest Stan the Killer.'

'So, if I were to tell you to go up to One-Eye and fire a revolver at his legs, would you do it?'

'Yes, Monsieur Maigrette. But you would have to give me a gun. I'm a very poor man and . . .'

'Now suppose I should ask you to go and tell the Beard or One-Eye that you've got some genuine information, that the police are coming to arrest them . . .'

'I'm quite willing, Monsieur Maigrette. I'll wait till One-Eye comes down the street and I'll give him the message.'

The Superintendent gazed intently at the thin little Pole, who displayed neither embarrassment nor anxiety. Maigret had seldom seen a man with so much self-assurance and so much composure.

Michel Ozep spoke of killing himself or visiting the Polish gang as though it were something perfectly simple and natural. He seemed equally at ease on the café terrace in the Rue Saint-Antoine or in the offices of the Police Judiciaire.

'You don't know either of them?'

'No, Monsieur Maigrette.'

'Well, I'm going to entrust you with a mission. Bad luck on you if things turn nasty!'

This time Maigret lowered his eyelids to conceal the extreme tenseness of his gaze.

'Presently we'll go together to the Rue Saint-Antoine. I shall wait for you outside. You'll go up to the room, choosing a time when the woman is there by herself. You'll tell her that you're a compatriot and that you've discovered by chance that the police intend to raid the hotel tonight . . .'

Ozep was silent.

'Have you understood?'

'Yes.'

'That's agreed, then?'

'I must confess something, Monsieur Maigrette.'

'You're funking it?'

'I'm not . . . what you call funking it, no! Only I'd rather arrange the business differently. You may think, perhaps, that I'm very daring – is that the word? . . . But with women I'm a timid fellow. And women are intelligent, far more intelligent than men. So she'll see that I'm lying. And because I know she'll see that I'm lying I shall blush. And when I blush . . .'

Maigret remained motionless, while the man tied himself up in an explanation that was both wordy and unconvincing.

'I'd sooner speak to a man . . . to the man with the beard, if you like, or the one-eyed one, or anybody else . . .'

Perhaps because a ray of sunlight was slanting into the room and falling directly on to Maigret's face, the latter seemed as drowsy as a man dozing after a heavy meal.

'It amounts to the same thing, Monsieur Maigrette . . .'

But Monsieur Maigrette made no answer, and the only sign of life he gave was the thin blue thread of smoke spiralling up from the barrel of his pipe.

'I'm very sorry. You can ask me to do anything you like, but you're asking me to do the one thing that . . .'

'Skip it.'

'What did you say?'

'I said skip it. Stop telling me tales . . . Where did you know this woman, Olga Tserewska?'

'Me?'

'Answer me!'

'I don't know what you mean . . .'

'Answer me!'

'I don't know the woman . . . If I knew her I'd tell you . . . I'm a former officer of the Polish army and if I hadn't been unfortunate . . .'

'Where did you know her?'

'I swear to you, Monsieur Maigrette, on the head of my late lamented father and mother . . .'

'Where did you know her?'

'Why are you suddenly so unkind to me? You speak to me so brutally! I only came here to help you, to keep my compatriots from killing French people . . .'

'Blah, blah!'

'What did you say?'

'I said blah, blah! That means you can go on with your blarney, but you won't take me in.'

'Ask anything you like of me . . .'

'That's what I'm doing!'

'Ask me to do anything else, to throw myself under a métro train or to jump out of the window . . .'

'I'm asking you to go and see this woman and to tell her that we are planning to arrest the gang tonight.'

'You insist?'

'You're free to accept or to refuse!'

'And if I refuse?'

'You can go and hang yourself somewhere else!'

'Why hang myself?'

'Just a figure of speech . . . In other words, you'll try to keep out of my way . . .'

'Are you really going to arrest the gang tonight?'

'Probably!'

'And you'll let me help you?'

'Possibly. We'll see about that when you've done your first job . . .'

'At what time?'

'Your job?'

'No! At what time are you going to arrest them?'

'Let's say one o'clock in the morning.'

'I'll go . . .'

'Where?'

'To see the woman.'

'Wait a minute! Let's go together!'

'It would be better for me to go alone. If we're seen together they'll know that I'm helping the police . . .'

Needless to say, the Pole had barely left the room when the Superintendent sent a detective after him.

'Shall I keep hidden?' asked the detective.

'No point . . . He's cleverer than you are and he knows very well that I'm having him shadowed . . .'

And without wasting a second Maigret went downstairs and jumped into a taxi.

'Quick as you can, to the corner of the Rue de Birague and the Rue Saint-Antoine . . .'

It was a radiant afternoon, and many-coloured awnings glowed brightly above the shop fronts. In the shade, dogs lay lazily stretching, and life flowed by in slow motion; the very buses seemed to move with difficulty in the sultry air, and their great wheels left marks on the overheated tarmac.

Maigret leapt from his taxi into the house at the corner of the two streets, and on the second floor he opened a door without knocking. Here he found Sergeant Lucas sitting at the window, still in the guise of a quiet, inquisitive little old man.

The room was shabby and not very clean. On the table lay the remains of a cold meal that Lucas had had sent up from a delicatessen.

'Anything new, Superintendent?'

'Are they there, over the way?'

The room had been chosen for its strategic position, for it afforded a view into the two rooms of the Hôtel Beauséjour which were occupied by the group of Poles.

On account of the heat, all the windows were open, including that of a neighbouring room in which a young woman lay asleep, very lightly clad.

'You seem to be having a good time . . .'

A pair of fieldglasses on a chair proved that Lucas was doing his job conscientiously and was anxious to observe details.

'For the moment,' the sergeant replied, 'there are two of them in the apartment, but soon there'll be only one. The man is getting dressed. He lay in bed all morning as usual . . .'

'The Beard?'

'Yes. Three of them had lunch together: the Beard, the woman and One-Eye. Then One-Eye left almost immediately. The Beard got up and began dressing . . . See! He's just put on a clean shirt, which doesn't happen often . . .'

Maigret went up to the window for a look. The shaggy giant was fastening a tie over the shirt that made an unexpected patch of brightness in the dingy room.

His lips could be seen moving as he looked at himself in the glass. And behind him the fair-haired woman was tidying up, collecting greasy papers which she rolled up into a ball, and finally extinguishing the spirit lamp.

'If we only knew what they're saying to one another!' sighed Lucas. 'At times it drives me crazy! I see them talking away endlessly; sometimes they gesticulate and I can't guess what it's all about . . . I'm beginning to realize what torture it must be to be deaf, and I can see why people who are afflicted in that way are considered spiteful . . .'

'Don't talk so much yourself in the meantime! Do you think the woman will stay there?'

'It's not her time for going out. If she meant to do so she'd be wearing her grey suit.'

Olga wore the dark woollen dress in which she went shopping in the mornings. As she did her casual housework she smoked a cigarette without ever taking it from her lips, after the fashion of those inveterate smokers who need tobacco from morning till night.

'She doesn't talk much!' commented Maigret.

'It's not her time for talking either. It's chiefly in the evenings that she talks, when they're all gathered round her. Or else on certain rare occasions when she's alone with the one I call Spinach. If I'm not mistaken, she's got a weakness for Spinach, who's the best-looking of the lot.'

It was a strange sensation being in an unfamiliar room looking across the street at people whose behaviour one got to know down to the last detail.

'You're growing into a regular concierge, poor old Lucas!'

'That's what I'm here for, isn't it? See, I can even tell you that the girl in the next room, who's sleeping so soundly, made love last night until three o'clock with a young fellow who wore a floppy bow-tie and who left at dawn, probably to creep back quietly into his parents' house . . . Look, the Beard is leaving now.'

'He's really almost smart!'

'Relatively speaking . . . He looks more like a fairground wrestler than like a gentleman.'

'Let's say a fairground wrestler who's done well in business,' Maigret conceded.

Over the way, there were no fond farewells. The man simply went off, that's to say he disappeared from that part of the room that was visible from the policemen's observation-post.

Shortly afterwards he emerged on to the pavement and made off towards the Place de la Bastille.

'Derain will shadow him,' announced Lucas, who sat there like a big spider in the midst of his web. 'But the man knows he's being followed. He'll simply take a walk and perhaps have a drink on the terrace of some café . . .'

The woman meanwhile took a road map out of a drawer and unfolded it on the table. Maigret reckoned that Ozep would not come by taxi but by the métro, and would therefore take another few minutes to get there.

'If he comes at all!' he corrected himself.

But the man came! They saw him arrive, hesitating; they saw him walk up and down the pavement, while the detective who was shadowing him pretended to be interested in a fishmonger's display in the Rue Saint-Antoine.

Seen from above in this fashion, the Pole's slight figure seemed even thinner and more insignificant, and Maigret had a moment's remorse.

He remembered the poor fellow's voice endlessly repeating his 'Monsieur Maigrette' as he struggled with complicated explanations.

The man was hesitating, unmistakably. One could have sworn, indeed, that he was afraid of something, and he kept looking round with apprehension.

'Do you know what he's looking for?' the Superintendent asked Lucas.

'The pale fellow? No! Perhaps for money so that he can go into the hotel?'

'He's looking for me . . . He thinks I'm probably somewhere in the neighbourhood and that if by some miracle I've changed my mind . . .'

Too late! Michel Ozep had just disappeared into the dark entrance hall of the hotel. One could follow him mentally. He must be climbing the stairs, reaching the second floor.

'He's still hesitating . . .' Maigret declared.

For the door should have opened by now.

'He's on the landing . . . He's going to knock . . . He has knocked . . . look!'

For the blonde young woman now gave a start, instinctively thrust the road map into the cupboard and went towards the door.

For a moment there was nothing to be seen. The two figures were standing in the unseen part of the room.

Then suddenly the woman reappeared and there was something altered about her. She walked with firm, rapid steps; she went straight to the window, closed it and drew the dark curtains.

Lucas turned to the Superintendent with a comical grimace.

'What about that?'

But he ceased joking when he noticed that Maigret was looking far more anxious than he had expected.

'What time is it, Lucas.'

'Ten past three . . .'

'In your opinion, is there any likelihood of some of our ruffians coming back shortly?'

'I don't think so . . Except for Spinach, as I told you, if he knows the Beard is out of the way . . . You're looking uneasy . . .'

'I don't like the way she closed that window . . .'

'You're anxious about your Pole?'

Maigret did not reply and Lucas went on.

'Have you considered that there's no proof he is in the room? We saw him go into the hotel, that's true, but he may well have gone into some other room . . . And it may be someone else who . . .'

Maigret shrugged his shoulders and sighed:

'Shut up! You bore me . . .'

III

'What time is it, Lucas?'

'Twenty past three . . .'

'D'you know what's going to happen?'

'Do you want to go and see what's going on over there?'

'Not yet. But I may be going to make an absolute fool of myself. Where can I make a call from?'

'From the next room. My neighbour's a tailor who works for a big dressmaking firm and they insist on his having a telephone.'

'Then go round to your tailor's. Try to manage so that he doesn't overhear the conversation. Ring up the Chief for me. Tell him to let me have twenty armed men as quickly as possible. They're to fan out round the Hôtel Beauséjour and wait for a signal from me.'

Lucas's expression reflected the gravity of this request, which in fact was not characteristic of Maigret's methods; he usually made fun of large-scale police intervention.

'Do you think something nasty's going to happen?'

'Unless it's already happened . . .'

He kept his eyes fixed on the window below, with its dirty panes and its old-fashioned crimson velvet curtains.

When Lucas returned after telephoning, he found the Superintendent still in the same place and still wearing the same worried look.

'The Chief begs you to be careful. There's been one inspector killed last week, and if there were to be another accident . . .'

'Shut up, will you?'

'Do you believe that Stan the Killer . . .?'

'I don't believe anything, old man! I've thought about this business so much since this morning that my head aches. Now I'm just getting impressions, and if you want to know the truth I've unfortunately got the impression that something unpleasant is happening or is going to happen. What's the time?'

'Three twenty-three . . .'

It seemed ironical that in the neighbouring room the girl was still asleep with her mouth open and her legs drawn up. On a higher floor, the fifth or sixth, somebody was trying to play the accordion, constantly repeating the same dance tune with the same wrong notes.

'Shall I go across?' suggested Lucas.

Maigret glared at him, as though his subordinate were accusing him of cowardice.

'What d'you mean by that?'

'Nothing! I can see that you're anxious about what's going on down there, and I offered to go and find out . . .'

'And do you think I'd have any hesitation about going myself? You forget one thing: once we're over there, it'll be too late to retreat . . . If we go there and discover nothing, we shall never discover anything about the gang. That's why I'm hesitating. If only that bitch hadn't shut the window!'

He suddenly frowned.

'Listen – at other times, she's never shut the window, has she?'

'Never!'

'So she can't have suspected your presence here . . .'

'She probably took me for an old dodderer . . .'

'So that it can't have been she who thought of closing the window, but the person who came in . . .'

'Ozep?'

'Ozep or another. The man who came in and who, before showing himself, told the woman to shut the window . . .'

He picked up his hat, which he had put on a chair, emptied his pipe and refilled it with a forceful forefinger.

'Where are you off to, Chief?'

'I'm waiting for our men to turn up. Look, there are two of them down by the bus stop. And in that stationary taxi I can recognize some of our boys. If I stay in there for five minutes without opening the window you're to come in with some of the men.'

'You've got your gun?'

A few minutes later Maigret crossed the street, while Inspector Janvier, who had caught sight of him, stopped wiping the tables on his terrace.

Lucas, in a state of feverish excitement, had his watch in his hand, but as happens when one is too anxious to do the right thing, he had forgotten to note the moment when Maigret entered the hotel, so that he was unable to say when the five minutes were up.

He did not in fact have to worry unduly about this, for after what seemed an incredibly short interval the window opposite opened. Maigret, looking more sullen than ever, signalled his sergeant to come over.

Lucas had had the impression that the room was empty except for the Superintendent, but when he entered it, after stumbling up a dark stairway that smelt of bad cooking and lavatories, he started back on discovering a woman's body prostrate at his feet.

A brief glance at Maigret, who replied:

'Dead, of course!'

It looked as if the criminal had wanted to leave his signature, for the victim had had her throat cut, like all Stan's victims. There was blood everywhere, on the bed and on the floor, and the murderer had wiped his hands on the towel, which was covered with dull red smears.

'Was it him?'

Maigret shrugged his shoulders, standing motionless in the middle of the room.

'Shall I give his description to our boys, so that he can't get out of the hotel?'

'Go ahead!'

'It might be as well to send an inspector up on to the roof, in case . . .'

'All right . . .'

'Shall I inform the Chief?'

'Presently . . .'

It wasn't easy to talk to Maigret when he was in this sort of mood! Moreover, Lucas remembered sympathetically that his boss had said he was going to make a fool of himself.

Now he would incur more than ridicule. For he had mobilized a considerable body of police, but at a moment when it was too late, whereas a crime had just been committed under Maigret's very eyes almost with his consent, since it was he who had sent Ozep to the Hôtel Beauséjour!

'Suppose any of the gang come back? Am I to arrest them?'

A half-hearted nod of assent. Lucas went out. Maigret remained alone in the middle of the room, where the open window let in the bleak afternoon light.

He wiped his brow and automatically relit his pipe, which he had allowed to go out.

'What time is . . .'

Then, remembering that he was alone, he pulled his watch from his pocket. It was 3.35, and up above the accordion was still playing, which did not prevent the girl next door from sleeping as peacefully as an animal.

'Where is Maigret?' asked the Director of the Police Judiciaire as he got out of his car and met Lucas.

'In the room upstairs . . . No. 19 on the second floor. The hotel people don't know anything yet.'

A few minutes later the Director found Maigret sitting on a chair in the middle of the room, with the body beside him; he was smoking, with a stubborn look on his face. He scarcely noticed the arrival of his Chief.

'Well, Maigret, this looks as if we were really in a mess . . .'

The only response was a growl which meant nothing.

'So the famous killer was none other than the fellow who came to offer you his services! . . . Admit, Maigret, that you should have had your suspicions, and that Ozep's behaviour was ambiguous, to say the least . . .'

Maigret's brow was furrowed by a deep vertical frown, and his sternly jutting jaw gave his whole face a look of remarkable power.

'Do you think he's been unable to leave the hotel?'

'I'm sure of that,' replied the Superintendent off-handedly.

'Haven't you looked for him?'

'Not yet . . .'

'Do you think he'll let himself be caught easily?'

Then Maigret's gaze slowly turned from the window and fastened on his Chief. There was something impressive about his very slowness and hesitancy, the ambiguity of his sentences.

'If I am wrong, the man will try to kill several people before he lets himself be caught. If I'm not mistaken, it ought to be plain sailing.'

'What do you mean? Have you still any doubts about Stan the Killer and your Ozep being one and the same person?'

'I am convinced that a short while ago there were two people in this room and that one of them was Stan the Killer . . .'

'So then . . .'

'I tell you again, Chief; I may be mistaken, like anyone else. In that case I beg your pardon, for we'll be in a mess. The way this case seems to have worked out bothers me; I feel there's something amiss. If Ozep was Stan, there's no reason why . . .'

'Go on, tell me!'

'It would take too long . . . What time is it, Chief?'

'A quarter past four . . . why?'

'Oh, nothing . . .'

'Are you staying here, Maigret?'

'Until further orders, yes . . .'

'In the meantime I'll go and see what our men are up to . . .'

They had arrested Spinach, who, as Lucas had foreseen, was on his way to pay a visit to the young woman. They had told the Pole that his compatriot had been killed, and he had turned pale, but he had shown no sign of emotion at the mention of Ozep.

'She can't be dead, she can't!' he had repeated while they took him off to the station.

When this capture was reported to Maigret he merely growled: 'As if I cared!'

And he resumed his curious tête à tête with the dead woman. Half an hour later the one-eyed man came back and he, too, was arrested as he entered the house. He also submitted without protest, but when he heard of the young woman's death he tried to get free of his handcuffs and rush upstairs.

'Who's done that?' he cried. 'Who killed her? . . . It was your lot, wasn't it?'

'It was Ozep, otherwise known as Stan the Killer . . .'

And the man calmed down as though by magic, repeating with a frown: 'Ozep?'

'Are you trying to make us believe you don't know your boss?'

The Director himself was in charge of this hurried interrogation, in a corridor, and he had the impression that a slight smile flitted over the prisoner's lips.

One of the confederates, the one they called the Chemist, was examined next, and he merely replied to every question with an air of bewilderment, as though he had never heard speak of the young woman, or of Ozep, or of Stan . . .

Maigret was still upstairs, going over the same problem, hunting for the clue which would at last enable him to understand what had happened.

'All right!' he muttered when he heard of the arrest of the bearded man, who, after struggling frantically, had finally burst into tears.

Then Maigret suddenly looked up at Lucas, who had brought him this latest news.

'Don't you notice something?' he said. 'Four of them have been arrested, one after the other, and not one has put up any real resistance, whereas a man like Stan . . .'

'But since Stan is Ozep . . .'

'Have you found him?'

'Not yet. We had to let all the gang come back before turning the hotel upside down, otherwise they'd have suspected something and they wouldn't have walked into the trap. Now that we've practically got the lot, the Chief has begun to put the place under martial law. Our men are down below and are going to search everywhere meticulously, from the cellar to the attic if there is one . . .'

'Listen to me, Lucas . . .'

The sergeant had been about to leave, but he waited a moment, and his feeling for Maigret was akin to pity.

'I'm listening, Chief.'

'One-Eye is not Stan. Spinach is not Stan. The bearded fellow is not Stan. But I'm convinced that Stan lived in this hotel and was the focus of the whole group!'

Lucas refrained from speaking, leaving the Superintendent to ride his hobby horse.

'If Ozep had been Stan he had no reason to come here and kill an accomplice. If he was not Stan . . .'

And suddenly, standing up so abruptly that the sergeant gave a start:

'Look at this woman's shoulder . . . The left shoulder, yes . . .'

He bent forward himself. Lucas drew aside the woman's dress and uncovered white flesh on which was the mark with which, in America, they brand criminal women.

'Have you seen, Lucas?'

'But, Chief . . .'

'Don't you understand? *She* was Stan! . . . I had read something of the sort, but I hadn't made the connection because I was so firmly convinced that our Stan was a man . . . Four or five years ago, in America, a young woman led a gang of criminals in attacks on lonely farms, just as has been happening here . . . And, just as here, the victims had their throats cut by this woman, whose cruelty was described with a certain relish in the American papers . . .'

'She was that woman?'

'Almost certainly . . . I shall know that within an hour, if I can lay my hands on the requisite documents . . . I had cut a few pages out of a magazine one day . . . Are you coming, Lucas?'

Maigret hurried down the stairs, dragging his second-in-command after him. On the ground floor he ran into the Director.

'Where are you off to, Maigret?'

'To the Quai des Orfèvres, Chief. I think I've got it. In any case I'm taking Lucas along, and he'll come and tell you . . .'

Maigret hailed a taxi, unaware that he was incurring curious glances in which anger and pity were mingled.

'But what about Ozep?' inquired Lucas as he took his seat in the taxi.

'It's Ozep that I'm after . . . I mean that I hope to get some information about him . . . If he killed that woman, he must have had his reasons . . . Listen, Lucas: when I suggested sending him in to face the others, he accepted immediately. On the other hand when I asked him to take a message to the woman, he refused, and I was forced to

insist and even to threaten him. In other words, the others did not
know him but the woman did . . .'

As might have been expected, it took over half an hour to lay hands
on the right file, for tidiness was not Maigret's strong point, for all his
placid bearing.

'Read this! . . . Make allowances for the exaggeration of the American papers, which always try to give their readers their money's
worth: "Vampire Woman . . . Polish Murderess . . . Gang Leader
aged Twenty-three" . . .'

The woman's exploits were related in detail and illustrated with
copious photographs.

Stephanie Polintskaia, at eighteen, was already known to the
Warsaw police. About this time she met a man who married her and
tried to curb her criminal proclivities. She had a child by him, but one
day, on his return from work, he found the baby with its throat cut. As
for the woman, she had run off with the money and the few valuable
objects the house contained.

'Do you know who this man was?' asked Maigret.

'Ozep?'

'Here is his portrait, and it's a perfect likeness. Which proves that
one ought to be closely acquainted with the criminal archives of every
country in the world . . . You understand now? Stephanie, known to
her circle as Stan, led a life of crime in America. How she escaped
from that country's prisons, I don't know. The fact is that she took
refuge in France, where she resumed her exploits, without altering her
methods, having gathered a set of brutal characters around her as she
had done in America . . .

'Her husband learned through the press that she was in Paris, that
the police were on her tracks. Was he really anxious to save her
another time? I don't think so . . . I rather believe that he wanted to
make sure that the woman who so brutally murdered their child
would not go unpunished. That's why he came to me with offers of
help . . .

'He had not the courage to act on his own. He's a weak-willed, un-
stable character. He wanted the police to act with his help, and it was
I who this afternoon obliged him, so to speak, to make a move himself . . .

'Alone with his former wife, what could he do? He could kill or be
killed, for on finding herself discovered the woman would certainly
have had no hesitation in doing away with the only man capable of
denouncing her.

'He killed, therefore! And shall I tell you? I'm convinced that he'll
be found in some corner of the hotel, more or less seriously injured;
after trying to kill himself on two occasions and failing on both of

them, it'll be surprising if he doesn't attempt and fail a third time. Now you can go back and tell the Chief . . .'

'No need!' said the latter's voice. 'Stan the Killer has hanged himself in a room on the sixth floor, the door of which happened to be open . . . A good riddance!'

'Poor wretch!' sighed Maigret.

'You're sorry for him?'

'I am indeed . . . Particularly as I am to some extent responsible for his death . . . I don't know if I'm getting old, but I took a very long time to discover the solution . . .'

'What solution?' queried the Director of the Police Judiciaire, with a suspicious glance.

'The solution of the whole problem,' declared Lucas, glad of the chance to put in his word. 'The Superintendent has just reconstructed the story in every detail, and when you came in he was telling me that Ozep would be discovered in some corner where he'd tried to commit suicide . . .'

'Is that true, Maigret?'

'It's true. You know, if one goes on brooding over a single question . . . I don't think I've ever been so frantic in my life . . . I felt that the solution was there, quite close to me, so that it only needed the slightest . . . You were all buzzing round me like big flies and talking about small fry who didn't interest me . . . Ah well!'

He took a deep breath, filled his pipe and asked Lucas for matches, since he had used up all of his during the afternoon.

'Say, Chief! It's seven o'clock. Why don't we three all go and have a cold beer somewhere? On condition that Lucas removes his wig and makes himself look presentable . . .'

They were sitting round a table at the Brasserie Dauphine when suddenly the Superintendent clapped his hand to his forehead. He had just cast an instinctive glance at the waiter.

'And what about Janvier?' he asked.

'What about him?'

'He's not been relieved of his duty! Poor fellow, when I think that while we're drinking our beers he's still having to serve them!'

THE DROWNED MEN'S INN

I

'Will you really not take shelter?' the captain of the gendarmes urged Maigret, with a certain embarrassment.

And Maigret, his hands in his overcoat pockets, the brim of his bowler hat full of water which spilled over at his least movement, Maigret at his moodiest, massive and motionless, growled between teeth still clenched round the stem of his pipe:

'No!'

It's a remarkable fact that particularly tiresome cases, the ones which are the most difficult to disentangle and which end up more or less unpleasantly, are always those in which one has become involved rather stupidly through chance, or simply through lack of the courage to say no while there was still time.

Maigret was, once again, in this situation. He had come to Nemours, the previous evening, on a matter of minor importance that had to be settled with Captain Pillement of the gendarmerie.

Captain Pillement was a charming, cultured and athletic man, who had been trained at the artillery school in Saumur. He had insisted on doing Maigret the honours of his table and his cellar, and then, as it was pouring with rain, had invited him to spend the night in the guest room.

Autumn was at its worst, and for the past fortnight rain and fog had prevailed, while the Loing in full spate carried along branches of trees in its muddy waters.

'This was bound to happen,' sighed Maigret when, at six in the morning, while it was still dark, he heard the telephone bell ring.

A few moments later Captain Pillement was at his door, saying softly:

'Are you asleep, Superintendent?'

'No, I'm not asleep!'

'Would you like to come along with me to a place fifteen kilometres away? A curious accident has occurred there during the night . . .'

Maigret had gone there with him, of course – to the banks of the Loing, where the highway follows the course of the river, between Nemours and Montargis. The landscape was of a sort to put one off early rising for good. A cold lowering sky. Heavy slanting rain. The river a dirty brown, and beyond it the line of poplars that edged the canal.

There was no village. There was a single inn, the Auberge des Pêcheurs, seven hundred metres away, and Maigret already knew that it was known locally as *L'Auberge aux Noyés*, the Drowned Men's Inn.

As for the people who had been drowned there on this occasion, nothing was known about them yet. The crane was at work, creaking away, and a diver had gone down; there were two men in seamen's oilskins working his pump. Cars had drawn up, five or six of them at the roadside. Others, coming from both directions, slowed down and sometimes halted to see what was happening; then they went on their way.

There were uniformed gendarmes, there were ambulances summoned during the night whose services would obviously not be needed now.

It was just a matter of waiting until the car which was down there, in mid-stream under the swiftly flowing water, could be firmly fastened to the crane and hoisted out of the river.

A ten-ton lorry, one of those stinking monsters that travel by day and by night along main roads, was drawn up just before the bend in the road.

Nobody knew exactly what had happened. The night before, this lorry, which travelled regularly between Paris and Lyon, had driven along this road shortly after eight o'clock. At the turning, it had run into a stationary car with all its lights switched off, and the car had been sent hurtling into the Loing.

The driver, Joseph Lecoin, had thought he heard cries and the skipper of the barge *Belle-Thérèse*, which was moored in the canal less than a hundred metres away, asserted that he too had heard someone shouting for help.

The two men had met on the river bank and had searched, after a fashion, with the aid of a lantern. Then the lorry driver had gone on his way as far as Montargis, where he had informed the gendarmerie.

The spot where this accident had occurred being within the jurisdiction of Nemours, the gendarmerie of that town had duly been informed, but since nothing could be attempted before daybreak it was not until 6 a.m. that the lieutenant had woken his captain.

The scene was a depressing one. Everybody was cold, and stood with hunched shoulders glancing at the muddy water without even very much anxiety.

The innkeeper was there, sheltering under a huge umbrella, and discussing the matter knowledgeably.

'Unless the bodies are wedged in the car, they won't be recovered for a long time, for all the weirs are down and they'll float as far as the

Seine unless they get caught in tree-roots.'

'They're surely not in the car,' retorted the lorry driver, 'because it was an open car!'

'That's odd!'

'Why?'

'Because yesterday a young couple in an open car came to stay the night and had lunch at the inn. They were to come back tonight but I haven't seen them again.'

Maigret was not really listening to this chatter, but he heard it and recorded it involuntarily.

Finally the diver emerged and the others quickly unfastened his big brass helmet.

'You can get going,' he announced. 'I've hooked on the pulley-block.'

Motorists were hooting on the road, puzzled by the sight of this gathering. Heads appeared at car windows.

The crane, which had been brought from Montargis, was making an intolerable din, and at last the upper part of a grey car was brought up out of the water, followed by the wheels . . .

Maigret's feet were wet and the bottom of his trousers muddy. He would have liked a cup of hot coffee, but he did not want to leave the place to go as far as the inn, and the captain of the gendarmerie did not venture to distract his attention.

'Careful, boys! . . . Keep it clear on the left . . .'

The front of the car showed clear traces of the collision, thus proving that, as the lorry driver had already said, the roadster had been facing towards Paris at the time of the crash.

'Up she goes! . . . One . . . Two . . . Up she goes! . . .'

At last the car stood on the bank. It looked strange with its twisted wheels, its mudguards crumpled like paper, its seats already covered with mud and rubbish.

The lieutenant of gendarmerie noted the registration number, while the captain searched the dashboard for the plate bearing the owner's name. It was inscribed: R. Daubois, 135 Avenue des Ternes, Paris.

'I'll call Paris, shall I, Superintendent?'

Maigret seemed to be saying: 'Do as you please, it's no concern of mine!'

This was a job for the gendarmerie, and not for the Superintendent of the Police Judiciaire. A sergeant on a motor cycle dashed off to call Paris. Everybody, including a dozen curious onlookers who had got out of passing cars, surrounded the wreck that had been brought up out of the water, and some of them automatically felt the coachwork or leaned forward to look inside.

It was one of the crowd, in fact, who out of curiosity turned the nandle of the luggage compartment. The car was so battered that it opened unexpectedly, and the man uttered a cry and started back, while his neighbours pressed forward to look.

Maigret went up with the rest, frowned, and for the first time that morning spoke instead of merely grunting.

'Now then, back, everyone! . . . Don't touch anything!'

He, too, had seen. He had seen a human figure curiously doubled up, crammed into the back of the luggage compartment as though some effort had been required to close the lid. A mass of platinum blonde hair showed that the bundle was the body of a woman.

'Captain! Clear the ground, will you? There's something new, something rather unpleasant . . .'

And an unpleasant task in prospect! To begin with, the dripping corpse had to be extracted from the car . . .

'Don't you smell something?'

'Yes . . .'

'Don't you think that . . .'

And they had the proof of it a quarter of an hour later. One of the motorists who had stopped to look happened to be a doctor. He examined the corpse on the bank beside the road, and the curious crowd of onlookers, including children, had to be kept back.

'She has been dead at least three days.'

Someone pulled Maigret by the sleeve. It was Justin Rozier, the innkeeper from the Auberge aux Noyés.

'I recognize the car,' he declared, deliberately assuming an air of mystery. 'It belonged to my young couple!'

'Have you got their names?'

'They filled in a form.'

The doctor spoke again. 'Do you realise that this woman has been murdered?'

'With what?'

'A razor. She's had her throat cut.'

And the rain still poured down on the car and on the corpse and on all the black figures moving to and fro in the greyness.

The motor cycle reappeared, and the sergeant jumped down.

'The car doesn't belong to Monsieur Daubois any longer; I spoke to him personally on the phone. He sold it last week to a garage owner at the Porte Maillot.'

'What does the garage owner say?'

'I called him too. The garage sold the car again three days ago to a young man who paid cash down and therefore left no name.'

'But I tell you I've got the name!' broke in the innkeeper, impatiently, obviously feeling that he was not getting enough attention.

'Just come up to my place and . . .'

Meanwhile a redheaded fellow had come on the scene, a journalist from the one local paper of Montargis who was also correspondent of a big Paris daily. Heaven knows how he carried out his inquiry, for Maigret sent him packing and so did Captain Pillement, which however did not prevent him, almost immediately afterwards, from spending over a quarter of an hour in the telephone booth.

An hour later, the policeman responsible for keeping inquisitive people from invading the inn was besieged by reporters armed with their press cards. Photographers were there too, climbing on to tables and chairs and taking pictures which had nothing to do with with the tragedy.

As for Maigret, he was on the phone to Paris, getting the answer to his request.

'The Criminal Investigation Department agrees. Since you're there, carry on with the inquiry unofficially. You'll be sent an inspector from the Rue des Saussaies later in the day . . .'

It was a curious affair, and the inn was a curious place, oddly situated at a sudden bend in the road. Hadn't Maigret just been told that this was the third car in the last five years to have fallen into the Loing at just this spot?

The other two cases had been less mysterious: cars being driven at top speed which had not anticipated the turning, and, unable to change course, had plunged into the river. In one of them a family of five had been trapped. In the other there had only been one victim.

The place had nonetheless earned its nickname, particularly as one Whitsunday a young woman had deliberately drowned herself there for personal motives while her husband was fishing a hundred metres further on.

The Auberge aux Noyés! A glance at the telephone booth, which journalists were occupying one after the other, told one that before the day was up it would be famous.

. . . *The Crime at Drowning Corner* . . . *The Mystery of the Auberge aux Noyés* . . . *The Body in the Car* . . . *The Puzzle of the Grey Car* . . .

Maigret, calm and stolid, went on smoking his pipe, devoured a huge ham sandwich with a glass of beer, and observed without the least curiosity the traditional agitation which invariably complicates the task of the police.

In all this crowd, two people alone interested him: the skipper of the *Belle-Thérèse* and the driver of the lorry.

The skipper had come to ask him humbly:

'You know we get a bonus for speed . . . I should have left this morning . . . So if I might possibly . . .'

'Where are you going to unload?'

'Quai des Tournelles in Paris . . . Another day on the canal, then nearly a day on the Seine. We'll be there by evening the day after to-morrow . . .'

Maigret got him to repeat his statement:

'We'd finished supper and my wife had gone to bed already. I was going to bed myself when I heard a queer noise . . . From inside the boat you can't quite make out what's happening. I stuck my head through the hatch . . . I thought I heard a voice calling for help . . .'

'What sort of voice?'

'Oh, a voice . . . The rain was rattling down on the iron roof . . . A voice that sounded far away . . .'

'A man's voice or a woman's?'

'More like a man's!'

'How long after the first noise?'

'Not quite immediately, because I'd been taking my shoes off and I had time to put on my slippers . . .'

'What did you do next?'

'I couldn't go out there in slippers. I went downstairs again; I put on my leather jacket and my rubber boots. I said to my wife, who wasn't asleep yet: "Maybe somebody's drowning . . ."'

Maigret pressed him: 'Why did you think it was somebody drowning?'

'Because, along the river and the canal, if we hear somebody calling for help, it generally means that! With my boathook, I've saved half a dozen of them.'

'So you made for the river?'

'I was practically there, you see, because at that point there's less than twenty metres between the canal and the Loing. I saw the lights of a lorry. Then I noticed a big fellow walking about . . .'

'The lorry driver . . . was that who it was?'

'Yes. He told me he'd run into a car and it had rolled into the river. I went to fetch my torch.'

'And all this took a certain time?'

'Yes, in fact it did!'

'What was the lorry driver doing meanwhile?'

'I don't know . . . I suppose he was trying to make out something in the darkness.'

'Did you go up to his lorry?'

'I may have done . . . I don't remember. I was chiefly trying to see if a body could have come to the surface . . .'

'So you don't know if the driver was alone in his lorry?'

'I suppose he was. If anyone else had been there they'd have come to help us.'

'When you realised there was nothing to be done, what did the driver say to you?'

'That he'd go and inform the gendarmerie.'

'He didn't specify where?'

'No . . . I don't think so . . .'

'You never thought of pointing out that he could telephone from the inn, which is only seven hundred metres away?'

'I thought of that afterwards, when I saw that he'd driven off . . .'

The driver was of Herculean build. He had rung up his employers to warn them that he had been detained by the police following an accident, and he was waiting quite patiently to see what would happen, being treated to drinks by the journalists in return for endlessly retailing his story.

Maigret took him aside into a small private dining-room with a couch in it which clearly suggested that the inn with the ominous name was welcoming to loving couples.

'I thought lorry drivers usually travelled in pairs, especially on long journeys?'

'Yes, we mostly do! My mate hurt his hand a week ago and he's on sick leave, so I travel on my own.'

'What time did you leave Paris?'

'At two o'clock. I've got a mixed load and I couldn't go fast on these slippery roads.'

'I suppose you stopped for dinner at a regular drivers' pull-up?'

'You're right there! We have our own places, and we meet there at more or less the same time. I stopped right after Nemours at Mère Catherine's, where the food's first class.'

'How many lorries were parked there?'

'Four. Two removal vans from Morin's, a petrol tanker and an express delivery van.'

'Did you eat with the other drivers?'

'With three of them. The others were at the next table.'

'In what order did you leave?'

'I don't know about the others. I left last because I was putting through a phone call to Paris.'

'Whom were you calling?'

'My boss, to have some piston-rings ready for me at Moulins. I'd noticed that the engine wasn't running smoothly and that the third cylinder . . .'

'All right! How far away from your mates were you?'

'I left ten minutes after the last of them, one of the removal vans. As I was going faster, he must have been four or five kilometres ahead of me . . .'

'And you didn't see the roadster until you ran into it?'

'When it was a few metres away, too late to avoid a crash.'

'There were no lights on?'

'None at all!'

'And you saw nobody?'

'I can't say. It was raining. My windscreen wiper isn't too good. All I know is that when the car was in the water I fancied I saw someone in the darkness, trying to swim. Then I heard a sort of cry for help . . .'

'One more question: just now, in the box under your seat, I noticed an electric torch, in good working order. Why didn't you pick it up?'

'I don't know . . . I was panicking . . . I was afraid my truck might skid into the river too . . .'

'When you passed the inn, wasn't it lit up?'

'It may have been!'

'Do you often take this road?'

'Twice a week.'

'Didn't it occur to you to telephone from the inn?'

'No! I remembered Montargis wasn't far off, so I went there . . .'

'While you were looking around, could anybody have hidden in your truck?'

'I don't think so.'

'Why not?'

'Because they'd have had to unfasten the ropes of the tarpaulin.'

'Thank you. You'll stay here, of course, in case I need you.'

'If I can be of any use to you!'

His only concern was to eat and drink his fill, and Maigret saw him go off to the kitchen to arrange for his midday meal.

The cooking was done by Madame Rozier, a lean sallow woman who was finding it hard to cope with the sudden rush of customers. Added to which, the journalists would not even let her get to the telephone to order supplies from the town.

A young barmaid, Lili, over-pert for her age, was joking with everybody as she served apéritifs, and the landlord, at the bar, had not a moment's breathing-space.

It was the off-season; whereas in summer the inn could count on tourists, lovers and fishermen, its autumn customers generally consisted only of a few sportsmen from Paris who hired a shoot in the neighbourhood and ordered their meals for a set day.

Rozier had stated to Maigret:

'The day before yesterday, in the evening, a young couple turned up in a grey car, the one that's been fished out of the river. I assumed they must be a honeymoon couple. Here's the form they filled in for me.'

The writing on the form was spiky and irregular. It read:

'Jean Vertbois, 20 years of age, advertising agent, 18 Rue des Acacias, Paris.'

He was described as coming from Paris and going to Nice.

Finally, when he had been asked to fill in a form for his companion, he had scrawled across his own: 'And Madame.'

The information had already been telephoned through to Paris, and an inquiry was in progress in the Rue des Acacias, in the 17th arrondissement, not far from the garage where the car had been purchased.

'A very pretty young lady, seventeen or eighteen,' the landlord answered Maigret's question. 'The chick, I called her privately! She was wearing a dress that was too thin for the time of year and a sports coat . . .'

'Did they have luggage?'

'One suitcase, it's still up there . . .'

The suitcase contained only a man's clothes and underwear, which suggested that the mysterious girl had left home unexpectedly.

'Did they seem nervous?'

'Not particularly . . . To tell you the truth they were chiefly thinking about making love, and they spent most of yesterday in their bedroom . . . They had their lunch taken up there, and Lili observed that it was an awkward business serving people who took so little trouble to hide their feelings . . . You see what I mean?'

'They didn't tell you why, if they were on their way to Nice, they stopped less than a hundred kilometres from Paris?'

'I fancy they'd have stopped anywhere, provided they could have a bedroom . . .'

'And the car?'

'It was in the garage. You've seen it. A classy car, but fairly old, the sort people buy who haven't a great deal of money. It looks rich and it costs less than a mass-produced car.'

'You never tried to open the luggage compartment out of curiosity?'

'I'd never have taken such a liberty.'

Maigret shrugged his shoulders, for the fellow had nothing worth while to tell him and he knew how inquisitive that type of landlord is.

'In short, the couple was expected back to sleep in the hotel?'

'To sleep and to dine. We waited until ten o'clock to clear away.'

'At what time was the car taken out of the garage?'

'Let's see . . . It was dark already . . . About half-past four . . . I assumed that after spending so long shut up in their bedroom the young people had felt like going off for a jaunt to Montargis or elsewhere. The suitcase was still there, so I wasn't worried about the bill.'

'You knew nothing about the accident?'

'Nothing until the gendarmes turned up about eleven at night.'

'And you immediately thought it must be something to do with your guests?'

'I was afraid of it. I had noticed how clumsily the young man had backed out of the garage. He was obviously an inexperienced driver. Now we know about the sharp bend by the river.'

'You noticed nothing suspicious in these people's conversation?'

'I didn't listen to their conversation.'

In brief, the situation was as follows:

On Monday, about 5 p.m., a certain Jean Vertbois, aged twenty, an advertising agent, resident at 18 Rue des Acacias, Paris, had bought from a garage near his home a luxurious but old-fashioned car, for which he had paid with five thousand-franc notes. (The garage owner, Maigret had just been informed, had the impression that there was still a thick wad of notes in his customer's wallet. Vertbois had not tried to bargain with him, but had mentioned that he would have the identity plate changed next day. He had been alone when he visited the garage.)

Nothing was as yet known about Tuesday's happenings.

On Wednesday evening the same Vertbois, with his car, had arrived at the Auberge aux Noyés, less than a hundred kilometres from Paris, accompanied by a very young girl whom the landlord, presumably an experienced judge, had taken for a girl of good social standing.

On Thursday the couple had gone out in their car as though for a pleasure trip in the neighbourhood, and a few hours later the car, with all its lights out, was run into by a lorry at seven hundred metres from the inn, and both the lorry driver and the skipper of a barge had apparently heard cries for help in the darkness.

Of Jean Vertbois and the girl there was no trace. The whole police force of the district had been searching since early morning. They had drawn blank at railway stations; and nobody corresponding to the description of the missing couple had been seen at any farm or inn, or on any of the roads.

On the other hand, in the luggage compartment of the car, the body of a woman had been found, aged between forty-five and fifty, well groomed and smartly dressed.

And the pathologist confirmed the observation made by the first doctor, namely that the woman had been slashed to death with a razor on the previous Monday!

With less certainty, the pathologist had suggested that the body had been somewhat clumsily packed into the luggage compartment of the car only a few hours after death.

The conclusion was that there was already a corpse in the car when the couple drove up to the inn!

Was Vertbois aware of this? And was his young companion?

What was their car doing at eight in the evening, all lights out, on the edge of the road?

Had there been a breakdown, which an inexperienced driver could not deal with?

Who had been in the car at the time?

And who had called out in the darkness?

The captain of gendarmerie, being the soul of tact, had not wanted to disturb Maigret in his inquiry, but was meanwhile endeavouring, with his men, to collect as much evidence as possible.

Ten flat-bottomed boats went to and fro along the Loing, which was being searched with hooks. Some men were splashing about on the river banks, others busied themselves around the weirs.

The journalists considered the inn as conquered territory and established themselves there, filling every room in the place with their din.

The *Belle-Thérèse* had set off towards the Quai des Tournelles with her cargo of tiles, and the truck driver, quite indifferent to all this excitement, was philosophically enjoying an unexpected holiday with pay.

The rotary presses of newspapers had begun to print their headlines, the most sensational being in the heaviest type, such as one reporter's effort:

Teen-age Lovers Carry Corpse in back of Car

then, in italics:

The muddy waters of the Loing engulf the guilty couple and their victim

This was the gloomy period of the inquiry, during which Maigret, on edge, spoke to nobody, growled, drank beer and smoked pipes, while he prowled about like a caged bear; it was the uncertain period, in which all the data that have been collected seem to contradict one another, and when one searches in vain amid a jumble of futile information for a guiding thread, in constant fear of picking the wrong one which will lead nowhere.

The crowning misfortune was that the inn was poorly heated, and with central heating at that, which the Superintendent particularly loathed. Furthermore, the cooking was poor and the sauces were diluted in order to cope with the increased demand.

'You'll forgive me for what I'm going to say to you, Superintendent . . .'

Captain Pillement, a sly smile on his lips, sat down at last in front of an excessively ungracious Maigret.

'I know you're annoyed with me. But I myself am delighted to have kept you here, for I'm beginning to think that this road accident which started off in so commonplace a fashion is gradually going to turn into one of the most mysterious cases imaginable.'

Maigret merely went on helping himself to potato salad, sardines and beetroot, the inevitable hors d'oeuvres served in bad inns.

'When we know the identity of the pretty girl who was so much in love . . .'

A big, mud-splashed car, driven by a chauffeur in uniform, drew up in front of the door, and a grey-haired man got out, instinctively recoiling before the relentless assault of the photographers.

'Look at this!' murmured Maigret. 'I bet that's her father!'

II

The Superintendent had not been mistaken, but if he apprehended a painful scene it was spared him, thanks to the remarkable dignity of the lawyer Monsieur La Pommeraye. After dismissing the journalists with a wave of the hand, like one used to displaying his authority, he had followed Maigret into the little private dining-room and introduced himself.

'Germain La Pommeraye, notary at Versailles.'

His profession, and the royal town where he practised it, were perfectly in keeping with his tall, elegant figure, his pale complexion, and the features which barely quivered as he inquired, with his eyes fixed on the floor:

'Have you found her?'

'I shall be obliged,' Maigret sighed, 'to ask you a certain number of questions for which I apologize.'

The notary waved his hand as though to say: 'Carry on! I know what you're going to ask . . .'

'Can you tell me, first, what made you think your daughter might be involved in this affair?'

'You'll understand. My daughter Viviane is seventeen and looks twenty. I said *is* although I suppose by now I should perhaps have said *was*. She's a creature of impulse, like her mother. And, rightly or wrongly, particularly since I became a widower, I have always been unwilling to thwart her instincts. I don't know where she made the acquaintance of this Jean Vertbois, but I think I recall that it was at the swimming pool, or in a sports club whose grounds are in the neighbourhood of the Bois de Boulogne.'

'Do you know Jean Vertbois personally?'

'I met him once. My daughter, as I said, is impulsive. One evening she suddenly announced to me: "Daddy, I'm going to get married!"'

Maigret rose, suddenly opened the door, glanced with contempt at the journalist who had his ear pressed to it.

'Go on, monsieur!'

'At first I took the thing as a joke. Then, seeing that it was a serious matter, I asked to see her suitor. That was how Jean Vertbois turned up at Versailles one afternoon. One detail displeased me from the start; he drove up in a fast sports car borrowed from a friend. Do you see what I mean? Young men have every right to be ambitious, but I object when at the age of twenty they indulge their taste for luxury at little expense to themselves, particularly for a luxury which is in rather bad taste . . .'

'In short, the interview was scarcely a friendly one?'

'It was definitely stormy. I asked the young man how he expected to support a wife, and he replied with disconcerting frankness that pending an improvement in his financial situation my daughter's dowry would at all events prevent her from starving. As you see, the very type of shameless little opportunist in words as well as in attitude! So much so that I wondered for a moment if this shamelessness could not perhaps be a pose concealing a certain timidity.

'Vertbois held forth to me at length on the way parents assume rights, and on the reactionary ideas of certain bourgeois of whom I was obviously considered the perfect representative.

'After an hour I flung him out.'

'How long ago was this?' asked Maigret.

'Barely a week. When I saw my daughter afterwards she declared that she would marry Vertbois and nobody else, that I didn't know him, that I had misjudged him, and so forth. And she actually threatened to run away with him if I would not agree to their marriage.'

'You stood firm?'

'Unfortunately I believed it was an empty threat. I counted on the lapse of time to settle things. And now, since yesterday afternoon, Viviane has disappeared. I went round that evening to the Rue des Acacias, where Vertbois lives, but I was told he had gone off on a journey. I questioned the concierge and I ascertained that he had been accompanied by a very young girl, who must have been Viviane. That's why, when I read in the midday papers the account of last night's happenings . . .'

He retained his quiet dignity. Yet there were beads of sweat on his forehead as, with averted eyes, he said:

'One thing I beg of you, Superintendent: be frank! I'm still tough enough to take a direct blow, but I shouldn't find it easy to stand up to a long period of alternating hope and despair. In your opinion, is my daughter still alive?'

There was a long pause before Maigret replied:

'Let me first of all ask you one final question. You seem to know your daughter well. It looks as if her love for Vertbois was a whole-hearted romantic passion. Do you think your daughter, if she learned that Vertbois was a murderer, would have become his accomplice out of love? Don't be in a hurry to reply. Suppose your daughter, on arriving at her lover's – which he was, in the fullest sense of the word, I'm afraid – learned that in order to be able to escape with her and find the money necessary for this elopement he had been driven to kill someone . . .'

The two men fell silent. At last Monsieur La Pommeraye sighed:

'I don't know . . . However I can tell you one thing, Superintendent, something that nobody else knows. I told you just now I was a widower. That is true. My wife died three years ago in South America, where she had gone to live with a coffee planter eight years previously. Now when she left me she took a hundred thousand francs out of the safe in my office. Viviane is like her mother . . .'

He was startled to hear Maigret say with a sigh:

'I hope so!'

'What do you mean?'

'Because if Jean Vertbois has nothing to fear from his companion, he has no reason to get rid of her. If, on the other hand, when your daughter discovered the body in the boot she displayed indignation and uttered threats . . .'

'I follow your argument, but I don't understand the sequence of events as described in the newspapers. When the collision took place the car was not empty, since the lorry driver and the bargee both heard cries. Vertbois and Viviane had no reason to separate. So it's likely . . .'

'The men have been dredging the river all day, so far without results. May I ask you to come with me for a moment into the room the couple occupied in this inn?'

It was a commonplace room with a floral-patterned wallpaper, a brass bedstead, a mahogany wardrobe. On the dressing table stood a few toilet articles, a razor, a shaving brush, and two toothbrushes, one of them new.

'You see,' Maigret observed. 'The man had his personal belongings. But the couple must have stopped somewhere on the way to buy a toothbrush for the girl, and those travelling slippers that I see beside the bed. But I should have liked to find some proof that it really was your daughter who . . .'

'Here's the proof!' the father said sadly, pointing to a piece of jewellery gleaming on the mat. 'Viviane always wore these earrings, which belonged to her mother. One of them fastened badly, and she kept losing it and finding it again as though by miracle. This is it! Now do you still believe I've any hope of finding my daughter alive?'

Maigret dared not answer by saying that in that case Mademoiselle Viviane La Pommeraye would probably be charged with complicity in a murder!

After much pressure, the notary had been persuaded to return to Versailles, and under the unceasing rain the Auberge aux Noyés had come to look more and more like an army headquarters.

Journalists, tired of standing about in the rain watching the watermen exploring the river, had resigned themselves to a game of *belote*. The captain of gendarmerie had put his car at Maigret's disposal, but the Superintendent made no use of it, and his haphazard activities were not such as to inspire confidence in anyone ignorant of his methods.

So, when they saw him go into the telephone booth, the reporters imagined they were about to learn something fresh, and, with professional indiscretion, they unhesitatingly surrounded the door.

But it was to the Paris Observatory that Maigret had been telephoning, asking first for the latest weather forecast, and insisting on certain details.

'You say there was no moon yesterday at about 8 p.m.? Will it be so again tonight? It rises at ten minutes past midnight? Thank you . . .'

As he left the telephone booth he seemed really satisfied with himself. He even took a mischievous pleasure in saying to the journalists:

'Good news, gentlemen; we shall have torrential rain for three more days.'

After which he was seen holding a lengthy conversation with Captain Pillement, who disappeared and was not seen again that day.

There was some hard drinking going on. Someone had discovered a bottle of Vouvray, and everybody wanted some of it; Lili, moving from one table to another, encountered roving hands which she did not repulse too sharply.

Darkness, falling at half-past four, put an end to investigations in the Loing and it was becoming unlikely that the body or bodies would be recovered, since by this time they would have been carried downstream as far as the Seine.

To clear the road, a breakdown truck had come to fetch the car that had been fished out of the river, and had taken it to Montargis, where it was impounded by the police.

It was six o'clock when a reporter called out to the innkeeper:

'What are you giving us for dinner tonight?'

And a voice was heard replying:

'Nothing!'

Nobody was more surprised than the innkeeper, who looked round to see who had dared to speak in his place and particularly in a way so damaging to his business. It was Maigret, who stepped forward calmly.

'I am going to ask you, gentlemen, not to dine here tonight. I don't forbid you to come back about ten o'clock if you feel like it, and even to sleep at the inn. But between seven and nine I am anxious for the place to be occupied only by those people who were here last night . . .'

'A reconstruction?' some smart-aleck interrupted.

'Not even that! I warn you straight away that it's no use hiding in the neighbourhood, for you would see nothing. On the other hand, if you behave well, you'll probably have a fine scoop for tomorrow's issue . . .'

'At what time?'

'Let's say before eleven . . . I know a place at Montargis where you can get a first-class meal: the Hôtel de la Cloche . . . Go there, all of you. Tell the proprietor that I sent you, and you'll be very well looked after. When I come to join you . . .'

'You're not dining with us?'

'I'm already engaged. But I shan't be late . . . Now, you can take it or leave it, and if anyone wants to play it smart I can guarantee he won't get the slightest bit of information. Well, gentlemen, goodbye and good eating!'

When they had left he breathed more freely, and cast a mischievous glance at the landlord, who was furious.

'Come, come! You make your money from selling drinks and not from serving meals. Now they've been drinking ever since this morning . . .'

'They'd have gone on!'

'Listen to me! It's essential that between seven and ten everyone should be in the same place as yesterday, and that the same lights should be on.'

'That's easy enough.'

There was still somebody there who seemed to have been forgotten. Joseph Lecoin, the lorry driver. He stared at Maigret in astonishment, and finally spoke up.

'What about me?'

'You're going to drive me to Nemours.'

'In the lorry?'

'Well, why not? Failing a ritzy limousine . . .'

And so Superintendent Maigret left the Auberge aux Noyés on the seat of a ten-ton lorry which kept up an infernal racket.

III

'Where shall I drop you?'

They had driven in silence, in the darkness, in the rain, meeting cars that dipped their headlights, and the windscreen wiper kept up a regular humming like a great bumble-bee.

'You're not going to drop me anywhere, old man!'

The driver looked at his companion in astonishment, thinking he must be joking.

'So what? Are we going back to Paris?'

'No! Let me just look at the time . . .'

He had to strike a light to see his watch, the hands of which stood at half-past seven.

'Good, we've got time. Stop at the first pub you see . . .'

And Maigret turned up his coat collar as they crossed the pavement; then he stood with his elbows propped in easy-going fashion on the bar-counter of a small tavern, while Lecoin, by his side, wondered at this sudden change of attitude.

Not that the Superintendent had become at all threatening, or showed the least trace of ill-humour; on the contrary, he was calm, and from time to time there was even a twinkle in his eyes. He was full of self-confidence, and if he had been asked he would readily have replied: Life's good!

He savoured his apéritif, looked at his watch again, paid for the drinks and announced:

'Off we go!'

'Where are we going?'

'First to have dinner at Mère Catherine's, as you did last night. You see! It's raining just as hard; it's just the same time of night . . .'

There were only three lorries outside the inn, which was unprepossessing in appearance but in which lorry drivers knew they could enjoy a well-cooked meal. The proprietress served it herself, assisted by her fourteen-year-old daughter.

'Hello, you back again?' she greeted Lecoin with some surprise.

He shook hands with his fellow-drivers and sat down in a corner with the Superintendent.

'Suppose we ordered the same thing that you had yesterday?' suggested Maigret.

'Here there aren't umpteen dishes to choose from. You have to take what's on the list . . . Look, it's *fricandeau* of veal with sorrel . . .'

'One of my favourite dishes . . .'

Had not the last few minutes revealed a certain alteration in the attitude of the big lorry driver? His mood seemed less forthright. He kept glancing stealthily at his companion, wondering no doubt what the policeman was getting at.

'Come on, Catherine! We haven't got time to waste . . .'

'You always say that, and then you spend a quarter of an hour over your coffee . . .'

The *fricandeau* was perfect, the coffee more like real coffee than what is usually served in bistros. From time to time Maigret pulled out his watch, and seemed to await the departure of the other drivers with some impatience.

They got up at last, after a round of old *marc*, and soon afterwards the purr of their engines was heard.

'*Marc* for us too,' ordered Maigret. To Lecoin he said:

'That's how it was yesterday, wasn't it?'

'Yes, indeed. Just about this time I was going off, I'd had my phone call . . .'

'Let's go!'

'Back there?'

'Do just what you did yesterday . . . Do you mind?'

'No; why should I mind? Since I've got nothing to hide . . .'

Just at that moment Catherine came up and asked the driver:

'Did you give my message to Benoît?'

'Yes, it's all settled!'

Once back in the lorry, Maigret asked: 'Who is Benoît?'

'He keeps a petrol pump at Montargis. He's a pal of mine. I always stop there to fill up. Old Catherine wants to have a pump fixed up at her place, and I was to tell Benoît . . .'

'It's raining hard, isn't it!'

'Even a bit harder than yesterday . . . Just think! when one has to travel all night in such muck . . .'

'We're not going too fast?'

'Same as yesterday . . .'

Maigret lit his pipe.

'We chaps always get the blame,' Lecoin was muttering, 'because we keep to the middle of the road or don't pull over fast enough. But if people who drive small cars had to cope with monsters like ours . . .'

He let out a sudden oath and braked so violently that Maigret was almost thrown head first into the windscreen.

'Good Lord!' cried Joseph Lecoin. And he looked at his compaion with a frown, muttering:

'Was it you who put it there?'

For there was, in fact, a car standing exactly where Jean Vertbois's car had been hit the day before. A grey car, too! and its lights were off, and the rain was falling, and the night was dark!

And yet the lorry had stopped more than three metres away from the car!

For a moment the lorry driver's face had betrayed incipient anger, but he merely growled:

'You might have warned me . . . Suppose I hadn't seen it in time . . .'

'And yet we were busy talking . . .'

'What about it?'

'Yesterday you were by yourself. You had nothing to distract your attention . . .'

And Lecoin asked, with a shrug:

'What do you want now?'

'We're going to get down . . . This way . . . Wait a minute . . . I want to try an experiment. Shout for help . . .'

'Me?'

'Since the people who were shouting yesterday aren't there, someone has to take their place.'

And Lecoin shouted unwillingly, scenting a snare.

His most anxious moment came when he heard footsteps and saw a figure moving in the darkness.

'Come here!' Maigret called out to the newcomer.

This was the skipper of the *Belle-Thérèse*, whom the Superintendent had summoned through the gendarmerie without telling anyone.

'Well?'

'It's not easy to say definitely . . . I think it was about the same . . .'

'What's that?' growled Lecoin.

'I don't know who shouted, but I'm saying it was more or less the same sound as yesterday.'

This time the big fellow was on the point of losing his temper and hitting out at the skipper, who was unaware of the part he was playing in this performance.

'Get back into the lorry!'

Someone else now came up, someone who had hitherto not stirred: it was Captain Pillement.

'It's going all right!' Maigret told him in a low voice. 'We shall see what happens next . . .'

And he went back to sit beside Lecoin, who was making no further effort to seem pleasant.

'What am I to do now?'

'What you did yesterday!'

'Go to Montargis?'

'Just as you did yesterday!'

'All right! I don't know what idea you've got in your head, but if you think I've anything to do with this affair . . .'

They were already passing the inn, where four windows were lit up, on one of which the telephone number was inscribed in enamel letters.

'So you never thought of stopping to telephone?'

'I've already told you so . . .'

'Carry on!'

Silence; Maigret smoked his pipe in his dark corner, beside the sullen man with his occasional abrupt movements.

They reached Montargis, and suddenly the Superintendent remarked:

'You've gone past it . . .'

'What?'

'The gendarmerie . . .'

'That was your fault, making all this fuss . . .'

He started to back the lorry, for the gendarmerie station was only fifty metres away.

'No, no, carry on!' Maigret protested.

'Carry on what?'

'Doing just what you did yesterday . . .'

'But I went . . .'

'You didn't go straight to the gendarmerie. The proof is that the times don't fit . . . Where is Benoît's filling station?'

'At the second turning.'

'Let's go there!'

'What for?'

'Nothing. Do what I tell you.'

It was a very ordinary filling station, in front of a house with a bicycle shop below. The shop was not lit up, but through the windows one could see at the back of it a kitchen in which shadowy figures were moving.

The lorry had scarcely stopped when a man emerged from the kitchen, having obviously heard the engine and the grinding of the brakes.

'How many litres?' he asked without glancing at the lorry. Then, a minute later, he recognized it, and looked up at Lecoin, asking:

'What are you doing here? I thought . . .'

'Give me fifty litres!'

Maigret sat still in his corner, unseen by the mechanic. Benoît, thinking himself alone with his friend, might perhaps have talked, but Lecoin, sensing the danger, remarked hastily:

'Is that all you want, then, Monsieur le commissaire?'

'Oh, is there somebody with you?'

'Someone from the police who's doing what he calls a reconstruction. I don't understand a thing about it. It's always people like us that get pestered, while . . .'

Maigret had jumped out of the lorry and gone into the shop, to the great surprise of its owner. He had caught sight of the man's wife in the room at the back.

'Lecoin wants to know how things are going . . .' he remarked on the off-chance.

She looked at him suspiciously and leaned forward to peer through the window.

'Is Lecoin there?' she asked.

'He's filling up.'

'He's not got into any trouble?'

Anxiously, puzzled by the intrusion of this bowler-hatted man, she went to the door.

It was difficult, in the bad light, to make out people's faces.

'Say, Paul . . .' she said to her husband, who was encumbered with his petrol hose. 'Is Lecoin there?'

Maigret, taking advantage of the shelter of the shop, quietly filled his pipe and lighted it, thus casting a momentary gleam on the nickel handlebars of the cycles.

'Are you coming in, Paul?'

Then the Superintendent clearly heard one of the two men asking the other:

'What'll we do?'

By way of precaution he seized his revolver and kept it in his pocket, ready to fire through his coat if necessary. The street was deserted and dark, and Lecoin was big enough to fell an adversary with one blow of his fist.

'What would *you* do?'

The woman was still standing in the doorway, her shoulders hunched against the cold. Joseph Lecoin climbed down heavily from his seat and took a couple of steps undecidedly along the pavement.

'Suppose we go and discuss things inside?' Maigret said calmly.

Benoît hung up his petrol hose. Lecoin, who seemed still undecided, was screwing up the stopper of his tank.

Finally he said gruffly, walking towards the door of the shop:

'After all, this hadn't been foreseen in the arrangement. After you, Superintendent . . .'

IV

It was a typical working-class home, with its carved oak sideboard, a check oil-cloth on the table and some horrible pink and mauve fairground trophies by way of vases.

'Sit down,' the woman muttered as she mechanically wiped the table in front of Maigret.

Benoît fetched a bottle from the sideboard and filled four small glasses in silence, while Lecoin slumped down astride a chair and leaned his elbows on the back of it.

'Did you suspect something?' he said sharply, looking Maigret straight in the eyes.

'For two reasons: first because the only shouts heard were in a man's voice, which was rather strange, considering that a girl was

present and that if she'd been drowning she was a good enough swim-
mer to stay on the surface long enough to call for help . . . Next, after
an accident of this sort, why should anyone drive twenty kilometres to
warn the police when there's a telephone close by. The inn windows
were lighted up. It was impossible not to think of . . .'

'Sure,' admitted Lecoin. 'It was he who insisted . . .'

'He'd got into the lorry, obviously?'

It was too late to retreat. In any case the two men had resigned
themselves and the woman, meanwhile, seemed relieved. It was she
who advised them:

'Better tell the whole story. It's not worth it, for two wretched thousand-franc notes . . .'

'Joseph'll tell,' put in her husband.

And Lecoin, after swallowing the contents of his glass, explained:

'Let's say that it happened just like this evening. You were quite
right. In spite of the rain and my bad wiper I've got good enough eyes
and good enough brakes not to run into a stationary car. So I drew up
a metre and a half away. I thought someone must have had a breakdown and I got off the lorry to lend a hand. That was when I saw a
young man who seemed very excited and who asked me if I wanted to
earn two thousand francs . . .'

'By helping him push the car into the water?' interrupted Maigret.

'At a pinch he could have pushed it by hand. That's what he was
trying to do when I turned up. But what he chiefly wanted was to be
taken off somewhere without anyone knowing. I really think that if
he'd been by himself I'd not have agreed. But there was the girl . . .'

'She was still alive?'

'Yes indeed! To persuade me, he explained that people were trying
to stop them getting married, that they were in love, that they wanted
to fake a suicide so that nobody would try to find them and separate
them . . . I don't much like that sort of game, but if you'd seen her, the
kid, in the rain . . . So, after all, I helped them shove the car into the
Loing. The young people hid in my lorry. They asked me to shout for
help, to make things more convincing, and I shouted . . . So that it
would seem as if they'd both got drowned . . . Afterwards I merely
had to drive them to Montargis . . .

'For that matter I noticed on the way that the young man was no
fool. He knew he couldn't stop at a hotel. He didn't want to take the
train either. He asked me if I didn't know someone who for another
two thousand francs would keep them a few days until the inquiry was
over. I thought of Benoît . . .'

The woman asserted:

'We believed that they were runaway lovers, too . . . So as our
brother-in-law, who's away with the army, has a room here . . .'

'Are they still in the house?'

'*She* isn't . . .'

'What?' And Maigret looked around anxiously.

'In the afternoon,' the motor mechanic began, 'when I saw the newspaper, I went upstairs and I asked if the story about the corpse was true. The girl tore the paper from my hands, glanced through it and suddenly, taking advantage of the door being open, she dashed out . . .'

'Without her coat?'

'Without a coat or a hat . . .'

'And the young man?'

'He swore he couldn't understand, that he had only just bought the car and hadn't thought of opening the luggage compartment . . .'

'Has your house any other door besides this one?'

At that very moment, as Benoît shook his head in reply, a crash was heard in the street. Maigret ran out on to the pavement and saw there a prostrate figure, a young man trying excitedly to get up and run away, although he had broken his leg jumping down from the upstairs window.

It was a dramatic and yet a pitiful sight, for Vertbois was mad with rage and would not yet admit himself defeated.

'If you come near I shall fire . . .'

Maigret, however, pounced on him, and the young man did not fire, from fear or through failure of nerve.

'Quiet, now . . .'

The young man was inveighing against the lorry driver, the garage mechanic and his wife, accusing them of having betrayed him.

He was the typical young delinquent, the sort Maigret knew only too well from dozens of specimens, devious, resentful, ready to go to any lengths to satisfy his greed for money and pleasure.

'Where is Viviane?' Maigret asked, as he put the handcuffs on.

'I don't know.'

'So you'd managed to convince her that you pushed the car into the river with the sole object of faking a suicide pact?'

'She stuck to me like a leech . . .'

'And it's tiresome, isn't it, to be landed with a corpse you can't get rid of?'

It had been the foulest, most stupid and revolting crime, the sort moreover which never pays!

Jean Vertbois, seeing that his marriage plans had fallen through and that the La Pommeraye fortune would never come his way, even if he abducted Viviane, had turned to a middle-aged woman who had been his mistress for a long time and got her to visit his apartment; he had murdered her and stolen her money, with part of which he had bought a cheap car, planning to dispose of the body in some lonely spot.

And then Viviane had turned up, with her young, whole-hearted passion, determined to run away from home and throw in her lot with her lover's.

She would not leave him for a moment! The hours sped by as they drove along, carrying the corpse with them.

Viviane believed she was enjoying a honeymoon, whereas she was deeply involved in a horrible drama!

While she embraced the man she loved, he was thinking only of the sinister load of which he must get rid at all costs!

It was then that, in desperation, he had invented this fake suicide, which the chance advent of a lorry had assisted and yet complicated.

'The news you promised us, Superintendent?'

The journalists had enjoyed a regular feast at La Cloche and their mood reflected this.

'The murderer of Marthe Dorval is in hospital . . .'

'Marthe Dorval?'

'A former light opera singer, who had some money put aside, and who was the mistress of Jean Vertbois . . .'

'He's in hospital?'

'At Montargis, with a broken leg. I give you permission to go and take his picture and ask him all the questions you like . . .'

'But the girl?'

Maigret hung his head. About her he knew nothing, and there was always the fear that she might have taken some desperate action.

It was after midnight, and the Superintendent was with Captain Pillement in the latter's house at Nemours, discussing events, when the telephone rang.

The captain, who answered it, displayed surprise and delight, and asked a few questions. 'You're certain of the address? Listen! To make quite sure, bring me the taxi-driver here . . . Even if he's tipsy . . .'

And he explained to Maigret:

'My men have just discovered a taxi-driver at Montargis who, some time during the day, took on a girl who was bare-headed and wore no coat. She had him drive her into the country, near Bourges, to a lonely manor-house. On the way, as the driver was getting worried about his fare seeing that she wasn't even carrying a handbag, she repeatedly told him: "My aunt will pay."'

For Viviane La Pommeraye, panting and exhausted, had taken refuge with one of her aunts, with whom, ever since childhood, she had gone to spend her holidays.

AT THE ETOILE DU NORD

1

A vague mumble over the telephone was the cause of it all, at any rate the cause of Maigret's involvement in this baffling case.

He had almost ceased to belong to the Police Judiciaire. In two more days he would have officially retired. He was expecting to spend these two days, like the previous ones, putting his files in order and sorting out his personal documents and his notes. He had spent thirty years in the office in the Quai des Orfèvres, and he knew every nook and cranny of it better than those of his own house. He had never looked forward impatiently to retirement. But now, forty-eight hours away from freedom, he felt like a boy who has completed his military service, counting the hours, dreaming constantly of the house on the banks of the Loire which was awaiting him and where Madame Maigret was already fixing things up for his arrival.

In order to work in peace he had just spent the night in his office, which was now blue with tobacco smoke. Dawn revealed rain on the embankment, where the street lamps were still burning, and this atmosphere reminded him of the many interrogations which, begun in this very room in the early afternoon, had gone on through the night until the same drab dawn, when a confession was finally wrung from an exhausted offender, while the man who had been questioning him was just as worn out himself.

The telephone rang in a neighbouring room. At first Maigret paid no attention, then he raised his head, remembering that the inspector on duty had looked in a few minutes earlier to say he was going out for a drink of hot coffee.

The big house was deserted, its lights burning low in the empty corridors. Maigret went into the inspectors' office, lifted the receiver and said: 'Hello?'

And a man's voice at the end of the line said: 'Is that you?'

Why, instead of saying no, or asking for details, did he merely reply with an indistinct mumble?

'This is Pierre . . . We've just been told at Emergencies about a mysterious crime committed at the hotel Etoile du Nord . . . Are you going over there?'

Maigret mumbled again, hung up and looked around him in some embarrassment. He knew the way these things happen. The inspector on duty had a friend called Pierre at Emergencies Central Office, and this friend was happy to be able to give him a tip.

Only two more days . . .

Maigret filled his pipe and went back to his room, but he lacked the courage to reimmerse himself in the pile of papers; a minute later he put on his bowler hat and his heavy overcoat with the velvet collar, and with a shrug of his shoulders went downstairs.

It was barely six o'clock in the morning. The telephone had worked fast, for when Maigret alighted from his taxi in the Rue de Maubeuge, a stone's throw from the Gare du Nord, there were no onlookers by the door of the hotel, at which a uniformed policeman was standing guard.

'Has the district Superintendent come?'

'Not yet. They've gone to fetch him from his home.'

'And the doctor?'

'He's just gone up.'

The Etoile du Nord was typical of the drab fourth-rate hotels to be found in the neighbourhood of all stations. In a small office to the right of the door, Maigret noticed an unmade bed, presumably the night porter's.

The dirty greyness of it all was intensified by the bleary light of a wet dawn.

'No. 32, on the third floor.'

A worn stair-carpet, held down with brass rods. In the passage on the first floor, a few people in their night clothes, some wearing overcoats by way of dressing-gowns over their pyjamas, half-awakened faces showing the kind of bewilderment which is a reaction to sudden catastrophe.

Maigret went up and almost collided with a young girl who was coming downstairs, dressed in a dark suit.

'Where are you going?' he asked automatically.

'To catch my train.'

'Go back into your room.'

'But . . .'

'Nobody is to leave the hotel before I give permission. There's a policeman at the door.'

He went on up, forcing her to go backwards up the stairs.

'Will it take long?'

'I don't know. I tell you again, go back to your room.'

At the start of an inquiry Maigret was often surly, and this time, into the bargain, he had not slept. A door opened, that of no. 32, and a

man emerged who had obviously dressed in a hurry, wearing neither
collar nor tie and with slippers on his bare feet.

'The Police Superintendent?'

'No! I'm from the Criminal Investigation Department: Superintendent Maigret.'

'Come in, please. I'm the proprietor of the hotel. It's the first time
anything like this has happened in the five years I've been in the business . . .'

This was a familiar type: a plaintive bore, a weak character who
had invested all his savings in this hotel in the hope of retiring after a
few years.

Maigret went into the room. The doctor was putting on his coat,
and a man was lying on the bed, stark naked, in a position which concealed his face but revealed a large wound in the middle of the back,
roughly on a level with the heart.

'Dead?'

'Almost instantaneously.'

'And the blood?'

The doctor pointed to a large pool on the floor, near the door.

'He crawled over there to call for help.'

The proprietor explained:

'My alarm clock had just rung, for I always get up at half-past five.
We cater mainly for travellers and they have to catch early trains. I
heard the sound of doors banging . . .'

'One minute. You said doors banging. Do you mean you heard
more than one door?'

'I think so . . . I can't be sure . . . I heard a lot of noise going on . . .'

'And footsteps?'

'Footsteps, certainly!'

'In the passage or on the stairs?'

'That's what I'm wondering . . .'

'Think carefully . . . footsteps on the stairs don't make the same
sound as on a floor.'

'There may have been both sorts? . . . What did strike me was a cry,
a cry that sounded like a man gasping. I was putting on my trousers
. . . I opened the door and . . .'

'Excuse me! Where do you sleep?'

'At the end of the passage on the second floor. There's a little closet
there which we can't let because it's not got a proper window.'

'Go on!'

'That's all! I hurried up. Some guests were opening their doors.
This door was standing open and on the threshold a man was kneeling
rather than lying, with blood pouring from him . . .'

'Was he naked?'

'I took off his pyjamas,' the doctor interrupted.

'Stabbed with a knife?'

'Yes, a heavy knife with a broad blade.'

The local police superintendent arrived at last and frowned when he saw Maigret already on the scene.

Maigret had a particular loathing for sensational happenings in hotels, and he was already regretting having automatically answered a telephone call which was not meant for him. As usual, travellers were becoming impatient. They came up to him one after the other.

'Excuse me, Superintendent . . . Here are my papers . . . I'm a respectable resident of Béziers . . . I've got to be at Brussels by midday and my train . . .'

The Superintendent could only reply: 'Sorry!'

Some of them lost their tempers. Women, after trying blandishments in vain, burst into tears.

'If my husband knew I'd spent the night in this hotel!'

'Be patient, madame!'

Finally, as the crowd was blocking up the passages, he grew angry, and forced them all to return to their rooms and keep the doors shut.

He had less than a quarter of an hour before him to do a good job. Presently the specialists from the Records Department would be there with their cameras and instruments of every sort.

Then there would be the examining magistrate and his assistant, and the forensic pathologist.

'Is that his luggage? He had nothing else?'

The pallid proprietor shook his head. There was only a small suit-case standing in a corner. Maigret opened it and found nothing but toilet articles and a change of underwear.

On the coat-rack hung an iron-grey suit of excellent cut, a half-belted overcoat and a soft felt hat marked with the initials G.B.

In the wallet was a visiting-card inscribed: *Georges Bompard, 17 Rue de Miromesnil, Paris*. The wallet contained no money, and there was none to be found anywhere else except some small change in the man's pockets.

Maigret had had the body turned over, and he now beheld a man of about forty-five, well groomed, with particularly finely cut features. Curiously enough his silvery grey hair gave the unknown man a look of remarkable youthfulness as well as a certain distinction.

'Fetch me his registration form!'

The proprietor brought it. The name and address were the same as on the visiting-card.

'Was he alone when he arrived?'

'I've just asked the night porter, for he came in at half-past three in the morning. He was alone.'

'Where is the night porter?'

'He's waiting downstairs.'

'Tell him he's not to leave the hotel until I've finished my inquiry.'

As he spoke, Maigret bent down and picked up a silk stocking which had been lying half hidden at the foot of the bed.

'Bring me the list of guests, particularly of the women guests.'

The silk stocking had been pulled off carelessly and dropped on the floor, as though in the course of hasty undressing. It was flesh-coloured, of smallish size and medium quality.

Leaving the local police officer to collect the data for his report and receive the gentlemen from the D.P.P., Maigret went out of the room, still wearing his overcoat, with his hat on his head and his pipe between his lips. But the pipe had gone out, and he was followed by the hotel proprietor rather like a colonel inspecting barracks.

'Who's in here?' he asked in front of one door.

'Madame Geneviève Blanchet, forty-two years of age, widow, from Compiègne.'

'Let's go in!'

A first glance showed him that Madame Blanchet was wearing lisle stockings, but he none the less obliged her to open her cases, after which, despite her protests, he searched the room.

'You heard nothing?'

She reddened, and he had to insist.

'I got the impression . . . You know! the walls are so thin! . . . I got the impression, as I was saying, that the gentleman was not alone and that he . . . that they . . .'

'Were making love in the next room?' Maigret put it bluntly, for he had a strong dislike of prudish women.

Two old English ladies, further on, gave him some trouble, for they were in possession of several pairs of silk stockings, new ones, which they were planning to smuggle through the customs for their niece.

A Swiss woman with dubious papers was sent to the Quai des Orfèvres to have her identity checked.

Time was passing, and Maigret had not yet discovered the second stocking. It was on the floor above that he found himself in the presence of the girl in the dark suit whom he had already met on the stairs. He immediately glanced down at her legs.

'Hello, so you don't wear stockings?' he asked with surprise. 'At this time of year?'

For the month was March and the weather particularly cold.

'I never wear stockings.'

'Have you any luggage?'

'No!'

'Have you filled in a registration form?'

'Yes.'

He picked it out of the file. It gave the name of Céline Germain, no occupation, Rue des Saules, Orléans.

'Your name is Céline Germain?'

'Yes.'

He observed her more closely, for there was an aggressive decisiveness about her replies.

'Age?'

'Nineteen.'

'You're quite sure you never wear stockings?'

He searched the room, pulled the bedclothes about, opened all the drawers of the wardrobe and suddenly snapped out an order:

'Will you lift up your skirt?'

'What? Are you mad?'

'Please lift up your skirt.'

'Look here! Aren't you afraid of my entering a complaint against you, filthy beast?'

'A man has been killed in this hotel!' was all Maigret replied. 'Come on! Hurry up!'

She was pale, and her great gold-flecked eyes – a redhead's eyes – expressed contempt and fury.

'Lift it up yourself if you're not afraid to,' she declared. 'I warn you I shall lodge a complaint!'

He went up to her and touched her hips.

'You're wearing a girdle,' he noted.

'So what?'

'You know very well that it's not a foundation garment but a narrow suspender belt . . .'

'What business is that of yours? Can't I dress the way I like?'

'Where's the other stocking?'

'I don't know what you're talking about.'

The hotel proprietor was listening with stupefaction to this peculiar dialogue.

'Find me a big monkey-wrench!' called out Maigret curtly.

And he used it to dismantle the drainpipe of the washbasin. As he apparently expected, he soon pulled out a small spongy ball which was in fact a silk stocking.

'Come along, my dear,' he ordered without displaying the least surprise. 'We can discuss things better in my office.'

'And suppose I refuse to follow you?'

'Come along!'

He pushed her into the corridor. She tried to put up some resistance. Then he paused for a moment outside no. 32 and glanced into

Maigret's Pipe

the room.

'I'm off to Headquarters,' he told the examining magistrate who had just arrived. 'I think I'm on to something interesting.'

At that moment his prisoner tried to move away suddenly. But the Superintendent was just as quick; he grasped her by the arm, and then, with her free hand, she started scratching his face.

'Come now! Quiet!'

'Let me go! . . . I tell you to let me go. You're a swine. You wanted to make me undress. You lifted up my skirt. It was because I refused that you're taking your revenge!'

Doors were being opened, bewildered faces appearing, while Maigret alone remained quite calm, holding the girl firmly by the arm.

'Will you shut up?'

'You've no right to take me away! I've done nothing! I want to catch my train . . .'

He led her forcibly down the stairs and, still undiscouraged, she went on shouting shrilly:

'Help! . . . I've done nothing! . . . I'm being ill-treated!'

Perhaps she was hoping for some support from the puzzled crowd, as is the case more often than one thinks. In his early days Maigret had been beaten up because a pickpocket whom he was arresting outside a big department store had started shouting: 'Stop thief!'

There were a great many people outside the Etoile du Nord. The Superintendent had taken the precaution of calling a taxi. He nevertheless needed the help of a policeman to control the girl, who went on struggling and trying to fling herself on the ground.

Finally the taxi door closed on them. Maigret straightened his hat and cast a sideways glance at his companion, who was now panting.

'I've seldom seen a more tiresome little bitch,' he observed.

'And I've never met a worse brute than you!'

She was a strange girl! The first time he had seen her on the stairs, looking young and slight in her navy blue suit, he had taken her for a respectable young lady. In her room, on the contrary, she had been as ill-tempered and brazen as a tart.

Now her attitude was changing again, as she remarked:

'If you're the famous Maigret, I don't congratulate you, for I thought you'd be cleverer than this!'

He lit his pipe, which had long been out. She sighed:

'I loathe tobacco smoke!'

'Which doesn't prevent you from having cigarettes in your bag!'

'That's my own smoke; I object to yours!'

He went on smoking nonetheless, while watching her from the corner of his eye, since she was quite capable of opening the taxi door and jumping out.

'How long has it been?' he suddenly asked.

'What?'

'That you've been on the game?'

He had the impression that a fleeting smile passed over her thin lips.

'Is that your business?'

'Please yourself! Perhaps you'll be more sensible in my office.'

'Shall you still want to look at my girdle?'

'Who knows?'

It was still raining. The streets of Paris were busier now. The taxi slowed down to cross the Halles, and finally reached the embankment.

Maigret was still undecided whether or not he was glad to have taken the telephone call that morning. At all events, he was interested in the singular little creature sitting stiffly by his side.

The battle was on between them, a strange battle in which each side seemed to feel some curiosity about the other.

'I suppose you're going to question me for hours on end without giving me anything to eat or drink? That's your practice, isn't it?'

'Who knows?' he said again.

'I may as well tell you right away that I'm not afraid. I've got nothing on my conscience. You'll be sorry some day for whatever you do to me . . .'

'All right!'

'What have you got against me?'

'I don't know yet.'

'Then let me go. That would be much more intelligent of you.'

The taxi drew up in the courtyard of Police Headquarters, and Maigret got out. He was about to pull out his wallet and pay when his eyes caught the girl's, and he realized that she was awaiting this opportunity to make a final attempt to escape. He told the driver:

'I'll have the money sent down to you.'

Police Headquarters was busy now, and voices could be heard in most of the rooms. Maigret opened the door of his, ushered in Céline Germain, and locked the door from the outside; then he went to see the Director.

They discussed the affair for some ten minutes and reached an aggrement about it, after which Maigret went to see the office messenger.

'Send me up coffee and croissants for two.'

At last he opened his own door and stood for a moment motionless, seeing all his papers, torn and crumpled, scattered over the floor, the window panes cracked and the bust of the Republic, which used to stand on the mantelpiece, lying shattered on the ground.

As for the girl, seated in the Superintendent's own chair, she stared at him defiantly.

'I told you,' she said. 'And I warn you there's more to come!'

II

This was probably the most disappointing interrogation in all Maigret's career. From beginning to end it took place in exceptional circumstances, in a setting of the utmost chaos, with torn papers on the floor and pieces of plaster which the Superintendent pretended not to see.

Added to which Maigret had not slept, and the girl confronting him was presumably in much the same condition. So that both of them were pale, their eyes shining with that hectic but exhausted brightness that follows long periods of wakefulness.

When he entered his office, Maigret had walked up to his armchair with perfect composure and grasped the girl's arm, saying quietly:

'Do you mind?'

And she had got up, aware that he would have the last word; she had sat down in the place he indicated, facing the window through which the bleak light shone on her as inexorably as a magnesium flare. Did she expect him to start speaking? In that case she must have been seriously disappointed, for the Superintendent began by filling a pipe with meticulous care, then he poked the stove, sharpened a pencil, and finally opened the door for the café waiter who brought in breakfast for two.

'Does it tempt you?' he said gently to his prisoner.

'Isn't there any milk?' she retorted sourly.

'I thought black coffee would keep you awake better.'

'I hate coffee without milk.'

'In that case don't drink it.'

She drank it nonetheless, trying to get accustomed to her companion's ominous placidity. After reviving himself, he lifted the receiver of the telephone.

'Hello! Give me the Orléans Flying Squad.'

And when he had his connection:

'Maigret speaking . . . Will you give me some unofficial information . . . If need be I'll send you a rogatory warrant . . . It concerns a certain Céline Germain, residing Rue des Saules in your city . . .'

He thought he saw a brief smile pass over the girl's lips. Meanwhile he frowned. 'What? . . . You're sure? . . . Nor in the suburbs of Orléans?'

When he replaced the receiver his gaze dwelt at some length on

Céline Germain's face. Finally he asked with a sigh:

'Where do you live?'

'Nowhere!'

'Where did you meet Georges Bompard?'

'In the street.'

Now the two of them had joined battle, and each watched the other tensely, while outside the rain still fell and the hooter of some tug-boat sounded occasionally as it passed under the bridge.

'In what street?'

'At Montmartre.'

'You were soliciting?'

'What about it?'

'What time was it?'

'I don't know.'

'Did you go back to the hotel with him?'

She hesitated, realized that he knew her companion had entered the hotel alone, and explained:

'I went in a little before him and took a room. He wanted it that way.'

'Where were you born?'

'That's nobody's business.'

'You've never been in trouble with the police?'

At the same moment there came a knock at the door. Inspector Janvier seemed reluctant to speak, but Maigret signed to him to go ahead.

'I've come from the Rue de Miromesnil, where I didn't find out much. Georges Bompard really does live there. For the past fifteen years he's occupied a two-roomed bachelor flat on the fifth floor rear, at a rent of 2,500 francs. The concierge says he's very seldom there, for he's a commercial representative and he travels a good deal.'

Maigret felt that the girl was wincing and was about to say something, but the moment passed and she immediately resumed her impassive air.

'Go on.'

'That's all! Bompard left his home yesterday morning.'

'Had anybody rung him up?'

'He doesn't have a telephone.'

'Nothing else?'

'Nothing else. Except for a personal impression. He must have been a gay dog, to judge by the photographs of women that practically covered the walls.'

'Did you see a picture of this one?'

'I'm trying to remember... I don't think so ...'

'Go and fetch me all the photographs and the letters, if there are any.'

When Janvier had left, Maigret stoked the fire again, patiently, passed a hand over his brow and yawned.

'So the long and the short of it is that you know nothing. Your name is Céline Germain and you're a street-walker. Bompard accosted you in the street and took you to the hotel . . .'

'Not right away. We went dancing in night-clubs first.'

'And once in the hotel?'

'I went to his room, as we'd agreed. We went to bed.'

'I know! A neighbour heard you . . .'

She must have been a nasty-minded snooper if she got up to listen. Perhaps she looked through the keyhole too?'

'And then? Did anyone come in?'

'I don't know . . . I went back to my room.'

'Undressed?'

'I'd got partially dressed. I must have forgotten the stocking I'd dropped under the bed. I was woken up by steps in the corridor and by doors opening and shutting. When I realized what was happening I guessed I should be suspected and I tried to leave. Then you prevented me from leaving. I remembered the stocking and I put the other down the plughole. Now do you know enough?'

Maigret got up, put on his hat but not his coat, opened the door and simply said: 'Come!'

He went along a number of corridors with the girl, keeping a close watch on her; they climbed up narrow stairs and at last reached the Criminal Records Department, where all those arrested during the night are subjected to anthropometric examination.

It was the women's turn. There were still a score of them about, mainly prostitutes of the lowest sort who were used to the ceremony and undressed of their own accord.

At this point, anyone who had not known Maigret would have thought he was just a big fellow automatically doing an uninteresting job.

'Get undressed . . .' he sighed, relighting his pipe.

But he had to turn aside his head so that his prisoner should not see the strange smile that came to his lips.

'Take everything off?'

'Of course!'

He anticipated a conflict. He waited with some anxiety. Finally she literally tore off her jacket and her cream-coloured silk blouse, then sat down to remove her shoes.

As he looked down at her, the Superintendent noted that her hands were shaking, and he almost called off the ordeal.

'You still insist that you solicited in the public street?'

She nodded, her eyes in a fixed stare and her teeth clenched; she let her skirt drop. Two small firm breasts were visible under her chemise.

'Now get into line . . . You're going to be examined.'

And with an apparently automatic gesture he picked up the clothes and took them into the next room. This was the laboratory where, amid test tubes and projectors, specialists were busy with meticulous research.

'Look, Eloi, what d'you think of this outfit?'

A tall young man picked up the tailor-made suit and felt it knowledgeably. He put his finger on the label first.

'It comes from a shop in Bordeaux. It's excellent quality cloth and it's well made. It must belong to a young woman of good bourgeois family.'

'Many thanks.'

When he went back to the women's section he heard sounds of loud argument, and shortly afterwards the photographer of the Records Department came over to tell him:

'There's nothing to be done about it! Every time I try to take a picture she shuts her eyes, blows out her cheeks, twists her lips, in a word she manages to make herself quite unrecognizable.'

'Let her get dressed again!' Maigret conceded wearily. 'No card with her fingerprints, of course?'

'No. She's never been in trouble with the police. Look, here's the doctor looking for you . . .'

The doctor was a young fellow whom Maigret knew well. The two men talked in low voices in a corner for a long time. When they had done the girl reappeared, wearing her suit, her gaze fixed and her face so pale that the Superintendent felt compassion for her.

'Have you decided to speak?'

'I've nothing to say.'

They were back in Maigret's office again, and curiously enough a sort of intimacy had grown up between the Superintendent and the girl. Although they did not look on one another as friends but rather the reverse, they were no longer strangers.

'You know what the doctor told me?'

She reddened and was on the verge of bursting into tears.

'I suppose you can guess? It's less than a month since . . .'

'Shut up!'

'You admit, then, that less than a month ago you were still a virgin. I should like you to admit, too, that you haven't given me your real name.'

She retorted, with an attempt at irony: 'If you're providing both the questions and the answers!'

'That's right! I shall ask the questions and provide the answers. Or rather I shall try to reconstruct events. You live somewhere in the provinces, I'm not yet sure where, but probably somewhere near Bordeaux . . .'

He noted that the girl betrayed a certain satisfaction: so it was not Bordeaux!

'You were a well-brought-up young girl, probably living with your parents, Georges Bompard came into your life. He made love to you. . . . You gave yourself to him and he persuaded you to follow him . . .'

She looked away, realizing that the Superintendent was only talking in order to watch her reactions.

'Are you writing a sentimental novel?' she jeered, trying, not very successfully, to assume a tone of vulgar mockery.

'Almost, since the next chapter is desertion . . .'

'I suppose Georges tells me we must part and I kill him, then I go and hide the knife. . . . By the way, where could I have hidden the knife?'

'Excuse me, who told you he was killed with a knife?'

'Why . . . People were saying so . . . in the passages . . .'

'In that case, since you've now become so talkative, go on and tell me where, in fact, you hid the weapon . . .'

'You think you're remarkable, don't you?'

'One thing I'm sure of, you're pretty remarkable yourself! You endured that examination this morning, amongst all those prostitutes, sooner than confess that you'd lied when you spoke of soliciting!'

'You're very naive!'

'Why?'

'Because the fact that I was a virgin a month ago doesn't prove anything. Are you going to keep on questioning me a long time?'

'As long as I need to. By way of warning, I must tell you that three years ago a man spent thirty-seven hours on the chair you're now occupying. He had come in to give evidence. He went off handcuffed, and he is now a convict in Guiana.'

She glanced at him with contempt.

'Just as you please!' she said. 'I shall wait patiently for your questions. You began by feeling my girdle. Then you managed to see me stripped. I'm wondering whether after all you're just a nasty old man. . . .'

Maigret made no reply but, perhaps by way of punishment, kept her for a quarter of an hour waiting for a word, while he studied unimportant papers.

Then he looked up suddenly. 'How much did Bompard give you for the night?' he said. 'Since he picked you up in the street, it's only to be expected . . .'

'That he should pay me! He gave me a thousand francs . . .'

'Yes, there's a thousand-franc note in your handbag. Were all your customers equally generous?'

'Some of them were.'

At such moments Maigret would gladly have slapped her face. The most notorious criminals of the last thirty years had passed through his office. One of them, a former lawyer who had tragically turned to crime, had been so crafty that the Superintendent had more than once had to leave the room to hide his fury.

But on the present occasion he was confronted by a slip of a girl! She said she was nineteen, but he'd not have been surprised to learn that she was only seventeen.

For hours now they had been closeted together, and he had learnt nothing, not even her name or where she came from. She was lying brazenly, hardly seeking to conceal the fact. Or rather, she seemed to be saying:

'It's not up to me to tell you the truth, is it? It's up to you to find it out!'

Janvier had returned from the Rue de Miromesnil with a pile of photographs, some of them more than suggestive. Maigret had examined them each in turn, slowly, and had been conscious of his companion's cold fury.

'Jealous?' he asked her.

'Of a casual pick-up!'

At all events, there was no photograph there resembling Céline, while information about Bompard was somewhat meagre.

The firm that employed him had been contacted; it was a music publisher's in the Boulevard Malesherbes. The publisher, when questioned, had replied:

'Bompard was an odd man; I saw very little of him. He was an excellent representative, but he had certain fads, such as constantly changing his itinerary. He liked to surround himself with mystery, and we in the firm thought he was given to bluffing. Sometimes he implied that he belonged to an illustrious family. He dressed with meticulous care and a certain eccentricity which I thought out of place in his profession . . .'

At three in the afternoon, Maigret's office still displayed the same chaos, to which were now added glasses of beer on the table, the remains of sandwiches, ash from Maigret's pipe all over the place and cigarette stubs, since the Superintendent had finally sent for some cigarettes for Céline.

All in all, the situation was almost ridiculous, and this must have become generally known at Headquarters, for Maigret's colleagues kept looking in on obvious pretexts.

At the Etoile du Nord, Sergeant Lucas, Maigret's best collaborator, was carrying out a thorough investigation, to no effect. Not only was the knife nowhere to be found (even though all the toilets had been dismantled!) but no evidence had brought in the slightest clue.

Altogether, the only established facts were these: shortly after 3 a.m. a girl called Céline, about whom nothing was known, had rung at the door of the hotel and asked for a room for the rest of the night.

Less than a quarter of an hour later, Georges Bompard, carrying an overnight case, entered the same hotel and took a room, in which Céline visited him shortly afterwards.

Finally, two hours after that, Bompard opened the door to call for help and collapsed, having been stabbed with a knife in the middle of the back; the girl, meanwhile, endeavoured to disappear.

The afternoon papers had just come out. They published a photograph of Céline on the front page, but she was unrecognizable, since she had persisted in making faces at the camera.

'Tell me, my dear, when Bompard accosted you in that street in Montmartre, the name of which you have forgotten, was he carrying his case?'

'No!'

'You went into two night-clubs. Was he still without his case? And yet when he came to the hotel he was carrying one . . .'

'We went together to fetch it from a small all-night bistro near the Place Pigalle, where he had deposited it . . .'

'In the bedroom, did he open the case in your presence?'

'No . . . Yes . . . I can't be sure.'

'Where did he take the thousand-franc note from?'

'I suppose from his wallet!'

'When we found that wallet it was empty. Presumably Bompard gave you all the money he had with him, keeping only enough change to pay for his room next morning . . .'

'That was no concern of mine!'

Obviously! She had an answer for everything, and the very incoherence of her thesis had its own logic.

What else could he try, to break her composure? Persuasion? Resignedly, Maigret assumed his most good-natured air:

'Don't you think we're both of us becoming rather ridiculous? I'm trying to make you say you killed Bompard, whereas you may not have done so; on the other hand you persist in declaring you know nothing, whereas you really know something . . .'

'I'm in the stronger position, then!' she remarked.

'Well, yes! Only that won't last. Lucas has just called me to say he's got hold of something significant. At any moment now the situation will change and you'll be in an awkward fix . . .

'Let's argue calmly, both of us, and stop me if I'm wrong. To begin with, an undeniable fact: Bompard was stabbed with a knife. Now it's hardly likely, unless we assume premeditation, that you'd have had a knife of that size in your handbag. It can't have been lying about on the table, either . . . And the overnight case, which might have contained one, was shut . . .'

'I never said that!'

'All right! . . . It doesn't matter whether it was open or shut. The fact remains that a woman of your sort is not likely to use a knife. If you had wanted to do away with a faithless lover or an unscrupulous seducer you'd have bought yourself a revolver.

'Therefore, you did not kill Bompard . . .

'We must assume, then, that someone came in from outside, and I shall prove to you that this person could only have come while you were present. . . .'

She had risen, and was standing with her face pressed against the window-pane, while dusk fell over rain-drenched Paris.

'For one thing, if you had gone off quietly, after those embraces that don't concern me, you would probably not have left one of your stockings under the bed. You'd have picked up your belongings carefully, like the sensible, self-possessed little person that you are . . .'

He was speaking ironically, for at that moment he saw a sort of shudder run down the back of her neck.

'Are you listening, Céline? For another thing, Bompard was stabbed in the back, which implies either that he was occupied with a third person – yourself – when the murderer appeared, or that he had no reason to mistrust that murderer . . .

'These are the conclusions to which logical argument leads us! Now I've a piece of advice to give you in your own interest: to speak the truth without delay. You want to make me believe that you are a professional street-walker, not to use a coarser term . . .

'If I were to let myself believe that, I should not fail to point out to you that in that case you've probably also got a steady boy-friend – there's another name for them too – who, seeing you go into the hotel with an apparently wealthy man, might have thought of robbing him . . .

'You see what I'm driving at? And do you understand at last that it's in your own interest to tell me straight what you saw?'

A long silence followed. The girl went on looking out of the window. Maigret was on the look-out for any reaction from her, but without much hope.

Finally she turned round, as pale as she had been that morning when she left the Records Department. She went back to sit down on her chair wearily, pushing aside with her foot the papers scattered on the floor.

'Is that all?' she sighed.

'Why not confess right away what you'll be forced to confess in an hour or two?'

A bitter smile curled her lips as she remarked drily:

'Do you think so?'

It looked as though she had given in and was about to speak at last. She sat there, staring at the floor, with her knees crossed and her hands clasped over them. Maigret dared not move for fear of influencing her.

At last she bestirred herself, looked for the cigarettes on the desk and took one, which she lit off-handedly.

'This is a queer job you're doing!' she remarked. 'Doesn't it embarrass you a bit?'

Maigret did not bat an eyelid.

'You think that's a clever story you've made up? And you really imagine you know something about me?'

'I imagine I'm going to find out something,' he said with deep earnestness.

'Really?'

It was discouraging. She changed from one minute to the next, reverting to the tone in which, that morning, she had spoken of herself as a street-walker.

'Is this how you always carry on your inquiries?'

Maigret felt pity rather than anger, for she at last betrayed a latent anguish, a despair which might perhaps overthrow the frail barrier of her will.

'Listen, Céline . . .'

'I'm not called Céline!'

'I know.'

'You know nothing at all! You shan't know anything! And if by any misfortune you should get to know anything, you'll bear the weight of it on your conscience. Now send me to prison if you like. Give interviews to journalists who'll write columns about the girl who won't tell her name . . .'

'What were you doing in Bordeaux?'

'When?' she cried with a start.

'Not very long ago. I'll give you the exact date presently. From your accent I'd say you don't come from the south at all, nor from the south-west. And yet . . .'

She sighed, overcome by a weariness which was perfectly genuine:

'I've had enough of it! If you sent me to prison I should at least be able to sleep there.'

'You can sleep as soon as you've told me . . .'

'Is this blackmail?'

In distress, he blurted: 'No, you little fool! Don't you see that what I'm doing is for your own sake? Don't you know that once you've gone out of this door you'll be an accused person and you'll be at the mercy of the D.P.P.? Have you seen me take a single note? Have you seen me write a report of this interrogation?'

She watched him with curiosity.

'You must realize that so long as you're here . . .'

But he did not complete his sentence. He had already said too much. He could have slapped her, like a disobedient child, and yet at other moments . . .

'Shall we begin again from the beginning? Shall I prove to you that your story doesn't hold water?'

She looked up at him and said: 'I know!'

'So then?'

'There's nothing else to be done. I'm really at the end of my tether. If you'd let me lie on the floor I'd go to sleep . . .'

The telephone bell rang and Maigret turned his back on the girl, who did, in fact, lie down on the floor and close her eyes.

III

'Hello! . . . Is that you? . . . Are you still working in the office? . . . The electrician has come and is asking whether he should instal a light in the tool-shed . . .'

Madame Maigret was ringing from far away, from the newly decorated little house at Meung-sur-Loire where he was due in forty-eight hours.

'What sort of weather?' he queried.

'Dry . . . There's a strong wind . . .'

In Paris it was still raining, and Maigret wished the wind from the Loire would come and sweep away the tense, unhealthy atmosphere of his office, where for hours on end an exhausting struggle had been going on.

He held the receiver to his ear, but let his gaze dwell on that enigmatic creature who had been standing up to him with the incredible energy of which only some women are capable, and who had lied as girls know how to lie.

'Yes, I'm listening . . .'

'Can I speak to you a moment longer? The electrician wants to know if he should fix a bell at the front door. I thought the knocker would be enough . . .'

'Sure!'

But his 'sure' applied not only to the front door of the Meung house and its electric bell. Maigret had stopped listening. He couldn't wait to hang up and think about something else. He replied noncommittally.

'Yes . . . Good . . . As you prefer . . . That's right . . . Goodbye, darling . . .'

And when he said 'darling' the girl's eyes turned to him again with curiosity, since feminine instincts persist in spite of tragic happenings.

Whew! . . . Maigret had a sensation of relief. It seemed to him that after going round in circles for so long without finding a way out, he had at last discovered one. He had recovered his rational powers. His mistake had been to remain too long shut up with this girl in a stifling atmosphere.

'Hello! . . . Is Lucas back? . . . Send him up to my office at once. . . . Yes, with all the reports of the Etoile du Nord case . . .'

He lit his pipe, took a drink of beer, and went over to the window, which he opened in spite of the rain.

'Just a minute, to clear the air,' he explained.

True, he had not discovered the murderer of Georges Bompard, and there was nothing sensational about the idea that had just occurred to him, but it served to release him from the vicious circle.

His idea was as follows: when the crime was committed the night porter had been on duty on the ground floor, and it was impossible to leave the hotel without his cooperation. Now this night porter declared that he had not opened the door for anybody and had not left his post.

Moreover, on the second floor, the proprietor had been up, putting on his trousers, so he said, and he had hurried upstairs as soon as he heard the cries for help.

Assuming then, as Maigret did, that the girl had not committed the crime . . .

Assuming that she had witnessed it and was keeping silence for some compelling reason . . .

Lucas came in, a bundle of papers in his hand.

'Come in! Sit down! Have you got the night porter's statement?' And he read it through, muttering the words to himself:

'Joseph Dufieu, born at Moissac . . . Heard the calls for help from the third floor almost at the same time as my boss's footsteps on the stair . . . It was I who rang Emergencies right away, then I called a policeman who was passing and who came to stand sentry in front of the hotel . . .'

Was Maigret deliberately pursuing his inquiry in the girl's presence? She seemed, at all events, to be listening intently, and she betrayed a certain anxiety.

'Have you questioned all the guests in the hotel, Lucas?'

'The statements are here . . . I'm certain that none of them knew the victim and therefore none of them had any motive for attacking him.'

'What about the proprietor? Where does he come from?'

'Toulouse.'

Maigret's ideas, though still vague, were beginning to take shape, and he walked up and down, his hands behind his back and his pipe between his teeth. He shut the window again, and from time to time took up his stand in front of the girl, who seemed disturbed by his change of attitude.

'Good! Now follow my argument carefully, Lucas! Assume that this young lady did not kill Bompard. It would seem from your inquiries that none of the hotel guests did so. Now two men have asserted that nobody left the hotel. These two are Dufieu the night porter, and the proprietor . . . How do we know that one or other isn't a former acquaintance of Bompard's, having an old grudge against him?'

He suddenly broke off, dissatisfied.

'No! It wasn't the night porter, since Bompard saw him on his arrival and handed over his registration form; he'd have had time to recognize the man, and if there had been an argument between them it would have taken place before half-past three in the morning.'

Why did the girl relax as though relieved? And why did Maigret go on, still thinking aloud:

'As for the proprietor . . . Let's see! Does he get the night porter to wake him? No, he's got an alarm clock . . . He hadn't gone downstairs when he heard the shouts . . . Dufieu hadn't gone upstairs . . . So the proprietor couldn't know that Bompard was in his hotel . . .'

He sat down, heavily. As often happens, he had started out confidently on a trail and now noticed that it led nowhere.

'Get them to bring us up something to drink, Lucas . . . What'll you take, my dear?'

'A coffee!'

'Don't you think you're excitable enough already?'

To think that with a single word she could have cleared up everything and that she remained obstinately silent! He glared at her resentfully. He wanted to solve the problem at all costs. He could not picture himself, at the end of his career, handing the girl over to the examining magistrate and declaring:

'She's either guilty or she isn't. I've been closeted with her for over twelve hours and I've got nothing out of her . . .'

As for Lucas, he knew that on such occasions it was better to remain in the background, and after ordering two beers and a coffee he kept quiet in a corner.

'You follow, Lucas? There's one character I keep coming back to: the night porter. Only he knew that Bompard was in the hotel. Only he could have seen the murderer come out of the room . . . Wait! . . .'

There was a knock on the door. He shouted:

'No! I'm not in! . . . To anyone!'

He was on his feet again, in a state of excitement.

'The list of hotel guests, quickly! You did say the porter came from Moissac? . . . And the *patron* from Toulouse? . . . Let's see about the guests . . . London . . . Amiens . . . Compiègne . . . Marseille . . . Mercy-le-Haut . . . Not one from Moissac! . . . Not one from Toulouse!'

He had scarcely uttered these words when, turning to the girl, he noticed a look of terror in her eyes, while her little teeth were feverishly biting her lower lip.

'Can you guess what I'm getting at, Lucas? Bompard, having made a conquest, as must be usual with him to judge by the photographs that were found in his flat, puts up at a hotel chosen at random near the Gare du Nord . . . Somebody recognized him, somebody who has a reason to bear him ill will . . . And this obstinate child knows that person, since she refuses to speak, since she invents all sorts of nonsense rather than tell the truth . . . We're getting warm, I'm sure. Damn it, we . . .'

He repeated dreamily:

'Moissac! Toulouse! And the suit comes from a firm in Bordeaux . . .'

He picked up the telephone receiver and passed it to Lucas.

'Get me the music publisher for whom Bompard worked. Ask him where Bompard went on his last round . . .'

At moments like this Maigret seemed to grow larger, to become broader and heavier. He took deep puffs at his pipe and his gaze settled on the girl with crushing power. He seemed to be saying:

'All right! When you saw me you thought I wasn't nearly as clever as some people said. An easy-going duffer, didn't you? Somebody whom a little girl could make randy and who got his fun taking her clothes off; a sentimental duffer into the bargain, soft-hearted and excitable! One minute, my dear . . .'

And to Lucas, at the telephone:

'What does he say?'

'Bompard must have spent the last few months in the south-west.'

'That's enough! Ring off!'

He emptied his glass at one gulp, poked the stove for a moment, turned round, suddenly calm, and said to Lucas in so unexpected a tone that the girl could not restrain a smile:

'You might have told me I was making a fool of myself!'

'But, Chief . . .'

'The hotel servants . . . Have you questioned them?'

'Yes, Chief . . . There are only two chambermaids that sleep in the hotel, on the sixth floor. Of course they heard nothing. They were the last to come down, when the hullabaloo woke them up.'

'Have you their names?'

'There's Berthe Martineau, nineteen years old . . .'

'Where from?'

'I'm looking . . . Here we are . . . Compiègne!'

'And the other?'

'Lucienne Jouffroy, forty-five, from . . . from Moissac.'

And Lucas, who was a short man, looked up at the Superintendent with an expression of mingled astonishment and admiration.

'You've got it, now? Jump into a taxi . . . Go and fetch her . . . Quickly, for heaven's sake!'

And he pushed the sergeant out, then closed the door with weary relief.

He looked at the photographs one after the other, and merely noted that Bompard's mistresses were all young girls, often very young girls.

'Which is she?' he asked his prisoner, amicably.

He was almost as sleepy as Céline. She sat hunched up, and instead of replying she shook her head.

'Is Lucienne Jouffroy's picture among these?'

'I can't say anything yet!' she sighed at last, with an effort.

'Why not? Are you waiting till the woman comes? Admit that you're from Moissac yourself!'

'I'll speak later!'

'Why not now?'

'Because!'

'Do you know what I'd do if I had a daughter like you? I'd give her a good smacking from time to time, to teach her a lesson. Now, I bet you began by collecting photographs of film stars, didn't you? No? Then you've read too many novels . . .'

Gently, she corrected him: 'I was keen on music . . .'

And she gave a start when Maigret declared emphatically:

'It comes to the same thing! You were romantic! You met Georges Bompard. What surprises me, now, is that you should have fallen for a commercial traveller . . .'

She corrected him again: 'He told me he was a composer. He played the piano wonderfully . . .'

Once again an intimacy had grown up between them, that strange intimacy that is formed oftener than one might expect between a

policeman and his prisoner. The room was overheated and thick with
smoke. The various noises of Police Headquarters could be heard
vaguely. phones ringing in neighbouring rooms, footsteps down the
long corridor, and in the background the hooting of cars on the bridge
near by.

'Did you love him?'

She hung her head without replying.

'You loved him, that's for sure! And I wonder whether it was he
who took you away or you that followed him, that hung on to him?'

She answered him straight, raising her eyes:

'It was me, afterwards!'

He understood. He was back in that everyday reality which under-
lies the most apparently complicated cases.

A commercial traveller with a taste for young girls who gave himself
glamour in their eyes by posing as a great composer . . .

A romantic provincial teenager who, after yielding to him, had
sought to safeguard her happiness . . .

'Was it he who brought you to Paris?'

'I came on my own.'

'Had he given you his address?'

'No . . . He kept everything rather mysterious . . . But he'd told me
he used to go to a certain café in the Boulevard Saint-Germain. That
was where I found him. I had no luggage and he went to fetch his overnight case. He asked me to stay a few days in the hotel, after which he
would be free of certain commitments and would be able to devote
himself exclusively to me.'

That morning, when she had tried to make herself out a low-class
adventuress, Maigret had almost believed her, so well had she played
her part. In the course of the day she had shown herself alternately
very childish and very much of a woman, now obdurate and now
dejected, now aggressive and now disheartened.

'Your inspector's taking a long time,' she suddenly said, looking at
her wrist-watch.

'He's a sergeant . . .'

'I don't know the difference.'

'Is it a long time since you left Moissac?'

'I'm not going to say anything yet.'

'Do you know Dufieu, the night porter?'

'I shall talk when the sergeant gets back.'

'So you believe Lucienne Jouffroy has gone away?'

'I've no idea . . . Can I have some more coffee brought up, please?
I'm dying with fatigue.'

He rang the messenger. Soon afterwards a call came through for
him.

'What?... what did you say? Well, can't be helped, my boy. It was only to be expected . . . Yes, we'll have her description sent to all the frontier posts.'

He turned to the girl.

'That was Sergeant Lucas. He tells me Lucienne Jouffroy left the hotel late this morning without informing anyone . . .'

And he spoke into the phone again: 'Come back at once . . All right . . .'

He hung up, and saw his companion looking mistrustful.

'I suppose there's nothing to prevent you from talking now?'

'How am I to know you're not lying? Perhaps there wasn't even anyone on the line?'

'Why, what a suspicious person you are! Well, my dear, since that's the way it is, we shall just have to wait till Lucas comes back. Will you believe *him*?'

'Maybe.'

They were both on edge by now. A quarter of an hour passed without either of them speaking, and finally Lucas appeared, uneasy and abashed.

'I should have thought of it this morning, Chief . . .'

'How could you have thought of it this morning when I didn't think of it myself? What about the night porter?'

'He's here in the passage.'

'What has he got to say?'

'Nothing. He declares he knows nothing . . .'

'Bring him in.'

The man came in, stoop-shouldered, and cast a stealthy glance at Maigret.

'What was your connection with Lucienne Jouffroy?'

'She's my sister-in-law.'

'Sit down. You needn't be afraid. But answer my questions frankly. Did your sister-in-law have a daughter?'

'Yes, Rosine.'

'What has become of her?'

'She died.'

'Of what?'

A stubborn silence. Maigret persisted: 'Of what?'

And then Céline said in a low voice, turning towards the porter:

'You can tell him, Joseph.'

'She died of an operation she had done because she was pregnant. She was sixteen . . .'

'And this happened at Moissac?'

'At Moissac, three years ago.'

'And Georges Bompard was travelling there at the time?'

'It was all his fault . . . It was he who took her to the abortionist, when she went to tell him she was pregnant.'

'One minute, Dufieu! I assume that it was following these events that your sister-in-law came to Paris, and that it was you who found her a job as chambermaid at the Etoile du Nord?'

The man nodded.

'Last night you must have been astonished when you saw a girl you knew turn up at that hotel at three in the morning, a girl of good family from Moissac . . .'

'Mademoiselle Blanchon,' he muttered involuntarily.

'The daughter of Judge Blanchon?'

Dufieu turned to the girl in alarm, and she replied clearly and composedly:

'Yes, I'm Geneviève Blanchon, Superintendent. My father knows nothing about it. It was only yesterday morning that I left Moissac. Bompard had promised to write to me there, and I'd had no news from him . . .'

'One minute, please. So, Dufieu, you were surprised when you saw the young lady, but you were far more surprised when Bompard appeared. As a night porter, you could not have been misled by the fact that he arrived a few minutes later than the girl.'

'No, Superintendent.'

'So you went up to the sixth floor to tell your sister-in-law.'

'Yes, I did.'

'Did you suspect that things might take such a dramatic turn?'

'I knew my sister-in-law wanted to be revenged on that man.'

Maigret turned to the sergeant.

'Lucas! Take him to your room, will you?'

He wanted to be left alone with the girl, who had now quite dropped her defiant air.

'Did Lucienne Jouffroy come in while you were there?'

'Yes.'

'Did you know her daughter had been Bompard's mistress?'

'Yes.'

'And that he had taken her to the abortionist?'

'Yes.'

'In spite of which you came to Paris to be with him?'

Unmoved, but lowering her voice, she replied:

'I loved him! He told me Rosine had had other lovers . . .'

'If I were your father . . .' growled Maigret.

'What would you do?'

'I don't know, but . . . So you left home without money and without luggage . . . And it was Bompard who gave you a thousand francs to keep you at the Etoile du Nord until . . .'

'I loved him,' she repeated.

'And now?'

'Now I don't know . . . I wanted to prevent Lucienne Jouffroy being arrested, and my father finding out . . .'

'You don't think that's going to be easy, do you?'

The telephone bell rang. Maigret answered, crossly:

'Yes . . . All right . . . Can't be helped . . . Of course . . .'

Then, replacing the receiver:

'Lucienne Jouffroy has not even tried to get across the frontier. She wandered about Paris for hours and she's just gone into a police station to give herself up and confess everything . . . She didn't mention you; she just declared that Bompard was in bed with a prostitute whom she didn't know . . .'

'What will happen?'

'If I know the jurymen of the Seine district, she'll certainly be acquitted . . .'

'And what about me?'

'You?'

He stood up and, suddenly yielding to a desire he had restrained too long, he slapped the girl's face. She was so taken aback that she remained speechless.

'Come along!'

'Where?'

'Never you mind.'

He took her along the corridors and into the dark courtyard of Police Headquarters.

'Hi! . . . Taxi! . . .'

He made her get in, muttering as though to himself:

'There are two doors . . . Suppose, in the midst of the crowd, somebody should get out of one of them . . .'

Then he fell silent. The car drove along the Rue de Rivoli. The girl sat motionless.

'Listen,' growled Maigret, 'have you lost your wits?'

'I'm sleepy,' she sighed.

'Well, you'll be able to sleep later . . . I warn you that if in one minute you don't . . .'

She opened one of the doors and hesitated.

And Maigret shouted furiously: 'Get off with you, for heaven's sake, you great goose! . . .'

The driver turned round, saw only one person in his taxi, and was about to stop, but the Superintendent lowered the pane between them and muttered:

'Draw up in front of some good brasserie . . . I've such a mighty thirst!'

MADEMOISELLE BERTHE
AND HER LOVER

I

'Monsieur le Commissaire,

'I am fully conscious of my boldness in disturbing you in your retirement, the more so since I have heard speak of your charming home on the banks of the Loire.

'But surely you will forgive me when I tell you that it's a matter of life or death for me. I live alone, in the heart of Paris, surrounded by its busy crowds. I go about my business like any other girl, and yet at any moment disaster may strike; maybe a bullet fired from heaven knows where, or a stab in the back? The crowd will see me fall; my body will be carried into some pharmacy before being taken to the morgue. The incident will only rate a few lines in the newspaper, should it deserve mention at all.

'And yet, Monsieur le Commissaire, I want to live, don't you understand? I am young and strong, I long to taste all the joys of life!

'You will no doubt be surprised to receive this letter in your country retreat, the address of which is not easily procured. Let me tell you, then, that I am the niece of a man who for a long time was your colleague in the Police Judiciaire, and who died by your side shortly before your retirement.

'I implore you, Superintendent, answer my call for help: give up a few days or a few hours for me! Listen to the heartfelt plea of a girl who appeals to you because she does not want to die.

'At 10 a.m. on Tuesday and Wednesday I shall be on the terrace of the Café de Madrid. I shall be wearing a small red hat. In any case, if you come I shall recognize you, since I have a photograph of you with my uncle.

'S.O.S.! . . . S.O.S.! . . . S.O.S.! . . .'

Maigret was furious. For one thing, because his first reaction, whenever he had allowed his feelings to be stirred, was always one of self-critical anger. For another, because he had irrationally chosen not to mention the letter to his wife, and he was slightly ashamed of having invented a pretext for coming to Paris. Thirdly, because the way he had hurried to keep this appointment was a proof that he was

less happy in his garden retreat than he tried to make out, and that
like any beginner he had become thoughtlessly involved in the first
mystery that had cropped up.

And finally, as so often happens in life, there was a material reason
for his anger, a trivial and ridiculous one. When he left Meung-sur-
Loire at seven that morning there had been an icy fog hanging over the
valley, and Maigret had put on his heavy winter overcoat.

Now, as he was sitting on the terrace of the Café de Madrid, the
Grands Boulevards were bathed in bright spring sunshine, and lightly
clad figures were strolling past.

'In the first place,' he reflected, 'that letter smacks too much of
literature. As for the colleague killed at my side shortly before my retirement it can only have been Sergeant Lucas, and he never mentioned any niece . . .'

The terrace was deserted. He was sitting all alone at a small table,
and, not knowing what to drink, since he had already had his coffee at
the Gare d'Orléans, he had ordered a beer.

'With luck she won't come, and I shall be able to go back on the 11
o'clock train!'

At the precise moment when the electric clock at the Carrefour
Montmartre showed ten o'clock, he saw a small red hat threading its
way through the crowd, and a minute later a rather plump young
woman, noticeably panting, sat down beside Maigret.

'Excuse me!' she gasped, putting her hand to her left side, where
her heart must have been thumping wildly. 'I'm always so frightened!'

And she added, looking up at him with an attempt at a smile:

'But now you're here it's all right! . . . I promise I'll be brave . . .'

All this had lasted only a few seconds, and Maigret still felt some
astonishment at finding this lively little person sitting beside him, her
hands nervously fiddling with her crocodile-skin handbag. As the
waiter was watching them, he asked her:

'What'll you have?'

'Something strong, if I may . . .'

'A brandy?'

'Yes, please . . . I was sure you would come . . . What frightened me
was thinking that you might not get here in time . . .'

'You're Lucas's niece?'

'Yes . . . I thought you'd guess that. His great-niece, more precisely . . . If I didn't give you my name and address it was because I
didn't trust the post . . .'

At the same moment she was staring at something, or rather at
somebody: a young man who had just sat down on the terrace a few
tables away. Maigret caught a fleeting glance of intense anxiety in the

girl's eyes, and he growled:

'Is that him?'

'Who?'

'The fellow over there . . .'

But she promptly regained her self-control, saying with a smile:

'Oh no! You're quite wrong . . . Only as soon as I catch sight of a man's figure, especially if he's wearing a fawn overcoat, I instinctively give a start . . .'

He noticed that instead of draining her glass she just dipped her lips into it slowly. He also observed the ironical and somewhat contemptuous attitude of the young man, and realized that he must look like one of those elderly gentlemen with a weakness for young girls.

'My name's Berthe . . .', said the girl, seemingly averse to silence. 'I'm twenty-eight . . . Since you've consented to take an interest in my affairs I'm ready to tell you everything . . .'

Her red hat gave her a springlike sparkle, but she was clearly a determined and self-assured little person.

'For you have consented, haven't you, Superintendent?'

'I know nothing as yet about your story . . .'

'You shall know it! You shall know everything! You won't leave me in distress much longer . . .'

Was it the presence of the young man in the raincoat which prevented her from feeling at her ease? She kept looking round in all directions. Her eyes fastened on passers-by in the crowd, returned to Maigret, to the glass of brandy, to the young man, and she still made nervous efforts to smile.

'Would you mind coming to my place? It's not far from here . . . Rue Caulaincourt, in Montmartre . . . With a taxi we can be there right away . . .'

And Maigret, still sulky because the situation seemed to him ridiculous, tapped on the table with a coin, and he noticed as they left the terrace that the young man in the fawn coat was also summoning the waiter.

It was no. 67b. not far from the Place Constantin-Pecqueur, between a bakery and an Auvergnat's bar. A typical Montmartre house, with the porter's lodge next to the front door, a worn reddish stair-carpet, walls of yellowish imitation marble and two doors with brass knobs on each landing.

'I'm very sorry to make you climb so high . . . It's right at the top, sixth floor, and there's no lift . . .'

Once on the doormat, she drew a key from her bag, and almost at once a magical sight was revealed. Spring in the Grands Boulevards was pale and insipid compared with the spring that one beheld from this dwelling perched high above the roofs of Paris. Down below, the Rue Caulaincourt was like a dark river along which buses and lorries drifted by, and one felt sorry for the people whose lives went on.so far from the air and sunlight.

A french window was open on to a long iron balcony. All along this balcony geraniums were glowing red in the sunlight, and a canary was hopping about in a cage that still contained a little of its morning birdseed.

'Take off your coat, Superintendent . . . Do you mind if I just go and tidy myself up? I dressed in such a hurry, wondering if you would come . . .'

All the doors were standing open, and the whole of the flat was visible. It consisted of three rooms, prettily furnished and meticulously clean, their cheerfulness enhanced by piles of brightly coloured dress materials. Mademoiselle Berthe, who had taken off her jacket, now appeared wearing a close-fitting yellow blouse patterned with tiny flowers.

'Let me take your coat . . . Do sit down . . . I'm all in a muddle . . . I'm so happy, you see! I feel that the nightmare's over . . .'

And indeed she was looking radiant. Her eyes were glistening; her full rosy lips were parted in a smile.

'You shall understand . . . I don't know where to start, but that doesn't matter, does it? for you're used to such things . . . When you saw this room with my sewing machine and all these bits of stuff you must have guessed that I'm a dressmaker . . . I'm even going to confess something else: I chiefly make dresses which my customers, who are all very nice ladies, ask me to copy from patterns which they bring me and which come from leading fashion houses. You won't give me away?'

She was so overflowing with life that she gave one no time to think, barely time to watch her changing facial expression. And Maigret once again felt somewhat embarrassed at being there, in that atmosphere of femininity and youthfulness, like a respectable married man on the loose.

'Now I've got a more serious confession to make . . . I'm ashamed, but it's got to be done . . . I could never have told my uncle Lucas . . . You see, Superintendent, I'm not a virtuous young person . . . I've got a boy friend, or rather I did have one . . . And it's precisely on his account . . .'

Maigret's embarrassment turned to confusion. Had he been fool enough to believe for one moment that something serious was involved, whereas this was just a case of a romantic girl being threatened by her boy friend in the hope of getting her to come back to him?

She chattered on: 'I met him last summer at Saint-Malo, where I

was on holiday. He's a young man of good family, the son of an indus-
trialist who had gone bankrupt. He'd always led the pampered life of
a rich boy and then suddenly, at twenty-three, he had to earn his
living . . .'

'What does he do?' Maigret asked sceptically.

'At Saint-Malo he was selling cars for a big garage . . . Or rather he
was trying to sell them, for things weren't going too well . . . And
Albert, that's his name, hates pestering people. Soon after I got back
to Paris he came here too and looked for a job . . .'

'Excuse me! Did he live here?'

And Maigret cast a glance towards the open door of the bedroom,
where he could see a wardrobe with a mirror and a carefully polished
parquet floor.

'No . . .' she said. 'I didn't want him to . . . He had a small room in
a hotel in the Rue Lepic. He often came here, but only in the day-
time . . .'

'He was your lover?'

She reddened and nodded, then she got up to offer Maigret a glass
of wine.

'I've only got some sweet white Bordeaux . . . I don't even know
where I've put it . . . My life's in such confusion . . . Listen! I'll be
brief, if I may, for I feel I'm going to get all worked up again . . . I
found out I'd been wrong about Albert. I soon realized that he wasn't
seriously looking for a job and that he spent most of his time in disre-
putable bars . . . I've several times seen him shaking hands with some
very shady-looking characters . . . You see what I mean? . . .'

She was walking backwards and forwards. Her voice grew muffled;
tears were clearly not far away.

'A week ago there was that business . . . you may have read about it
in the papers but you probably didn't pay much attention to it . . .
Four young men robbed a radio dealer's shop in the Boulevard Beaumarchais. They weren't after the stock, which was too unwieldy, but
the money, which they'd somehow discovered was in the safe. They
took away sixty thousand francs. As they were making off they were
seen by the police. One of the youths fired a shot which killed a policeman.'

Maigret had suddenly regained his self-possession, and his figure
seemed to have become more substantial, his gaze firmer. Automatically, he lit his pipe, which hitherto he had not ventured to take
from his pocket.

'And then?' he said in a tone which was as yet unfamiliar to Mademoiselle Berthe.

'Two of the thieves were arrested . . . two men well known to the
police, one who's heavily pock-marked, the other who's known as the

Marseillais . . . They were young fellows, practically beginners, and their headquarters is near the Place Blanche, where Albert often went . . .'

'Who fired the shot?' asked Maigret, staring through tobacco smoke at the canary.

'It's not known . . . Or rather, the gun was found on the pavement and it was Albert's . . . It was easy to recognize as he'd borrowed it from his father, whose name was on it. The father came forward when he read about it in the papers. He was questioned at Police Headquarters . . .'

'And Albert?'

'They're looking for him . . . You know better than I do how these things are done. I suppose they've sent out his description. And that's why . . .'

She wiped her eyes and went over to stand for a moment at the balcony, with her back to Maigret, who saw her shoulders shaken by a sob.

When she turned round again she was pale and tense-featured.

'I could have gone to the police and told them the truth, but I was afraid to . . . I trust you, Monsieur Maigret, because I know you won't betray me . . . Look at this!'

She raised the lid of a soup tureen of imitation Rouen pottery standing on the sideboard, and took out a letter which she showed Maigret. It was written in violet ink in an irregular hand:

> *Dear Berthe,*
> *As you'll see from this letter I'm at Calais, and I've got to get across the frontier as quickly as possible. But I'm determined not to leave without you. So I shall expect you. All you've got to do is put an ad. in the* Intransigeant *saying: 'Albert, such and such a day, such and such a time,' and I'll be at Calais station. I'd better warn you right away that if you were to show this letter to a nark I'll have my revenge. What I've done has been for your sake. So you know where your duty lies.*
> *I hold you responsible for whatever may happen to me. I warn you, moreover, that sooner than go off alone I shall prevent you from ever belonging to someone else.*
> *Understand this if you can.*
>
> *Your Albert*

'Why didn't you go to Calais?' Maigret asked with seeming innocence.

'Because I don't want to be the wife or mistress of a murderer. I thought I loved Albert. I took him for a decent boy who was down on his luck. I helped him as much as I could.'

Her lower lip was quivering. Tears were imminent.

'Now I know that all he wanted, all he still wants is my money. For he's well aware that I've got some put by, over fifteen thousand francs in the Savings Bank!'

She burst into tears:

'He's never loved me, you see! And I'm so unhappy! I'm frightened! I don't want to go there . . . The thought that he . . . that he . . .'

Maigret got up awkwardly and patted Berthe's shoulder as she sat weeping with her elbows on the table and her face buried in her hands. She quickly pulled herself together.

'Somebody from the police came to question me . . . They very nearly took me off as an accomplice. I didn't tell them about the letter, because I was sure that would have meant trouble for me . . . But I'm frightened! I'm sure he'll come back and do me some harm! . . . Once when the cat was rubbing against his legs he picked it up so roughly that the poor thing has been lame ever since . . . I'd have done anything for him . . . If you had seen him you'd have believed, as I did, that he was . . .'

'And you really don't know the young man who was sitting near us at the Café de Madrid?' interrupted Maigret.

'I swear I don't!'

'That's odd . . .'

'Why?'

He had gone on to the balcony, from which he could see out over the Place Constantin-Pecqueur. And there, just at the corner of the Rue Caulaincourt, he saw the familiar fawn-coloured raincoat pacing up and down.

'I don't know . . . Just an idea . . .'

'What's in your mind? . . . Tell me! . . . Reassure me! . . . Promise me, Superintendent, that you're going to protect me . . . I've got to know where Albert is . . . If only I was sure that he'd crossed the frontier! . . .'

'What would you do?' he growled.

'I should breathe more freely. Otherwise I'm sure he'll kill me, as he . . .'

His present surroundings seemed to Maigret an epitome of the humble workaday life of Montmartre, with its delight in simple things. On a kitchen table he saw the cutlet which was to provide the girl's lunch and a carton of *céleri rémoulade* from a dairy shop, together with a cream cheese in a blue earthenware dish.

Beside the sewing machine was a half-made dress, an evening dress of organdie dotted with spring flowers. In a china cup there were pins and buttons, a pencil, some tailor's chalk and a few stamps.

And this modest existence was brightened by the sunlight streaming in from the balcony that overlooked the city.

Mademoiselle Berthe was sniffling, unashamedly showing a reddened nose and tear-smeared cheeks.

'I know I'm a blunderer, I say things too straightforwardly, just as they occur to me . . . All the same, unless you help me, I'm sure, I tell you, that one of these days you'll come and identify my body at the morgue . . . He's my first lover, Superintendent . . . There had never been anyone else before, believe it or not . . . I wanted to get married and have children . . . Specially to have children! And now . . .'

'I'll see what I can do, my dear,' Maigret promised somewhat haltingly, for he hated emotional effusions.

But even before he had finished speaking she seized his hand and kissed it.

'Thank you, Superintendent! But tell me one thing more . . . I'm not a monster, am I? I did love him, it's true . . . But what I loved was the decent boy I took him for . . . I'm not betraying him deliberately . . . The proof of that is that I've said nothing to the police . . . It's different with you . . . I appealed to you to protect me, because I'm afraid, because I'm too young to die . . .'

He had moved away from her again and was standing on the balcony with his back to her, his head haloed by tobacco smoke.

'What shall you do?' she went on. 'Of course I'll stand the expenses. I'm not rich, but I told you I had a little money . . .'

'Isn't that a hotel over the way?'

'Yes, the Hôtel de Concarneau . . .'

'Well, I shall probably go and take a room there . . . One piece of advice: don't go out any more than you can help.'

'I won't go out at all if you like except to buy food . . .'

'Can't you get the concierge to do that?'

'I'll ask her . . .'

'I shall come back and see you this evening . . . A pity you don't know that young man . . .'

'Which young man?'

'The one who followed you to the Café de Madrid and who's keeping watch at the corner of the pavement.'

'Unless . . .' she began, her eyes widening.

'Unless?'

'Unless he's an accomplice of Albert's . . . Suppose, instead of coming himself, he's got one of his friends to . . .'

'I'll see you later!' growled Maigret, making for the door.

He was not satisfied. He did not know why. On the landing he picked a piece of white cotton off his sleeve. And as he went down the six floors he was wondering what he should do.

On seeing him, the young man in the raincoat dived into a bistro at the corner of the square, and Maigret followed him, ordered a large glass of beer, made sure the phone booth was in the bar-room itself and went into it, deliberately leaving the door ajar.

'Hello! . . . P.J.? Get me Inspector Lacroix, please . . . Yes, Jérôme Lacroix. It's his uncle Maigret . . . Hello! That you, son? How are things? What's that? Well, can't be helped, it'll have to wait . . . Jump into a taxi and come to see me here in the Rue Caulaincourt . . . Wait a minute.'

He leaned out of the phone booth and asked the *patron:*

'What's your place called?'

'The Zanzi-Bar.'

Maigret spoke into the phone once more: 'At the Zanzi-Bar . . . Yes . . . I'll be expecting you . . . No, no, your aunt's as fit as a fiddle . . . So'm I . . . See you soon . . .'

As he returned to the bar counter he thought he noticed an ironic flicker in the grey eyes of the young man, who was wearing a light-coloured suit, two-toned shoes and a snakeskin belt.

'Like a game of poker-dice?' he asked the *patron.*

'No time . . .'

'What about you, monsieur? Play you at poker-dice for the next drink?'

Maigret hesitated, and finally picked up the dice-box with a gesture as menacing as though he had already slipped the handcuffs on to the young man's wrists.

II

'Three kings at a throw!' the young rascal announced, adding, after a glance at the Superintendent who was picking up the dice:

'Your throw, Monsieur Maigret!'

Maigret threw two nines and a ten, then queried as he made a second throw: 'You know me?'

'We all know the cops!' the other retorted smoothly. 'Three jacks! You're staying in? What's your drink? You can't have been offered much up there, apart from that sweet wine that tastes like gooseberry syrup.'

On such occasions there is only one thing to do: to keep calm and not betray one's irritation. Maigret went on smoking his pipe in brief puffs, and picked up a second match, for his opponent, with angelic suavity, had just turned up three queens.

'You really don't remember me? After grilling me that night from nine o'clock till five in the morning!'

He was jauntier than ever. He was a good-looking scamp and he knew it. Above all, he had such a candid smile when he chose that it was difficult to be angry with him.

'Something to do with dope . . . You're not there yet? It was a few years back . . . I was a messenger at the Célis in the Rue Pigalle, and you were set on getting me to talk . . . Three kings in two throws! That's better. Good! Two nines . . . Pass me a match.'

And after ordering an apéritif with the same nonchalant and good-humoured air, he attacked:

'Well, what d'you make of my little sister?'

The bistro was practically empty, save for one drunk who was obstinately playing with the fruit machine, and the *patron* took advantage of this to fill his carafes with the dregs of his bottles.

'You surely cottoned on from the start, didn't you?'

It was over four years since Maigret had heard the familiar accent of the underworld, and he almost broke into a smile, like an exile meeting a compatriot.

'With all due respect, between you and me, I hope you didn't let yourself be taken in?'

Softly, softly! To gain time Maigret could always drink a mouthful of beer, or knock out his pipe and fill another.

'I knew she'd be at it again one of these days. You can always tell when that sort of attack is coming on. But I'd not have expected her to bother a big shot like yourself . . . Careful, Monsieur Maigret! You're taking a queen for a jack . . . Four jacks! You're staying in?'

He shook the dice.

'Four kings! You're not in luck, are you? As for little sister, it's not her fault if she's a bit crazy . . . When she was only a kid she was a bit odd, used to walk in her sleep.'

And, glancing at the door, he exclaimed:

'Why, here comes your mate . . . Better perhaps leave you two alone together.'

He drew back to let in Jérôme Lacroix, who had just alighted from a taxi. The two men stared at one another, the young rascal still wearing his engaging smile and the policeman from the Quai des Orfèvres with a puzzled frown.

'Morning, Uncle . . . What's that fellow doing here?'

'Who is he?'

'Louis the Kid . . . You must have known him when he was a pageboy in the Montmartre nightclubs . . . He thinks he's a joker, but I'm going to get him one of these days . . .'

Jérôme Lacroix, whom Maigret had brought into the Police Judiciaire, was a big bony fellow with thick hair and a stubborn expression. He had a long nose, small eyes, huge hands and feet, and he gave the impression of being morose, obstinate, ready to let himself be cut in pieces rather than fail in his duty in the least degree.

'Come and sit over here, son!' said Maigret, choosing a table from which he could see no. 67b. 'Do you know his sister?'

'Whose? Louis the Kid's? Actually I called on her just lately.'

The news did not please Maigret, but he showed no reaction.

'You do mean Mademoiselle Berthe, don't you?'

'Yes. A dressmaker who lives over the way . . . Is my aunt quite well?'

'You asked me that over the telephone.'

'So I did . . . I'm sorry . . .'

'What d'you know about this Mademoiselle Berthe?'

And Maigret observed with some satisfaction that his nephew was somewhat at a loss to reply.

'She's a dressmaker.'

'So you've just told me.'

'She's the mistress of a man called Albert Marcinelle, who's wanted for the murder of a policeman in the Boulevard Beaumarchais.'

'Anything more?'

'Well, that's all I managed to get out of her. Her place seems well kept. Her concierge speaks highly of her. Apart from that Albert she never has a man to visit her, not even her brother, whom she's thrown out once and for all . . . But . . . By the way . . . That's not what brings you to Paris?'

'It is.'

Jérôme, surprised, stared thoughtfully at his glass. He could not understand what interest such a case could have for his uncle, who had repeatedly refused to get involved in more serious affairs.

'You know . . . In my opinion . . . We shall pick him up one of these days and that'll be the end of it . . . A lowdown little scoundrel who's not worth bothering about. We've sent out his description everywhere, and I'd be most surprised if . . .'

'You ought to put an advertisement in the *Intransigeant*.'

Jérôme was becoming increasingly puzzled.

'To try and find him?'

'Make a note of the wording: "Albert Wednesday 3.17 p.m." Arrange to have a policeman at Calais station at that time. If our Albert turns up . . .'

'Is that all?'

'That's all.'

'D'you think he'll be there?'

'I bet you ten to one he won't.'

'So what then?'

'So nothing! Kiss your wife and son for me . . . By the way, if anything new turns up, give me a call at the Hôtel de Concarneau, will you? It's three houses further on . . .'

'Goodbye, Uncle.'

As Maigret paid for the drinks, he was already looking sprightlier than he had been earlier that morning, for he felt things had begun to move.

Roughly speaking, his impression was that the police were over-simplifying the situation and Mademoiselle Berthe was complicating it. Not far off there was a small restaurant favoured by taxi-drivers, with a couple of tables on the terrace, and as one of them was free he sat down and discovered on the menu *fricandeau à l'oseille*, veal with sorrel, one of his favourite dishes.

The atmosphere was so redolent of spring, with light puffs of air so warm and fragrant that, particularly after a bottle of Beaujolais, he felt light-headed and wanted nothing better than to lie down on the grass with a newspaper over his head.

By two o'clock he was at the Hôtel de Concarneau and, not without some difficulty, secured a room on the sixth floor front, exactly opposite Mademoiselle Berthe's balcony.

When he went up to the window he almost blushed, for the girl was busy trying a dress on a customer whose figure, more than partially undressed, could be made out in the bluish darkness of the room.

He asked himself repeatedly if she was doing this on purpose, and even if she might not have caught sight of him in his room. But the warmth of the day was enough to account for her open window.

Maigret practically never took his eyes off her, and he saw nothing in her behaviour which was not absolutely natural.

When the first customer's fitting was over she set to work on a blue dress, patiently, removing pins from between her lips one by one, kneeling for a long while in front of a tailor's dummy covered with black cloth. Then she poured herself a glass of water, did some stitching on her machine, raised her head when she heard a knock on the door and let in a second customer, who was bringing her some dress material. From Maigret's observation post it was almost possible to guess the words spoken from the movements of the women's lips, and he realized that they were arguing about prices and that the customer had to give way in the end.

Not until four o'clock or thereabouts did Maigret think of letting his wife know that he would not be home that night nor, possibly, for the next few days, and he rang for the chambermaid to hand her a telegram and at the same time to order a bottle of beer, since the Brie with which he had followed up his *fricandeau* had made him thirsty.

'Either that girl's very astute,' he muttered to himself, chewing the stem of his pipe, 'or else . . .'

Or else what? Why had he got involved in this business? Why had he not gone home by the eleven o'clock train as, at one point, he had thought of doing?

'Let's assume that she's speaking the truth, as seems plausible.'

If that were the case, what was he to do? Act guardian angel, like those American private detectives who are hired to follow nurses and children to protect them from gangsters?

It might go on for a long time. Albert seemed in no hurry to return to Paris to kill his mistress, and Maigret suddenly realized that he did not even know the man by sight.

And suppose it were not true? What had made her appeal to him? Why had she lured him out of his quiet country home into this drab corner of Paris?

He left his heavy overcoat in his room and went down. He stopped to ask the concierge at no. 67b if Mademoiselle Berthe was in.

'She is . . . As it happens I'm just going out to do her shopping for her, as she's got too much work . . . Would you be kind enough to take up this letter for her, while you're about it?'

He recognized Albert's writing and saw the stamp, postmarked Boulogne.

'So there!' he muttered as he climbed the stairs, in answer to an objection he had raised to himself.

He knocked. He was kept waiting for a moment on the landing and, when she opened the door to him, he had to go into the kitchen, since there was still a customer being fitted. The kitchen was as spotless as the rest of the flat. In one corner there was an opened bottle of white Bordeaux and a dirty plate. He overheard:

'A little tighter at the waist . . . Yes, like that . . . It's younger looking . . . When can you let me have it?'

'By next Monday . . .'

'You can't manage sooner?'

'With the best will in the world, no . . . At this time of year everybody's in a hurry.'

Then Mademoiselle Berthe released him, with a sad smile.

'You see how it is!' she said. 'I do my utmost to look cheerful. Life has to go on, in spite of everything. But if you knew how scared I am! or rather how scared I was, because now that you're here . . .'

'I have a letter for you.'

'From him?'

He gave it to her. She read it, dry-eyed but with trembling lips. Then she handed him the paper.

My darling,
I'm beginning to get worried. I warn you my patience is running out. I

dare not stay all the time in Calais, where I'd be spotted eventually. I have to keep moving about. I had lunch in Boulogne today and I don't know where I shall sleep. But I know that if you don't turn up I shall do what I said, at the risk of being caught.

   It's up to you.

                                                                            Albert

'You see!' she said dejectedly.

'What does your brother have to say about it?'

She gave no start; she did not even show surprise, only an increased sadness.

'He's spoken to you?'

'We had a drink together.'

'I ought to have told you everything this morning! He's not really a bad lot, but he was left on his own too young . . . He tries to act like a tough guy, although he wouldn't hurt a fly. All the same I had to stop him coming here because of the way he behaves . . .'

'All the same, too, you lied to me this morning . . .'

'I was afraid you might think . . .'

'Think what, for instance?'

'I don't know . . . That I was a girl of the same sort! . . . You might have refused to help me.'

She pointed to the letter: 'You've read that . . . It's dated yesterday . . . There's no proof that he hasn't taken the train since then.'

It was beginning to get cooler and the sun had set behind the houses. Mademoiselle Berthe went to close the french window and then returned to Maigret.

'Can I give you a cup of tea? No? . . . As you realize, I work for my living . . . I've always worked on my own, to try and establish myself in a job. When I met Albert I thought that meant happiness . . .'

She swallowed her sobs as she mechanically set about tidying the scraps of material strewn about.

'Haven't you any girl friends?' he asked, glancing at the photograph of a fair-haired young woman on the mantelpiece.

Her glance followed his.

'I had Madeleine, but she's married now . . .'

'You don't see her any more?'

'She lives outside Paris . . . Her husband is an important person . . . What Albert meant for me was . . .'

'Couldn't you let me have a picture of him?'

She did not hesitate for a moment.

'It's true that you wouldn't recognize him if you saw him!' she said. 'Wait a minute . . . I've got a photo we had taken at Saint-Malo. It was on the beach . . .'

And she took it from the soup tureen, which evidently served as her treasure-chest. It was a little snapshot taken by some holiday photographer. Albert, in white trousers, bare-armed, a linen cap on his head, looked like any young fellow one might meet at the seaside. As for Mademoiselle Berthe, she was clinging to him as though anxious not to let her happiness escape.

'It's dark, isn't it? As soon as the sun goes down the apartment is very dark. I'll put on the light.'

Just as she switched it on there came a knock at the door. It was the concierge with a basket of provisions.

'Here you are, Mademoiselle Berthe . . .'

'Just put it all in the kitchen, Madame Morin . . .'

'The lettuce is very nice. But as for the Gruyère, I had to . . .'

'I'll see you by and by! . . .'

And when she was once more alone with Maigret, she sat down, threaded a needle and put on her thimble.

'What did the police tell you? I hope you didn't mention that letter?'

Deliberately, he delayed answering, and she looked up and went on speaking more rapidly:

'I'm afraid I'm not very sure how these things are done . . . When I wrote to you . . . I suppose, you see, that when I consulted you it was rather as a lawyer . . .'

'What do you mean?'

'I mean about professional secrecy . . . I've been telling you everything, showing you letters . . . Oh, it wouldn't worry me if they arrested him, in fact it would be the best way to set my mind at ease! But I wouldn't want it to be my responsibility . . . So if they were to start investigating at Calais and Boulogne now . . .'

He gave her no assistance, and she was finding explanations difficult. She hemmed a dress with exaggerated assiduity.

'Which would you rather?' Maigret asked her slowly.

'What d'you mean?'

'That he should be caught or that he should get across the frontier?'

She looked at him with calm, trustful eyes.

'What do you think about it?'

'What would happen to him if he were caught? What danger is he in, exactly?'

'If it's proved . . . If he fired the shot, there's a risk of the death penalty . . .'

She averted her head and bit her lips.

'Then . . . I'd sooner he got across the frontier . . . Although, one of these days, he'll come back to fetch me . . . And if I refuse he'll . . .'

Maigret was holding the photograph of the two lovers, studying chiefly the young man's face, a fairly ordinary face with a mop of curly hair.

'Obviously you haven't written to him yourself . . .'

'How could I have written to him, since I don't know his address? . . . And what could I have told him?'

It was hard to imagine that tragedy lay just round the corner, so peaceful was the atmosphere. There were moments when Maigret could have fancied himself sitting at home opposite Madame Maigret as she stitched or darned his socks, for there was the same sense of calm, the same subdued light, the same order and neatness everywhere.

The only difference was that Mademoiselle Berthe was younger and prettier, and dressed with a certain fastidious good taste.

'Has he ever slept here?' he asked just to say something.

To which she replied, with quaint naiveté: 'Never at night . . .'

'On account of the concierge?'

'And the neighbours. Next door there's an old couple who are sticklers for propriety. There used to be a young woman on the fourth floor who had a great many visitors, and they wrote to the landlord to get her thrown out . . .'

She recalled her duties as hostess:

'Will you really not take anything? What do you usually drink?'

'I don't want anything, I promise you . . . I'm beginning to think you've been worrying unnecessarily . . .'

Now he was walking about as he used to when he was questioning somebody in his office at Police Headquarters, in the days when he was still Superintendent Maigret. He kept touching things automatically, fiddling with the most trifling objects, playing with the pins in the china bowl, setting the soup tureen exactly in the centre of the sideboard.

'In my opinion, when he sees there's no hope, he'll try to cross the Belgian frontier, and it'll be all over . . .'

'Do you think he'll succeed?'

'That depends. Obviously customs officers and policemen all have his description. But if he can get out by some smugglers' route . . .'

'How easy would that be?'

'I think it would be very difficult, because that's the sector where tobacco smuggling is carried out on a large scale. Come now, admit that you're still in love with him . . .'

'No!'

'At any rate that you'd be unhappy if you heard he was caught . . .'

'Isn't that natural? . . . It's ten months since . . .'

'An old married couple, evidently! . . .' he sighed, his voice softening a little. 'Now I'm going to leave you . . .'

'Already?'

'You needn't be afraid! I shan't be far off; just over the way, in fact, on the fifth floor of the Hôtel de Concarneau. I must confess that this afternoon I saw your customers in their slips, and even one of them without . . .'

'I didn't know . . .'

Mademoiselle Berthe's hand, when he grasped it, was soft and warm.

'I trust you . . .' she sighed rather sadly. 'This is the first evening I shall go to bed with my mind at ease.'

Going down the narrow staircase, Maigret felt like a clumsy giant. On the pavement, where it was still daylight, he almost collided with Louis the Kid, who raised a finger to his grey felt hat and said in a bantering tone:

'Excuse me, Superintendent, sir!'

Then Maigret had a sudden attack of ill humour. He felt he was floundering about in a hopeless bog. He wanted to get out of it at all costs, above all to extricate himself from the absurd position he had got into.

'Come here, you . . .'

'Do you want your return match at poker-dice? At your service!'

'What about paying a little visit to the Quai des Orfèvres?'

'That's not a very good idea . . .'

'Whatever you think, I'd like you to follow me there and answer a few questions which Inspector Lacroix will put to you.'

Louis was not enthusiastic.

'Are we going by métro?' he asked.

'We're taking a taxi.'

Maigret had never known a more ridiculous affair, and he reflected that if his wife had seen him a few minutes earlier in Mademoiselle Berthe's apartment she would scarcely have believed that he was there in a professional capacity. He was hardly sure of it himself!

'In you get. To the Quai des Orfèvres, yes, Police Head-quarters . . .'

Jérôme would worm things out of the impertinent young rascal, and then they'd see what would happen. As for Mademoiselle Berthe, it was difficult to believe that she was in any real danger, seeing that Albert was still on the run between Calais and Boulogne.

'You know the way . . . Right, now . . . Last room at the end of the passage . . .'

A room which Maigret had occupied at the start of his career, when there was still no electric light in the building.

'Wait for me a moment . . .'

Jérôme was there, drawing up a report.

'Would you like to grill the young scamp I've brought you? He knows more than he appears to . . .'

'Right, Uncle . . .'

The scamp still wore his jaunty air, and he had deliberately kept on his hat. He treated himself to a cigarette, which Maigret removed from his lips.

'Tell me now, kid . . . Where were you on the night of the burglary in the Boulevard Beaumarchais?'

'What night was that?'

'A Monday night . . .'

'Which month?'

He was acting the simpleton. Maigret found himself longing for the old days when one could stamp on such a fellow's toes to teach him to be serious.

'Where I was? . . . Wait a sec . . . I think there was a Marlene Dietrich picture at the cinema in the Rue Rochechouart . . .'

'And then?'

'And then? Wait a sec! There was a cartoon and then something about the plants that grow at the bottom of the sea . . .'

Jérôme would have had sufficient patience to keep on questioning him for hours on end. Maigret, however, had had enough of it.

'Were you in on it?'

'On what?'

'That job!'

'What job?'

Maigret felt like punching him in the face. He restrained himself in time.

'Have you got an alibi?'

'A good one! I was in bed . . .'

'You were at the cinema or you were in bed?'

'I was at the flicks first . . . Then I went to bed . . .'

Maigret had brought many others to heel, but here he had no authority to act, and his nephew seemed ill at ease.

'You wouldn't by any chance be the fourth guy, the one they didn't catch?'

The youth solemnly spat on the floor, declaring: 'I swear I wasn't!'

At that same moment the telephone bell rang. Jérôme lifted the receiver and knit his brows:

'What's that? . . . You're sure? . . .'

He hung up again, rose to his feet, and not knowing what to do with Louis left him in the office while he dragged Maigret into the passage.

'That was Emergencies: a woman has just been attacked on the sixth floor of . . .'

'67b Rue Caulaincourt!' his uncle completed the sentence.

'Yes. The concierge declares she saw a man leave the house, bleeding profusely. There's blood all over the stairs ... What are we going to do with *him*?'

For Jérôme, who had a great respect for regulations, was embarrassed by the somewhat unofficial presence of Louis the Kid.

III

Jérôme Lacroix could not resist constantly turning to Maigret and murmuring uneasily: 'What do you think about it, Uncle?'

And the ex-Superintendent would reply, while the shadow of a smile made his words even more enigmatic:

'You know, son, I never think ...'

He was taking up as little room as possible. For a long time he sat quite still in a corner beside the dressmaker's dummy, smoking his pipe with an absent-minded air.

Nonetheless his presence embarrassed everyone. The local police superintendent, fearful of appearing ham-fisted in front of the famous Maigret, sought the latter's approval incessantly.

'That's what you would do in my place, isn't it?'

Every landing was crowded, and a policeman was with difficulty preventing people from entering the apartment. Another, at the front door of the house, was vainly repeating: 'Since I tell you there's nothing to see!'

Many inhabitants of the Rue Caulaincourt went without their dinner that evening so as to remain on the watch in the street or at their windows. The weather, as a matter of fact, was ideal, and from time to time one could see shadows passing behind the drawn blinds of the room on the sixth floor.

Down below an ambulance had drawn up. It stood waiting for about an hour and then, to everyone's surprise, drove off again empty.

'What do you think about it, Monsieur Maigret?'

A problem had arisen. Mademoiselle Berthe, who had recovered consciousness, refused to let herself be taken to hospital. She was weak, for she had lost a great deal of blood through a scalp wound. But she displayed the intensity of her feeling by her gaze and by the nervous clenching of her moist hands.

'It's up to the doctor,' said Maigret, who did not wish to assume any responsibility.

And Inspector Lacroix consulted the doctor.

'Do you think we can leave her here?'

'I think that when I've put in a few stitches she can be left to sleep till tomorrow morning ...'

All this was taking place amidst the usual confusion. Only the injured girl's eyes remained obstinately fixed on Maigret, and seemed to be appealing to him fervently.

'You heard what the concierge said, Uncle? As I see it, things must have occurred after this fashion: Mademoiselle Berthe went downstairs, probably to buy a few provisions . . .'

'No!' Maigret said quietly.

'You don't think so? Then why did she go down?'

'To post a letter . . .'

Jérôme wondered how Maigret could be so certain of this detail, but he put off the question until later.

'It's unimportant . . .'

'It's very important. But carry on . . .'

'She had scarcely left the house when the concierge saw a man come into the building. The corridor was dark. The concierge assumed he was a friend of one of the tenants. Mademoiselle Berthe came back almost immediately . . .'

'There's a letter-box a hundred metres away, in the Place Constantin-Pecqueur,' specified Maigret, dotting his i's for his own satisfaction.

'All right! . . . She came back . . . She found the intruder in her flat. He attacked her and she defended herself. The man, seriously injured, to judge by the traces of blood on the stairs, hurried down, and the concierge caught sight of him running off, clutching his stomach . . .'

Jérôme looked round somewhat uneasily, and added with less assurance:

'The trouble is that the weapon has not been found . . .'

'The weapons!' Maigret corrected him. 'One blunt instrument with which Mademoiselle Berthe was struck, and another, probably a knife, used to wound the intruder . . .'

'Perhaps he took them away with him?' ventured Jérôme.

And Maigret turned his head away to hide a smile.

Orders had been given to look for an injured man throughout the neighbourhood. The doctor finished dressing the wound on the girl's head; in spite of the pain she strove not to take her eyes off Maigret.

'Do you believe, Uncle, that it may have been her lover?'

'Who did what?'

'Who came here and attacked her . . .'

Why did Maigret reply with such surprising certainty:

'I'm sure it was not!'

'What would you do in my place?'

'Since I'm not in your place I find it hard to answer.'

The local superintendent came up next, in quest of encouragement or approval:

'This is what I've decided; the doctor's going to send a nurse round presently to stay with the patient. Meanwhile I'll put an officer on duty below. Tomorrow we'll consider whether it is possible to question her, and whether there's any point in doing so . . .'

The girl had overheard. She was still looking at Maigret, and she had the impression that he gave her a slight wink. Then, reassured, she yielded to the torpor that was engulfing her.

The two men, uncle and nephew, walked past the inquisitive spectators on the neighbouring doorsteps, and Maigret filled a fresh pipe.

'Suppose we go for a bite?' he suggested. 'It strikes me that we haven't had any dinner yet. There's a brasserie along the street, and I must say a *choucroute garnie* would . . . You've just got to ring up your wife . . .'

During the whole meal Jérôme never ceased to watch his uncle, like a schoolboy in dread of being caught out. And little by little this was making him bad-tempered, even resentful towards Maigret for being too calm, too self-assured.

'Anyone would think you find this case amusing!' he remarked, helping himself to sausage.

'It is amusing, you're quite right!'

'It may be amusing for the person who's not responsible for finding the solution.'

Maigret was enjoying his meal: thickset, broad-shouldered, he picked up his glass of beer with such obvious greedy delight that he might have served as a brewer's advertisement.

As he wiped his lips, he treated himself to the sly pleasure of remarking:

'I've found it . . .'

'What?'

'The solution . . .'

'You know who attacked Mademoiselle Berthe?'

'No!'

'Well then?'

'That isn't important . . . I mean that it isn't important either for her or for me . . .'

Jérôme's face grew longer still and, but for the respect he felt for Maigret, he would have been red with anger.

'Thanks a lot!' he grumbled, bending over his plate.

'Why?'

'Because, instead of helping me, you're making fun of me. If you've really discovered something . . .'

But he tried in vain to provoke his uncle; Maigret had relapsed into stolid impassivity. He ordered a second helping of *choucroute*, with a couple of frankfurters, and a third beer.

'But look here, do you think I've done all I had to do?'

'You did what you thought you had to, didn't you?'

'There's a nurse in the room . . .'

'Yes . . .'

'And a policeman at the door . . .'

'Of course!'

'What d'you mean?'

'Nothing . . .'

Maigret paid for the meal; he refused his nephew's invitation to go home with him for coffee. And half an hour later he was at his window in the Hôtel de Concarneau.

On the other side of the street he could see Mademoiselle Berthe's room, where a dim light shone behind the blinds, and he could glimpse the figure of the nurse, huddled in an armchair reading. Down below on the pavement a policeman was pacing up and down, and looking at his watch every quarter of an hour.

'It's up to her to manage now,' Maigret muttered as he closed his window.

And just as he was pulling off his socks, sitting on the edge of the bed, he remembered his nephew, and added:

'It's up to him to work out his plan!'

The room was full of sunlight at nine o'clock next morning as he went up to Mademoiselle Berthe's bedside, while the nurse was tidying up the room.

'I've come to say goodbye to you,' he announced, assuming a falsely innocent air. 'Now that wretched Albert has failed in his attempt, I suppose you're no longer in danger . . .'

Then he read anxiety and almost panic in the wounded girl's eyes. She tried to raise herself up to find out where the nurse was. Then she stammered:

'Don't go yet . . . I implore you!'

'You're really anxious I should stay here?'

'Yes . . .'

'And you're not afraid, for instance, of my giving a few hints to my poor bewildered nephew?'

There was something both gruff and fatherly about Maigret that morning. And yet he was well aware that Mademoiselle Berthe was hesitating between smiles and tears. She was watching him. The previous evening she had been feverish and she might have misunderstood.

The presence of the nurse complicated things still further, for the girl could not speak as openly as she would have liked.

'By the way,' Maigret asked, 'you didn't get a letter this morning?'

She shook her head, and he declared confidently:

'You'll get one tomorrow . . . Yes, you will! . . . A letter postmarked Calais or Boulogne . . . And I can give you one detail: there'll be a couple of pinpricks in the stamp . . .'

He was smiling. Standing up in the sunlight, he was playing, just as on the previous day, with the china bowl that held pins, buttons and stamps.

He did not need to press his point, for Mademoiselle Berthe's blushes showed that she had understood.

Once more she looked round anxiously, for she was afraid of the nurse overhearing, but Maigret's glance told her that the woman was in the kitchen, where the hissing of the gas stove could now be heard.

'Do you know your next door neighbours?' he asked, changing the subject suddenly. 'You mentioned an old couple, didn't you? Have they a servant?'

'No. The wife does her own housework.'

'And her shopping too?'

'Yes. Every morning about nine or ten o'clock . . . I know she goes to the market in the Rue Lepic, for I've met her there several times.'

'And the husband?'

'He goes out at the same time and spends his morning hunting in secondhand book shops in the Boulevard Rochechouart.'

'So that their apartment is empty!' Maigret concluded in an unnecessarily loud tone of voice.

And once again the injured girl hesitated between smiles and tears. She was still uncertain whether Maigret was for her or against her. She dared not decide.

'Just fancy,' he said in a friendly tone, though still speaking very loud, 'they've put a policeman on duty on the pavement. And do you know what orders he's been given?'

He did not even seem to be addressing Mademoiselle Berthe. He had turned to face the opposite direction.

'To prevent you from going out, if the fancy should take you. And to prevent your enemies from coming in. I said coming in, mind you! The police, you see, are afraid they might come and attack you in bed . . .'

Thereupon he went to open the window wide, knocked out his pipe against his heel and filled another.

There was a longish silence. It seemed as if the girl, as well as the Superintendent, were waiting for something. Maigret paced anxiously up and down the balcony, leaning over to peer into the street, then shrugging his shoulders impatiently.

He even muttered between his teeth: 'The young fool!'

Suddenly he stood motionless, looking down into the street. Mademoiselle Berthe seemed on the point of getting up, in spite of her weak state. The nurse was watching both of them, wondering what it all meant and probably thinking they were a bit crazy.

'There's a métro station at the corner of the street,' sighed Maigret. 'And a bus stop fifty metres away! . . . And a taxi cruising by, into the bargain. So why? . . .'

This time Mademoiselle Berthe could not resist questioning him: 'Has he gone?'

And Maigret grumbled:

'He's taking long enough about it, at any rate! . . . You'd think he was tied on by elastic . . . At last!'

'By bus?'

'By métro . . .'

Then Maigret came back into the room, went into the kitchen to fetch the bottle of white wine, and sighed as he poured himself a drink:

'If only it had been dry!'

Mademoiselle Berthe was weeping uncontrollably. She was weeping her heart out, as they say, while the nurse tried to comfort her:

'Calm down, Mademoiselle! You'll do yourself an injury . . . I promise you your wound isn't serious . . . You mustn't be unhappy . . .'

'Idiot!' growled Maigret.

For that goose of a nurse had not understood that these were tears of joy that Berthe was shedding so wildly, while the sunbeams played over her sheets.

IV

When the doctor came, Maigret had taken his hat and left without a word. With the nonchalant air of one who has nothing better to do, he had gone to the Zanzi-Bar, and shortly afterwards had seen his nephew pass by on his way to subject Mademoiselle Berthe to close questioning.

Suddenly Louis the Kid had come in; he tried to draw back on seeing the Superintendent, who, however, called out:

'I've come to take my revenge at poker-dice . . . Give us the dice, *patron*. An anis for this gentleman . . . that's what you like, isn't it, Louis? . . . Your turn to start . . . Three queens . . . I'm afraid that's not good enough . . . What did I tell you? Three kings . . . One up to me . . .'

And without a change of tone he went on, bending towards his companion, who was trying hard to keep his countenance:

'Was the money in the soup tureen?'

Louis the Kid shook his head.

'Was it in Albert's pocket?'

A fresh, even more vigorous shake of the head, and finally Louis confessed:

'He ran off along the embankment and threw the notes into the Seine . . .'

'You're sure of that?'

'I swear it's true!'

'Then why did someone come yesterday?'

'Because he didn't believe me . . .'

Maigret smiled. It was a very special moment, not only on account of the spring weather, the sunshine, the lively atmosphere of the Rue Caulaincourt and his cool beer, but because a single remark had just now reassured him.

It was such a relief that he felt a sudden hot flush of retrospective fear.

Now he could go ahead. He was in a strong position.

'Who fired?'

'The Marseillais . . . Albert had given him his gun . . .'

And Maigret laughed to himself as he watched his nephew gloomily emerging from no. 67b and waiting for the bus a few metres away from the Zanzi-Bar.

'What are you going to do?' asked Louis the Kid, anxiously, still clutching the dice-box.

'Me? I'm going to say goodbye to your sister and catch my train.'

The bus passed, carrying away Jérôme Lacroix. Maigret crossed the street, and on the sixth floor found the nurse packing up her things.

'I'm not needed any more,' she announced. 'The doctor's going to call once a day and the concierge will look in from time to time . . .'

Maigret's eyes were gleaming with merriment. He paced about the room as though he were at home, waiting for the nurse to leave. Seldom had an inquiry given him as much delight, and yet it was a trivial affair about which, into the bargain, he would never be able to talk.

He recalled his reaction on receiving the letter from Mademoiselle Berthe at Meung-sur-Loire.

'It's odd,' he had observed, 'it seems sincere and yet at the same time it doesn't . . .'

And the young woman in the red hat who had joined him on the terrace of the Café de Madrid had given him the same impression. She was really frightened, that was obvious. But it was obvious, too, that she was lying when she spoke of being terrified of her lover. She did not put on the right tone of voice when she uttered Albert's name. Against her will she spoke it too gently, too tenderly.

Then why had this determined young person ventured to disturb ex-Superintendent Maigret in his rural retreat? And why had she shown him, rather than the police, those letters sent from Boulogne and Calais?

He had not understood to begin with, particularly since he had watched her for hours on end through the window, calmly carrying on her fittings like someone who is not in the least afraid of a vindictive attack. The stamps in the china bowl had given him an idea, and he had pierced them with a pin.

'Why are you smiling, Superintendent?'

'And why are you?'

They were alone together now. The nurse had left. The noise of the street rose towards them, somewhat diminished, with the first hint of that smell of heated asphalt that is typical of Paris in the summer.

Maigret, nonetheless, tried to put on a serious air and assumed his most ominous voice to say:

'Do you know that if the sixty thousand francs had been here and if it was Albert who'd taken them I'd have had you arrested?'

'And yet you were, so to speak, acting on my behalf . . .'

'That's just it! That's what I realized . . . I realized that you had sent for me not to protect you against your Albert but to protect Albert against himself . . . And if you had loved him a tiny bit less, I give you my word that last night I'd have hauled him out of his hiding-place . . .'

'I don't see what my love . . .' she murmured, reddening.

'You may not see it, perhaps, but that's how it is. I argued thus: here's a young person who's got plenty of cheek, but who seems to me straight enough. She's trying to save a boy who's got into a bad fix, she tries to save him out of love. And I'm convinced that if the boy had really committed a murder she'd have been revolted . . .'

'He gave me his solemn word that he never fired, Superintendent. In any case, it was all my fault in a way. I knew he was friendly with my brother Louis, and that some of Louis's associates were shady people. Albert had been unable to find work in Paris, and he was eager to marry me; so he was easily persuaded. The others, whom I don't want to know, took him along to keep watch. One of them borrowed Albert's revolver in case anything should happen. When the police turned up and they all ran away, they left the gun on the spot and they thrust the money into Albert's hands as they went by . . .'

'I know.'

'How did you guess where he was?'

'To begin with, I made sure there was no cellar or attic here. Then I noticed that when you spoke to me you sometimes raised your voice, as though you wanted to be heard by someone else . . . Originally there was only one apartment on this floor. When they subdivided it they left the communicating door, but made it a double one, I mean that there's a door on each side of the wall with a gap between the two . . . Albert was in there . . . Only . . .'

'Only I was sure that the police, who had already come once, would search the house a second time. I didn't know if it was being watched. In order to find out . . .'

'You appealed to me, knowing that I would keep you informed as to the course of the official inquiry. I was here to serve as a screen . . . I prevented suspicion from falling on your home and at the same time I provided you with information . . . I came to realize this . . . Do you know it was extremely bright of you?'

'Oh! Superintendent,' she murmured, shamefaced, 'I had to save Albert, didn't I? His accomplices would never have confessed the truth . . . He'd have taken the rap . . . Particularly as they were convinced that we'd kept the money . . . I learned that from my brother . . .'

'Who was trying to protect you! . . . Yesterday evening you went out to post the double letter you sent to your girl friend in Boulogne' (he pointed to her photograph) '. . . that Madeleine, whose job it was to send back the threatening letters to you. Meanwhile one of the accomplices took the opportunity to slip in here and look for the money. You came back, and he knocked you out with a bludgeon. Albert came out of his hiding-place and rushed at him with a knife in his hand . . . That's it, isn't it?'

He had anticipated her story. And he knew, furthermore, that it was Albert who had taken the two weapons into his hiding-place.

'I bet they're still there!' he growled. He opened the communicating door and, as he had expected, found a rubber bludgeon and a bloodstained knife.

'Where are you planning to meet him?' he asked, looking round for his hat.

She hesitated, then stammered:

'Must I tell you? Can I be quite sure that . . .'

Then he laughed outright.

'That I won't have you both arrested at the frontier? Is that what you're trying to imply?'

'No . . . But . . .'

'But you love your Albert so much, don't you? that the very idea that somebody else might . . .'

He was close to the door, had his hand on the knob.

'Actually, you're jealous . . . Yes indeed, Mademoiselle

Berthe! . . . And jealous of me, moreover, because you'd wanted to save him all by yourself . . . Come to that, I can't prevent you, as soon as my back's turned, from getting up in spite of your injuries and taking the train to Brussels . . . I'm even willing to bet that a boutique selling Paris models will open there shortly. Goodbye, Mademoiselle Berthe!'

And because he wanted some small revenge after all, he called out as he left the room:

'I shall send you my bill . . .'

THE THREE DAUGHTERS
OF THE LAWYER
I

Nobody could have been any further from any thought of adventure or surprise than Maigret that July morning, in his low-walled garden by the banks of the Loire.

From those white-washed walls, covered with espalier fruit-trees, from the flower-beds watered the previous evening, from the squares of pale lettuce and the melon frames, from the whole garden there seemed to rise into the sunlight a sort of transparent heat-haze, and the very flies seemed too drowsy to move through the close air.

His pipe between his teeth, an old straw hat on his head, Maigret was padding about blissfully in a patch of tomatoes so ripe that they dropped to the ground and spilled their scarlet juice, when he raised his head, surprised in the first place to hear a car drive up along the lane that led nowhere and even more surprised to hear it stop at his own front door.

He turned towards the kitchen where, in the blue shade, he saw Madame Maigret, as surprised as himself, stop short with a saucepan in her hand.

The brass knocker sounded on the door. Madame Maigret instinctively untied the strings of her cotton apron and straightened her knot of hair.

Maigret was loth to go and meet the visitor. He stayed there in his garden; he heard doors opening and closing, steps sounding on the grey flags of the passage, then in the dining-room, and, finally, his wife's voice saying:

'You'll find him in the garden . . .'

Beside the house there was just one rectangle of shadow, in which there were an iron table, a green-painted bench, an enamel wash-basin and a towel hanging by the wall to wash one's hands after working in the garden.

Maigret moved forward ponderously, screwing up his eyes against the sun, and saw before him a man of fifty to sixty, dressed in black, with that extreme, chilly formality of bearing that Maigret had met in certain high-ranking magistrates.

'I apologize for disturbing you in your retreat,' the stranger began, laying his bowler hat on the table and mopping his brow, which was crowned with thick white hair. 'My name is Motte; I am a lawyer from Châteauneuf.'

And with a slight mechanical smile which Maigret was to observe again frequently, he added:

'Oh, you have certainly never heard of me, although I have often heard of you . . .'

'Please sit down.'

'Thank you . . . I have come . . . Hm . . . I may as well tell you right away and get my task over, mayn't I? It's not an agreeable request to have to make to a man whom one finds, like the traditional philosopher, smoking a pipe in his garden! And yet my purpose in coming here is to beg you to leave your garden and your home for a few days and come to stay with me.'

Twice more that strange smile had appeared, a mechanical curl of the lips. Perhaps he was trying in this way to counteract the icy and over-solemn effect of his appearance?

Madame Maigret had retired silently and gone up in order to put on a clean dress, just in case. Her husband guessed as much when he heard her open the wardrobe in the bedroom, the window of which was wide open.

'I know that on leaving the Police Judiciaire you did not choose to set up as a private detective. So I am asking your assistance as an exceptional favour. I will put the situation to you as simply as possible and you shall decide . . .'

He closed his eyes for a minute as though to set his thoughts in order, and Maigret sensed that here was a man accustomed to express his thoughts clearly, indeed to enjoy hearing himself speak.

'As I was telling you, I am a lawyer at Châteauneuf, some forty kilometres from here. I have never been an ambitious man, and the look of your house and garden leads me to think that we resemble one another, at all events in the simplicity of our tastes. In a word, I am only happy in my own home, in the house which was my parents' and my grandparents' before me, and my greatest joys are derived from my three daughters, Emilienne, Armande and Clotilde. Emilienne is now sixteen, Armande nineteen and Clotilde twenty-three. Only one of them is engaged, Armande, and the wedding should be taking place next month.'

Maigret made a passing note of that 'should be'; he continued to show a polite attention, which did not prevent him from watching the progress of an army of ants crossing the gravel in a narrow stream.

'I don't know if you have children yourself . . .'

Maigret shook his head, reflecting that if his wife had heard from up in the bedroom she would be sad all day, for this was her great grief.

'My own principle has always been to give my daughters the utmost freedom. I want to be able to trust them completely. And although provincial lawyers are usually held to be prejudiced people there is one point on which I have no prejudice whatsoever: the question of wealth. In a word . . .'

This was one of his favourite phrases, which recurred in his conversation as frequently as did those little automatic smiles on his face.

'In a word, I should never dream of preventing my daughters from marrying men who were not rich. I have always said so, and when the situation arose, when Armande made the acquaintance of Gérard Donavant, I did not even point out to her that the young man was not only penniless but, furthermore, had no social position. In a word . . .'

'Again!' thought Maigret.

'He is a painter; for the past year he has been living in a small rented house beside the Loire and preparing for an exhibition of his work next winter, on which he is counting to make a name for himself. Armande is in love with him. She refuses to wait until after the exhibition to get married. I think it is a matter of personal pride with her to insist on the wedding taking place before it, and also a touch of superstition.'

He broke off when he saw Maigret leaning forward slightly as though falling asleep.

'Am I boring you?'

'Not at all. I was watching that ant carrying a load ten times its own size. That does not stop me from listening to you. You had got to "a touch of superstition" . . .'

Nonetheless he was inwardly cursing this black-suited bore who had thought fit to violate the privacy of the Maigret garden in order to relate his family affairs in such touchingly minute detail. Emilienne? Armande? Clotilde? Armande and Gérard were going to get married? Good luck to them! And good luck to Gérard's show! Maigret had been so happy a short while ago among his tomatoes.

'May I offer you a glass of white wine?'

'I'll have a glass of water, if I may.'

That was his own business; Maigret, however, wanted his white wine.

'Now I shall soon have done, never fear. I hope I have given you the picture of a happy home, a united family where everyone enjoys life. To complete it I must add a touch that may seem slightly ridiculous: I am a collector.'

With that, a twitch of a smile, as though by way of apology.

'A collector of carved and engraved ivories . . . I possess about eighteen hundred pieces, some of which are extremely rare. Now, for the past month, I have noticed that two or three times a week a thief has been at work in my house. You will probably think it very bold of me to bother you on account of thefts which you may consider unimportant. But apart from the fact that some of the objects which have disappeared are worth thousands, even tens of thousands of francs, there is something more serious, Monsieur Maigret, namely the moral consequences of these thefts. I have considered every possibility, you must realise. I am not a man who panics readily, nor am I fanciful. Our old cook was born in the house, like myself; her husband, the gardener, has been with us for thirty-two years. As for our little housemaid, I have watched her and I am convinced that she is incapable of stealing objects which, in any case, she would not know what to do with. I also thought of my head clerk, whom you will meet presently . . .'

Maigret gave a start, but uttered no protest.

'I have a second assistant whom you will also meet, and you will realise why I could not possibly suspect him . . . As you will have guessed, there remains Gérard Donavant, and that is why I am here. I have no right to ruin my daughter's happiness and that young man's just because I've imagined things, but neither have I the right to let Armande marry a thief. Moreover you'll agree that I cannot bring in the official police . . .'

'Where are these ivories of yours kept?' asked Maigret abruptly.

And this time Monsieur Motte's smile was less fleeting, for he realised that his task was going to be easier from now on.

'In my study . . . I mean in my private study, on the first floor, and not in my business office which is on the ground floor. I'll show you, when we go there, what precautions I took and what traps I laid . . .'

'And which served no purpose?'

'Which did not prevent the thefts taking place at an ever increasing rate.'

'Are these things easy to sell?'

'Practically impossible. As soon as I noticed the first thefts I warned all dealers likely to buy such pieces, and I wrote to the handful of collectors I know in Paris and in London. I must emphasize that the wedding is due to take place in a month's time, in twenty-nine days to be exact, and that I am becoming increasingly anxious as the date draws nearer . . .'

'Have you told your family about these thefts?'

'Only on the first occasion, for I then assumed that someone had moved the object accidentally. Later I said nothing.'

'What size are these objects, as you call them?'

'They are of various sizes, but the ones in which I am chiefly interested are the miniatures. Certain Chinese ivories are no bigger than a walnut and yet contain a number of figures, delicately carved . . .'

'Another question: does your thief choose the most valuable pieces?'

'Yes.'

'Are these easy to recognize?'

'On the contrary, it is very hard to decide whether a given piece is very valuable or a commonplace article. Now I should just like to say . . .'

'He's going to mention money,' thought Maigret. But the lawyer from Châteauneuf determinedly pursued his idea.

'. . . to say how, in my opinion, the problem should be approached. It will obviously be necessary for you to spend a certain period of time in the house. It will also be necessary to avoid arousing suspicions and I can consequently not introduce you as the famous Chief Superintendent Maigret.'

Maigret seldom made fun of people, and yet Monsieur Motte's solemn composure provoked an irresistible desire to tease. With the utmost seriousness he murmured: 'Shall I put on a false beard?'

But the lawyer remained imperturbable; he pretended not to have heard.

'I shall therefore introduce you to my family as an old Army comrade who lives at some distance and has a few days to spare. What town are you particularly familiar with?'

'What about Bergerac?' suggested Maigret.

'Very well. You are my friend from Bergerac . . . Monsieur what shall we say?'

'Legros?'

The odd thing was that Maigret was not taking the thing at all seriously. He replied with a straight face, but was secretly making fun of the proposed plan.

'Can you drive?'

'A car? No.'

'A pity.'

'Why? Must Monsieur Legros own a car?'

'It's absolutely essential. You shall see why. I drive. All my girls drive, even the youngest who has not yet got her licence. My chief clerk uses the car and so does Gérard . . .'

'And I shall have to be able to shadow him,' growled Maigret, whose eyes were aching from watching the procession of ants.

'We'll make a different arrangement. Since you cannot drive you shall have a chauffeur. My friend Legros might very well have a chauffeur. By the way, what profession shall he have?'

'I don't care . . .'

'A profession about which you can talk knowledgeably?'

'A wholesale timber merchant? I've always longed to be a wholesale timber merchant because of the smell of newly sawn boards . . .'

'All right. I will take you with me to Orléans, where we'll hire a chauffeur-driven car. You will arrive a quarter of an hour after me.'

Only then did Maigret wonder if he might not be dreaming. He stared with stupefaction, as though for the first time, at this peculiar man who in a few minutes had laid down plans for him with such uncanny coolness. Then he wondered whether his wife, who had gone down into the kitchen again, had overheard the conversation. Finally, to gain time, he emptied his glass and knocked out his pipe against his sabot.

'But . . .' he began.

He realized at last that he had let himself be spellbound. It seemed too late now to destroy the edifice that had been so skilfully constructed by the imperturbable lawyer from Châteauneuf.

'I suppose,' the latter remarked, 'that you won't take long to get dressed? You had better bring a case with a change of clothes.'

He looked Maigret straight in the eyes, and Maigret looked back. This was the moment of decision. It would have been just as easy for Maigret to say: 'Get the hell out of here' as to get up and go off to dress, as the man had suggested.

'Well, you see . . .'

'Remember that Armande is to be married in twenty-nine days!'

So what? Did he, Maigret, know this Armande or her Gérard? Did *he* collect ivory knicknacks with tiny carved figures?

He was at home in his garden, with his sabots and his straw hat, and the line of shade was creeping forward over the ground, getting narrower beside the wall until at noontime there would be none at all.

'I know a garage which will provide a reliable chauffeur . . .'

Monsieur Motte was so sure of everything! He sat there on the bench staring at the tips of his well-polished shoes. For two pins he would have said to his companion:

'Well, what are you waiting for?'

What happened next was that Maigret got up and went into the kitchen. At a glance he realized that his wife had been listening, for she began shaking her head violently as though to say: 'You're not to go!'

And he, for no reason, at any rate for no reason that he could have defined, nodded his head just as forcibly, thereby declaring:

'I'm going!'

Then he said aloud:

'Come up and help me pack my suitcase . . .'

Going up the stairs, she grumbled:

'And I'd made a *fricandeau* for you!'

Once in the bedroom, however, she had to keep silent, because Monsieur Motte could hear them through the open window. Maigret leaned forward to look at him. This strange, self-possessed man with his measured speech, his meticulous politeness, impressed him, he did not know why.

'Emilienne, Armande and Clotilde . . .' he muttered.

'That's why you're going there?'

She was not really jealous, but she sometimes pretended to be because this delighted Maigret, who would then smile and shrug his
shoulders.

He frowned, however, when he looked at himself in the glass, to
think that he'd become Monsieur Legros from Bergerac, the timber
merchant!

He tried to picture the dining-room where he was presently going to
lunch in company of people whom he did not know and who would
scrutinize him with curiosity.

He was soon ready, went downstairs and found Monsieur Motte
still in the same spot.

'I don't suppose we need call one another *tu*?' he growled, as though
in revenge for his own meekness.

'No . . . After such a long time . . .'

'Where did we do our military service?'

'I did mine at Orange, with the spahis.'

Incredible, but true: this frigid little gentleman had worn the gor-
geous uniform of the Algerian cavalry and pranced about the streets of
Orange on an Arab charger!

'The spahis be it,' said Maigret. 'After all, there's no reason why I
shouldn't have been a spahi too, provided I'm not required to ride a
horse . . .'

These jokes, however, called forth no reaction save the automatic
smile from the Châteauneuf lawyer, who was now waiting politely for
Maigret to be ready to go.

Madame Maigret brought the suitcase which Maigret had lugged
around on so many official inquiries. He felt like saying to it:

'Well, old thing, this is a queer job they've given us . . . You belong
to Monsieur Legros now, and . . .'

Madame Maigret was asking: 'When will you be coming home?'

'In a few days, Madame,' put in Monsieur Motte. 'I promise to let
you have him back soon, for I'm convinced that it won't be long before
he discovers the truth . . .'

'Thank you very much!' breathed the ex-Superintendent.

And he got into the car beside Monsieur Motte, who announced as
he took the wheel:

'You need have no fear . . . I never drive fast . . .'

'I couldn't care less . . .'

They soon reached Orléans and stopped in the main square, in
front of a garage. While the lawyer called in here, Maigret found his
way into a brasserie where they served the best brown ale in the whole

department.

'Emilienne, Clotilde and Armande . . .' he recited. 'No, Armande is the middle one . . . Emilienne, Armande and Clotilde . . . I'm longing to see whether they look like their father.'

For actually, although he grumbled and cursed at the lawyer, he felt curious to see that house which had belonged to Monsieur Motte's father and grandfather, with its office on the ground floor and its study on the first floor, its garden – presumably, since there was a gardener – its seventy-year-old cook and the little housemaid who was above suspicion.

'Why,' he reflected, 'there was no mention of his wife. Perhaps she's dead?'

Monsieur Motte had left the garage and was looking for his companion. Not knowing that he was being watched, he displayed a certain anxiety and the nervous smile was quite forgotten.

At last he caught sight of Maigret on the terrace, and informed him that his car and chauffeur would be ready in a quarter of an hour. The ex-Superintendent took advantage of this respite to drink another glass of beer and smoke his pipe in the sunshine in front of his marble-topped table.

'Well, if the house proves gloomy and the daughters ugly . . .'

Two hours later, as he left the exceptionally bright dining-room and followed Monsieur Motte into the drawing-room, where he was offered a cigar, he was no longer in a joking mood.

He would in fact have been much surprised if anyone had told him that he had only been there for a hundred and twenty minutes, and that only that morning he had never heard speak of Emilienne, Armande and Clotilde.

Emilienne was the one who offered him his cup of coffee with a charming little curtsey and a smile which was peculiarly her own. Clotilde drew the blinds to soften the hot afternoon sun, and in the tempered light, Armande was beautiful, with a fresh simple beauty, unaffected and unself-conscious.

'If you'd rather smoke your pipe . . .' the lawyer was saying.

Of course he'd rather have smoked his pipe! But he chose not to, because of the three girls and because of Madame Motte, who sat there in her armchair, a mild smile on her lips.

For there *was* a Madame Motte, a gentle, retiring woman who seemed to wander through life smiling vaguely as though in a dream.

'Two lumps?'

'Just one, please . . .'

How often, as he passed those large houses on the banks of the Loire, with their subtle harmonious lines, Maigret had said to himself:

'It must be easy and pleasant to live there, surrounded by pretty things . . .'

And the Mottes' house was typical of the country houses of an earlier period, with nothing either mean or showy about it, nothing ugly or aggressive. Tufts of grass grew between the flagstones in the courtyard. From time to time a heavy cart could be heard lumbering along the narrow lane. The walls were panelled in light wood, with just the right amount of patina, and when one walked through the drawing-room the crystal drops of the chandelier tinkled discreetly.

'Presently, if you like, my dear fellow, Armande shall give you a little music. But I think she'd rather wait until her fiancé comes. Are you fond of music?'

To be sure! Why not? But he had never had the time to hear much.

'Are you fond of Schubert?' Armande pressed him, as she turned the pages of a volume of music.

'Yes, indeed, mademoiselle!'

He did not yet call her Armande, but he felt that this would come, and that he would soon be saying Emilienne, Armande and Clotilde as though he were a member of the family. He cast a glance at the lean figure of Monsieur Motte, silhouetted against the pale gold of the drawn blind.

He noticed that peculiar tic, that fleeting smile; and he was sure that the lawyer was trying to say to him:

'You see that I had told you the truth!'

He had indeed! And the very perfection of it all was disturbing; Maigret felt himself becoming imperceptibly involved in a world that was too perfect, too happy, where there was no place for the sordid aspects of life with which he had been concerned for over thirty years.

And it was then that he understood, and gave a sudden start as though there, amid all that surrounding sweetness and serenity, he had caught sight of something horrid and repulsive, a scorpion for instance or a reptile.

Someone had stolen!

And this phrase, which at the Quai des Orfèvres was anodyne enough, denoting an offence which was an everyday affair in the life of a policeman accustomed to dealing with far worse depravities, here assumed a different meaning.

Someone had stolen!

Could that confounded little lawyer read his thoughts? Maigret caught a sudden look of sadness on the man's face.

Someone had stolen!

And it was rather as if someone had deliberately defiled, degraded a splendid thing, had for instance outraged Emilienne's innocence by treating her as a whore, or soiled those perfect panels, broken the grand piano, or torn the Persian carpet with its incredible blue tints.

Someone, in the house, had stolen!

And Maigret almost felt like apologizing to his host for the light-hearted tone he had assumed that morning.

For he had just come to realize that the mere purloining of some ivory objects can in certain atmospheres assume an intenser emotional significance than all the violent crimes with which the Police Judiciaire has to deal.

II

The lawyer's gilt escutcheon-sign was not set close to the great front door flanked by two stone posts, but a little further on, where his office had its private entrance; its green panes distinguished the windows from the others in the house.

They were still drinking their coffee, when Armande gave a start on hearing footsteps in the street, and Gérard Donavant need not have troubled to ring at the door, for his fiancée recognized his step from afar. A bell sounded nonetheless in the porch, a deep resonant bell, and the girl rushed out unceremoniously to open the door. She returned with her young man, radiant, and seeming to say to Maigret – or rather to Monsieur Legros:

'You see that Gérard deserves to be loved!'

What embarrassed the ex-Superintendent more was feeling Monsieur Motte's insistent gaze fixed on him, and particularly as he had not been able to restrain a start of surprise on Gérard's entrance.

The young man was really a magnificent specimen, tall and strong with a sun-tanned face, bright-eyed, his movements easy and flexible in the casual thin sweater which enhanced his athletic appearance.

'Gérard, let me introduce you to a friend of Father's, an old friend of his army days, Monsieur Legros, who's come to spend a few days with us.'

The two men exchanged an energetic handshake. Their eyes met, and Maigret was aware of a momentary unease clouding the young man's cheerful look.

'Delighted to meet you,' he said.

As he went back to his seat Maigret noticed that somebody was missing from the drawing-room, the youngest sister Emilienne. who had left the room silently. Clotilde, meanwhile, remarked:

'Armande was waiting for you to begin playing. All morning she's been practising that Schubert song you love so much . . .'

Why did Monsieur Motte keep looking at him as though to say:

'Well, what's your impression? Have you noticed anything?'

Maigret made a little sign to him, and he understood.

'Will you excuse us if we don't stay for the music this afternoon? My friend Legros has some rather important questions to discuss with me.'

They went up a staircase so perfectly polished that it reflected their foreshortened figures. Monsieur Motte showed Maigret into a huge study whose windows overlooked the courtyard, drowsy under the heavy sunshine, and beyond it a green garden, which still contained the swings and seesaws that the girls had played with as children.

As for the study, it was austerely furnished in ebony, in order – as was immediately evident – to set off the hundreds of tiny ivories set out in glass cabinets which covered the walls right up to the ceiling.

'I guessed that you had something to tell me,' said the lawyer, offering his guest an armchair of tawny leather.

Unfortunately Maigret could henceforward no longer enjoy wholeheartedly the quiet and harmony of a house where such patient care had been lavished to ensure order and happiness. He avoided looking at his host, who had now sat down at his desk.

'I rather thought it was you yourself who might have some details to add to the confidential story you told me this morning,' he retorted.

The opening remarks of this conversation would scarcely have been understood by an eavesdropper.

The lawyer said: 'You know him?'

Maigret replied: 'You knew the facts?'

And Monsieur Motte went on:

'He told me everything himself . . . I did not want to influence your judgement beforehand . . . I wanted to see . . .'

It was almost like a trap, and Maigret could now account for the peculiar effect that Monsieur Motte had had on him.

'Has the young man told you his real name?'

'Yes, Gassin . . . Gérard Gassin . . .'

'Did he tell you that his father was better known by the nickname "the Commodore", or by that which has now become so notorious, of "the Dutchmen's swindler"?'

'He told me . . . When I gave you my word this morning that I had no prejudices, I meant something more than you may have realized. I don't believe it follows that a thief's son must be a thief . . . The extreme frankness with which Gérard told me his whole story, in this very room, won him my sympathy . . . And now I think you are truly in possession of all the factors necessary to your inquiry.'

His tic was no longer a smile, it was a curt grimace.

'I leave you absolutely free . . . I promise not to try and influence you in any way and I will accept your judgement, whatever it may be . . . This was what was in my mind when I appealed to such a man as yourself . . .'

The situation was genuinely moving, and yet it contained an element which Maigret could not yet define, something disturbing, as it were discordant.

Three times he had arrested the Commodore, an extraordinary man who frequented only grand hotels and fashionable clubs and who, by some curious obsession, confined his swindling to Dutch bankers and big business men.

Was it because such people are often somewhat naive? Or simply because, having once been successful, the Commodore had not thought it worth while changing his tactics? Was there an element of superstition in it?

The Commodore, a handsome man, as tall and as strong as his son but more elegantly dressed, with a halo of snowy hair, sought out his dupes in Pullman cars between Amsterdam and Paris, and his frauds were so skilfully prepared that only once had it proved possible to bring him before the court.

'Do you know where the Commodore is now?' asked Maigret, lighting his pipe at last.

The lawyer nodded.

'Gérard told me. His father has been living for the past two years in luxury in a villa he has built for himself at San Remo. Gérard himself has always refused to profit by such ill-gotten wealth and has tried to make himself independent. Do you understand now, Monsieur Maigret? . . . forgive me, Monsieur Legros! we'd better get used to the name, even when we're between ourselves. Do you understand what's so tragic about my situation? If the young man is sincere, if he's honest, my suspicions are liable to discourage him permanently and so to break my daughter's heart. On the other hand if I've been taken in . . .'

This time he smiled, a thin bitter smile as though to explain:

'What's the point of a life like mine, a constant striving towards the perfection with which one is surrounded, if I end by bringing a bandit into the bosom of my family?'

Maigret went downstairs alone, at his own request. For some little time past, the notes of the piano and the sound of Armande's voice had ceased. To his surprise, there was no one in the drawing-room but Emilienne, who gave a start when she saw him come in.

'Are you looking for my sister and Gérard?' she asked.

'Well . . .'

'They're walking in the garden . . . I think Armande had a bit of a headache . . .'

What sort of conversation could he have had with her? As a child he

had had no sisters, and his girl cousins lived at the farther end of
France. As a young man he had had little contact with respectable
girls, and he had chosen for his wife as uncomplicated a person as he
could find. Moreover, during the years he had spent in the Police
Judiciaire, he had seldom had to deal with conventionally brought up
young ladies of fifteen or sixteen.

Emilienne baffled him, with the mingled daring and timidity in her
gaze, the mingled childishness and femininity of her appearance, and
her sudden changes of mood.

'I shall go out for a walk too,' he announced, prudently. He went
past the old gardener, who was raking a path; the gravel glittered
much more than his own at home, and he decided to ask the lawyer
where he got it from. He reached an arbour of roses, and saw
Armande there, wiping her eyes with a handkerchief which was obviously not her own, for she immediately gave it back to her companion.

The couple, moreover, showed no surprise or embarrassment when
Maigret appeared. On the contrary, as he was about to go on his way,
Armande called him back, her voice still tremulous with tears.

'Monsieur Maig . . .' she began.

He entered the bower of greenery and blossom through which delicate sunbeams filtered.

'I'm sorry . . . it escaped me . . . I promise you I'll be more care-
ful . . . I would like you to speak to Gérard, or rather to listen to him.
With the car you can be in his studio in a few minutes, can't he,
Gérard?'

And so a few moments later Maigret was introduced into a small
house standing alone on the river bank, a peasants' cottage which had
been considerably transformed. Most of the inside walls had been
knocked down to make a large studio which was lit from three sides
and simply furnished in light pine. Easels stood in the middle of the
room and the walls were covered with sketches or nearly finished
paintings.

'So you knew who I was?' asked Maigret, as he sat down on a stool.

'Your picture was in the papers at the same time as . . .'

As the Commodore's, of course! Maigret remembered.

He had even been rather angry with the journalists who had
thought fit to publicize his sturdy figure, thus putting thieves and
murderers on their guard against him!

'I must confess,' the young man went on after a brief silence, 'that I
was expecting some such surprise as this. Monsieur Motte is only
doing his duty. As for Armande, she is so sensitive, so intuitive that as
soon as you arrived she guessed what was happening. When I confirmed her suspicions she couldn't help weeping, womanlike. She has
a rather simplistic idea of the police and she almost expects you to

arrest me without more ado . . . What can I offer you? I've got some quite good beer and I think I remember that . . .'

'How long has Mademoiselle Armande known who you are?' asked Maigret.

'Since the first day . . . or say the third day, when I discovered that I was in love with her . . . You know that Monsieur Motte allows his daughters a good deal of freedom. She came here to see my paintings. I told her the whole truth, and promised I would tell her father everything next day. She was a little hesitant about this, I must admit, and if I'd listened to her I'd probably have postponed my confession . . .'

'In your opinion, how many ivories are missing from the lawyer's collection?'

'I sense the trap you're setting me, you know. Monsieur Motte only mentioned the first theft to his family, so as not to be impeded in his investigations. But, as I have told you, Armande is amazingly intuitive. She soon realized that other thefts were being committed. So every day she manages to make an inventory of the collection secretly, and thus we know just what's going on . . .'

'Of course, considering your profession and your knowledge of art, you are in a position to assess the value of the different pieces in the collection?'

'So much so that I was able to point out to Monsieur Motte that no. 33 in his catalogue is clearly a German copy, and after writing to the British Museum, he had to agree that I was right.'

Maigret drank his beer, which was cool, since there was a refrigerator in a corner of the studio. For all its simplicity the cottage was comfortable, and there was an elegance about it which owed nothing to furnishers or antique dealers.

'I see that you paint chiefly portraits,' he observed tentatively.

'That's to say that I take the local people as models. The way things are going, they'll soon have all passed through my studio.'

'Have you never painted Mademoiselle Armande's portrait?'

Gérard looked slightly embarrassed; he said no, but with less forthrightness.

'And this portrait, the girl in pink . . . Isn't it Mademoiselle Emilienne?'

'Yes, it is . . . I may as well admit the truth. At first I was rather hesitant about letting Armande visit me here alone . . . I thought up the excuse of painting her sister's portrait so as to avoid ill-natured gossip. Then, when we no longer needed a chaperone, well, the portrait was dropped . . . A little more beer?'

And suddenly perching on a table in front of Maigret, with his glass in his hand, he went on:

'You may be wondering why I've brought you here? Please believe me, it's not to plead my own cause nor yet to show you all the nooks and crannies of my house so as to prove that the stolen ivories aren't here. I may add that I'm never sure that they aren't, and that every morning and every evening I make a thorough search of the place.'

'You're afraid that . . .'

'I'm not merely afraid, I'm almost certain that the person who takes the trouble to steal unsaleable objects with the sole aim of preventing my marriage will find a way, sooner or later, to produce a proof of my guilt by revealing those damned ivories carefully hidden away in my house.'

'So you're convinced that the thief's sole aim is to prevent your marriage?'

'I can think of no other explanation. It's been going on for a month now and I've had plenty of time to think over the problem . . . I know your reputation well enough to be sure that you've already caught the atmosphere of the house. Monsieur Motte lives only for his family and his collection. He is consequently somewhat reluctant to introduce strangers into his home. They haven't many friends. That explains why Clotilde, the eldest daughter, who's twenty-three, has not yet had a single offer of marriage.'

'What are you driving at?'

'My point is that there are not many people whom I can suspect. One man, the chief clerk, whose name is Jean Vidier and who is twenty-eight years old, is able both to be in contact with Armande and to have access to Monsieur Motte's study unaccompanied . . .'

'What is this meant to prove?'

'No, Monsieur Maigret! It's not what you think! I know that I must sound like a guilty person trying to cast suspicion on an innocent one. I should never have brought up the subject if it had only involved myself, but Armande's happiness is at stake. I tell you – and I'm not a fool – that this Jean Vidier, who's a handsome fellow and an ambitious one, would welcome the chance to become the lawyer's son-in-law and perhaps some day inherit the practice. I must also tell you that for the past two years he has missed no opportunity of waylaying Armande, and on such occasions his looks have been deliberately eloquent. I maintain that I've a right, indeed a duty, to defend myself.

'I've studied the question with more passionate involvement than yourself, of course, but also with a closer knowledge of the house and its inhabitants.

'I'm not trying to lull your suspicions or win you over to my side. What I want is to have the situation cleared up, for it's intolerable . . .'

Maigret took advantage of the silence to light a fresh pipe and pour himself another glass of beer. He decided to find out from Gérard where he got it from, for it was of a better quality than is usual in a wine-growing country.

'According to you, then, this Jean Vidier?'

Why did Gérard once more betray embarrassment?

'No, Superintendent . . . I don't want you to start from any preconceived idea . . . Look, I'll be completely frank with you. Before I came here, Vidier may possibly have stood a chance. Not a chance of any real, deep love . . . But Armande is too alive, too greedy for life, if I may put it that way, to stay unmarried for long. In a few years she might have come to accept the offer of a peaceful, unexciting affection.'

'Couldn't your clerk have tried for Clotilde?'

'No! Clotilde is prouder than her sister and would have scorned the thought of marrying her father's employee. For that matter, she's the only one of them who cold-shoulders me a bit because, after all, I'm only a penniless dauber.'

'Does she know who you really are?'

'No!'

'Which members of the household know?'

'Only Monsieur Motte and Armande. I don't think Monsieur Motte has told his wife, for he doesn't talk much to her about his affairs.'

'And Jean Vidier?'

'Now you're getting warm. For a long time I wondered whether he knew. I'm sure, now, that he does. After my confession, Monsieur Motte, who is very meticulous, took the trouble to collect a file with all the press cuttings that referred to my father. Well, one morning, when Jean Vidier was alone in the study, I saw that file on the desk . . .'

'So that in your view the situation is clear-cut?'

And Maigret was astonished to hear him reply with a categorical 'No!'

He looked with surprise at the young man, who seemed abashed by his own assertion.

'What do you mean?'

'Listen, Monsieur Maigret . . . I have taken a very special interest in police cases, and you can understand why . . . So I've studied attentively the press reports of your inquiries . . . I have observed that – please don't take offence – you've always been very straight, even with people like . . . like . . .'

'Like your father!'

'Yes . . . And that's why I believe you'll be straight with me too. I might have left you to conduct your inquiry by yourself, but when I recognized you I immediately told Armande I wanted to speak to you. I'm impatient, don't you see? In theory I'm getting married in twenty-nine days. But actually I'm at the mercy of some happening, some cunning plot of my enemy, since I clearly have an enemy although I don't know for certain who it is. I have told you now what I had to tell you about Jean Vidier. And now I must add, with equal frankness: although all the presumptive evidence is against him, my intuition tells me he is not the guilty person . . .'

A big fly kept passing to and fro between them. Through the window Maigret could see a racing skiff with four oarsmen speeding like an arrow down the Loire; the cox was leaning forward and his 'One . . . Two . . .' was almost audible through the still, close air.

'I repeat, I've been over every conceivable explanation again and again. I even wondered whether Madame Motte . . . But that's out of the question, it's ridiculous. You've seen her. One would think her husband had deliberately chosen her in keeping with his home, gentle and welcoming and utterly uncomplicated. Don't you see, he's a man with a lofty conception of happiness, who has sought persistently all his life to create and administer such happiness for himself, for his family, for his clan . . . I've not had a great deal of experience, Superintendent. I'm only a young man. But I've lived in widely differing social milieux and nowhere have I ever witnessed such a resolute quest for harmony in all the smallest details.'

Maigret was the more uneasy in that he recognized here the echo of his own thoughts, more passionately expressed.

'If I knew that what I am about to say might be repeated outside these four walls, I'd bite off my own tongue. Once again, I'm trusting you to play fair with me. My love for Armande is true and honourable, I swear, and I've got to protect it. At my age it's hard to believe in human treachery, and that was why I felt almost ashamed when I was speaking about Jean Vidier. I sought for another explanation . . . This one is even more appalling. Suppose that Monsieur Motte . . .'

Maigret gave a start, then endeavoured to remain still and expressionless.

'Suppose that this man who pursues his ideal of happiness with so much intelligence, taste and determination should suddenly become afraid of an intruder, an outsider, worming his way into his home . . . And suppose him to be determined that his behaviour shall on no account be inconsistent with his principles, anxious to maintain his reputation in the eyes of the world as a broad-minded, enlightened man . . . That's what I worked out finally . . . I've nothing to add . . . I can see no other explanation for a situation which is so absurd that at times I wonder if I've not gone mad.'

As he spoke these last sentences he had got up and was striding up and down the studio. Automatically, he opened the drawer of the table.

And then he suddenly took something from it, an object no larger than a walnut, and flung it carelessly towards Maigret, saying:

'Look here! What did I tell you would happen?'

It must have been the precious piece of which the lawyer had spoken, a tiny fragment of ivory on which an Oriental artist had succeeded in carving with great delicacy a scene with six figures.

Maigret held it in the palm of his hand, enjoying the perfect smoothness which ten or twelve centuries of handling had imparted to the ivory.

'It should be easy, now,' he said, 'to determine who has been in your house.'

'Do you think so?' the young man laughed bitterly.

'Has Monsieur Motte been here lately?'

'He was here only last night, with his three daughters . . .'

'And Jean Vidier?'

Gérard hesitated. This final admission seemed to distress him. At last he said with a sigh:

'I don't have a servant. A woman comes in every morning for a couple of hours to clean the place. I eat at the inn.'

'I don't see how . . .'

'My cleaning woman, Mathilde, is Jean Vidier's aunt. He comes from a very humble home. It's surprising indeed that he shouldn't be more embittered. I've nothing to add . . . I'll drive you home.'

'If you don't mind, I'd rather walk . . .'

'Whatever you prefer. But I'll have to take them back their car.'

And Maigret found himself alone in the streets of Châteauneuf, which were now divided into two almost equal sections by the midday sun: on the one side a zone of light and heat, where an occasional dog or cat lay drowsing, on the other cool shade, with tradesmen sitting in their doorways.

'What was he trying to tell me?' he wondered.

Had Gérard Donavant, in fact, been trying to direct him on to the trail of the lawyer Motte or on to that of Jean Vidier?

'In which case,' he growled to himself as he skirted the marketplace – as empty now as a skating-rink – 'he's even cleverer than his father . . .'

So clever that . . .

There was no suspicion of a corpse in this case, no threat, apparently, to any human life. These were just a set of happy people resolutely defending their happiness, as they conceived it, against one another.

And now, by the oddest chance, this contest for happiness had taken the form of a criminal offence, the theft of some curious little objects brought from China by traders and bought at a high price by an obsessive collector.

'What was he really trying to tell me?'

Then Maigret noticed that he had unconsciously pocketed the tiny piece of ivory which, for connoisseurs, was worth tens of thousands of francs.

He stopped at the front door, between the two stone posts against which all the dogs of the neighbourhood were wont to relieve themselves. He rang the bell, and took a certain pleasure in hearing its deep mellow reverberation. The little maid opened the polished door, stepped aside, closed the door and told him:

'Everybody's in the garden.'

Maigret, however, made his way into the drawing-room, where he knew they would all forgather after dinner. He laid the ivory on the delicately-veined green marble top of the central table.

Then he decided to go into the lawyer's office to make the acquaintance of Jean Vidier.

III

He was considerably disappointed. He could not have said exactly how he had pictured Jean Vidier, but in any case the reality corresponded to no notion he could possibly have formed.

In spite of the green panes, which took up a third of the windows, the office was as light as the rest of the house; the walls were covered with notices of public auctions of farms and houses, of agricultural material, of livestock and farm implements. A single piece of furniture seemed to belong to another epoch, a high desk of black wood with an incredibly long-legged stool.

A glance at the occupant of that stool, however, explained its character: the lawyer's second clerk was a grey-headed old man wearing a black silk cap; in every detail, down to a pair of cotton oversleeves, he seemed to have come straight out of a nineteenth-century engraving.

He did not even bother to turn round when Maigret entered. Jean Vidier, on the other hand, rose hastily, bowed, smiled, bowed again, fussed about trying to do the honours of the place.

'I am . . .' began the Superintendent.

'I know! I know! Monsieur Motte warned me . . .'

Warned him of what? And how, precisely, could one define this young man? His very ordinariness was discouraging. He must have been a good pupil at school, indeed a model pupil; he had certainly been teacher's pet, held up as an example to the rest. Certainly, too, he must have been the one who did little jobs in class such as filling the teacher's glass of water, sharpening pencils, wiping down the blackboard.

He was the 'deserving young man' in every sense of the term, and one could picture him running a Church club or taking boy scouts camping in the summer. Who knows? He might have taken part in amateur theatricals, and he was sure to have a pleasant baritone voice.

Neat, spruce, sleek-haired, always ready to oblige, ready to bow and scrape and to say thank you, in a word to make himself both useful and agreeable.

'Needless to say I'm at your disposal,' he declared. 'Will you excuse me a moment?'

He was putting his initials to a document which he handed over to his fossilized colleague, then indicated by appropriate gestures that he would rather talk to the Superintendent elsewhere.

'May I show you round the place? As a timber merchant, I am sure you will find it interesting and . . .'

They were in a little passage which gave on to a spiral staircase. The young man's tone changed, as he suggested more diffidently:

'Shall we go upstairs? Monsieur Motte is in the garden.'

The little staircase, as Maigret now discovered, led directly into Monsieur Motte's study. Jean Vidier seemed completely at home there, and invited Maigret to sit down in the same leather armchair that he had occupied earlier that afternoon.

'I may as well tell you, Chief Superintendent, that I guessed who you were as soon as you arrived. I knew, in any case, that my employer wanted to call in a private detective. I've recently seen newspapers lying open at the "small ads" page, with crosses marked against the names of detective agencies.'

He was so pleased, so proud of himself! He did not realize for a moment that Maigret was by no means flattered by this comparison with detectives who advertise themselves at a rate of twenty francs the line.

'You see I'm being perfectly frank with you! I might have pretended to be taken in by this timber merchant story. I'm frank, I repeat, probably too frank, for in this life it's never wise to show one's true feelings . . .'

Why are these bumptious fellows so unlikable? wondered Maigret, watching him.

'So I know why you are here. And I tell you straight, without beating about the bush: "Take care, Chief Superintendent! The person who summoned you did so with the best intentions. But did he suspect what you might discover? You have seen a happy home; what would you say if, suddenly, tragedy were to strike it?"'

Napoleon, at historic moments, could not have taken a more important air than this young man, who had shamelessly settled down in his employer's armchair and was toying with a paper-knife.

He cared little whether or not he received an answer. He was keyed up, and he had probably been rehearsing his speech ever since the morning; now, at last, he could declaim it, with an occasional glance at his own reflection in a glass cabinet.

'I must point out,' he corrected himself, 'that I have no precise information, otherwise I know my duty well enough to have assumed my responsibilities. But Monsieur Motte has relied on me completely for the past ten years. I venture to add that for some time past the running of the office has been in my hands. So has the responsibility for all the critical correspondence connected with the collection that you see in this room. And so! . . .'

Which implied: 'And so don't be misled into taking me for an ordinary clerk! I don't know what you may have heard about me, but now you have been warned!'

'Excuse me . . .' began Maigret, who had not yet been able to open his lips.

'One moment . . . I must emphasize my deep conviction that this inquiry is not only useless but dangerous. You could surely, without any loss of face, find that your commitments require your presence elsewhere . . .'

'Thank you!'

'I mean no offence. But I know the household and you don't. And you will have to take the responsibility for what may occur if you should persist, and if your efforts should happen to be successful.'

He was probably not malicious. A malicious person could not, in so brief a space, have thought up so many wounding things to say to the ex-Superintendent of the Police Judiciaire. No! He was just a self-satisfied little fellow, who believed in his own merits, his own judgement and probably too in his own honesty.

'Now, if you don't mind, I'd sooner that what I have just said should remain between ourselves. Note that this is only a request. There is nothing to stop you from repeating to Monsieur Motte all that I have been telling you, and, once again, you'll only have yourself to blame . . .'

'I know . . .' sighed Maigret, whose head was buzzing.

'What do you know?'

'Nothing, Monsieur Vidier. I know that I know absolutely nothing and I am grateful to you for your help . . .'

'You mean to say?'

'I mean nothing. I assume, of course, that you haven't been amusing yourself stealing ivories . . .'

'You suspect me?'

'No, no! Rest assured . . .'

'Because, in that case, I would prefer to put the matter immediately in the hands of the police . . .'

He was scarlet, glistening with sweat.

'I assume, too, that apart from your most impressive little lecture you have nothing important to tell me?'

'Absolutely nothing!'

'Why, then you see we understand one another perfectly. Our interview is at an end, Monsieur Vidier. You are free to . . .'

'But . . .'

'I say you are free to . . .'

'You are going to remain in this study?'

'With your permission. And I should like to remain here alone.'

'Very well . . .'

He rose reluctantly, repeating; 'Very well . . .'

'Goodbye, Monsieur Vidier.'

'Goodbye, Superintendent!'

Barely had the door closed behind him when Maigret broke into uncontrollable silent laughter.

In spite of what he had just announced, he had no purpose in staying there, and he was not even interested in looking at the ivory objects that crowded the glass cabinets in such numbers that he felt slightly sick.

He merely filled himself a pipe and lit it, then went to stare out of the open window, from which he could see in the distance the glittering gravel on the garden paths.

'I mustn't forget to ask him where he gets such fine gravel from . . .'

His own garden was smaller, of course! So was his house! And he hadn't three daughters like that peculiar Monsieur Motte . . .

Emilienne, Armande and Clotilde . . .

The evening meal was choice and perfectly prepared, without extravagant abundance, the table exquisitely laid and the wines knowingly selected.

Gérard Donavant was present, and Maigret gathered that this was the case every evening, that since the young couple's official engagement he joined the family party regularly at dinner.

For this occasion he had put on a town suit, with a white shirt which set off his tan, and Madame Maigret would undoubtedly have been reminded of some young film star.

Nobody had yet been into the drawing-room, and the ex-Superintendent assumed that the tiny ivory people were still sitting on the green marble table. Monsieur Motte had a somewhat higher colour than that morning, for he had been lying out in the sunshine in the garden, where refreshments had been brought out.

Maigret himself was somewhat flushed, as happened nowadays
when he bestirred himself a great deal on a hot day. Possibly
Donavant's beer had contributed to this, as well as the increasing embarrassment of his situation.

For in fact, who was still taken in by the tale of the timber-
merchant-old-army-pal invented by Monsieur Motte? Neither
Gérard nor Armande, nor even Jean Vidier! At most, then, Madame
Motte, who seemed to take no interest in anything, Emilienne and
Clotilde. Even so, the two girls had a way of looking at their guest
which embarrassed him, particularly when the lawyer obliged him to
talk about the timber trade.

He felt rather as if he had rashly wandered into a shop full of ex-
quisite china where he could only just thread his way through by
tucking in his stomach and avoiding the slightest gesture.

At midday, he had been impressed by the discreet and refined elegance that surrounded him. By the evening he had begun to have
enough of it, and decided he would smoke his pipe in the drawing-room after dinner.

For after all, what had they brought him here for? Gérard and
Armande were in love! Monsieur Motte, who had no prejudices,
chose to fill his glass cases with objects that Maigret considered really
rather hideous, as well as perfectly useless. He himself might just as
well have filled his cupboards with toy soldiers!

He had been fetched in a car, driven by a chauffeur, made to mas-
querade under another name and a different profession!

And everybody he saw privately immediately told him:

'You know, I'm not taken in. I know perfectly well who you are and
why you're here . . .'

And yet . . .

He could not have explained his feelings, but he was strangely
uneasy in spite of it all, as though he smelled tension in the air. He
could not get used to this Châteauneuf lawyer whose manners were as
smooth and polished as his ivories, and whose faint nervous tic must
surely imply something.

Could he be deceiving them all? Was there another personality
hidden behind that enigmatic mask?

At all events, he never took his gaze from his guest, and his eyes
sometimes held a questioning look that was truly pathetic.

As for Armande, she avoided looking directly at the Superintendent, for then her face instinctively assumed a suppliant expression, as though her fate lay in his hands.

'That girl,' thought Maigret, 'would follow her lover to the ends of
the earth, even if he had stolen all the ivories ever made.'

Gérard, alone, talked volubly, with a good humour which was not affected but quite spontaneous. He had the same easy manner as his father, the same stylish distinction which had enabled the Commodore to bamboozle so many thickheaded bankers.

He just cast a brief glance at Maigret from time to time, as one might glance at the barometer to make sure nothing sensational was happening.

Clotilde was as commonplace as her mother. The best thing she could hope for was to get married and have three or four children, amidst whom she could find uncomplicated happiness or, at any rate, tranquillity of body and mind.

As for Emilienne . . . She was too young . . . or too wide awake for her age. One couldn't treat her as a little girl, and yet it seemed ridiculous to treat her as a young woman.

She had a long pale face, large greenish eyes, and fingers so long and slender that Maigret, who had never seen their like, kept looking at them involuntarily.

'Tomorrow,' Monsieur Motte announced, 'you can go boating on the Loire with the girls. I'm sure Gérard will be glad to go with you . . .'

Why not suggest blind man's buff or tag while they were about it?

'I don't know, ' he mumbled unenthusiastically.

'Of course you're perfectly free to do what you like . . . I just wanted you to know that we have a motor-boat and a boat-house by the river . . .'

And Maigret wondered: 'Is he trying to get me off the trail already? Or does he want to suggest that there may be something in the said boat-house? In that case, why hasn't he gone to look himself?'

Everyone rose from table. As usual, there was a certain polite indecision about moving into the drawing-room, and eventually it was Emilienne who went in first. She went up to the table to ring for coffee.

When Maigret, in his turn, came up to that table, the ivory object was no longer there.

And when he turned round he saw Emilienne kissing her father's forehead, then her mother's; she made him a curt little bow, but avoided saying goodnight to the others.

'She always goes to bed early,' Armande explained, offering Maigret a cup. 'One lump, isn't it? Father tells me you would like me to play something . . .'

The girl had been at the piano for about half an hour, when the Superintendent left the room, moving carefully so as not to set the springs of the armchair or the floorboards creaking. The drawing-room, with its lighted chandelier, looked like an eighteenth-century print, and the family sat as still as waxworks in their separate armchairs.

A good deal earlier, the Superintendent had noticed a pool of light in the courtyard which was presumably cast by a lamp in the lawyer's study on the first floor.

The piano was still playing as he crept silently up the stair and turned the handle of the door. A first glance showed him Jean Vidier sitting at his employer's desk, his face wreathed in smoke from a cigarette which threatened to drop ash all over the documents he was examining.

'Did you want something?' he asked without stirring.

Maigret closed the door, realizing from the young man's attitude that he was accustomed to work thus in the evenings in the study, where the lawyer would join him presently.

'I have some rather urgent work . . .' went on the clerk, rather impatiently.

'Will it take long?'

'I am expecting Monsieur Motte presently, and we shall have to work at it together until late into the night . . .'

'That's a pity!'

'Why?'

'Because you won't be allowed to go on working so long . . .'

'What do you mean?'

'You've got the telephone? Yes, I see you have. I propose to ring up the police at Châteauneuf and ask them to come and arrest you.'

'Me?'

Vidier had leapt to his feet in stupefaction.

'You want to arrest *me*?'

Fortunately the piano was still playing and drowned his indignant cry.

'Indeed I am! You are well aware, Monsieur Vidier, that complicity in a theft is an offence, just like the theft itself. Now the mere fact of allowing the theft to be committed without saying anything about it can be considered as complicity . . .'

'But . . .'

'Let me finish. You know who has stolen your employer's ivories . . .' Jean Vidier burst into a sarcastic laugh:

'They haven't been stolen at all!'

'That's just what I mean. Let's say that you know who has removed your employer's ivories. You are well aware that the disappearance of these objects may be very damaging to a certain person, that they may cost him his happiness . . .'

'No!'

'What did you say?'

'I said no!'

His temper was rising and he glared defiantly at Maigret.

'You see, Monsieur, you needn't think you impress me with your threats! Armande was quite determined to go off with her lover if Monsieur Motte had withheld or withdrawn his consent . . . I know, because I heard her say so . . .'

'To whom?'

'To Gérard. So you see nobody's happiness was at stake. As for the ivories, you know perfectly well that they'll be restored sooner or later, since it's impossible to do anything with them. In any case . . .'

'In any case?'

The piano, which had stopped for a moment, began again less loudly, and Armande's low, slightly husky voice was heard singing a Schubert song.

'In any case, nothing! As for arresting me . . . And suppose I tell you that I'm quite prepared to face your policemen? Admit that you wouldn't dare telephone? . . . Admit that you're in a weak position, Chief Superintendent Maigret!'

And Maigret replied, simply: 'You're quite right.'

It was his composure that quelled the chief clerk's fury and took away his self-confidence, his swagger.

'What do you mean?'

'I'm saying that you're quite right . . . You cannot be prosecuted for complicity . . .'

'Why?'

Maigret's movements now became very leisurely. He hunted about for a sharp instrument to clean his pipe, then bent down to look at the waste paper basket.

'Because one cannot be an accomplice in a non-existent offence.'

'I don't understand . . .'

'Of course you do! You are familiar enough with the statute book to know that a theft between members of the same family does not constitute a legal offence . . .'

The fellow was as easily deflated as excited. He was miserable now, on the verge of tears. He cast a hangdog look at Maigret.

'How did you find out?'

'Who else could it be? Not Madame Motte, surely?'

Jean Vidier gave a smile.

'Not Clotilde either, she's not clever enough.'

'Don't say anything against Mademoiselle Clotilde. If one were free to choose one's love . . .'

And Maigret realised that Vidier would rather have fallen in love with the elder of the Motte girls than with the second.

'You see! That doesn't leave many people . . .'

'She's not responsible . . .' muttered the clerk.

'Did I say she was responsible? She's still a minor, isn't she?'

'She's very highly-strung . . . One evening I caught her with one of
the ivories in her hand and she swore that if I told anyone she would
kill herself . . .'

'Of course, of course! That's typical of her age!'

'To kill oneself?'

'No, to talk of doing so! To be in love the way she is! To be as jealous as she is, so jealous that she'd rather have the man she loves
driven away than see him happy with her sister . . . And anyhow,
what a crazy idea to take her as a chaperone and paint her portrait . . .'

'You heard about that?'

But at the same moment Vidier became suddenly attentive, rushed
past Maigret so quickly that he almost knocked him over, and opened
the door, which closed again behind him. A second later, sounds of a
scuffle were heard in the next room and suddenly a shot rang out, followed by a great silence.

Downstairs the piano stopped playing.

IV

The night was warm, even though the study windows were wide open,
letting in the fragrance of the garden. In the distance an occasional car
flashed along the main road.

In the street, in front of the main doorway with its two stone posts,
Maigret's car was waiting, its headlights on, and the chauffeur in uniform standing beside it on the pavement.

Monsieur Motte was very pale. His lip twitched more frequently
than ever, and he was trying hard to give the impression of a smile.

'I apologize, Superintendent . . . But it's better this way, isn't
it? . . . Much better than if . . .'

He could not finish his sentence. He was a little afraid of his voice
breaking.

'I wanted to know the truth at all costs. And I was far from guessing
that the cause of it all was a little girl's romantic attachment. I'm an
old man and Emilienne is very young; that explains, I suppose, how
although I spoiled her I understood her less than her sisters . . .'

He turned towards Jean Vidier, who sat there in a corner, not fully
recovered from his agitating experience.

'But for you, my good Jean . . .'

'Oh no, Monsieur! I'm convinced that she would never have fired.
When I heard a noise in your room I immediately thought, I don't
know why, that it was not you. Mademoiselle Emilienne had just

taken the revolver from your bedside table. I flung myself upon her, and it was I who let the gun go off in the struggle. I'm sorry about your mirror . . .'

Then, after a resentful glance at Maigret:

'If this gentleman hadn't come . . .'

Monsieur Motte managed his little smile at last.

'If my friend from Bergerac had not come,' he corrected.

He did not finish what he was going to say. On the desk were spread out the missing pieces of his collection, which Emilienne had given back after keeping them hidden for a long time in her cupboard.

He rose.

'Tomorrow I'll have a new mirror put in . . .'

He might have been about to mention money, but changed his mind.

'I'll write to you tomorrow, Monsieur Maigret . . . I'm too weary tonight . . . I'm sorry you feel you must leave so soon . . .'

An hour later, Madame Maigret switched on the light hurriedly when she heard the sound of an opening door, and she was reaching towards the drawer where the revolver was kept when Maigret's deep voice sounded up the stairway: 'It's me!'

'Have you found that old lunatic's ivory whatnots already?'

'Oh yes!'

'Where were they?'

'I'll tell you all about it later . . .'

He was still so steeped in the atmosphere of the place that he found it hard to believe that he had been away from home only a day. And that night he dreamed, not only of glittering white pebbles, but of the three daughters of the lawyer of Châteauneuf . . .

Emilienne, Armande and Clotilde . . .

STORM IN THE CHANNEL

I

It looked as if fate had taken advantage of Maigret's recent retirement to confront him, ironically, with the most glaring proof of the unreliability of human evidence. And this time the famous Superintendent, or rather the man who had borne that title only three months earlier, was on the wrong side of the counter, so to speak, facing a policeman's searching gaze and being asked the question:

'Are you sure it was half-past six, or a little earlier, and that you were sitting beside the fire?'

Now Maigret realised with appalling clarity how a small handful of human beings, half a dozen in this case, were suddenly going to be paralysed by this simple question:

'What exactly were you doing between six and seven o'clock?'

If only it had been a question of disorderly, or dramatic, or tragic incidents! But it was nothing of the sort; merely a matter of half a dozen people hanging about, waiting for dinner on a wet night in the two or three public sitting-rooms of a boarding-house!

And Maigret, when he was questioned, hesitated like a forgetful schoolboy or a false witness.

'A wet night' is putting it mildly. At the Gare Saint-Lazare there had been a notice: 'Storm in the Channel. The Dieppe–Newhaven crossing may be delayed.'

And a good many English travellers turned around and went back to their hotels.

At Dieppe, in the main street, it looked as if the wind would tear down the street signs. You had to lean against the street doors to open them. The water came down in bucketfuls, with a noise like waves crashing on shingle. Sometimes a figure would dart past, someone who had to go out, clinging close to the walls, his head covered with a coat.

It was November. The lights had had to be put on at four o'clock. At the harbour station, the boat which should have left at two lay alongside the fishing-smacks whose masts were clashing together.

Madame Maigret had resignedly fetched from her room a piece of

292

knitting which she had started in the train. She was sitting close to the stove, while an unfamiliar ginger cat, the boarding-house cat, had come to nestle in her lap.

From time to time she raised her head and cast a woebegone glance at Maigret, who was wandering about like a lost soul.

'We ought to have gone to the hotel,' she sighed. 'You'd have found someone there to play cards with.'

Obviously! But Madame Maigret, ever thrifty, had got from some friend or other the address of this god-forsaken boarding-house at the end of the quay, amid the gloomy desolation of the summer visitors' district, where in winter all the shutters were closed and all the doors barred.

And yet this was supposed to be a holiday trip, the first, really, that the pair of them had taken since their honeymoon.

Maigret was free at last! He had left the Quai des Orfèvres and he could go to bed at night secure in the knowledge that he would not be disturbed by a telephone call summoning him to examine a corpse that was not yet cold.

And so, as Madame Maigret had long wanted to visit England, he had made up his mind:

'We'll go and spend a fortnight in London. I'll take the opportunity to look up some of my colleagues at Scotland Yard with whom I worked during the war.'

Just their luck! A storm in the Channel, the boat delayed, and this gloomy boarding-house, remembered on the spur of the moment by Madame Maigret, its very walls exuding meanness and boredom!

The landlady, Mademoiselle Otard, was a spinster of fifty who tried to disguise her sourness behind honeyed smiles. Her nostrils twitched involuntarily every time she came across the trail of tobacco-smoke that followed Maigret in his wanderings to and fro. Several times she had been on the point of commencing that it was not the thing to smoke a pipe incessantly in small overheated rooms where ladies were sitting. On these occasions Maigret, feeling a row imminent, looked her in the eyes so calmly that she preferred to turn her head away.

She was equally disgusted when she saw the Superintendent, who had never been able to break himself of the habit, hovering about the stoves, then seizing the poker and raking the coal so energetically that the chimneys roared like furnaces.

The house was not a large one. It was a two-storey villa converted into a boarding-house. There was a passage by way of entrance hall, but for economy's sake it was rarely lighted, nor was the staircase leading to the first and second floors, so that every now and then you would hear people stumbling up the stairs, or a hand groping for the door-knob.

The front room served as a lounge, with funny little armchairs of greenish velvet and tattered old magazines on the table.

Then there was the dining-room, where guests were also allowed to sit except at meal-times.

Madame Maigret was in the lounge. Maigret wandered from one room to the other, from one stove to the other, from one poker to the other.

At the back was the pantry where Irma, the fifteen-year-old maid, was busy that afternoon cleaning knives and plate with silver polish.

And finally there was the kitchen, the domain of Mademoiselle Otard and of Jeanne, the older of the two maids, a slattern in her late twenties, perpetually slipshod, unkempt and of dubious cleanliness, and moreover perpetually embittered, looking about her resentfully and suspiciously.

The only other member of the household was a bewildered little boy of four who was always being pushed around, scolded and slapped: Jeanne's son, as Maigret learned by questioning the younger servant.

Elsewhere, in such weather, time might not have passed very cheerfully. Here it dragged funereally, and there must have been far more seconds to the minute here than anywhere else, for the hands seemed not to move at all on the face of the black marble clock standing under its glass case on the mantelpiece.

'Try to take advantage of a lull to go to the café. You're bound to find someone there to have a game with,' suggested Madame Maigret.

One couldn't even have a quiet chat in the place, for there was always somebody about. Mademoiselle Otard bustled from kitchen to lounge, opening drawers or cupboards, sitting down, going off again as if she had to keep an eye on everyone or a disaster would happen. As though if she stayed away for a quarter of an hour somebody would take the opportunity to pinch her old copies of *La Mode du Jour* or set fire to the sideboard!

From time to time Irma came in too, to put away knives, spoons and forks in that same sideboard and take others out.

As for the sad lady, as the Maigrets called her because they did not know her name, she sat bolt upright on a chair beside the dining-room stove, reading a book whose title could not be seen because it had lost its cover.

As far as they could discover, she had been there for several weeks. She seemed to be about thirty, and in poor health; perhaps she had come to convalesce after some operation? At any rate she moved about with the utmost caution, as if she were afraid of damaging herself. She ate little, and always sighed as she ate, doubtless regretting the minutes wasted in such a vulgar activity.

As for the other lady, the young bride as Maigret called her with a sardonic smile, she was quite the reverse, and she was forever making a draught as she swept from one armchair to another.

The 'young bride' was probably in her early forties. She was short and stout and definitely not easy-going; the proof was that her husband came hurrying up at her slightest summons, assuming beforehand an obedient, sheepish air.

This husband was about thirty, and it was obvious from a glance that he had not married for love but had sacrificed his freedom in order to ensure for himself a comfortable old age.

Their name was Mosselet: Jules and Emilie Mosselet.

Though the clock hands did not move fast, they must have moved a bit, for Maigret remembered afterwards having looked at the time when Jeanne brought the sad lady a peppermint tisane; it was a few minutes past five, and Jeanne was looking surlier than ever.

It was shortly after this that the young Englishman, Mr John, came in from outside, letting the cold wind and the rain into the house and bringing trickles of water into the lounge off his dripping raincoat.

He looked flushed with the keen air and the news he was bringing. He announced in a strong English accent:

'The boat's going to sail . . . My luggage can be taken out, Mademoiselle.'

He had been restless ever since the morning, for he was eager to get back to England, and now he had just come from the harbour station where he had learnt that the Channel steamer was going to attempt the crossing.

'Have you got my bill ready?'

Maigret hesitated for a moment. He was on the point of following his wife's advice, at the risk of a soaking, and running down the street as far as the Brasserie des Suisses, where at least there would be some life and activity.

He even went as far as the coat-stand in the hall, and noticed in the semi-darkness the Englishman's three big suitcases. Then he shrugged his shoulders and went into the lounge.

'Why don't you go? You're just getting irritable unnecessarily,' said Madame Maigret.

This remark was enough to make him subside heavily into an armchair, pick up the first magazine he saw and begin to turn over its pages.

The remarkable thing was that he had strictly nothing to do and nothing to preoccupy him. Logically, he should have been in a state of perfect relaxation.

The house was not large. From any point in it you could hear the slightest sounds; in fact in the evening, when the Mosselet couple retired to their bedroom, it became quite embarrassing.

But Maigret saw nothing, heard nothing, had not the faintest presentiment.

He was vaguely aware of Mr John paying his bill and going into the pantry to tip Irma. He made some vague reply to the Englishman's vague goodbye and realized that Jeanne, being heftier than the young man, was going to carry two of the cases to the boat.

But he did not see her go. It didn't interest him. He happened to be reading a long article in tiny print on the habits of field-mice – the magazine he had picked up at random being an agricultural journal – and he had ended up by becoming absurdly fascinated by it.

After that, the minute hand could creep forward on the grey-green clock-face without anybody noticing. Madame Maigret, counting the stitches in her knitting, was moving her lips in silence. From time to time a lump of coal crackled in one of the stoves or a gust of wind howled in the chimney.

The clink of china indicated that Irma was laying the table. There was a vague smell of frying that heralded the traditional evening dish of whiting.

And suddenly voices rang out in the night, excited voices that seemed to spring from the storm itself and that drew nearer, sounded right up against the shutters, stopped at the door and were brought to a noisy close by the most violent ring of the bell ever heard in that house.

Even then Maigret did not give a start. For hours he had been longing for a break in the day's monotony. Now that it had come, far more sensational than anything he could have expected, he sat absorbed in stories about field-mice.

'Yes, this is the house . . .' Mademoiselle Otard's voice was heard saying.

She ushered in air and wetness and damp clothes, and red excited faces. Maigret was obliged to raise his head. He caught sight of a policeman's uniform and the black overcoat of a little man with an unlighted cigar in his mouth.

'I think this is where a certain Jeanne Fénard was in service?' said the man with the cigar.

Maigret noticed that the little boy was there, having crept in from heaven knows where, probably from the depths of the kitchen.

'She has just been shot dead with a revolver as she was going along the Rue de la Digue.'

Mademoiselle Otard's immediate reaction was one of incredulity and suspicion. She was patently not the sort of person to be taken in easily and, tight-lipped, she let fall the magnificent comment:

'Really?'

But the sequel left her in no doubt, for the man with the unlighted cigar went on:

'I am the police inspector. I want you to come with me to identify the body . . . And I want nobody else to leave the house.'

Maigret's eyes were twinkling mischievously. His wife looked at him as if to say:

'Why don't you tell them who you are?'

But Maigret had retired such a short time ago that he was still savouring the delights of anonymity. He sank back into his armchair with real enjoyment. He scrutinized the inspector with a critical eye.

'Kindly put on your coat and follow me . . .'

'Where to?' Mademoiselle Otard protested again.

'To the morgue . . .'

There followed loud screams, a genuine or else a well-simulated fit of hysterics, with a moan from the sad lady visitor, whom Maigret had forgotten.

Irma darted in from her pantry, holding a plate in her hand.

'Is Jeanne dead?'

'It's none of your business,' declared Mademoiselle Otard. 'I shall be back presently. You can serve dinner in the meantime.'

She glanced at the little boy, who had not understood what was going on and was wandering about among the grown-ups' legs.

'Shut him up in his room . . . Put him to bed.'

Where was Madame Mosselet at that moment? The question would seem an easy one and yet Maigret couldn't have answered it. On the other hand Mosselet, who wore ridiculous red felt slippers indoors, was standing there somewhere near the hall. He must have heard the noise from his room and come down.

'What's happening?' he asked.

But the local inspector was in a hurry. He said a few words in a whisper to the uniformed policeman, who took off his cape and cap and settled down by the fire, like someone who has come to stay.

Meanwhile Mademoiselle Otard was being hurried out, wearing a yellow waterproof coat and rubber boots. She turned round once more to call out to Irma:

'Hurry up and serve dinner! The fish'll be burnt!'

Irma was weeping mechanically, as though out of politeness, because somebody had died. She wept as she handed round the dishes, turning her head away so that her tears should not fall into the food.

Here, Maigret noticed that Madame Mosselet was at table, showing no other emotion than curiosity.

'I wonder how it can have happened . . . Was it in the street? . . . Are there gangsters in Dieppe?'

Maigret was eating hungrily. Madame Maigret could not understand how her husband could seem so uninterested in this affair, when his whole life had been spent investigating crimes.

The sad lady was staring at her whiting and the whiting was staring back at her. From time to time she opened her mouth, not to eat but to breathe out a little air by way of a sigh.

As for the policeman, he had taken a chair and was sitting astride it, watching the others eat and longing for a chance to show off.

'It was I that found her,' he said with pride to Madame Mosselet. who seemed the most interested.

'How?'

'Quite by chance . . . I live in the Rue de la Digue, a little street that runs from the quay to the far end of the harbour, beyond the tobacco factory. That's as good as saying that nobody ever goes down it. I was walking fast with my head bent and I saw something dark . . .'

'How dreadful!' said Madame Mosselet, without conviction.

'At first I thought it might be a drunk, for there's always some of them lying about the pavement . . .'

'Even in winter?'

'Particularly in winter, because people begin drinking to get warm . . .'

'While in summer they drink to get cool!' Jules Mosselet said jokingly, with a sly glance at his wife.

'That's about it . . . I touched the body . . . I found it was a woman . . . I called for help, and when she had been carried into a pharmacy, the one on the corner of the Rue de Paris, we saw that she was dead . . . And that was when I recognized her, because I know all the faces in the neighbourhood. I told the Chief: "That's the maid from the Pension Otard . . ."'

Then Maigret inquired hesitantly, as if reluctant to interfere in what did not concern him:

'Were there any suitcases beside her?'

'Why should there have been suitcases?'

'I don't know . . . I wonder, too, if she was facing towards the harbour or in this direction . . .'

The policeman scratched his head.

'Wait a minute . . . I believe, the way she was lying, she must have been coming this way when it happened.'

He hesitated a moment, then made up his mind to take hold of the bottle of red wine and pour himself a glass, murmuring:

'May I?'

This action had brought him close to the table. There were still two whiting lying flat on the dish. He hesitated once more, took one of them, ate it without knife or fork and went over to throw the back-bone into the coal scuttle.

Then he looked questioningly round the table, made sure that nobody wanted the second whiting and ate it like the first, took another drink and sighed:

'It must have been a crime of passion . . . That girl was a really fast one. She was always hanging around the dance-hall at the far end of the harbour . . .'

'Well, that makes it different,' murmured Madame Mosselet, who seemed to think that if passion was involved the whole thing was quite natural.

'What surprises me,' went on the policeman, while Maigret never took his eyes off him, 'is that it was done with a gun. Sailors, you know, are more likely to use knives.'

At that moment Mademoiselle Otard reappeared, and the wind, which had given a flush to other people's faces, had made hers pale. The incident, moreover, had given her a sense of her own importance, and her whole attitude proclaimed:

'I know certain things, but don't expect me to tell you . . .'

Her glance swept round the table, the diners and their plates, taking stock of the fish-bones. She said severely to Irma, who stood glued to the doorway, snivelling:

'Why don't you get on with serving the veal?'

Finally she turned to the policeman:

'I hope they've given you something to drink? . . . Your chief will be here in a few minutes. He's telephoning to Newhaven.'

Maigret gave a start and she noticed it. It struck her as odd, and an obvious look of suspicion crossed her face. Consequently she felt bound to add:

'At least I suppose so . . .'

She did not suppose so; she knew. So the local inspector had heard about Mr John and his hurried departure.

For the time being, then, the official line followed the trail of the young Englishman.

'All this is going to make me ill again!' the sad lady murmured plaintively. She opened her lips scarcely three times a day except to sigh.

'And what about me?' asked Mademoiselle Otard indignantly, for she could not endure that anyone else should be more affected by the event than herself. 'You think this is going to be convenient for me? A girl I spent months training after a fashion . . . Irma! When are you going to bring that gravy?'

The most obvious result of these comings and goings was to let

wafts of cold air into the house; instead of merging in the surrounding
warmth, it formed little fluttering draughts that crept round the back
of your neck and aroused a shiver between your shoulder blades.

So much so that Maigret got up and, disregarding the empty coal-
scuttle, went to poke the stove. Then he filled his pipe, lit it with a
paper spill held close to the flame and automatically took up his
favourite attitude, in which Headquarters at the Quai des Orfèvres
had so often seen him, pipe between his teeth, back to the fire, hands
clasped behind his back, with that indefinable air of stubbornness
that he assumed when apparently unrelated facts began to group
themselves in his mind and form, as it were, a still unsubstantial germ
of truth.

The arrival of the Dieppe inspector did not rouse him from his
immobility. He heard:

'The boat hasn't got there yet . . . They're going to let me
know . . .'

And one could readily imagine the steamer tossed in the darkness of
the Channel, where nothing could be seen but the pale crests of huge
waves. And the seasick passengers, the deserted buffet, anxious
shadows on the darkened deck, with no other guide than the flash of
the Newhaven lighthouse.

'I shall be obliged to question all of these ladies and gentlemen in
turn,' said the inspector.

Mademoiselle Otard understood, and decided:

'We can shut the communicating doors. You can sit in the lounge
and . . .'

The inspector had had no dinner, but there were no more whiting
left on the table and he did not like to thrust his fingers into the dish
where slices of veal were congealing.

II

It happened by chance. The policeman had looked round to decide
whom he should begin with. His glance had met that of Madame
Maigret, who seemed calm enough to set an example.

'Come in,' he had said to her, opening the door of the lounge and
then closing it behind her, while a faint smile flitted across the lips of
the former Superintendent her husband.

Although the door was shut you could hear practically everything
that was being said on the other side, and Maigret's smile grew more
marked when his colleague in the next room asked:

'Spelt *ai* or *é*?'

'*Ai.*'

'Like the famous detective?'

And the admirable wife merely replied:

'Yes!'

'You're not related to him?'

'I'm his wife.'

'But then . . . In that case . . . It's your husband who's here with you?'

And a minute later Maigret was in the lounge, facing the little fellow who looked radiant and at the same time a trifle anxious.

'Now admit that you were trying to have me on! . . . When I think that I was going to question you like all the rest . . . I must point out that what I'm doing now is just to carry out normal procedure and also in a way to kill time till I get news from Newhaven . . . But you were on the spot. You must have seen the whole thing coming in a way – surely you've got more definite ideas and I'd be grateful if you . . .'

'I assure you that I haven't the slightest idea.'

'Well, who knew that the murdered girl was going out?'

'The people in the house, of course. But this is where I realize how hard it is to be a witness; I'm quite incapable of stating definitely who was in the house at that moment.'

'You were busy?'

'I was reading . . .'

He did not care to add that he had been reading an article on the life of moles and field-mice.

'I was vaguely aware of noise and bustle . . . Then . . .'

'Madame Mosselet, for instance! Was she downstairs or wasn't she? And if she was, which room was she in? What was she doing?'

The Dieppe inspector was not satisfied. He was almost convinced that his illustrious colleague was enjoying letting him struggle on his own, and no doubt he promised himself secretly to show Maigret how he, a provincial detective, could conduct an inquiry.

The sad lady was sent for; her name was Germaine Moulineau and she was a schoolteacher on convalescent leave.

'I was in the dining-room,' she mumbled. 'I remember thinking it was unfair to let that poor girl carry the Englishman's cases when there were strong men sitting about killing time.'

This was aimed at Maigret, as was proved by the glance she cast at his broad shoulders when she referred to 'strong men'.

'After that you didn't leave the dining-room?'

'I went up to my bedroom.'

'Did you stay there long?'

'About a quarter of an hour . . . I took a tablet and waited for it to take effect . . .'

'Forgive the question I'm going to ask you, but I'm asking all the

guests in the house the same thing and I consider it a mere formality. I
suppose you have not been out today, so that your clothes must be
dry?'

'No . . . About the middle of the afternoon I went out for a
moment.'

Yet another proof of the unreliability of evidence! Maigret had not
noticed that she had gone out, nor that she had left the dining-room
for a quarter of an hour.

'Perhaps you went to the chemist's to fetch your tablets?'

'No . . . I wanted to look at the harbour in the wind and rain . . .'

'Thank you . . . Next, please!'

The next was Irma, the young maid, still sniffling and crumpling
the corner of her apron between her fingers.

'Do you know if your friend Jeanne had any enemies?'

'No, Monsieur.'

'Had you noticed any change in her behaviour, suggesting that she
was afraid because of some threat?'

'Only that she told me this morning she wasn't going to stick in this
hole much longer. That's what she said . . .'

'You're not treated well here?'

'I didn't say that,' Irma declared hastily, with a glance at the door.

'Well, then, do you know if Jeanne had any lovers?'

'She must have done.'

'Why d'you say she must have done?'

'Because she was always afraid of having a baby.'

'Do you know any of their names?'

'There was one fisherman who sometimes came and whistled in the
alley, a chap called Gustave . . .'

'What alley's that?'

'The alley behind the house. You can get out that way, across the
courtyard behind the kitchen.'

'Did you go out this evening?'

She hesitated, nearly said no, hesitated again and then admitted:

'Just for a second. I went to the baker's to get a croissant.'

'What time was that?'

'I don't know . . . I suppose about five.'

'Why did you have to get a croissant?'

'We don't get a lot to eat,' she muttered in a barely audible voice.

'Thank you.'

'You won't tell on me?'

'You needn't worry . . . Next, please! . . .'

This time Jules Mosselet made his appearance, looking completely
self-possessed.

'All yours, Inspector!'

'Did you go out this afternoon?'

'Yes, Inspector . . . I went to get some cigarettes.'

'At what time?'

'It must have been five or ten minutes to five . . . I came back almost immediately. The weather was shocking.'

'You didn't know the dead woman?'

'I didn't know her at all, Inspector.'

He was thanked, as the others had been, and his wife took his place and was asked the question that had now become a ritual:

'Did you go out this afternoon?'

'I suppose I've got to answer?'

'You'd be well advised to do so.'

'In that case I only beg you not to mention it to Jules. You'll see why. He's very attractive to women and because he's a weak character, I don't trust him. When I heard him go out I followed him to find out where he was going . . .'

'And where did he go?' asked the Inspector with a wink at Maigret.

The answer was somewhat unexpected.

'I don't know . . .'

'What d'you mean, you don't know? You've just admitted that you followed him . . .'

'That's just it! I thought I was following him. Don't you understand? By the time I had put on my coat and opened my umbrella he had already got to the corner of the first street. And when I got there myself I saw a figure in a brown raincoat in the distance and I followed it. It wasn't until five minutes later, when the person went past a lighted shop window, that I realized it wasn't Jules . . . So I came back and behaved as if nothing had happened . . .'

'How long after you did he come back?'

'I don't know . . . I was upstairs. He may have stayed downstairs for a while.'

Just then there was a sharp ring of the bell and a policeman in uniform handed a note to the inspector, who opened it and presently handed it over to Maigret:

Nobody answering to the name or description of John Miller landed from the Dieppe boat at Newhaven.

The police inspector had politely invited Maigret to accompany him on his investigation if he was interested, but did not seem particularly enthusiastic, in view of his colleague's apparently unhelpful attitude.

However, as they walked together along the street, in constant danger of tiles falling on their heads – there were broken pieces lying here and there on the pavements – he explained to Maigret:

'I don't want to leave anything to chance, as you'll have noticed. I shall be very surprised if there isn't something fishy about that John Miller. The landlady tells me he had been at her *pension* for several days, but that he had never given anything but evasive answers to her questions. He paid his bill in French money and – this is interesting – with an unusual quantity of small change. He went out very seldom, and only in the mornings. On two consecutive days Mademoiselle Otard met him in the market place, taking an apparent interest in butter, eggs and vegetables . . .'

'Or perhaps in the housewives' purses!' cut in Maigret.

'You think he's a pickpocket?'

'At any rate, that would explain how he might have got into England under a different name and in different clothes from those you had described to the English authorities.'

'That won't stop me from keeping on trying to get hold of him. And now we're going to Victor's, the café close to the fish market. I should like to meet that Gustave the little maid told us about, and to know whether he's the same as a certain Gustave Broken-Tooth with whom I've had a lot of dealings . . .'

'According to your man, the men hereabouts use knives rather than guns,' Maigret objected again, as he jumped over a deep puddle of water and got splashed nonetheless.

A few minutes later they went into Victor's, where the floor was thick with grease and a dozen or so tables were occupied by sailors in jerseys and clogs. The café was glaringly lit, and a juke-box was dispensing shrill music, while the proprietor and two slovenly waitresses bustled about.

It was obvious from the men's glances that they had recognized the local inspector, who went to sit with Maigret in a corner and ordered a beer. When one of the girls served him, he caught hold of her apron and asked her in a low voice:

'What time did Jeanne come in this afternoon?'

'What Jeanne?'

'Gustave's girl . . .'

The waitress hesitated, glanced at one of the groups of men, and then pondered:

'I don't think I saw her!' she said at last.

'She often comes, doesn't she?'

'Sometimes. But she doesn't come in. She opens the door a crack to see if he's there and, if he is, he goes to join her outside.'

'Did Gustave spend the evening here?'

'You'll have to ask my friend Berthe . . . I had to go out.'

Maigret was smiling to himself. He seemed delighted to find that he was not the only person who could not provide definite evidence.

Berthe was the other waitress. She squinted; possibly that was what gave her such a disagreeable air.

'If you want to know,' she told the inspector, 'you'll have to ask him yourself. I'm not paid to do police work.'

By now the first waitress had already spoken to a red-headed fellow in rubber boots, who stood up, hitched up his duck trousers, which were fastened with a piece of string, spat on the floor, walked up to the inspector and, when he opened his mouth, revealed a broken tooth right in the middle.

'Is it me you're talking about?'

'I want to know whether you've seen Jeanne this evening . . .'

'What's it got to do with you?'

'Jeanne is dead.'

'It's not true . . .'

'I tell you she's dead. She was shot dead in the street.'

The man was genuinely surprised. He looked round at the others and shouted:

'Here, what's all this about? Is Jeanne really dead?'

'Answer my question. Did you see her?'

'Oh well, can't be helped. I'd sooner tell the truth. She came here . . .'

'At what time?'

'I don't know . . . I was playing for drinks with Big Joe.'

'Was it after five?'

'Must have been!'

'Did she come in?'

'I don't allow her to come into the cafés I go to. I saw her face in the doorway. I went and told her to leave me alone.'

'Why?'

'Because!'

The proprietor had stopped the juke-box and silence reigned in the room. The other customers were trying to overhear snatches of the conversation.

'Had you been quarrelling?'

Broken-Tooth shrugged his shoulders, like someone who knows he's going to have a hard time making himself understood.

'We had and we hadn't . . .'

'Explain yourself!'

'Let's say that I had my eye on another girl and she was jealous.'

'What other girl?'

'One who came to the dance-hall with Jeanne once . . .'

'What's her name?'

'I don't even know it . . . Well, can't be helped, if you really want to

know . . . I've never even touched her, so I can't get into trouble for
that, in spite of her age . . . It's the kid that works at the boarding-
house with Jeanne . . . That's all! When Jeanne came, I just went outside and told her that if she didn't leave me alone I'd hit her.'

'And after that? You went straight back into the café?'

'Not right away. I went to watch the Newhaven boat leaving . . . I
thought it might get into difficulties on account of the current . . . Are
you going to arrest me?'

'Not yet . . .'

'You needn't stand on ceremony, you know! We're getting used to
always taking the rap for other people . . . And so Jeanne's dead! I
hope she didn't suffer?'

It was a strange sensation, for Maigret, to be there and to have
nothing to do. He was not used to being merely a member of the
public. He heard a voice that was not his own asking the questions,
and he had to make an effort not to break in, approving or dis-
approving.

Sometimes a question was on the tip of his tongue and it was a real
torment to have to keep silent.

'Are you coming along?' the inspector asked Maigret, as he stood
up and laid some money on the table.

'Where are you going?'

'To the police station. I've got to make out my report. Afterwards, I
might as well go to bed. There's nothing more I can do today . . .'

Out on the pavement, however, he murmured as he turned up the
collar of his overcoat:

'Of course I shall put a man on to tail Broken-Tooth. That's my
method, and I think it used to be yours too . . . It's a mistake to try to
get immediate results at all costs; one only gets tired and flustered.
Tomorrow I shall have to deal with the Public Prosecutor's lot.'

Maigret chose to part company with him under the red light at the
police station. There was nothing for him to do in the office where his
colleague was going to settle down quietly to writing a meticulous
report.

The wind had dropped a little, but the rain was still falling, seeming
even wetter because it was falling vertically. Few people were passing
in front of the shop windows, which were still lighted up.

As he always used to do when a case was starting badly, Maigret
began by wasting time. He went to the Brasserie des Suisses and spent
a quarter of an hour uninterestedly watching a game of backgammon
at the next table.

His shoes had let in water and he felt he was catching a cold. That
decided him, after finishing his glass of beer, to order a rum toddy that
sent the blood racing to his head.

'Oh, well,' he sighed as he got up.

It was none of his business! It was rather sickening, but he had looked forward to his retirement for so long that he wasn't going to grumble now it had come.

Out of doors, at the end of the quay beyond the harbour station, which was deserted and lit only by a single arc-lamp, Maigret caught sight of a blur of violet light on the wet pavement and remembered a certain dance-hall that had been mentioned.

Without having really made up his mind to go there, and although he was still resolved to keep out of this business, he found himself in front of a garish façade, vulgarly painted and lit by coloured lamps. When he opened the door a waft of dance music hit him, but he was disappointed to find the place almost empty.

Two women were dancing together, two working girls probably, out to get their money's worth, and the three musicians were playing for them alone.

'By the way, what day is it?' he asked the proprietor as he sat down at the bar.

'Monday. Today, of course, we shan't get a big crowd. Here, it's chiefly Saturdays and Sundays, and a bit on Thursdays. There'll be a few couples presently, when the cinema shuts down, although in this weather . . . What'll you drink?'

'A toddy . . .'

Maigret regretted his choice on seeing his toddy concocted from an unknown brand of rum and water boiled in a dubious-looking kettle.

'You haven't been here before, have you? Are you passing through Dieppe?'

'Just passing through, yes . . .'

And the man, misinterpreting his intentions, explained:

'You know, you won't find anything of that kind here. You can dance with these young ladies and offer them a drink, but as for anything else, well . . . Specially today!'

'Because there's nobody here?'

'Not only that . . . Look, you see those kids dancing? D'you know why they're dancing?'

'No.'

'To get rid of the blues. A little while ago one of them was crying and the other sat staring straight in front of her. I stood them a drink to cheer them up . . . It's not very pleasant to hear suddenly that one of your friends has been killed . . .'

'Oh, has there been an accident?'

'There's been a crime! In a little street not a hundred metres from here. A servant girl was picked up with a bullet in her head . . .'

And Maigret reflected:

'And it never occurred to me to ask if she'd been shot in the head or in the chest!'

Then he said aloud:

'So the shot was fired at close quarters?'

'Very close, I'd say. In this darkness and in such stormy weather it would have been hard to aim from as much as three steps away. All the same I'll bet it wasn't a local man. They're ready enough with their fists, of course. Every Saturday I have to chuck somebody out before they get to fighting. Look, ever since I heard about it I haven't felt quite myself . . .'

He poured himself a little drink, and smacked his lips.

'Would you like me to introduce you?'

Maigret did not refuse quickly enough, and the proprietor had already summoned the two girls with a friendly wave.

'This gentleman's feeling lonely and would like to offer you a drink . . . Come over here. You'll be more comfortable in this corner . . .'

He winked at Maigret, as though authorizing him to take a few liberties unseen.

'What shall I bring you? Hot toddies?'

'That'll do . . .'

It was awkward. Maigret couldn't think how to handle this. The two girls were scrutinizing him stealthily and trying to make conversation.

'Won't you dance?'

'I can't dance . . .'

'Wouldn't you like us to teach you?'

No! There were limits, after all! He couldn't see himself gliding about the floor under the amused gaze of the three-man band!

'Are you a commercial traveller?'

'Yes. I'm just passing through. The boss has just told me that your friend . . . I mean, that there's been a tragedy . . .'

'She wasn't a friend of ours!' retorted one of the girls.

'Oh? I understood . . .'

'If she'd been a friend of ours we shouldn't be here! But we knew her, same as we know all the girls that come here. Now she's dead we don't want to say anything against her. It's quite sad enough without that . . .'

'Of course . . .'

He had to agree with them. Above all he had to wait patiently without scaring his companions.

'Was she not very respectable?' he ventured at last.

'That's putting it mildly . . .'

'Shut up, Marie! Now she's dead . . .'

A few customers appeared. One of the girls danced several times with strangers. Then Maigret caught sight of Gustave Broken-Tooth, dead drunk, leaning against the bar.

The drunken man stared at Maigret as though he were on the point of recognizing him, and Maigret anticipated an unpleasant scene. But nothing happened. The man was too tipsy to see anything clearly and the proprietor was only waiting for a chance to throw him out.

In exchange for the favour he had done Maigret by introducing him to a couple of local beauties, he expected him to stand a round of toddies every quarter of an hour.

Consequently when the former Superintendent left the place at one o'clock in the morning, he lurched through the doorway, had some difficulty in fastening his overcoat, and splashed in all the puddles.

He forgot that the boarding-house guests who came in after eleven at night were supposed to ring a special bell which sounded in Mademoiselle Otard's room. He rang the front door bell violently, woke everybody up, and was given a most unfriendly welcome by the landlady, who had thrown on a coat over her nightgown.

'Today of all days!' he heard her muttering.

Madame Maigret had gone to bed, but she switched on the light when she heard steps on the stairs and gazed in astonishment at her husband, who seemed to be walking with exaggerated clumsiness and who tore off his collar with unwonted violence.

'Where on earth have you been?' she murmured, turning over towards the wall.

And he echoed her:

'Where have I been?'

Then he repeated, with a peculiar smile:

'Where have I been? . . . Supposing I've been to Villecomtois?'

She frowned, searched her memory, and felt sure she had never heard the name before.

'Is that near here?'

'It's in the Cher . . . Villecomtois!'

Better wait till next morning before bothering him with questions, she thought.

III

Whether at home or on her travels, whether she had gone to bed early or late (which seldom happened), Madame Maigret had a mania for getting up at an impossibly early hour. Maigret had already had an argument with her on the subject the day before, when he found her up and dressed at seven o'clock in the morning with nothing to do.

'I can't get used to staying in bed,' she had replied. 'I always feel I've got the housework to do.'

And the same thing happened that morning. He opened an eye, at one moment, because the yellow glare of the electric light was shining into it. It was not yet daylight and already his wife was making timid splashing noises in the room.

'What was that name?' Maigret wondered, half asleep, realizing to his annoyance that he was getting a headache.

The name he had triumphantly announced to his wife the night before, the name of some village or small town, had obsessed him so much that, as often happens, he had forgotten it by dint of thinking of it.

He thought he had only half fallen asleep, for he was still conscious of certain small facts; thus he noticed that the electric light had been switched off and that a bleary daylight replaced it. Then he heard an alarm clock ring somewhere in the house, somebody's footsteps on the stairs and the front door bell ringing twice.

He would have liked to know if it was still raining and whether the storm had died down, but he could not bring himself to open his mouth and ask. Then suddenly he sat up, for his wife was shaking him by the shoulder; it was broad daylight; his watch, on the bedside table, showed half past nine.

'What's up?'

'The local police inspector is downstairs . . .'

'What's that to do with me?'

'He's asking to see you . . .'

Of course, because the night before he had maybe drunk a toddy too many – and that quite unintentionally! – Madame Maigret felt bound to assume a protective and maternal air.

'Drink your coffee while it's hot . . .'

On such mornings it's always a bore getting dressed, and Maigret almost put off the task of shaving to another day.

'What was the name I told you last night?' he asked.

'What name?'

'I mentioned a village . . .'

'Oh yes, I remember vaguely; it was somewhere in the Cantal . . .'

'No, no, in the Cher . . .'

'D'you think so? . . . I believe it ended in *on* . . .'

So she couldn't remember either! Well, it was no good worrying. He went downstairs still only half awake, his head heavy, and his pipe had not the same taste as on other mornings. He was surprised to find nobody in the kitchen or in the pantry; however, when he opened the dining-room door he discovered all the inmates of the house, sitting frozen into stillness as if for some ceremony, or to have a group photograph taken.

Mademoiselle Otard gave him a nasty reproachful look, doubtless because of his noisy entrance last night. The sad lady, in her arm-chair, was as remote as a dying woman who has lost touch with this world. As for the Mosselets, they must have quarrelled for the first time that day, for they avoided looking at each other and seemed to be blaming the whole world for their row.

Even little Irma was not the same, and seemed to have been steeped in vinegar.

'Good morning!' said Maigret, as cheerfully as possible.

Nobody answered, or made the slightest gesture in acknow-ledgement of his greeting. Meanwhile, however, the lounge door opened, and the police inspector, looking pleased with himself, held out his hand to his illustrious colleague.

'Please come in here . . . I had an idea I should find you still in bed . . .'

The door had closed again. They were alone in the lounge, where the fire had only just been lit and was still smoking. Through the window Maigret could see the grey quayside, still windswept, with clouds of spray flying from every big wave.

'Yes, I was tired,' he grunted.

And seeing the inspector's smile, he chose to show right away that he knew what the man was hinting at. He had not thought of one point last night, but now it recurred to him.

'Of course, your Gustave Broken-Tooth was there! So there was a policeman at his heels. And this policeman told you . . .'

'I assure you I had no intention of making the slightest reference to it . . .'

Idiot! So he thought that if Maigret had spent the evening at the dance-hall with those two girls, it was because . . .

'I've taken the liberty of disturbing you this morning because the Dieppe police have made a discovery which, if I may say so, is of a somewhat sensational character . . .'

Maigret poked the fire, out of habit. He would have liked a drink, something refreshing, lemon juice for instance.

'Didn't you notice anything when you came downstairs?' went on the inspector, who was in the seventh heaven, like an actor who has just been applauded tumultuously and who is about to deliver his best speech.

'Do you mean the people waiting in the dining-room?'

'Yes. I was anxious to get them all together in one room and prevent them from coming and going . . . I've got a piece of news which may perhaps surprise you: the man or woman who murdered Jeanne Fénard is one of them!'

It would have taken more than that to stir up Maigret on a morning like this, and he merely stared at his colleague with a heavy, almost listless gaze. And the local detective would have been greatly surprised if he had known that at that precise moment what was worrying Maigret was to remember the name of a village ending in *ois*.

'Look at this ... Don't be afraid of touching it ... The fingerprints, if there were any, have been washed away hours ago by the rain.'

This was a small card with which Maigret was already familiar, an oblong, greyish card bearing the printed word *Menu* surrounded by decorative scrolls.

The letters written in ink had been almost obliterated by the rain, but it was still possible to make out: Sorrel soup ... Mackerel with mustard sauce ...

'That was the menu for the day before yesterday's dinner,' he commented, still showing no surprise.

'So I have just been told. One thing is certain, then: this is a menu from the Otard boarding-house, and a menu which was used the day before yesterday, namely the day before the crime. Let me tell you now that it was picked up this morning, by the merest chance, on the pavement in the Rue de la Digue, less than three metres away from the place where Jeanne was killed ...'

'Evidently! ...' grunted Maigret.

'You agree with me, don't you? You noticed that last night I was in no hurry to arrest Broken-Tooth, in spite of his past record, as some might have felt bound to do. My method, as I've told you, is not to hurry things at any price. The presence of this menu on the scene of the crime proves, in my opinion, that the murderer is staying in this house. And I'll go farther! In the midst of the storm that's still raging this morning, I tried to reconstruct his actions. Imagine that your hands are wet with rain and that you've got to shoot straight. What do you do? You take out your handkerchief and wipe your fingers. As he took out his handkerchief, the murderer dropped ...'

'I understand ...' sighed Maigret, lighting his second pipe of the day. 'And have you also worked out the meaning of the figures written on the back of the card?'

'Not yet, I must confess. Somebody who was here the night before last must have used this menu to make a note of something. I can read the pencilled figures: 79×140. And underneath that: 160×80. I thought at first that it might be the score of some game, but then I gave up that explanation. Nor can it be the time of a train or a boat, as had occurred to me. As far as that goes, the thing is still a complete mystery, but it is nonetheless evident that the murderer is one of the people in the boarding-house. That is why I have collected everybody in the dining-room under the eye of one of my officers. I wanted, before going any further, to ask you one question:

'Since you were here the night before last, did you at any time during the evening notice anybody using a pencil to make notes on a menu-card? . . .'

No! Maigret had noticed nothing of the sort. He remembered that Monsieur and Madame Mosselet had played draughts on a small table in the lounge, but he had already forgotten where the rest were. He himself had read the paper and gone to bed early.

'I think,' went on the inspector, pleased with his little sensation, 'that we can now examine our people one after the other.'

And Maigret was still hunting for that wretched name, growing thirstier and thirstier, and sighing:

'Not until I've had something to drink, please!'

He opened the communicating door and saw Madame Maigret, who had virtuously come to sit with all the rest. In the grey light, the atmosphere was that of a small-town dentist's waiting room. They sat behind half-drawn curtains, with sullen faces, not daring to stretch out their legs, surreptitiously exchanging cautious or mistrustful glances.

Madame Maigret could obviously have avoided this ordeal. But it was just like her to want to behave like everybody else, to take her place in the line, having armed herself with her knitting, which kept her lips moving in silence as she counted her stitches.

Out of politeness, the inspector had brought her in first, had apologized for bothering her again, and had shown her the menu without attempting to catch her out.

'Does this remind you of anything?'

Madame Maigret glanced at her husband, shook her head, then re-read the figures and frowned, as if reluctant to admit to a fantastic idea.

'Absolutely nothing!' she said at last.

'The evening before last, did you see anybody scribbling on a menu?'

'I must admit that as I never stopped knitting I didn't notice what was going on around me.'

While she was saying this she made a little sign to her husband. And he, realizing that she had something to add but that she would have liked to do so confidentially, said out loud nevertheless:

'What is it?'

She felt annoyed with him. She was always afraid of making a blunder. Now she blushed, feeling intimidated; she hunted for words and apologised profusely.

'I don't know . . . I'm very sorry . . . Perhaps I'm wrong . . . But I immediately thought, when I saw those figures . . .'

Her husband sighed, reflecting that she was incorrigible in her touching humility!

'You'll probably laugh at me . . . A hundred and forty centimetres is the width of some dress materials. Eighty centimetres is the width of some others. And the first figure, seventy-nine, is the length you'd need for a skirt . . .'

She felt quite proud as she caught a gleam in Maigret's eyes, and now she went on volubly:

'The first two numbers, 79 × 140, represent exactly the amount of material needed for, say, a pleated skirt. But you can't get all materials in that width. For stuff that's eighty centimetres wide you'd need double the length to get in the pleats . . . I don't know if I'm making myself clear . . .'

And turning to her husband, she exclaimed:

'D'you think it could have ended in *ard*?'

For she was still hunting for that wretched name which she blamed herself for having forgotten.

'Yes, that's one of my house menus. But I didn't write those figures,' Mademoiselle Otard replied to the inspector's questions. 'And I'd like to say that if my house is to be kept in a state of siege I shall be obliged to . . .'

'Please forgive me, Madame . . .'

'Mademoiselle!'

'Forgive me, Mademoiselle, and I will do my best to cut this state of siege, as you call it, as short as possible. But let me tell you that we are certain that the murderer is a guest in this house and that in the circumstances we are entitled to stay . . .'

'I'd like to know who!' she retorted.

'So should I, and I hope that it won't be long before we find out. Meanwhile I have a few questions to ask you which did not occur to me during yesterday's upheaval. How long had the Fénard girl been in your service?'

'Six months!' Mademoiselle Otard replied, curtly and reluctantly.

'Will you kindly tell me how she came into your house?'

And the woman, perhaps because she felt Maigret's sardonic gaze on her, retorted:

'Like anybody else: through the door!'

'I didn't expect a wisecrack at a time like this. Did the Fénard girl come to you through an employment agency?'

'No!'

'She came on her own initiative?'

'Yes!'

'You didn't know her, did you?'

'I did!'

Deliberately, she now answered with only the barely essential syllables.

'Where did you know her?'

'At home.'

'Meaning?'

'She worked for some years at the Anneau d'Or, where I was cashier.'

'Is that a restaurant?'

'A hotel-restaurant.'

'Whereabouts?'

'I've told you; at home, in Villecomtois . . .'

Maigret had to restrain himself not to give a start. So that was the crucial name, rediscovered at last: Villecomtois, in the Cher! And at this point he forgot the promise he had made himself to stay in the background.

'Did Jeanne come from Villecomtois?' he asked.

'No. She just happened to turn up there, as a maid-of-all-work . . .'

'Had she a child then?'

She retorted contemptuously:

'That was seven years ago, and Ernest is four . . .'

'Seven years since when?'

'Since I left to settle down here.'

'But what about her?'

'I don't know . . .'

'If I understand you rightly, she stayed there after you had left?'

'I suppose so.'

'Thank you!' said Maigret in the threatening tone of a lawyer who has just been cross-examining a recalcitrant witness in court.

For form's sake, the Dieppe inspector added:

'So in fact, she turned up here this summer and you engaged her on recognizing a girl from your part of the world, or more exactly a girl whom you had known at home? I understand your action. And it was all the more generous in that, for one thing, this Jeanne had a child, and for another, her manners and her behaviour were not exactly in keeping with the reputation of your boarding-house . . .'

'I did what I could!' was all Mademoiselle Otard would say.

A minute later it was Mosselet's turn to come in, a cigarette between his lips, his expression sly and condescending.

'Still at it?' he asked, perching on the corner of the table. 'You must admit that for a honeymoon trip . . .'

'Did you write this?'

He turned the menu over and over between his fingers, and

inquired:

'Why should I be drawing up menus?'

'I'm talking about the pencil notes on the back . . .'

'I hadn't noticed . . . Sorry . . . No! It wasn't me. What's this all about?'

'Oh, nothing . . . I suppose you didn't see anybody writing on one of the menu cards the evening before last?'

'I must admit that I wasn't watching . . .'

'And you didn't know Jeanne?'

Then Jules Mosselet raised his head and said simply:

'How d'you mean I didn't know her?'

'I mean you didn't know her before you came here?'

'I had seen her before.'

'In Dieppe?'

'No! At home . . .'

The name was going to recur! Maigret, although a silent actor in this scene, was as jubilant as though he had been its hero.

'Where is your home?'

'Villecomtois!'

'You are from Villecomtois? Do you still live there?'

'Of course!'

'And you knew Jeanne Fénard there?'

'Everybody knew her, seeing she was the maid at the Anneau d'Or. I knew Mademoiselle Otard too, when she was cashier there. And that was why, when we came through Dieppe, my wife and I, we thought we'd be better off staying with somebody from our own part of the world . . .'

'Your wife is from Villecomtois too?'

'From Herbemont, a village five miles away. Comes to the same thing! When you're travelling you may as well do a good turn to people you know . . . And so when Mademoiselle Moulineau was ill . . .'

Maigret had to turn his head away not to smile, and this movement, as he realized, offended the inspector, who could not understand it. So all the characters involved in this Dieppe affair were from Villecomtois, a remote village of which nobody had heard tell until now!

Maigret reflected:

'It's pretty sure that the friend who gave my wife this address must come from Villecomtois too!'

As for the local inspector, completely baffled, he tried to maintain his dignity as he mumbled:

'Thank you. I shall probably need you again. Please ask your wife to come in.'

As soon as Mosselet's back was turned, Maigret picked up from the table the menu which provided such crucial evidence, slipped it into his pocket and laid a finger on his lips as though to tell his colleague:

'Don't mention this to her . . .'

Madame Mosselet took her husband's place with the dignified air of a woman for whom the law holds no terrors.

'What is it now?' she asked.

The Dieppe detective, deprived of the menu card, was at a loss what to say. He began:

'Do you live at Villecomtois?'

'Villecomtois, in the Cher, yes. My father bought the Anneau d'Or hotel there. He died, and I was left on my own and needed a man to run the house, so I got married . . . We closed down for a week for our honeymoon, but if this sort of thing is going on . . .'

'Excuse me!' interrupted Maigret. 'You were married at Ville-comtois?'

'Of course . . .'

'How far is it from the nearest large town?'

'It's forty-three kilometres from Bourges . . .'

'Was it at Bourges, then, that you bought your trousseau?'

She stared at him for a moment in amazement. She must have been wondering:

'What business is it of his?'

Then, with an imperceptible shrug, she replied:

'No! I'm going to buy my trousseau in Paris.'

'Oh! So you're going to finish your honeymoon in Paris?'

'We were going to start it there. But I wanted to see the sea. So did Jules. We had never seen the sea, either of us. If it hadn't been for the rate of exchange we might have gone on to London . . .'

'So you brought as little luggage as possible with you. I see your point . . . In Paris, you'll have plenty of time to fit yourself out . . .'

She could not understand why this man, who was as broad and solid as a wardrobe, insisted on talking about such futile things. And yet he went on, puffing gently at his pipe:

'It'll be particularly convenient since you've practically got a model's figure. I bet you're size twelve.'

'A biggish twelve. Only as I'm rather short I have to have my dresses taken up . . .'

'You don't make them yourself?'

'I've got a little dressmaker whose work is as good as anybody's, and who only charges . . .'

At last she was struck by the abnormal character of this interview, and stared at the two men; she saw Maigret smiling and the other, rather ill at ease, seeming to wash his hands of the business.

'But what's all this about?' she suddenly asked.

'How much material would you need, one metre forty wide, to make a skirt?'

She was unwilling to answer. She did not know whether to laugh or to be angry.

'For a single skirt-length, seventy-eight or seventy-nine centimetres, wouldn't you?'

'So what?'

'Nothing . . . Don't worry . . . Just an idea of mine . . . We were talking about dresses, my wife and I, and I said you'd be easier to dress than she is . . .'

'What else do you want to know?'

She was glancing towards the door, as if afraid that her husband might take advantage of her absence to be off on some escapade.

'You are absolutely free to leave . . . The inspector is much obliged to you.'

She went out, still uneasy and anxious, with the suspicious look of some women who are so convinced of human perfidy that they cannot imagine they've been told the truth, even by chance.

'Can I go into the town?'

'If you want to . . .'

When the door had closed again the inspector got up, intending to rush into the dining-room and order a policeman to follow her.

'What are you doing?' asked Maigret, going over to the stove which he had not poked for a long time.

'But I assume . . .'

'You assume what?'

'You're not going to tell me . . . Remember, she was the one who gave us the weakest evidence yesterday . . . According to her, she went out to follow her husband, but she asserts that she mistook a stranger's figure for his and, after following it, came home disappointed . . . All this business about dress materials . . .'

'Exactly!'

'Exactly what?'

'I tell you these notes on the menu card prove that she is not guilty, that no woman in the house is guilty and that's why it's unnecessary to interview the "sad lady"—that's what my wife and I call the schoolteacher. Remember that a woman carries her own measurements in her head and knows the width of materials well enough not to need to note them down. If, on the other hand, she has asked a man to buy something of the sort for her, or if that man wants to give her a surprise . . .'

He pointed to the old copies of *La Mode du Jour* lying on the table.

'I'm willing to bet,' he said, 'that we should find in here the pattern that took Madame Mosselet's fancy. She and her husband must have discussed dress materials . . . The husband made notes, with the intention of making her a present. It's specially important for him to be nice to her because, as we've been told, she's got the money, that's to say the Anneau d'Or hotel. He was picked because she needed a man about the house . . . and also, no doubt, because Madame Mosselet belatedly developed some romantic feelings. But she must keep a tight hold on him. She watches him. He comes here to stay with an old acquaintance without suspecting that Mademoiselle Otard has taken in an unfortunate creature who also once lived at Villecomtois . . .'

It was still raining. Transparent drops chased one another down the panes. From time to time a black mackintosh went past on the pavement, hugging the wall.

'It's none of my business, is it?' went on Maigret. 'But I didn't get an entirely favourable report on this woman Jeanne from those girls last night. She wasn't a nice type of girl. She was cantankerous, embittered by her misfortunes. She hated men, blaming them for her downfall, and she always managed to make them pay. For she was one of the rare habituées of the dance-hall who was willing to spend the rest of the night out . . . Rum toddies may stupefy one, but not as much as you seem to think . . .'

The other man felt ill at ease, remembering his behaviour that morning, his mocking, supercilious smile when Maigret had appeared.

'You can see the course of events for yourself . . . You'll discover that Jeanne, back home, was the mistress of this Mosselet, who's quite nasty himself. You'll find out that he was the father of her kid and that she has had more cuffs from him than thousand-franc or even hundred-franc notes . . . Then she suddenly sees him turn up here with a wife rolling in money and jealous as a tigress . . . What does she do?'

'Blackmails him,' the local inspector sighed regretfully.

And Maigret lit a fresh pipe, his third, muttering:

'It's as simple as that. She blackmails him, and as he's scared of losing not his love but his bread-and-butter . . .'

At that moment he opened the dining-room door and saw them all still sitting in their places, as if they were at the dentist's.

'Come here, you!' he said in a changed voice to Jules Mosselet, who was rolling a cigarette.

'But .'

'Come on, now!'

Then to the policeman, who was nearly six foot tall:

'You come in too . . .'

And finally he gave the local inspector a look which meant:

'With that sort of fellow, you know . . .'

Mosselet was less bumptious than he had been earlier, and seemed almost ready to hold up his arms to ward off blows.

Maigret was anxious to keep out of it. The women, on the other side of the door, jumped as they heard voices raised, vehement protests, and then strange bumping noises.

As for Maigret, he was looking out of the window. He was thinking that perhaps the Newhaven boat would leave at two. Then, by a curious association of ideas, he reflected that he'd have to go and have a look at Villecomtois one of these days.

When he felt a tap on the shoulder he did not even turn round.

'Is it okay?' he asked.

'He's confessed.'

Maigret was obliged to stay a minute longer looking out of the window so as not to let the local inspector see his smile.

Sometimes it's better not to seem too clever . . .